NAZI GERMANY HAD ONE LAST CHANCE TO WIN THE WAR. A VERY GOOD CHANCE.

In London, the Allied Powers' prize Nazi prisoner, Rudolf Hess, had convinced his captors to fly him to Chicago.

Off the Maine coast, three extraordinary German commandos—a brilliant Wehrmacht officer, a giant SS trooper, and an immensely gifted killer—had emerged from a submarine to begin their journey to the American heartland.

In Chicago itself, an exquisitely tooled terror team had begun to operate under perfect cover.

Their common goal: to kidnap the one man who could give Germany the first atomic bomb, Enrico Fermi.

And God help anyone who tried to stop them . . .

THE HESS CROSS

THE HESS CROSS

James Stewart Thayer

POPULAR LIBRARY • NEW YORK

THE HESS CROSS

Published by Popular Library, a unit of CBS Publications, the Consumer Publishing Division of CBS Inc., by arrangement with G. P. Putnam's Sons

ISBN: 0-445-04286-9

Printed in the United States of America

10 9 8 7 6 5 4 3 2 1

To
Joseph Thomas Thayer

I

May 10, 1941

A hundred feet above the tomato patches, oat fields, and dairy barns of southwest Scotland, a German Messerschmitt 110 streaked toward Glasgow. The howl of its dual engines pierced the green Scottish countryside as they pushed the plane 300 miles an hour.

The pursuit-fighter had departed from Augsburg, near Munich, at 6:00 P.M. and had flown in an unwavering course across the channel. At the English coast the plane had descended from 15,000 feet and begun hedge-hopping to avoid detection by English spotters. A British Spitfire would have made an easy kill of the Me 110, because the Me's three fuselage cannons and four wing machine guns would never be fired. The three-man fighter carried only a pilot. This was the plane's first and last flight.

The Luftwaffe serial card in the flight purse identified the pilot as Hauptmann Alfred Horn. Unlike most fighter pilots, Horn was a big man, and his broad, beefy shoulders strained sorely against the side panels of the cockpit. A minor irritation during the first hour of the flight, this discomfort had evolved into a pain that began between his shoulderblades and seared down both arms. But this was the only blemish in a journey that had thus far been flawless.

German coastal weather stations had promised excellent flying conditions over England. Broken clouds at 10,000 feet forecast for the English coast had not materialized, which made flying by landmarks even easier than the Hauptmann had hoped. The packet of maps of England and Scotland in the leather compartment by his knee was unopened. For weeks before the flight he had studied maps and pictures of British towns. Shapes of steeples and town halls had been committed to memory. Now a glance at a distinctive building or lake or mountain would immediately confirm his location and course.

Flying the Messerschmitt was an intense physical experience. Horn's senses were assaulted by the fighter. On each side of the cockpit was a Daimler-Benz twelve-cylinder 1,350-horsepower engine. Their combined effect was to produce a roar, an endless piercing bellow of such ferocity that only with concerted effort could Horn prevent the cacophony from overwhelming him.

Air in the cockpit was thick with oil and exhaust. During his first flight in an Me 110 five months ago, Horn had prematurely landed the plane and vaulted from the cockpit almost before it rolled to a stop on the runway. He ran toward the hangar, frantically waving for the fire team. With sirens screaming, the fire trucks dashed to the fighter, but found it warm, ready to run, and distinctly not on fire. Horn asked the amused ground-crew sergeant why the Me 110, the crux of the Luftwaffe fighter force and the scourge of Poland, was devoid of such refinements as padded seats, breathable air, and a bearable decibel level. The sergeant explained that in 1938 Hermann Göring and his retinue visited Augsburg for a tour personally conducted by Professor Willi Messerschmitt. Göring was delighted by the Me 110 and posed for photographers while sitting in the pilot's seat of a plane that had just rolled off the production line. As he climbed out of the cockpit, the obese Reich Marshal became wedged in the hatch. Although this embarrassing incident lasted only a minute, the flushed Göring and the frantic Willi Messerschmitt pulled and grunted

8

at each other just long enough for scores of photographs to be taken. Göring's aides immediately rounded up most of the photos for reasons of state security, but Himmler was rumored to have two or three. Funds for the comfort of Me 110 pilots became one of Göring's lower priorities. This incident, the sergeant added, was not mentioned above the rank of lieutenant to that day.

So now Hauptmann Horn was paying for the Fat One's fat. The engines' howl, the acrid cockpit air, and the increasingly sharp shoulder and back pain began to dominate and muddy his thoughts. Scottish countryside, so breath-taking from 15,000 feet, swept past at a mesmerizing pace as the Messerschmitt screamed toward Glasgow a few hundred feet above the ground.

Dusk made hedge-hopping even more dangerous. Horn peered intently through the windshield, trying not to lose the land's contour. At this elevation the altimeter was useless. He suppressed the urge to yank back the stick and climb to a safer altitude. Treetops and hills flew at him in an unending, numbing stream.

Dusk dimmed to darkness. Horn could now see only the land's silhouette against the deep purple sky. Fewer landmarks were recognizable. His eyes flashed to the instrument panel. The directional gyro and magnetic compass, glowing in muted green light, showed his flight to be on course, directly northwest. All other instruments checked out. He smiled grimly as he saw the fuel gauge registering eighth capacity. This, it said, was a one-way flight. Years would pass before he would again see his lovely Ilse and their four-year-old son, Wolf.

In the weeks before his flight, Horn had bid a silent good-bye to his family. Wolf would be much older when his father returned and Horn worried that his son's memories would not survive the absence. The boy was young. Memories didn't last. And so during April and early May, Horn had left home late and returned early each day to be with him. They walked for hours

9

in the zoo at Hellabrunn and along the Isar River. Evenings were spent playing games in the study of their home at Harlaching. At Horn's request, his wife used rolls and rolls of film capturing father and son together.

Horn sadly remembered his wife's many questions during this time. Why during the war should he come home early? Why the new radio transmitter-receiver in the work-room, contrary to war regulations? And why the long hours reading in the study at night, door bolted from the inside? Not telling his beloved Ilse about the plans had pained Horn. But a few hours from now she would know. The entire world would know. And they would not believe.

Horn looked up from the panel and instantly knew he was in peril. There was no purple sky, only blackness. *Gott in Himmel.* The ground. He jerked back on the stick and slammed the throttle to full. The Daimler-Benz engines erupted with sound and Horn was thrust back into the metal seat as the Messerschmitt shot upward. For three timeless seconds the fighter screamed into the blackness. And then the curved, dark indigo line of the horizon dropped into view and rushed under the plane. The Me 110 skimmed over the crest of a large hill.

Horn fought back the euphoria that drugs men who have cheated death. There was no time for it, because he instinctively knew that the small mountain which almost took his life was his target, Dungavel Hill.

Horn leveled the straining plane and banked it southwest toward the Firth of Clyde. He throttled back until it was cruising toward the sea at 150 miles per hour. A few minutes later he reached the firth and turned south, to follow the coastline. He spotted Ardrossan, the small spur of land jutting out from the Ayr County coast. His flight had been exactly on course. He pulled a catch under the panel and the auxiliary tank dropped from the fuselage and fell toward the sea.

Night was almost total as the plane banked left to make the final approach to its destination. He cinched up the front buckles of his parachute and for the last time checked the position of the release cord. To have attempted to land the plane in a rough Scottish meadow in pitch blackness would have been fatal. And he was too good a German to give the Tommies a chance to closely examine an intact Messerschmitt with its new and secret innovations. Pilot and plane would part company at 3,000 feet.

Several lights flickered below. This was Eaglesham, a tiny town eight miles west-by-southwest of Dungavel House. Anyone so flagrantly violating the blackout laws in Germany would have been arrested.

Horn's eyes darted between the panel clock and the ground-speed indicator. He could no longer see landmarks, so to gauge distance he counted slowly, unaware he was mouthing the seconds. Twenty-eight. Twenty-nine. Thirty.

He thrust the stick ahead. The fighter plunged downward in a power dive, accelerating faster and faster toward the ground. At 1,000 feet he pulled the plane up into a tight arc. Centrifugal force crushed him into the seat and ground pain into his shoulders. The plane swept toward the stars.

Horn had rehearsed the bail-out maneuver in his mind a hundred times. He tugged the hatch release on the wind-shield frame and slid the cabin roof back over his head. Cold, violent wind poured into the cockpit. He flicked the engine tumbler switches and feathered the props. The mills died abruptly.

The chilling silence heightened the German's sense of impending danger. Penetrating engine rumble had been a source of confidence, and now there was only rushing wind. The plane was pushed by momentum and it slowed rapidly as it climbed. Timing was critical. At stall speed the flaps and rudders would be useless and the plane paralyzed. Horn had to anticipate the loss of maneuverability by several seconds, because the Messerschmitt had one final, vital act to perform.

An instant before the stall, Horn rolled the plane onto its back. Black Scotland turned upside down. He jammed his left arm against the cockpit wall to brace himself and then popped the safety-strap buckle. Twisted by the wind, the straps dangled crazily and the buckles slapped Horn's chin. Blood rushed to his head. Gripping the window frame, he let himself drop to a standing position on the seat. Even at this low speed the crash of wind pummeled him against the hatch cover as he emerged from the cockpit. The German waited until the plane was almost motionless, released his grip, and fell into space.

A thudding jolt ripped through Horn and sucked out his breath as the chute burst open and the billowing white cloth strained against its rope environs.

Crystalline silence. Stillness. Horn's taut muscles unwound. The night air was brisk as he gently swayed to and fro in the harness. His chute was an ephemeral vision, a pale, ghostly presence obscured by the darkness above him. Time was suspended. Maybe only seconds passed. Maybe minutes. Horn had no sensation of descending, just a comforting calmness as Scotland came to him.

Horn hit the pasture, and something cracked in his ankle. He rolled twice, then lay still for several seconds, trying to orient himself. The grazing grass was damp and cold. Just as he raised himself to his knees, a wind gust caught the chute and jerked him backward into the air and heavily to the ground. The parachute bloomed and raced along the pasture. Horn was pulled like a sled at a frantic pace across the field. His hands automatically reached for the release buckles. His one thought: he did not want history to record he had been pulled through a Scottish cow pie.

A new squall blustered the chute into a swirl and whirled it across the field like a cartwheel. The lines twisted and spun Horn onto his stomach, then onto his

12

back, and finally into a bumpy roll. Plow rows, gopher mounds, and creeping blackberry vines bruised and tore him. Damp rye grass splashed his face. His arms bounced and jarred against the ground, reducing his efforts to release the harness to a wild flailing of his chest. He skidded across the pasture.

The parachute suddenly collapsed. Horn quickly stood, tore off the harness, and stepped toward the spiritless chute. His right leg crumpled and he dropped heavily to the ground. He sat upright and painfully reached for his ankle.

"Who ae ye?" The yell was unnaturally loud over the still pasture. "Ae ye German?"

A winded, partially clothed farmer stood ten yards from Horn, whooping great lungfuls of air and nervously rubbing his hands. From his craggy, weather-beaten face, Horn guessed the man was a plowman who had spent his entire life walking behind a team of horses.

As if in answer, the sound of a metallic, screeching, rending crash lashed out across the pasture. Metal tore from metal, and glass splintered violently. The grinding jumped to a high-pitched wail, which ended four seconds after it had begun. There's the crash, thought Horn, but where's the explosion?

The farmer turned from the sound to the pilot, who was trying to stand again, and said, " 'Twasn't an RAF plane, was it?"

"No," Horn grunted as he cautiously tried weight on his right leg, "it was a Messerschmitt." His English was webbed with a guttural German accent.

"Where'd it come froom?" the farmer asked, glancing again toward the wreckage.

"From Germany."

"And where'd ye come froom?"

"From Germany."

"Jaysus." The plowman could not move. He was frozen by the history of this moment. A German had landed on Scottish soil. The invasion had begun.

"Where're yer goons?"

"I have no weapons. I am alone. There are no others," answered the German as he stooped to unlace his boot. "I think I have broken my ankle."

The plowman ran forward and put his arm under the pilot's to help take weight off the injured leg.

"Me 'ut's o'er there." He pointed to the small cottage barely visible in the darkness. Just as the plowman and pilot took the first arm-in-arm step, the sound of a dull, thudding explosion reached them from the remnants of Horn's fighter. Both men looked over their shoulders, to see a brilliant flame shoot up from the silhouetted wreckage and sputter and die just as suddenly. Horn smiled to himself. Now there would be very little left of his plane.

Tea was brewing when Horn and the farmer reached the house. The plowman's mother had put her white-lace doily on the lamp table and was scooping sugar into a bowl when he pushed open the door with his foot. He was utterly exhausted and used both arms in a clumsy attempt to keep weight off Horn's bad ankle. Despite the farmer's efforts, Horn winced with each slow step. The plowman hauled Horn to the best chair in the cottage, a grainy, horsehair-stuffed leather affair whose springs had long ago conformed to the bony protrusions of the peasant's thin backside. The pilot gratefully slumped into it as the old woman brought him a cup of steaming tea. She was a little, intense woman with gray hair pulled back into a severe bun. She wore an oft-repaired night robe the same color as her hair.

"No, thank you, madam. May I have a glass of water."

It was meant to be a question, but it wasn't. The old lady knew from his first accented word that the man seldom asked for anything. His appearance reinforced this. German pilots wore blue-gray uniforms made of the poorest-quality wool. Horn wore a single-piece fine leather jumpsuit that fit him as if made by a Bond

14

Street tailor. The supple leather of his boots was capped by a dark fur lining that ringed the boot tops. On the silken collars of his azure shirt were patches edged in twisted aluminum cord and embroidered with oak leaves.

"Who ae ye?" The plowman managed to blurt out the question through great quaffs of air. He had fallen into the wooden rocking chair near the fireplace, and his gasping efforts to catch his breath spastically rocked the chair.

"I am Captain Alfred Horn of the Luftwaffe."

When the pilot failed to contribute more information, the farmer awkwardly volunteered, "Weel, I'm David McLean, and this here's me mother."

The pilot nodded. "I must see the Duke of Hamilton immediately. Tonight."

"The Duke o' Hamilton? Now, why would a fighter pilot be wantin' to see the duke?" McLean asked. He knew whatever answer he got would only be partially true at best. Horn may have come in a Messerschmitt, but he was no fighter pilot. He was too old. Must be forty-five or forty-six. And fighter pilots of all countries were short, thin men who could fit into cramped cockpits. Large men were made waist gunners on bombers. McLean had seen several downed German fighter pilots being paraded near the Glasgow city hall by their Home Guard captors when he was in town three weeks ago. Without their planes wrapped around them, they were nothing. Horn was big, over a head taller than the farmer. And heavy. After half-carrying the German across two fields, McLean could testify to that.

McLean's glance dropped to the thin gold wristwatch on Horn's left hand. The farmer had seen only a few watches as expensive as this, and they were all worn by Members of Parliament touring the county, reluctantly extending their dainty hands to farmers to demonstrate they were humble enough to be elected again. In Lanark County they usually weren't.

The McLeans sensed there was more to the German than the trappings. Horn projected commanding competence, an aura of dignified, noble ability. It was an element which so rarely entered their peasant lives that it was not defined or understood but was overwhelmingly impressed upon them. The man was of the social stratum that transcended national boundaries and was as inaccessible to the McLeans as a foreign country.

It was his eyes. Almost hidden behind overpowering thick black eyebrows which grew together over the bridge of his nose, the eyes missed nothing. They were sharp and unrelenting. Never did they slip out of focus, clouded by a fatigue or a passing reverie. They contacted, analyzed, accepted or rejected, and flashed to another subject. The eyes, more than the leather boots or the gold watch, were the indicia of Horn's station.

"I have a message for the duke. I must speak to him tonight. How far is his home?" Horn asked, speaking slowly, molding the words with his German accent.

"Weel, 'tis aboot twelve miles or so froom here. But 'tis unlikely ye'll be seein' the duke tonight. 'Tis past . . ." McLean glanced at the wall clock and saw that the pendulum hung lifeless behind the beveled lead glass. This was the cap to an already bizarre evening. He had lived in the cottage all his life, and this was the first time the pendulum had stopped. "It moos be ten-thirty or so."

Horn's wristwatch sparked reflected light from the ceiling bulb. "Oh, no," he said, "it is nine-thirty. I set this watch before I left Augsburg."

"Ye ferget," McLean said, a small smile coming to his craggy face, "Scotland is on Dooble Soommer Time. We use the extra hour o' light each day to load the antiaircraft goons."

The little victory was not savored long.

"That must be why the British gunners are doing such a good job protecting London from our nightly
16

bombings, *nicht wahr?*" Horn asked, but as soon as he saw McLean's face drop and, perhaps more importantly, the old lady pick up a pair of scissors from the mantel, he quickly added, "That was ungracious of me. Please accept my apology. My flight tonight is an act of peace, not of war. Here, look at my son I left behind."

Horn fumbled into his jumpsuit and extracted a billfold. "This is Wolf. He is four." Horn paused and added softly, "I don't know when I'll see him again."

The aristocracy and authority fell away from Horn's voice as he spoke of his son. The photograph showed Horn dressed in slacks and a white shirt, kneeling next to a small dark-haired boy. Both were smiling, enjoying the moment. McLean knew the pilot would not see his son again until after the war was over.

The cottage front door shuddered from the force of a beating meant to be a knock.

"Open up, McLean. There's a kroot 'idin' aroon' 'ere."

McLean recognized the high-pitched voice of Archie Clark, the local Home Guard. The thudding came again. "McLean. Open up."

"Jaysus," McLean said as he leaned to the side of his chair, flicked the door handle, and slumped again back into his seat. He didn't look up as Clark burst into the room, waving his World War I Webley pistol wildly.

"McLean," Clark yelled, oblivious of the closeness of the small room, "there's a kroot 'idin' oot aroon' 'ere, and . . ." He saw Horn and froze, speechless.

Horn pointed to the closet door and with his deep German accent said, "You might look in that closet."

Clark's head thrust forward as if to get a better look at the German officer. The paralysis vanished. He jerked the heavy pistol at Horn and shouted, " 'Ands oop. Get those 'ands oop."

Startled by Clark's sudden recovery, Mrs. McLean raised her hands above her head.

"God's teeth, poot the bloomin' goon away, Archie,"

McLean said. "Last time ye 'ad it oot, ye shot woon o' Widow Hightower's goats in the arse."

Clark was quickly reassured by McLean's sardonic command. He knew from their long friendship it was a tone McLean used only among friends and in controlled situations. But who was the big man sitting in McLean's chair? He was dressed in a pilot's jumpsuit, yet he was too old. From the twigs clinging to the fur on his boots, Clark guessed the pilot had crawled to McLean's doorstep. Clark's confused thoughts were disrupted by bootsteps on the cobblestone walkway.

Two soldiers loudly stomped through the open door. The distinctive blue-and-white flashes on their shirt sleeves marked them as signalers from the Royal Signal Corps, probably posted to Eaglesham. Both were clean-shaven and wore newly pressed uniforms. They had no doubt been called from Saturday-night plans to aid in the search. Except for size, the two looked remarkably similar, and neither was in good humor.

"So, ano'er woon shot doon, eh? Ye're a wee bit astray, me friend," the shorter one said, not expecting the German to understand.

"Yes," said Horn, "I was ordered to bomb the signal station near here but could not find it, so I began looking for the nearest church to drop my payload. We never waste a bomb."

David McLean laughed, and was joined by his mother and Archie Clark, who holstered his pistol. The soldier went red in his face and his eyes hardened. He grabbed Clark's pistol and pointed it at Horn's head. The German's smile vanished. He saw the veins stick out on the signaler's neck and the corners of his mouth turn down. Unlike Clark, this was a man who didn't point a gun unless he was seriously considering using it. Horn slowly raised his hands.

"Easy," he said softly. "I am unarmed and I am here on official business and must see the Duke of Hamilton tonight. I will go with you to his home."

Horn put the right amount of obsequiousness into

his voice, to satisfy the signalman, who slackened the pressure on the trigger but did not lower the Webley. The malevolent smile returned.

Horn lumbered up from the deep chair, carefully keeping the weight off his right foot. He turned to Mrs. McLean and said, "I am apparently going with these gentlemen. Thank you, madam, for your kindness. You and your son"—he turned to McLean—"will be remembered."

The larger signalman put his arm under the German's and helped him out of the house. The smiling soldier followed without returning the pistol.

Archie Clark snapped the holster cover shut and said, "I moos say, the Home Guard acted bloody swift this night, wha' say?" He paused to brush unseen dust from the epaulet straps on his khaki shirt and looked to McLean for approval.

McLean yawned widely, stretched, and clasped his hands behind his neck. "Donna ferget to mention yersel' in yer report."

Ignoring the comment, Clark continued, "Migh' e'en be a promotion in this."

"Wha' does a farmer get promoted to?" McLean asked as he winked at his mother. Home Guard promotions were unheard of.

"Good na, General," Mrs. McLean said, escorting Clark to the door. "And, Archie, thank ye." She affectionately patted his shoulder as he walked out.

"Wha'll happen to him, David?" she asked as she bolted the door and turned to her son, who was thoughtfully rocking in the chair and staring at the clock.

"Oh, he'll go down to the McTavish Pub and yarn how he's just shot down three or four bombers wi' his pistol," McLean replied, anticipating his mother's hearty laugh.

Not this time. "Nae, nae, no' Archie. Be serious. Where'll they take the German?"

"Why, Mama, I do believe ye've been charmed," he

19

said. Seeing the concern which wrinkled her eyes, he continued, "Pe'eps to the Eaglesham jail foor a time. And then into the POW camp near Glasgow."

"Foor how long?"

"A long time. At least till the end o' the war. But there's woon thing foor certain: Horn'll nae see the Duke o' Hamilton."

Douglas Douglas Hamilton, the fourteenth Duke of Hamilton, Marquess of Douglas and Clydesdale, Earl of Angus, Arran, and Lanark, eleventh Duke of Brandon, and on and on, lay on the canvas cot in the whitewashed corridor outside the fighter-command operations room at Turnhouse. Layers of regulation RAF blankets warded off the chill of the Scottish May dawn. He had lain awake most of the night expecting the bell that had rung repeatedly during the previous four nights. Hamilton knew the alarm would sound before sunrise. Germans never did anything in fours, always in threes and fives. They would make it five in a row, and this certainty kept him awake.

For the last four successive nights the thirty-four-year-old duke had patrolled southwest Scotland in his Hurricane. The German bombing runs had been sporadic, without pattern, but with lethal effect. Glasgow and suburbs had been hit, as had the airfields on the firth. The RAF was reeling under the Luftwaffe's attacks.

Fighter squadrons impressive on command charts were in reality painfully undersupplied and undermanned. Planes were robbed to keep other planes operable. Parts were promised, but rarely arrived. Many of the Hurricanes in Hamilton's squadron were kept together with bailing wire and curses.

The pilots were chronically fatigued. A night's sleep was unheard of. Irregular catnaps, gobbled food, and a sense of duty made hazy by tension and uncountable hours in the sky kept the pilots running to their planes at the alarm bell.

Hamilton was pushed not so much by loyalty to the Empire as his desperate desire for revenge. For weeks London and other English cities had been the bomber's targets, and duty argued for his efforts. Now Scotland too was on fire, and loyalty became a burning. When the alarm bell rang, Hamilton was always first to his plane and first in the air. Rarely did he return with ammunition in the belts. His ground crew was perpetually overworked, because Hamilton's plane required more service and care than any other at the airfield. The reason: Hamilton flew harder, longer, and with more ferocity than any other pilot in the squadron.

"Sir, wake up." The controller rounded the corner from the ops room and approached the duke's cot. His boots echoed in the hallway. "Wake up. It's urgent."

"What's urgent, Corporal?" Hamilton responded without moving in the bed. If it wasn't the alarm, it wasn't urgent.

"A German pilot has parachuted down near Eaglesham. He's asked to speak to you."

Hamilton lifted his head off the pillow to look at the controller, but still didn't commit himself to leaving the bed. "Corporal, I suggest you mix a little water with it next time."

"His name is Captain Alfred Horn, and he's asked to see you personally."

"I don't know a Captain Alfred Horn. I don't know any German pilots, for God's sake. Can't this wait, Corporal? It's four in the morning."

"No, Sir. The chief wants you at Maryhill Barracks immediately."

The corporal was not usually this insistent, and Hamilton could see he was not leaving until the duke's feet were on the ground.

"All right, all right. Get the staff car ready and out front."

"It's already there. So's the driver."

The efficiency by his subordinates was typical. The Duke of Hamilton had been appointed RAF wing

21

commander at the outbreak of the war. Because he was the premier peer of Scotland, many airmen believed Hamilton would treat the position as an honorarium. They joked that any man who could trace his ancestors back to the thirteenth century must be genetically adept at staying alive long enough to procreate. The duke hadn't.

His detractors didn't know him. Hamilton had been in love with flying since age fourteen, when he spent hours watching the British pilots train in their biplanes. At age eighteen he was a skilled pilot. In 1933, as chief pilot on the Houston Everest Expedition, he became the first man to fly over Mount Everest. He had owned several planes before the war and flew them incessantly. He was now respected throughout the RAF as one of the most capable fighter pilots. His origins and reputation commingled and produced a mystique which caused junior officers and airmen to revere him.

Hamilton sat upright on the cot. The tension that had kept him awake did nothing to revitalize him. He was so exhausted he seemed as if in a cloud. The cot pulled at him, begging his return. His feet were a hundred miles away, and the lines of communication were scrambled by fatigue. The duke switched his mind off and began the routine. Feet into the pants already open and in position on the floor. Shirt off the wall hook. Flight jacket. Leather helmet. The helmet was almost strapped when his brain caught and he remembered that a car, not his Hurricane, waited for him. He threw the helmet onto the bed and numbly marched out the ops-room door toward the waiting automobile.

Since the outbreak of the war, Maryhill Barracks had grown from a single barracks to a small encampment of soldiers training for the front. No one considered dropping the name "barracks," however, because it so aptly described the camp. Everything was single-ply—the walls, paint, blankets, barbed-wire fence, and toilet paper. Maryhill Barracks had been designed to last for the duration of the war, and the Army Architect Corps had great faith in Britain's war machine. Five seconds after England's victory, the barracks would crumble to the ground in a fine, forgettable powder.

There was an affinity between the barracks and his stables, thought the Duke of Hamilton as the staff car slid to a stop in front of the Barracks' headquarters' door. He stepped out into a knee deep haze of dust churned up by the car's abrupt halt. The dust was the driver's last effort to break the land-speed record on the road from Turnhouse to Maryhill Barracks. From the car's squealing start Hamilton knew he would not catch up on his sleep during the jolting ride. An authority superior to the duke had ordered the driver to get the duke to the barracks as fast as possible. The lane-and-a-half-wide twisting country roads had become a Grand Prix circuit. When Hamilton had ordered the driver to slow, the private had grinned fiendishly and embedded the accelerator pedal even farther into the fire wall. Now it was over, and Hamilton was intact.

"Will that be all, sir?" called the private from the driver's seat. Without looking, Hamilton knew the driver was still wearing the wolf's grin and probably checking his watch for an elasped time.

"Yes, Private. Thank God."

The car shot away, raising another film of dirt, which clung to Hamilton's pants and gave his uniform a two-tone appearance. An RAF interrogation officer met him at the barracks' headquarters' door.

"Thank you for coming, sir. At 2200 hours, May 10, a Messerschmitt 110 crashed into a field in Lanark County, six miles from Eaglesham. The pilot bailed out and has suffered a broken ankle."

The officer was well trained. His welcome had been short, rudely short from anyone other than an interro-

23

gation officer. Within thirty seconds the duke knew all the officer knew about the flight.

"Here's what the pilot carried with him," said the officer as he pointed to an assortment of objects on the table in the middle of the room. There were several photographs, a gold wristwatch, a camera, a flight purse, and an identification card. More interestingly, there was a small syringe with several needles. Hamilton opened a small, ornately carved wood box that contained an assortment of vials and capsules.

"Is the man ill?" asked Hamilton, nodding to the needles and bottles.

"No, sir. Our company doctor said those are homeopathic drugs."

"Homeopathic?"

"Yes. The capsules and bottles contain extremely weak toxins that in large doses produce symptoms of diseases the man who takes them is trying to avoid. In the seventeenth century, people believed that by taking these drugs the diseases could be escaped."

"Is Horn a kook?"

"I don't believe so. He's lucid and acts with a purpose. That purpose is to speak with you."

"Perhaps I should see this Captain Horn."

Horn had spent the night in the Maryhill stockade, the official title for a six-by-ten-foot room fastened to the headquarters building seemingly as an afterthought. The only furniture was a wood-and-canvas cot. He had slept with his flight uniform on. And slept well. The rigors of his cross-channel flight and night jump, combined with the interrogation officer's incessant late-night questions, had taken their toll. He had been asleep before the door on his cell closed that night.

The sound of the bolt grating against its catch propelled Horn from sleep. The importance of his mission cleared his head like a breath of ammonia. He immediately knew where he was and whom he was expecting.

Nor was he disappointed. Horn had studied numer-

24

ous photographs of the Duke of Hamilton, and the duke now stood before him in the open doorway. The duke's strikingly handsome face was unmistakable. He was the highest-ranking Scottish nobleman and he looked it.

Hamilton entered the cell and closed the door behind him without saying anything. Horn stood, stepped gingerly forward, and said, "We met, sir, during the 1936 Olympics in Berlin. I have come as Adolf Hitler's emissary with proposals for peace. I am Deputy Führer Rudolf Hess."

If Rudolf Hess had been expecting to be treated as a visiting dignitary, he was immediately and sorely disappointed. Rather than the prime minister or foreign secretary, Hess was visited by a series of psychiatrists, intelligence agents, and other assorted interrogators. When he wasn't being questioned, Hess was confined in tiny cells in various prisons and secret houses.

Two weeks after his flight, Hess stopped jumping off his cot every time the cell door opened, expecting an emissary from Churchill coming to negotiate the future of Europe. His captors took his shoe laces and belt and returned his pill kit only when he stopped eating in protest. He was allowed to shave only when a guard hovered over him. The dim light bulb in his cell was always on, so that intent eyes could watch him twenty-four hours a day through the brick-size slot in the iron door. He was given only a spoon to eat with, which was taken from him as soon as he swallowed his last bite of each meal. When the doctors found spectacularly unsuccessful slashes on his wrists, the MP's searched his cell for an hour and finally removed his bed springs. Then they pulled out the light fixture and lit the cell with a spotlight shining through a thick glass shield in the ceiling. He was shown how to salute his guards and how to properly address his superiors, which included everyone who visited his cell. His diet,

25

exercise routine, and toilet habits were rigidly controlled.

Thus the British professionally and thoroughly reduced Germany's deputy führer to a prisoner of war. The world thought it had heard the last of Rudolf Hess.

II

November 6, 1942

Chicago is the gray city, and Hyde Park is the grayest of the Gray City. This neighborhood eight miles south of the Loop is downwind of the steel mills and foundries in Gary, Indiana, and other steel towns along the southwest shore of Lake Michigan. The sky above Hyde Park is the repository of the mills' airborne effluent. The neighborhood suffers from the worst sulfur-dioxide smog in the country.

The air is gray. On most days, anything over a block away appears through a mist. Smog completely hides buildings four blocks away. Lines are vague and subdued. Edges and corners in Hyde Park have an ethereal blur, like the French Impressionist paintings in the Art Institute on Michigan Avenue. The shroud seldom lifts.

The University of Chicago dominates Hyde Park. Its immense neo-Gothic buildings stretch from Washington Park ten blocks west to Lake Michigan. The hub of the university is the Quadrangle, several acres of grass dotted with small trees surrounded by the five- and six-story classroom buildings, dormitories, and libraries. Here is the Class of 1904 Drinking Fountain and Senior Bench and other college necessities.

"Neo-Gothic" is a pleasant euphemism for "confused." The university buildings rise six stories, unadorned by the least bit of frivolousness. The walls are plain gray block. But the buildings go berserk when they reach roof level. Most have circular towers at each corner, the conical roofs of which rise to sharp points festooned with flags or crosses. Medieval parapets with archers' slits ring the roofs. Gargoyles peer from entrenched positions near the parapets.

It is unlikely that Marshall Field foresaw the future value of the property when he gave several acres of Hyde Park swamp to the Baptists in 1890. Nor did John D. Rockefeller foresee the growth of the university when he succumbed to three years of subtle pressure and endowed the university with start-up grants. The Baptists, being pure of heart as Baptists are, had been appealing to Rockefeller's philanthropy and could not find it. Finally, William Rainey Harper, later president of the university, asked Rockefeller if he was going to be outdone by Leland Stanford, who was building a college in California. He was not, and in 1890 the founder of Standard Oil Company gave one million dollars to the University of Chicago and continued to grant it large sums of money over the next three decades.

The transition from swampland to one of the world's leading universities was not without its travails. Hyde Park never became part of corrupt Mayor Bill Thompson's machine, and therefore fights for garbage collection and street repair were constant and bitter during his tenure as mayor from 1915 to 1931. Hyde Parkers also feared that the Levee, a boiling pot of street violence, prostitution, drugs and illegal gambling situated between Hyde Park and the Loop, would spill over into Hyde Park. The university prayed that the Everleigh sisters, Bathhouse John Coughlin, and Hinky Dink Kenna could be contained in the Levee. And the Negroes were coming. In 1937 most Hyde Parkers opposed funding of the federal low-income-housing project on the South Parkway two miles west of the university. The university had no official position, but it began buying land around the campus as a buffer zone against encroachment by undesirables.

Many alumni attributed the declining neighborhood

to the University of Chicago's withdrawal from Big Ten football. In the early 1900's, Amos Alonzo Stagg built the most powerful college football team in the nation. He invented the T formation, the end-around play, and man-in-motion, and many others. In 1905, the Chicago Maroons scored 245 points against 5 points for all their opponents combined. They remained the Big Ten powerhouse in the 1920's, but after Stagg retired in 1933, the Monsters of the Midway began to slide. Nineteen thirty-nine proved fatal for the team. Scores were unbearable; Illinois trounced Chicago 46–0; Virginia 47–0, Ohio State 10–6, Michigan 85–0, and Harvard 61–0. President Robert Hutchins withdrew the university from the Big Ten and announced that his school would concentrate on scholastics. Loyal alums blamed the pullout for the climbing crime rate in Hyde Park, for the increase in social diseases in South Chicago, and for the bad winters.

John Crown dipped his chin against the bite of this year's bad winter and turned his back to the blowing cold. He fingered the car's door handle, tempted to climb in and hide from the icy blast. But he was waiting for Miguel, and he owed Miguel a lot, so he stayed out in the wind, where his friend could see him. Tiny, needle-tipped ice shards, which Chicagoans blithely called hail, blew down his collar and burned his chest. He stamped back and forth, trying to push the blood through his feet. His teeth began to rattle. Elm trees played with the streetlight and sent shadows across Crown's face, emphasizing its angular features, the sharp nose and thin face, making him look almost gaunt. Only the full head of brown hair mitigated this harshness. He popped his elbow several times. Got to get that fixed, he thought.

Crown was thoroughly wet and cold, but he didn't mind. He was comfortable with himself for the first time since disastrous June. He was out of the depression that had almost killed him. The mist that had sunk into his mind and anesthetized him for all those weeks had lifted.

As he rubbed his hands together to fight the chill, once again, for the thousandth time, his mind sped back to the beginning of his sickness, to Operation Reinhard. The chief, who was called the Priest and who said his name was Richard Sackville-West, had assigned Crown and Maura to the mission. They had arrived in Newcastle-on-Tyne almost a year ago and had driven to the camp in the Northumberland Hills along the North Tyne River. The partisans were already bivouacked and anxious to begin the training. Ten of them, the finest in the Free Czech Army, had been handpicked for a mission they would have very little chance of surviving. For the next six weeks, Jan Kubis, Josef Gabcik, and the others spent ten grueling hours a day sharpening their skills under the tutoring of John Crown, the small-arms expert, and Miguel Maura, the knife-and-fist specialist. The Priest and his British counterpart determined the Czechs were ready, and on December 28, 1941, the commandos were parachuted into Czechoslovakia for their mission—the assassination of Reinhard Heydrich.

Perhaps no man in history deserved to die more than SS Obergruppenführer Reinhard Heydrich. As head of the Reich Security Service, Deputy Reich Protector of Bohemia and Moravia, and chief administrator of all German concentration camps, Heydrich was responsible to only two men, Hitler and Himmler. He was regarded by inner circles as Hitler's successor. At the Wannsee Conference in January 1942, Heydrich was selected to administer the Final Solution of the Jewish question, which he did with cynical brutality from his office in Prague. He ruled Eastern Europe with a cold sadism and a merciless iron hand. Heydrich, the tall, blond nightclub devotee and Mozart and Haydn addict, murdered thousands of people.

On May 29, 1942, as Heydrich's limousine slowed

for a corner at the outskirts of Prague, Gabcik leaped into the street and pulled the trigger of his Sten gun. Nothing happened. The weapon had jammed. As Heydrich and his chauffeur stood to draw their pistols, Kubis lobbed a bomb into the rear seat. The explosion ripped open the Reich Protector's back and embedded horsehair from the seat deep into his flesh.

Heydrich lived for nine painful days. News of his death was greeted with hearty applause at the ops room in England, where Crown and Maura had been praying for the infection to spread. As German bombs tore London apart and as most of Europe suffered under the Nazi boot, they had proved to the world that the Nazi criminals were not inviolable, not invincible. They could be reached. Vengeance could be had. A wave of hope spread through the conquered lands. Crown and Maura shared in the euphoria.

Then came the first reports from Lidice, a small mining town fifteen miles west of Prague, unconfirmed reports of German retaliation for the death of Heydrich. Rumors of burning and shootings. On June 10 the Germans confirmed the worst in their proclamation to the Czech people. The entire town of Lidice had been razed, and the remnants of the buildings had been plowed into the ground. The entire male population, 173 men, was shot. Two hundred women were shipped to concentration camps, and a hundred children were sent to Germany for reeducation and resettlement. Hitler ordered that Lidice be erased from the maps.

John Crown disappeared for two weeks. When Miguel Maura found him in the poverty ward of the Leeds hospital, Crown was close to death from drink and lack of food, and his elbow had been shattered from a drunken fall down a stairwell. The Priest relieved them from further assignments, and Maura spent the next weeks standing by Crown, helping him fight the dulling depression that ruled his waking moments and pierced his sleep.

Crown's recovery was long and painful. Miguel was

31

his link to sanity during those weeks. Maura, whom Crown had worked with since meeting him in San Sebastián during the Spanish Civil War, argued and cajoled Crown out of the lethargy and melancholia. At times it was a kicking, screaming struggle, but Maura finally dragged Crown through the layers of depression and made him function again. Chicago was their first assignment since he had recovered. The Priest's first team was whole again.

Crown's thoughts returned to cold Chicago when he saw Maura bob around a clot of university students. A few women turned to watch him pass, a typical reaction. Maura was a classically handsome Basque, with a finely chiseled nose, gleaming even teeth, and large dark eyes.

"You ready to do some business?" Miguel greeted his partner with the phrase that had come to mean a lot to them.

"Just as you are," Crown answered, and meant it. "It's good to be back at work, whatever the Priest has in store for us."

"Well, whatever it is," Miguel added with his slight Spanish accent, "we've got some serious carousing to do between now and then. I know this interesting little place downtown, and I'm thirsty."

The little place was Lip's Lower Level, a notorious Loop saloon that catered primarily to sailors from the Great Lakes Naval Station north of the city. For some reason Crown didn't understand, Maura loved the smoky, raucous atmosphere of this dive. They spent the evening pitching down schooners of beer and enjoying each other's company. An accurate gauge of Maura's inebriety was the number of times an hour Crown had to prevent him from showing his prowess with his throwing knife to the surrounding sailors. When it reached four, Crown dragged the Basque from Lip's.

Chicago November slapped them as they stepped

from Lip's onto the sidewalk. Crown pulled the coat collar tight around his neck. Maura seemed oblivious of the biting wind. His coattail flapped around his knees.

"I forget, amigo. How did we get here tonight? Your car or mine?"

"You don't own a car. Mine's parked across the river."

Crown and Maura turned into the wind and walked north on Dearborn Avenue. The street was strangely vacant. The freezing temperatures had chased most people from the Loop. Even the lunatics and alcoholics who surface after the rush hour each day to fester on the sidewalks had been beaten into hiding by the cold. A few sailors hurried to the buses that would return them to the Naval Station.

Lake Michigan wind lost none of its chill as it streamed from the lake and poured around Loop buildings. Maura hurriedly buttoned his coat. Pitted against Chicago's wind, the beer had kept him warm for only a few minutes. He dug his hands farther into his coat pockets. He and Crown walked in brisk unison on Dearborn toward the river.

"Have you figured out why we were brought here, John?"

"No, but whatever it is, it isn't going to be the usual. Hyde Park smells of a boring assignment. The Priest didn't say anything other than it's important."

"I hope the job makes up for being in this miserable city."

"Don't knock Chicago. There are a lot worse places. The last time I got out of a cab, a man rushed up to me and asked where I came from and how much I paid the cabbie. If a cabbie is caught twice screwing a fare, he's suspended for a week. In New York, a cabbie will drive you around the block for as long as he thinks he can get away with it."

Crown was not sure Maura was listening, but he went on, "And you seem to get along with the sailors

33

at Lip's. In Norfolk, Virginia, all the boardinghouses have signs saying 'No Dogs or Sailors Allowed.' If a Spaniard came looking for a room, one of those old ladies who runs the boardinghouses would have a conniption fit. Chicago's not a bad town. You've even got a room."

Both men laughed, and their breath rolled in frozen waves as it hit the air. They approached the Dearborn Street Bridge and the temperature dropped. Or maybe it was the sight of the river and bridge.

The Dearborn Street Drawbridge was the apex of architectural theory that form must be subverted to function. The bridge was utilitarian ugly. It was too short to require inspiring, sweeping suspension spans and not high enough above the river to need towering understructure. The Dearborn Bridge was a plank laid on dwarf pylons. As if in recognition that the bridge was beyond aesthetic help, it had been painted vomit ocher. The paint was thoroughly chipped, and rust splotches grew under the paint flakes. Crown thought of a giant metal Goliath felled not by a rock from a sling but from terminal skin disease.

As they stepped onto the bridge catwalk, the brown odor of the Chicago River caught them.

"Mother Madonna, how can the people of this city put their sewage into their beautiful lake?" Maura asked, wrinkling his nose against the smell.

"They don't," Crown said. "In 1900, Chicago engineers built a series of dikes and channels in order to get ships from Chicago up the Chicago River to the Mississippi. To do this, they made the river flow backward. It now flows from Lake Michigan to the Mississippi."

"What about the sewage?" Maura asked.

"They still dump it into the Chicago River, as you can tell from the smell. But now it goes to St. Louis and New Orleans, not out into their precious lake."

Maura laughed heartily. "And I thought Chicagoans were stupid."

34

Looking back, John Crown would always say the car sounded sinister. Something about its high-revving motor or the squeal of its tires as it turned onto the bridge from the north caught his ear, but he readily discarded the hunch. Hundreds of cars crossed the bridge every hour. This one swerved wildly as it came toward them. The black automobile was low-slung and streamlined, and its polished grille reflected the bridge lights. It wove back and forth like a mole frantically looking for its hole.

"If you think you had a lot to drink tonight, Miguel, look at the two gents in the Buick. They're snockered."

But as the Buick crossed the drawbridge center line it focused on Crown and Maura. It no longer veered erratically, as if driven by a man intoxicated beyond seeing. It bore down on the two pedestrians and clearly intended to crush them against the bridge guardrail.

Miguel Maura lunged forward and hit Crown and thrust him ahead with his arms. Crown stumbled out of the auto's range, but the front fender caught Maura's legs as it slammed into the guardrail. Crown heard his friend's knees pop like crushed walnuts. He turned, to see Maura rebound from the rail onto the car's hood. The Buick bounced away and Maura slid heavily to the concrete sidewalk.

Crown rushed to him. He could see bone splinters protruding through the Basque's torn pants. Blood rushed from the mangled knees onto the walkway. Maura calmly stared at the car as Crown lifted him to a sitting position.

"Jesus, Miguel. Don't move. I'll get help."

Through teeth clenched with pain, Maura slurred, "Watch the window, John."

"Watch" was the word. Five years of assignments together had taught Crown that anything Miguel Maura said to watch was deadly and imminent. Crown spun toward the car and saw through the glare of headlights a black-gloved hand carrying a pug-nosed revolver emerge from the passenger window. The gun

35

fired, and metal hit metal six inches from Crown's sleeve. The gunman and the driver opened the car doors. Their aim would be more accurate from a standing position. Crown and Maura were trapped between them.

"Let's go, Miguel. One way out for us."

Crown grabbed Maura's torso and hoisted him to the rail. He lifted his friend over the pipe, pushed him outward, and dropped him into the Chicago River. As soon as he released Maura, Crown vaulted onto the railing, balanced precariously for an instant, and kicked out from the bridge. The sound of a second shot chased him as he fell toward the black river.

Water as cold as the Chicago River in November is not just cold. It is numbing. Crown tried to fight to the surface, but his limbs seemed disconnected from his body. His legs were impersonal and apart. His forehead throbbed from the cold. Thumbs of freezing water pushed his eyeballs deep into their sockets. His lungs were paralyzed. But somehow he rose and broke the surface of the river.

Crown shook the water from his eyes. Maura was bobbing eight feet away and was gagging from inhaled water. His arms beat the river, trying to keep himself afloat. As he reached Maura, warmth brushed Crown's leg. It was Maura's blood, drifting away in the Chicago River.

"No way to treat a friend." Maura coughed as Crown grabbed his collar and pulled him into a floating position on his back. The freezing water had taken the glaze from Maura's eyes. He was badly hurt, maybe dying, but he was thinking.

"Let's make it to those boats," Crown said as he tasted the oily film of the river water.

Crown began a one-arm swim to the concrete river shore lined with fishing vessels listing against their moorages. Small waves splashed against the swimmers, and Crown's wet scalp was so cold it felt as if an invisible hand was tearing his hair. Coldness gripped his
36

chest like a vise and made breathing a concerted effort. He kicked against the water and pulled the Basque behind him. Maura stiffened when Crown's leg jabbed a mangled knee.

"God damn, John," Maura gasped in pain, "easy. My legs have been on the short end already tonight."

They fought through a few yards of freezing water, and Crown was already out of breath. He tried to time his breathing with the waves, gulping air in the troughs. Maura sputtered as a wave drowned his inhale.

The Basque's hand slapped wildly at Crown's head. Crown stopped his awkward struggle and saw Maura pointing to the wooden steps connecting the bridge to the river shore below. The driver and passenger of the Buick were scrambling down the stairs to the shore and boats. Through the watery film in his eyes, Crown saw that they each carried a black pistol. The leader stopped at the landing and stared down at the swimmers to gauge their direction. He intended to complete his job while Crown and Maura were perfect targets bobbing helplessly in the Chicago River.

There was no choice. Crown side-kicked, pulled Maura around, and began to swim back to the center of the river. Fatigue and intense cold were quickly draining his strength and made the river feel like molasses. One of the henchmen aimed his pistol. His partner nudged him and nodded to the nearest fishing boat tied to the riverbank.

The leader ran to the trawler and climbed over the gunwales. He descended the cabin ladder, and the boat's interior light flashed on. The high whimper of a frightened voice wavered across the river. Then a short, corpulent man, dressed in wool long johns, climbed to the deck. The gunman followed, his pistol dug into the fisherman's neck. They climbed the steep ladder to the controls above the cabin. The second assassin untied the mooring lines and jumped on board. The boat's diesel engine boomed. Stern water boiled as

37

the propeller whipped the river water. The boat pulled away from shore.

The vessel ominously turned toward Crown and Maura. The wooden hull split the water into frothing halves as the boat bore down on its targets. The second gunman walked to the bow, leaned against the bow railing, and casually revolved the cylinder of his weapon. He stared down at the floating men as the boat closed the gap. Crown saw the assassin's thin smile.

Even without his friend anchoring him, Crown could not have escaped. He was forty yards from the shore opposite the boat moorage. Evasive swimming maneuvers, even if successful a time or two, would quickly sap his strength. The boat would simply herd him like a cowboy herds cattle, until the bowman got him in his sights or the trawler ran over him. There was nothing to divert the gunmen's attention. No escape route. No offensive maneuver. By any calculation, he and Maura were dead. The boat was twenty yards off and lunging toward them. The bow gunman raised his pistol again.

"One of us can make it. Two cannot. Leave," Maura shouted above the engine. He craned his head toward Crown and commanded in a lower voice, "Leave."

It was the diversion, a simple tactic used when all other routes were closed. The mathematics of the diversion were plainly and succinctly stated by Maura. It demanded immediate action. No farewells.

Crown kicked off and swam frantically away from Maura. When he was three yards out of the boat's course, he stroked toward the moorage from where the fishing boat had just come. The boat plunged by him. Its wake lifted him above the waterline as the trawler bore down on Maura. The gunman's steady arm pointed at the Basque as if the boat's bow alone would not do a thorough job on its floating target.

Three seconds before impact, Miguel Maura's arm lashed out. Crown saw a steel glint flash in the air. The gunman lurched and clutched his neck. Blood spurted through his fingers. Maura's throwing knife was embedded in the assassin's throat. The gunman stumbled blindly against the bow railing, lost his balance, and toppled over the rail into the river. The boat plowed into Maura and the henchman at the same instant.

Crown swam wildly toward the river shore. He knew the remaining murderer could easily see him as the boat swerved port to make another pass. The handgun popped, and a shaft of inky water shot into the air two feet from his head. His arms churned the water. Crown's back was an easy target for the gunman's next shot. His spine tightened in anticipation of the bullet.

Crown's knuckles slammed into the stern of a fishing boat moored to the river shore. Skin ripped off three fingers. He reached for the deck of the boat to pull himself on board, but he didn't have the strength to kick himself high enough, and he slipped back into the water. The assassin fired again, and wood chips burst from the boat near the waterline.

The trawler was now thirty yards from the moored boat. Crown kicked to the moored boat's stern. The boats were lined bow-to-stern in a long row along the shore. Twelve inches separated the stern of the boat from the bow of the next. Crown grabbed the hull of the next fishing cruiser and pulled himself through the gap.

The gunman's trawler abruptly throttled back. Crown heard the muted clang of the gear lever being rammed into reverse. The engine growled and strained as it slowed the fishing boat.

Crown was trapped in the water between the boats and the vertical slope of the concrete dock. The mooring lines were out of his reach. No steps descended from the shore to the waterline. He pulled himself along the slip of water. The moored boat drifted to shore. To avoid being crushed against the concrete, Crown inhaled deeply and dipped beneath the surface.

He came up ten feet farther along the slip, where the boat's listing could not catch him. He paddled to the stern, paused, wiped the oily water from his eyes, and peered through the boats into the center of the river just as the gunman's boat glided into view. Maura's murderer was casually patrolling the shore, knowing Crown was trapped. The line of boats was endless. There was no way to climb out of the water. The gunman was leisurely waiting until Crown either showed himself and was shot or froze to death.

Crown plunged into the next gap between moored boats and kicked at the water to propel him to the cover of the next fishing vessel. A bullet crunched into the bow of the boat that now shielded him. The prowling trawler's wake rolled into the moored boat, which then drifted against the concrete. Crown's hand was caught and cruelly pinched between wood and concrete. He yanked it free. Two disjointed fingers were bent at right angles to his hand. Cold blocked the pain.

He drifted toward the stern of the boat. There was no hurry. He had no plan. There was only an endless line of boats to shield him from the gunman's shots. Cold penetrated to his bones. His strength was nearly gone, and his body had almost quit responding. Breaths came in short spastic gasps.

Once again Crown felt a warm rush against his legs. His mind flashed to his friend's blood wasting away in the river. But this wasn't blood. Warm fluid was pouring into the river. Crown spread his hands along the shore wall, feeling for the outlet. His knees smashed against the wall as he groped for the pipe and tried to keep his head above the water. A fetid stench wafted toward him. Wisps of odorous steam rose from the water. He inched along the wall, his exhausted legs pushing him through the increasingly warmer water.

His right hand grasped an edge, an indentation in the shore wall. He gripped and pulled himself to a hole in the concrete wall. The tunnel's tepid effluent pushed against his body and rolled around him into the river. The top of the corrugated-sheet-metal opening was twelve inches above the waterline. He grabbed the lip of the tunnel opening, tucked his legs under him, and lifted himself into the shaft. The sound of another shot reverberated in the tunnel.

The shaft was four feet high, three of which were filled with slowly flowing sewage. Crown duck-walked upstream. His head rhythmically bumped against the metal roof of the tunnel as he tried to keep his mouth and nose above the sewage. Blackness was absolute. Sewage vapors seared his nostrils. Methane gas emitted by the human waste would kill him in a few moments, but his exertions forced his aching lungs to gasp great quantities of the gas. An age passed. His body was airy and distant. Concentrate. Walk. Keep alive. Hurry. Thoughts came in simple, weak pulses. Survive. Walk. His mind was failing, victim of the gas. Thought was fog.

The bumping stopped. Crown's head no longer hit the top of the tunnel. Rising slowly to his full height, he saw dark purple sky strained through a manhole grating above him. He reached blindly for the wall and found an iron rung. With the last of his mental reserve, he willed his weak legs to climb. Hand over hand, step by step, he ascended the ladder. Near the top, he hooked one leg over a rung to prevent falling and lifted the manhole cover out of its slot and to one side. His head emerged from the hole. He was at a warehouse truck-loading dock. No one was in sight.

III

Chicago's first winter snow fell two nights later. By next morning, smog had discolored the white blanket. The sky was ash-hued, and the trees were gray and lifeless. Crown's eyes searched in vain for some relief from the monotonous juxtaposition of drab on drab as he walked across the midway, passed Frank Lloyd Wright's Robie House, and north on Woodlawn. He had received the telephoned summons a few minutes before. Meet the Priest at a home on Woodlawn and Fifty-sixth Street. That the Priest had flown in from Washington was an indication of the importance of the assignment. Operatives went to the Priest. He did not go to them.

Crown hadn't given the present mission his attention. He was obsessed with one question: Who killed Miguel Maura? In the two days since his friend's death, Crown had secluded himself in his bleak studio apartment on the corner of Sixtieth and Woodlawn, asking that question over and over. When he reported Maura's death to Sackville-West, he had been ordered not to search for the killer. Crown's mission was too important to draw attention to himself by investigating a murder. So he sat in his room drinking Blue Ribbon and trying to piece the puzzle of Maura's death together. None of their old adversaries knew they would be in Chicago, because they had come to the Midwest in utmost secrecy. And they hadn't been here long enough to have made enemies. Had they been followed from Lip's Lower Level? No, not followed. They would have known within two blocks. Crown could not remember anyone watching them with undue interest at Lip's. Yet, it couldn't have been a random killing. The murderers had been too persistent and ruthless for that. The pieces didn't fit.

Crown knew he had not been analyzing the killing clearly. Grief numbed him. He tried to push it aside, but it returned again and again with aching persistence. He had worked with Miguel for four years. Their assignments had been hazardous and important, and they had risked their lives together on occasions too numerous to recall. They had developed an intuitive knowledge of the other's actions. This unerring sense had made them the Priest's most valued team.

Miguel was gone and Crown was left with a rush of emotion. His mind was sodden. His thoughts wandered to Spain, France, and Norway, where he and Miguel had worked together. The comradeship and the accomplishment they had shared in those places returned to sharpen the grief. Crown couldn't put Miguel's death into a compartment and force it into a corner of his mind. It pervaded him and spread to all corners of his thoughts like a winter blizzard.

For two days he had sat in his dim little room mechanically working through a case of warm beer, and there had come a certainty. The killer was somehow connected with his reason for being in Chicago. He would meet Miguel's murderer again. Crown had no doubt of the outcome of that encounter.

Crown climbed the front steps of the home to a large porch. The house was typical of others along Woodlawn. It was a large red-brick single-family unit that covered most of its lot. The front yard was very small and was encircled by an iron seven-foot-high spike fence broached by a swinging black iron gate. Crown could not see the guards, but there was no question the gate was closely watched by men ordered to let only him through. The Priest was cautious.

A tall, drawn man Crown vaguely recalled seeing once in Sackville-West's office in Washington answered the door, said a smileless hello, and led him toward the study. The window shades were drawn, and it took a few seconds for Crown to adjust to the dim light. The tall man opened the study door and gestured Crown inside.

Richard Sackville-West stood next to a large table that was covered with the papier-mâché reproduction of a battlefield. Several acres of hills and fields had been constructed in miniature with infinite care. A blue stream meandered down from the hills and cut through the pastures near a cluster of toothpick-and-paper houses. A tiny bridge on each end of the town crossed the stream. The hills were made of papier-mâché and covered with green-tinted cotton and small twigs, a believable mock-up of a forest. The remainder of the board was open field bisected by hedgerows made of a brown rubbery substance.

Located in strategic positions on the battlefield were squadrons of colorfully uniformed and helmeted ancient Greek troops. The metal soldiers were no more than half-inch high, and were positioned in orderly phalanxes of ten men across and four rows deep. Each soldier carried a glittering sword in an upraised position. The Greeks were elaborately and authentically hand-painted. Even the soldiers' eyes had been carefully drawn on the lead. Behind the foot soldiers were squadrons of cavalry. The riders sat erect, with their shields turned toward the opposing hill.

Facing the rows of Greeks were enemy troops wearing darker, more somber uniforms. The enemy front row carried spears and shields, and following rows had swords held across their chests. The darker soldiers were backed by platoons of archers kneeling on a papier-mâché hill overlooking the action. The battle was frozen, waiting instructions from the players.

Richard Sackville-West strode around the table and

extended his hand to Crown. "Good to see you, John. I hope you found your apartment suitable."

Crown already wondered at the conversation. Verbal amenities had never been the Priest's forte. He believed in short, economical discussion, touching only on matters at hand. The efficiency was an extension of the man's appearance. He was wearing a dark blue conservative suit and was sporting the habitual tweed tie. His wing-tip shoes enjoyed the typical mirror polish. His face was cultured. A pepper-gray, closely clipped mustache stopped precisely at the line of his thin upper lip. The mustache was a shade darker than his steel-colored hair. Only the eyes were unrefined. They were too hard, too quick. He could have been a successful banker or lawyer from LaSalle Street. But Crown knew he was one of the most dangerous men alive.

Another man sat on a velour couch near the battle-field table. The pleasant niceties had probably been for his benefit. Sackville-West continued, "John, I'd like you to meet Everette Smithson, head of the Midwest Division. This is his home, and he was kind enough to let us use it today. Everette will be working with you during the next few weeks."

The plump Smithson gathered his legs under him and with considerable effort lurched up from the couch. He smiled ingratiatingly with small even teeth set between fleshy jowls and shoved his hand toward Crown. It was damp and clammy, and it pumped Crown's enthusiastically, making his elbow snap like popcorn.

"Welcome to my game room," he said, still working on Crown's hand. "Your boss and I are recreating the Battle of Arbela, fought by Alexander the Great in 331 B.C. Of course, we don't have all of Alexander's forty-five thousand men, but we make do. I'm directing Alexander, and he is doing his best with Darius' Persians."

"Who won the real battle?" Crown asked, not knowing what else to say.

Smithson staged a hearty laugh that flapped his cheeks and said, "Alexander, of course, but we don't let that influence the game. In fact, Richard has already changed the course of history."

Crown had never heard anyone call the Priest "Richard" in the six years he had been working for him.

Smithson pointed to a long line of Greek soldiers and said, "I'd been hoping to use Alexander's Arbela maneuver. I was advancing my men in a long diagonal line against the left center of the Persians, and then I closed them together in an arrow formation."

Smithson picked up an intricately molded and exquisitely painted soldier on horseback, squinted at the plume on his helmet, and said, "Half the Persian squadrons advanced against the light troops, opening a gap in Darius' line. At that point, the Greek heavy cavalry dashed through the gap and flanked the Persians from the rear. Unfortunately, Richard marched forward with the left line of troops and didn't open the gap. As you can see, I'm in a quandary now. I was counting on Richard to do as Darius had done. Of course, my wedge may merely be a feint while I prepare some other nasty maneuver."

Smithson stared intently at the Greeks, and then his eyes darted to each of the Persian squadrons. If a nasty maneuver existed, he wasn't aware of it yet.

"Well," Sackville-West said, interrupting Smithson's concentration, "to business."

He sat in a chair behind the study's massive desk. It was a subtle reminder to Smithson of their respective ranks. Neither had Sackville-West heard a subordinate call him by his first name.

After Crown and Smithson were seated in the uncomfortable metal chairs facing the desk, Sackville-West began, "I was grieved to hear of Miguel Maura's death. He was half of our best field team. And, after a

46

rather . . . uh . . . faltering start, I had grown to like the man. I understand how you feel."

"Thank you, sir." The condolences were much more than Crown had expected.

"John, do you remember reading about Rudolf Hess's flight into Scotland in May of last year?"

"Sure. It was on the front pages for a week. It would've been hard to miss."

"Quite so. It was in the papers in Scotland, England, the U.S., and almost everywhere else. But not for long in Germany. I'll get to that in a moment. Let me fill you in on Herr Hess."

Sackville-West referred to a sheet of paper on the desk and said, "Hess was born in Alexandria, Egypt, where his father was in the importing business. He attended schools in Alexandria, Godesberg, Neuchâtel, and Hamburg. In the Great War he served on the western front and was wounded at Verdun. Later he was transferred to the German Air Force and became a pursuit pilot. After the war he studied at the University of Munich."

"Sounds undistinguished so far," interrupted Smithson. Sackville-West's eyes shot to Smithson in answer. A hard look from the Priest would silence anyone.

"Hess first heard Hitler speak in 1921 and soon became one of the first non-thugs to join the Nazi party. Hitler displayed him just as he displayed Göring, to give credibility to their movement. In 1923 Hess participated in the Beer Hall putsch, and in 1924 he was jailed with Hitler and several of his Nazi cronies in the Landsberg prison, where Hitler dictated his political testament, *Mein Kampf,* to Hess."

Sackville-West paused to reach for the pitcher of water on the desk, and Crown asked, "Was being Hitler's secretary Hess's primary role?" Crown wanted to ask what Hess had to do with his being assigned to Chicago.

"Yes, but much more than that. He was also Hitler's confidant. Until 1932 he held no rank in the party, but he was seen everywhere with Hitler. Hitler soon allowered him to emerge, and Hess became chairman of the central commission of the Nazi party in December 1932. In April 1933 he was promoted to deputy führer, and a few months later to Reich minister for party affairs. Other Nazi leaders came and went, usually violently, but Hess was a permanent fixture. When he flew to Scotland in 1941, he was the third most powerful man in Germany, behind Hitler and Göring."

"If he was in such a favored position, why did he desert Germany?" Crown asked.

"We don't know. Apparently it took Hitler by surprise, and the Nazis were extremely embarrassed. At first the German press said nothing, but soon they had to face his absence and explain it to the German people. Goebbels bungled this propaganda job. At first the official line was that Hess had a history of mental disturbances and that he was hallucinating on the night he flew to Scotland. But this was even further embarrassing, because it was an admission that someone who had risen so high in the party had been insane. So the Reich minister for people's enlightenment and propaganda clarified the derangement stories by saying that injuries received at Verdun had flared up and hampered Hess's thought processes. So the German press said Hess was a good German, an idealist, who couldn't help what he did. Five days after Hess landed in Scotland, his name disappeared from German newspapers and has not been seen since. He had officially ceased to exist."

"That's what the Germans were told. What does Hitler actually believe?" Crown asked.

"We don't know that, either. But three days after the flight, Hitler called in Nazi leaders and gave them a pep talk. Hess's journey apparently shocked and demoralized the Nazi party."

"Imagine how sorry I am to hear that," Crown said.

Sackville-West laughed softly and went on, "The popular belief in England and the U.S. is that Hess
48

wanted to contact Tory appeasers who might consider a bargain with Germany whereby Hitler would attack the Soviet Union if Great Britain made peace with Germany. With a nonaggression pact with England, Hitler could concentrate his forces on Stalin. Hitler has been lusting after Russia's natural resources for a decade."

"Could Hess have had Hitler's secret approval for the flight?"

"Perhaps. But Hess didn't have concrete proposals for peace or suggestions for further contact. In addition, such intercountry contacts can be made through Switzerland or Spain. It wasn't necessary to forfeit the third most important man in Germany to do so. No, the embarrassment of Hess's flight more than outweighed any benefit he could have supplied as a courier of a peace feeler."

Smithson swiveled his bulk to Crown and said, "Hess was thrown into an English prison soon after he arrived. And then he started to crack up."

"Well, Everette," Sackville-West said as he continued to look at Crown, intending to keep this a two-way conversation, "that's only partly correct. In the year after his flight, Hess was given the most intensive psychological tests ever conducted on a human being. The foremost psychiatrists in England spent months with him. I have their reports here." He lifted a bulky loose-leaf volume off the desk. "It's dry reading, so let me summarize. Hess began showing a breakdown of his thought processes several weeks after his flight. These were characterized by rambling speech and lapses in memory. At times he said he couldn't remember his wife's name or the names of his close associates in the Nazi party. He also developed an increased psychological dependence on homeopathic drugs, which are regarded by doctors as useless. But if they are taken away from Hess, he assumes an infantile behavior pattern. He won't eat, he won't participate in interviews with the psychiatrists, and on and on."

"Why don't they just let him starve?" Crown asked.

"It's a rare man who can starve long enough to do himself any damage."

"Because Hess has become an invaluable source of information, and we don't want to stop the flow of facts and figures by angering him. Have you ever heard of the European Documentation Center?"

"No. It sounds like a purposefully vague title."

"It is. The EDC is associated with Oxford University and is officially in charge of cataloging information about Nazi Germany gleaned from German newspapers. It does some of this to maintain its front. Actually, the EDC is the British government's organization to interrogate Nazi defectors."

"Does 'interrogate' mean polite questions or something harsher?" asked Crown. In many countries the gentle questions are routinely followed by brutal and usually effective methods of eliciting information. In Spain he had once been on the painful receiving end during such a question-and-answer session conducted by the infamous Dr. Bull, as the torturer liked to call himself. Dr. Bull was dead. Miguel Maura had seen to that.

"Merely questions, of course. The British don't engage in other types of activity," Sackville-West answered as he smiled thinly. When pressed hard enough, all countries resort to torture. "Seriously, EDC questions only defectors who voluntarily give information. This requires specialists, though, because most enemy soldiers who cross want to give only enough information to prove the sincerity of their defection. Other information can be pried from them after meticulous questioning, always with the understanding the defector will be sent back to his homeland if he withholds facts."

"Cross" referred to crossing the English Channel. England's topography dictates that an enemy who defects must cross the channel. In the intelligence world, "cross" had come to mean a defector who was in his heart a defector, a genuine article ready to provide in-
50

formation. Crossers are distinguished from enemy plants, who are ordered to act as if they have defected to give false information.

Sackville-West carefully opened his attaché case on the end of the desk. He was the only person alive who knew how to open it without being injured. He took out a thin manila folder and leaned over the desk to hand it to Crown. Crown saw three green stripes across the top of the folder. These indicated a 3A security clearance, the only clearance he did not have. He was forbidden to look at the contents unless directed to do so by one who had a 3A. There was no English or American clearance Sackville-West did not have, and he instructed, "Please review the first page."

There were several onionskin pages in the folder, each with three green stripes. The first page read:

* * *

EUROPEAN DOCUMENTATION CENTER PERSONNEL

Josef Ludendorf, chief, born 1883, Munich, Germany. Parents: Karl Ludendorf, central-post-office official, and Gerda Botsch Ludendorf, housewife. Middle-income. Owned a small home.

Josef Ludendorf educated in Munich public schools. Excellent marks. Entered University of Munich in 1901. Studied romantic languages and history. From studies and travels after graduation in 1905 learned French, Spanish, English, and Italian.

Offered post at University of Munich in languages department. Taught at university for next thirty years. No reports of early political activity.

Ludendorf appointed chairman of University of Munich student newspaper in 1928. Guided editorial policy of the newspaper. In 1933 newspaper began publishing editorials critical of new National Socialist German Workers' party and its leader, Adolf Hitler. Editorials continued until

1934, when Ludendorf fled Germany after threatened with indefinite sentence in concentration camp for political prisoners.

Ludendorf joined Oxford University faculty in 1935. Taught graduate-level languages and German history. Made a full professor in 1938, a remarkable achievement.

In 1939 Ludendorf asked by British government to form European Documentation Center. Reduced his classwork at Oxford and assumed EDC responsibilities. In March 1940, at urging of the British government, requested leave of absence from Oxford to assume full-time work at EDC. Headed EDC since that time.

Never married. Both parents died 1918 of flu. One brother has managerial position with small foundry near Munich.

When Crown looked up from the file, Sackville-West continued, "What that doesn't tell you is how successful the EDC has been. Since 1939 they have questioned over seventy Germans. Some, of course, don't give much information, but others have been invaluable sources of not only general knowledge about the German economy and government, but often of specific military information."

Again Sackville-West reached into his attaché case and opened a folder. He laid it on the desk in front of him and leafed through several pages. Each had green stripes. Crown glanced at Smithson, whose substantial bulk was perched anxiously on the edge of the metal chair. Different grades of security clearances between the three men and different needs to know were the reasons for the paper shuffling. Sackville-West had not read the Ludendorf biography aloud because in the agency one was told only what he needed to know. Apparently Crown needed to know about Ludendorf. Smithson did not.

After arranging the papers, Sackville-West produced

a pipe from the case and tapped various pockets of his suit to find his tobacco. "Are you familiar with the Libyan campaign?" he asked.

"No, other than it was a tremendous British success in late 1940," Crown answered, wanting to suggest that the tobacco might also be in the briefcase.

"Well, in the fall of 1940, General Wavell was in command of the British expedition in Africa. He had only fifty-one thousand troops, a partly equipped tank brigade, and an air force that was laughable."

Sackville-West paused to reach into the case to find the tobacco. He put a pinch in the pipe and tamped on it with his index finger and said, "This crippled British force was facing two-hundred-fifteen thousand Italians in Libya and another two-hundred thousand in Italian East Africa. Wavell was ordered to avoid skirmishes because of the predictable result of such a manpower imbalance. In July the Italians invaded Sudan, Kenya, and Gallabat, forcing Wavell to evacuate. It looked grim for the British. Wavell, by the way"—he paused to puff several times—"is a personal friend of mine."

No surprise here. In Sackville-West's Washington office, only one picture sits on the mahogany desk. It shows Winston Churchill and Sackville-West dining together and obviously enjoying each other's company.

Through billowing smoke the Priest continued, "Because of the unhealthy odds against the British if a full-scale battle began, Wavell was ordered to make one man look like ten, make one tank look like ten, and to build airplanes out of wooden boxes so Italian flybys would report exaggerated figures of British strength. Things were that bad. The Italians leisurely built a string of seven heavily armed fortresses north to south across the front.

"Then Wavell received two incredible pieces of information. First, there was a gap between two of the Italian forts, Sofafi East and Sofafi Southwest, which was difficult to defend because of the topography. And second, for some reason, the Italians weren't even try-ing to defend the gap at all.

"Wavell assigned Major General R. N. O'Connor to take his thirty-one thousand men through the virtually undefended space. To make it short, O'Connor dashed five hundred miles across Cirenaica and destroyed the Italian army. It was a military feat unparalleled in the desert war."

"And the European Documentation Center's role?" Crown asked.

"A big one," Smithson volunteered uncertainly.

"Precisely," Sackville-West went on as he relit the pipe. "A week before O'Connor began his offensive, a Major Johann Wesel crossed to England. He was inter-rogated by the EDC, and they discovered that Wesel had been assigned to the German Army's Italian li-aison office. Because of his position, Wesel knew in de-tail the strength and weaknesses of the Italian army in Africa, including the gap between the forts. The EDC immediately gave Wesel's information to the British High Command, which passed it on to Wavell.

"In other words, Wavell and O'Connor had the ex-act details of the Italian positions. As a result, the greater parts of five Italian divisions were destroyed. Thirty-eight thousand prisoners, four hundred heavy guns, and fifty tanks were taken. O'Connor's sprint turned into a major British campaign which drastically weakened the Italian hold on Africa."

"I hope the men at the EDC are being paid salaries commensurate with their work," Crown said at his boss's pause.

"That would be impossible. The Sofafi gap is only one example, albeit the most dramatic. There are several other instances where information gleaned from crossed Germans has saved British lives and has cost the Germans dearly." Sackville-West stood from his chair, his pipe gripped firmly in his teeth. He looked through the window curtains at the Chicago weather. New lines around the Priest's eyes were visible in the window light. Sackville-West had told Crown as early as 1938 that the United States would fight Hitler. The wrinkles were manifestations of the work and worry of the secret war that began years before most Americans had heard of the Nazi party.

"I tell you all this, John, so you'll realize the importance and effectiveness of the European Documentation Center. Now, let me mention several other classified items, and then I'll try to draw them together. The reason you are in Chicago will become clear as I do."

Crown noted the smirk that crossed Smithson's face, a reflection of the power the Chicago man felt because he possessed information Crown as yet did not. Sackville-West was lecturing Crown, not him. It equalized the conversation.

"Does the name Otto Hahn mean anything to you?" Sackville-West's questions interrupted Crown's thoughts.

"No, it doesn't."

"Professor Hahn is a German chemist presently involved in weapons experiments that we know extremely little about. In fact, what I'm told, I don't understand, but let me tell you anyway.

"You know that some atoms are radioactive—uranium, for example. Professor Hahn and his colleagues in Germany are experimenting with ways of splitting the atom, causing particles to break off and shoot away from the atom. Their hope is to start a chain reaction, one atom hitting another, and it hitting another, and on and on. This is nuclear fission."

"Where are you when you have nuclear fission?" Crown asked, sorry to see the conversation take a scientific turn.

"London and Washington speculate that the chain reaction could balloon violently, causing a massive explosion. The German research is designed to produce a bomb."

"That's just what the goddamn Germans need, another bomb."

"This one is different. Our scientists believe that just like a conventional explosion, when an atom bomb is detonated, there will be an extremely rapid rise in temperature, which will result in the complete vaporization, or gasification, of the products of the explosion and also of the container. These very hot gases produced in the restricted space will start to move outward immediately following the detonation. But there are several ways an atom bomb will differ from TNT. First, the amount of energy released will be a thousand or more times that of our largest current weapons. The scientists figure that the wind velocity a quarter-mile from the explosion site will reach eight-hundred miles per hour, and that all structures within two miles will be flattened."

Sackville-West looked up from the ominous statistics, and a shadow of fear crossed his face, something Crown had never seen before.

"Second," the Priest continued, "the explosion will be accompanied by a highly penetrating and deadly invisible ray. The scientists are only beginning to guess the effects of this ray, but they suspect it will have the effect of a massive overdose of X ray, that is, sickness and deterioration of the body parts. And third, radioactive particles will remain in the air and on the ground after an explosion. The particles will sicken or kill people coming in contact with them."

Sackville-West raised his hand to prevent an expression of disbelief, and said, "We know the Germans are spending millions on atom research right now. We also know that the Reich Ministry of Economics has forbidden the exportation of radioactive materials. The location of German stockpiles of uranium has become a German state secret of the highest priority. Even more frightening is that the Germans first produced heavy water in 1937 and split a uranium atom in 1938."

Sackville-West anticipated the question and went on, "Heavy water is water that has been made fractionally

56

more dense by passing electricity through it. It's used to slow down the neutrons and divert them back into the reaction, thus allowing the reaction to build. The fact the Germans first produced it five years ago indicates they are far ahead of us in nuclear-bomb research."

The Priest was warming to his subject. His usually conservative gestures were now more animated, and his voice lost its hard, articulated edge. He was the United States government's premier operative. His agency was given information and told to act. Act secretly, swiftly, and surely. It was inconceivable that his data had not been analyzed and sifted by the best minds in the country, who had been trained to look for weak spots, inconsistencies, and planted information. That Sackville-West had been ordered to act made it clear that the United States was deeply concerned about this German research. Crown's doubt of the unbelievable tale of a city-destroying bomb the size of a basketball disappeared.

"Now, to Hess's role in this affair. Rudolf Hess has always been viewed by us as Hitler's faithful, do-anything dog. Our studies of him done before his flight to Scotland showed him to be of medium intelligence with a rather shallow personality. We believed he rose to his powerful position in the Third Reich simply because of his unquestioned, blind obedience to Hitler. Hitler spoke, Hess jumped. Take a look at excerpts from some of Hess's speeches made before his crossing." Sackville-West produced another manila folder and passed it to Crown.

The thin sheets in the folder had only one green stripe. The first page was entitled, "EXCERPTS FROM SPEECHES BY RUDOLF HESS SHOWING HIS ATTITUDE TOWARD ADOLF HITLER." Crown glanced down the sheet. Each quotation was preceded by a date, a place, the name of the audience, and the purpose of the speech. The quotations were thickly obsequious:

Hitler is simply reason incarnate.

One must want the Führer.

With pride we see that one man remains beyond criticism, that is the Führer. This is because everyone feels and knows: he is always right, and he will always be right. The National Socialism of all of us is anchored in uncritical loyalty, in the surrender to the Führer that does not ask for the why in individual cases, in the silent execution of his orders. We believe that the Führer is obeying a higher call to fashion German history. There can be no criticism of this belief.

"This is sickening," Crown said as he handed the folder back. "Hess can fawn like no one I've ever heard of before."

"My thoughts, too. So the psychiatrists in England began their studies of Hess almost with their tongues in their cheeks. They had Hess figured out before he landed. He was a slobbering puppet.

"His mind seemed to deteriorate in his cell. As I mentioned earlier, he would at times completely withdraw from human contact, refusing to talk or to listen to the doctors. He suffered hallucinations and short spells of complete amnesia. He would spend hours staring at a blank wall."

Everette Smithson raised his hand slightly, as if he were asking a teacher for permission to speak. "It sounds like he may have been crazy all along. What's more crazy—saying idiot things about Hitler or staring at a wall?"

"Few of the top Nazi leaders were ever sane," Sackville-West said as he smiled at Smithson, who beamed, grateful for the recognition.

Sackville-West returned to the folder. "A few months after the amnesia and hallucinations began, Hess started dropping phrases like 'fission,' 'heavy water,' and 'uranium.' At first the doctors thought nothing of it, thinking it was the wandering of a deranged man. But the more Hess's mind seemed to deteriorate, the more these scientific words cropped up. The doctors soon realized they were not qualified to question Hess further, because they had no idea what he was talking about."

"So the European Documentation Center was called in?"

"Yes. Normally, Hess would have been referred to them immediately after his arrival. But he was clearly having mental troubles, and it was thought that psychiatrists would be more efficient gaining whatever information Hess could offer.

"The EDC produced a report after interviewing Hess one week. Mind you, the doctors were also present during these interviews. The EDC people, as good as they are, do not have psychiatric training, and we didn't want to lose whatever strands of sanity Hess still possessed.

"The EDC report indicates that Hess, far from being a do-nothing party speechmaker, had a very important role. For some reason unknown to us, he understood the potentials of what Professor Otto Hahn told the German leaders about an ultimate bomb long before other Nazi leaders did. He became interested in nuclear physics. Perhaps as a pacifier, Hitler assigned him to oversee the nuclear experiments and to act as liaison between the scientists and the Führer. Hess apparently kept a close watch on the experiments and became knowledgeable about them. For several years Hahn and the other German physicists told him immense amounts of scientific data in order to convince Hess to keep money coming to the experiments."

"How technical is Hess's information?" Crown asked.

"We don't know. The EDC men don't know anything about nuclear physics, so they can't ask intelligent questions. The best they can do is to scribble down what Hess mutters and pass it along."

"It wouldn't seem possible that a fanatic Nazi bootlicker never known for any intellectual prowess could have data that would help us."

"Perhaps not," Sackville-West replied, "but all information, no matter how general, must be extracted from Hess. The very least he knows is how much emphasis the Nazis are putting on the nuclear experiments, and that information alone is vital.

"There is only one man qualified to question Hess, and he is here at the University of Chicago. His name is Enrico Fermi. I'll be brief with his biography."

Sackville-West picked up a 3A sheet and summarized. "Fermi was born in 1901, the son of a railroad administrator. He quickly outgrew traditional education and began the study of physics as a hobby. He purchased and borrowed physics texts, and he decided to become a physicist before his high school ended. In 1918 Fermi went to Pisa to begin his higher education at the Reale Scuola Normale of Pisa. In 1922 he received his doctorate in physics. Fermi then taught at various institutions and studied with the world's leading physicists. In 1924 he became a lecturer at the University of Florence, and two years later he went to the University of Rome as a professor of theoretical physics. He made important discoveries involving the behavior of electrons in solids, electrical conductivity, electron emission, and thermoelectric effects.

"In 1928 he was married to his present wife, Laura. This apparently didn't slow him down, because in 1934 he developed a theory of radioactive beta-ray disintegration. He was awarded the Nobel Prize in physics in 1938." Sackville-West lowered the 3A. "What I'm trying to impress you with is that Enrico Fermi is a heavyweight."

"You've succeeded admirably," Crown replied. The prospect of meeting a Nobel laureate intrigued him.

"Mussolini began cracking down on the Jews and intellectuals in the late thirties. Fermi is a Catholic, but he found he couldn't carry on his research and teaching in the repressive atmosphere of fascist Italy.

He fled in 1939 and accepted a post at Columbia University in New York. A while ago he came to Hyde Park."

"Where he is working on research similar to the Germans', research on the ultimate bomb," Crown guessed. His assignment was beginning to take shape.

"Yes. His research is too important to take the time to fly him to London to interview Hess. So Hess is coming here. Fermi will interview him, and then Hess will return to England. European Documentation Center personnel will also come to Hyde Park to assist Fermi. In fact, Peter Kohler, the assistant chief of EDC, has been in Hyde Park for over a week preparing a safe house. Your job is to transport Hess from England, to ensure his safety while he is in Chicago, and to get Hess back to England. This must be done with unprecedented security. The Germans, and everyone else for that matter, must not even have slight suspicions of Hess's travels.

"As you know," Sackville-West went on, cutting off the opportunity for questions, "Smithson here is in charge of mid-States antisabotage. He has the resources you need, like automobiles and the like. He'll cooperate in every way, and you're to call him if you need anything. You have one week to work with Peter Kohler to make your preparations for Hess's confinement in Hyde Park. Next Monday, we have transportation for you to London to pick up Hess. I've prepared a packet of further instructions, which you can read downstairs. They are not to leave the building."

When the flurry of orders ended, Sackville-West rose and walked around the desk, indicating the meeting was over. He put his hand on Crown's elbow and said, "I'll walk you downstairs," meaning he had further instructions out of Smithson's hearing. As Crown left the room, he saw Smithson busily sweeping tobacco crumbs from the desk just vacated by the Priest. Smithson carefully dropped them into the wastepaper basket.

As they slowly descended the stairs, Sackville-West said, "I was a little hard on Smithson back there. Don't underestimate his value. He's in charge of our entire Midwest effort. And for some reason which escapes me, he's very good at it. The Germans are busy in the U.S., but Chicago has less instances of so-called accidental power blackouts, explosions, and missing personnel than any other area in the country. Smithson knows his job."

"What about Miguel's killer?"

"You don't have time to look for him. Stay away from that. That's an order."

"I want him dead." Crown could not keep the fever out of his voice.

Sackville-West said in a softer voice, "John, the importance of your assignment can't be overstated. The stakes are enormous. Your job is to escort Hess from London to Chicago. Miguel is gone, and you've got to forget him for a while."

Not very likely, Crown thought. Not very likely at all.

IV

Iron Mike was made to carry bombs, not passengers. The huge Flying Fortress, official USAF designation B17D, was the most sophisticated bomber in the world.

Boeing engineers in Seattle had been given three short guidelines: speed, payload, and protection of the crew. They produced a bomber that soon became the backbone of the Allied air forces. Speed: the B17D was powered by four 1,200-horsepower Wright Cyclone turbo-supercharged engines capable of propelling the plane at 325 miles per hour at 20,000 feet. Payload: over eight tons of bombs. Protection of the nine crewmen: three machine guns forward, two amidships, and two in a bulge beneath the fuselage.

The most distinctive feature of the B17D was its glass nose, in which the bombardier was stationed. This green-house was also one of the most vulnerable targets on the plane. The pilot and copilot sat side by side in the cockpit above the fuselage just ahead of the leading edge of the wing. Above the cockpit was an astro-hatch lookout post, resembling a bubble, where a crewman watched for diving enemy fighters.

Iron Mike was RAF Wing Commander Thomas Stratton's Fortress. He had flown it from the Boeing plant in Seattle to Wichita, where the oxygen system, automatic pilot, homing equipment, and machine guns were installed. Then on to London's Croyden Airport, where it had been assigned to the RAF's Hell Fire Fifteenth Squadron.

Stratton had personally painted "IRON MIKE" on the plane's nose behind the bombardier's greenhouse. The fierce cartoon boilermaker raised a steel mallet above his head for another blow at the black anvil he stood behind. Below the cartoon was the inscription "IRON MIKE—ONE MORE STRIKE," followed by fourteen bomb decals, each representing a mission over Germany.

On Monday, November 16, Stratton received orders to remove *Iron Mike's* bomb racks and install nine wicker seats. He protested loudly to Group Captain Benchley that his Fortress was a bomber, not a bus, but was told only that *Iron Mike* was being assigned to an extremely important mission that would only last several weeks. Stratton was not placated. His crew was enraged. Waist gunner Jimmy Toland threatened to reverse his .30-caliber machine gun so its barrel pointed at the passengers. Bombardier Lou Budwig promised to drop the nine passengers and their bloody wicker seats through the bomb bay somewhere over the freezing channel.

Despite the complaints, the bomb racks were removed with the alacrity which naturally follows an order given to an RAF group captain from an air chief marshal. Benchley had been sworn to secrecy by Air Chief Marshal Hilling. Neither the group captain's superior nor his superior's superior was to know of the work on *Iron Mike*. For security reasons, Stratton and his boiling crew were confined to quarters for the three days until the mission. Profits at the Goat's Head Pub near the airfield plummeted.

* * *

John Crown's safety harness strapped him tightly to the wicker seat. He was wearing a leather flight coat, and he was cold. The Fortress's cabin was not heated. And because it was not pressurized, *Iron Mike* could not climb above the weather. Adding to Crown's discomfort was the tough little waist gunner who sat on the bicycle seat near his machine gun, glowering at him.

Many times during the flight Crown questioned his choice of the B17 over a conventional passenger plane, say, a Boeing Stratoliner. The Stratoliner had padded seats, a heated and pressurized cabin, hot meals, and even bunks. But the drawbacks to the passenger plane were substantial and dangerous. It had a range of only 1,750 miles, which would have required a fueling stop at the RAF airfield in Greenland, one of the most hazardous fields in the world. And a more dangerous factor: scheduled passenger service between Croyden and New York's La Guardia had been suspended due to the heavy German air raids on London. A passenger plane would have been highly conspicuous. Crown didn't want a curious Luftwaffe fighter pilot investigating an unarmed Stratoliner.

A Fortress crossing the North Atlantic was routine. Hundreds of them flew from the U.S. to England as the States became increasingly involved in arming the British. Many of the B17's returned from England to Wichita to be reoutfitted and refurbished. To make *Iron Mike* look as if it needed repair, Wing Commander Stratton had been ordered to paint strings of black spots on the plane's wings and fuselage to resemble bullet holes and to blacken one of the engine encasements to appear as if it had been on fire. Enraged bombardier Budwig greased and regreased the bomb bay-doors.

Wing Commander Stratton climbed down from the cockpit and squeezed through the short aisle between seats toward Crown, who wondered how the 25-year-old Britisher had risen to the rank of wing commander at such a young age. Air Chief Marshal Hilling had promised him the best pilot available. Crown was an inexperienced flier, so his only gauge of Stratton's competence was the obvious high regard his crew had for him. Even the surly waist gunner straightened up as Stratton walked past.

"We're just over Lake Michigan, sir. We'll be arriving at Midway in thirty minutes or so," the wing commander said, just loud enough to be heard over the engine rumble. "The runway is clear, and the fog has let up, so there'll be no problem."

"Thanks, Commander," answered Crown. "Have you contacted our ground escort?"

"Yes, sir. They're in place and ready."

"Did the Hurricanes have any problem?" Crown asked, referring to the twelve RAF fighters that had accompanied the Fortress until it was out of the war zone. An hour after *Iron Mike* lifted off from Croyden, Crown had climbed into the observer's bubble atop the cockpit to view the escort. The shark-nosed fighters were flying in two six-plane V formations, one two miles off the bomber's starboard wing and the other at ten o'clock off the port wing. The formations had been ordered to maintain a substantial distance from the bomber to reduce the possibility an enemy spotter would see the entire procession and attach significance to it.

"No. They turned back two hundred and fifty miles out, and they're all back at Croyden. And the Greenland fighter escort returned to base in good shape, too."

Only during the last few hours of the transatlantic flight, when the plane had been well beyond the range of any German fighter, had *Iron Mike* been unescorted. It touched down at La Guardia for fueling. No one had been allowed to leave the plane.

"Good. Say, Commander, I understand your crew wasn't very enthusiastic about this flight."

"No, they weren't. Neither was I. No one would tell me who we were going to transport, but I took a look at the bloke when he boarded *Mike,* and I placed him." The commander bent closer and said, "This is one very important cargo."

"That's right. I toyed with the idea of confining you and your crew during our stay in Chicago, which may last several weeks. But I've got enough problems without a mutiny. So I want you to impress upon the crew that this flight and anything they may have seen on it must be kept an absolute secret. If I get wind of any leaks—and believe me, I will—everyone will be put into a barracks with a twenty-four-hour guard until the court-martial. That sounds harsh, Commander, but secrecy is vital here."

"There'll be no problem with the men. My engineer is an RAF volunteer from Chicago. He's been salivating ever since I told him our destination. He and the others don't want barracks duty."

As Stratton wove his way back to the cockpit ladder, Josef Ludendorf, sitting in the seat of Crown's left, leaned toward Crown and asked in a voice fraught with tension, "Is everything all right?"

"Yes, of course. The commander just told me we'd be landing in Chicago shortly."

Ludendorf had been nervous throughout the flight. He had not tried to hide it, and told Crown that he had flown only twice before. Both prior flights had been accompanied by heaving sickness. He had managed to contain himself thus far. The EDC chief was a slight man, perhaps five feet, five inches tall. He was losing his hair, and he slicked down long strands on the side of his head over the bald spot. He wore rimless spectacles and constantly shoved them back on his nose. A small red spot glowed from both sides of his nose where the ill-fitting glasses kept the skin perpetually raw. His mouth was small and pinched. At first Crown attributed the constant cringe on Ludendorf's face to his fear of flying, but later, as the bomber left the turbulent air of the North Atlantic and the ride became smooth, Crown realized the fearful expression was chronic.

Ludendorf was a bifurcated man. Crown's first impression of a hesitant, retiring, and anemic individual was dispelled soon after their conversation about Hess's interrogation began. Somewhere over the North

Atlantic, Ludendorf had launched himself into the briefing, happy to be diverted from grim thoughts of the flight. Ludendorf's cracking voice firmed. His presentation had been systematic and complete. And he had made what could have been a weary account of Hess's medical condition fascinating.

Crown now saw that Ludendorf was beginning to lose himself to the terror of the approaching landing. The EDC chief sucked on his lower lip and gripped the chair arms as if he were visiting a dentist. Crown attempted to shift Ludendorf's thoughts by asking, "You say you're convinced Hess isn't insane?"

Ludendorf wheeled in his seat to Crown, his eyes wide and his left hand ready to gesture for a conversation that would not require gestures. He pitched into a speech. "Yes. Yes. I'm told by psychiatrists that although he shows symptoms of several mental disorders, most of the time he is lucid." Ludendorf spoke with the soft German accent of one who has spent years trying to overcome that last vestige of his origin. "I did not have trouble communicating with him. That is to say, he had no difficulty complaining to me about various things. It was often hard keeping his mind on the subject at hand. . . ."

To slow Ludendorf down, Crown interjected, "What did Hess complain about?"

"Numerous grievances. His most frequent was that secret agents were trying to poison his food. He would not specify whether they were German or British agents, but he mumbled things like Himmler was out to get him. He began losing weight, so one of the guards agreed to sample Hess's food before Hess ate it. This quieted him a little, but even when he dined with us, he was very suspicious. If the food was served from a common tray, he would select a portion, but never one nearest him. He also accused the jailers of plotting to destroy his sanity by pumping the sounds of motorcycles, airplanes, and machine guns into his cell. These sounds were hallucinations. Then he complained

68

that his cell was electronically bugged. We could not convince him otherwise."

"Was it?" asked Crown.

"Of course. But it should not have concerned him." Ludendorf managed a weak smile. He knew why Crown had asked the same questions he had answered hours before. He was grateful for it.

"Hess's favorite topic is Hitler," the professor continued. "He often recounts that when he first heard Hitler speak he had a vision that Hitler could lead Germany to greatness. Hess enjoys telling how he became a fervent worker in the Nazi party. He regards Hitler as a god, the only man who can save Germany. In his cell, Hess gave speeches to the guards or psychiatrists about the glorious Hitler. Have you read the excerpts from his speeches made before the flight?"

"I read as far as I could."

"Well, these talks in his cell were similar to them. In fact, so similar they sounded memorized. We began looking more closely at this drivel and discovered that most of it *was* memorized. Hess gave almost the identical speech day after day. None of it was spontaneous. Hess was not searching for new and increasingly eloquent statements about Hitler, as a true flatterer will. So we began digging a little deeper into Hess's true feelings." Ludendorf released his grip on the chair and used both hands to animate his lecture.

"We discovered that Hess was bitter and frustrated during his last year or two in Germany. He felt he was being pushed aside, manipulated out of favor by people he considered upstarts in the party. People like Martin Bormann, who took over Hess's positions and titles after Hess flew to Scotland. Hess found himself doing less and less decision-making and more and more ceremonial appearances. He began to feel he was just a legitimate front for less-than-desirable elements that were rising to power in the Nazi party. He resented that his enormous popularity with the German people was being exploited by these people, whom Hess occasionally calls criminals."

Rudolf Hess rose from his seat in the row ahead of Crown. Hess had stared stonily at the seat in front of him during the entire trip. The only thing he had said since boarding was to request to use the makeshift lavatory at the back of the cabin, to which he walked now. He carried his leather shaving kit under his arm. It was filled with pill bottles. Ever since the British doctors had told him the pills were useless, Hess had been sheepish about taking them in public. He still took about forty pills a day, but now only when he thought he was not being watched. As Hess walked past Crown and Ludendorf, a guard stood and followed him. The guard was one of five crack commandos sitting near Hess. This man, a burly six-footer dressed in street clothes and a heavy overcoat, had the unpleasant task of watching Hess through the peephole in the lavatory door while Hess relieved himself and swallowed his pills. At no time, day or night, during Hess's seventeen months in England had he not been watched.

Heather McMillan unbuckled the safety straps and rose from her seat next to Hess's.

"How much longer until we land, Mr. Crown?" she yelled above the drone of the plane.

For the first time since they had met two days ago, Crown looked at her squarely. Her large eyes were deep green and contrasted with her shoulder-length, muted auburn hair. Her mouth was wide, perhaps too wide. A few light freckles were splashed over the thin bridge of her nose. She purposely kept her full lower lip tucked in, reflecting the business of the question.

"The commander said we'll arrive within thirty minutes. How are your conversations with Herr Hess?" Crown asked, knowing Hess had said almost nothing.

"Wonderful," Heather replied, showing him the yellow pad. "I took down everything he said verbatim and used a quarter of a page. Occasionally I ask him to
70

pause so I can flex my worn-out fingers." She lifted her right hand and made a series of fists. Ludendorf joined them in the small laugh.

Crown had reviewed her dossier during his first hour in England. RAF Lieutenant McMillan was Air Chief Marshal Hilling's adjutant. She had initially been assigned to Hilling as his typist, but soon displayed skill at distributing orders, rough-drafting correspondence, and turning away unwelcome junior officers beset with minor problems. Soon she was making decisions for the air chief marshal. Each day she submitted a list of orders she recommended. Hilling reviewed them briefly, occasionally penned in a change, signed them, and returned the sheet to Heather. She would then send them off. The air chief marshal discovered he had more time for major decisions. As his adjutant, Heather became one of the few women non-nurses to hold an officer's commission in the RAF.

Because of the absolute trust the air chief marshal had in her, and because of the strict security of the mission, he had assigned Heather, rather than an outsider, to assist Crown. Her primary duty was boring: take down on a legal pad every word Hess uttered en route. She would also transcribe the conversations between Hess and Enrico Fermi in Chicago. Thus far, her job had been easy. On her pad appeared the only thing Hess had said since he was put on the plane, twelve identical questions: "Do you think it might be possible for me to use the bathroom?"

The Fortress lurched as it hit an air pocket, and she grabbed for the back of her wicker seat. The woolen scarf, wrapped several times around her neck, and the tight flight coat made her movements awkward. She wore regulation RAF gray-brown flight pants, designed for warmth, not style. Their legs made her look bottom-heavy. The RAF commando sitting across the aisle from her straightened in his seat and tried to catch her eye. He failed, just as he had failed in his

71

clumsy attempt to meet her as they boarded the bomber.

Rudolf Hess walked from the head, his feet wide apart in an exaggerated sailor's gait to prevent losing his balance. He grabbed the back of Crown's chair, expecting the plane to lurch, and when it did not, he said, "Excuse me," and slipped past Heather to his seat. She made an elaborate production of writing "Excuse me" on her pad, smiled brightly, and sat down.

Ludendorf said to Crown, "I think she is telling us she's underemployed."

The snapping of Heather's seat buckle and the unsnapping of the commando's were almost simultaneous. The soldier rose from his seat, smiled knowingly to the commando sitting next to him, and then leaned across the aisle to Heather. He was a large man with a hard-bitten face, the face of a professional soldier. His flattop hair was brown and close-cropped.

Crown couldn't hear what he said, but her shaking head left no doubt of the nature of his proposal. He spoke again, this time holding up a note pad and riffling it with his thumb. Again she shook her head, this time more insistently. The commando's smile vanished, and he exposed his lower teeth as he spoke.

Crown tapped the commando's leg with his hand. The soldier looked at him, then looked away, as if dismissing a servant, and returned his overbearing attention to the reddening Heather. Crown tapped again, and now the soldier couldn't ignore the man he had been told was his superior on this journey. Crown leaned forward and said in a low voice, "How about leaving the lady alone? She's had a long day."

"Listen, Yank, you may be my boss here, but you can't bloody well run my life, now, can you?"

"I'm telling you to back off." The soldier didn't recognize the thin warning smile that crossed Crown's face.

"Fuck off, Yank."

No one in the plane saw Crown's hand move. Not

even the offending commando, who jerked upright, paled, then slumped clumsily back into his seat with his mouth opening and closing like a fish out of water. His friend in the next seat had to help him with his safety straps.

Heather only knew the soldier was no longer pestering her. Crown must have said something. She looked over her shoulder at him and smiled her confused thanks.

Ludendorf again wanted an escape from his fear. "Can you tell me how you got Hess out of the hospital?"

"Sorry, Professor. Perhaps when this is over I can let you know. I've been instructed to tell no one."

"Of course," replied Ludendorf, "but I'll bet it was interesting."

Very interesting. Hess had been interned at Maindiff Court Hospital in June. The hospital had been chosen because it was suitable for the accommodation of a psychopathic personality, although no severe mental cases were treated there. In addition, many British officers were undergoing treatment and recovering from war wounds at the hospital. Removing Hess from the hospital without raising suspicion was Crown's first task when he arrived in England. He assumed that Nazi agents, ordered to discover why the deputy führer made the flight, were closely tracking Hess. And then there was the insatiable British press.

On November 18, after Crown and Heather painstakingly searched RAF officers' files, Lieutenant Chauncey Stewart, a supply officer in the Tenth Wing, stationed at Croyden, received a phone call from Air Chief Marshal Hilling ordering him to report to the base commander's headquarters at 1100 hours the following morning. The lieutenant, a tall, thick-set man with bushy black eyebrows and a full crop of black hair, was nervously wringing his service cap when he entered the quonset hut. He glanced about quickly, and

73

was only slightly relieved to see a civilian. He nevertheless stood stiffly at attention.

"No need to be formal, Lieutenant. You outrank whatever rank I ever had in the service. Will you please read this?" Crown handed the lieutenant a sealed envelope.

Crown's assurances of his inferior rank did not assuage Lieutenant Stewart. He fumbled as he tore open the envelope and read:

EYES ONLY

Nov. 18, 1942

Lieutenant Chauncey Stewart
Supply Station
Tenth Wing, RAF
London, England

Lieutenant Stewart:

The person delivering this letter to you is John Crown. You will follow his orders as if they were my orders.

You will accompany Mr. Crown to Maindiff Court Hospital and remain there for as long as he determines.

I have cleared your absence with your superiors and you are not to discuss this with them or anyone else.

Yours very truly,

J. R. Hilling
Air Chief Marshal
Royal Air Force

Lieutenant Stewart looked up from the letter, no less puzzled and tense. "Sir, may I ask, why to a hospital? Am I sick?"

"No, Lieutenant. Air Chief Marshal Hilling is arranging for a very important man to leave the hospital in strict security. No one must suspect he has gone.

You'll be that person's stand-in during his two- or three-week absence. We want someone in his cell, or more correctly, in his ward, while he is gone, to give the impression he's still in the hospital. You were chosen simply because of your physical resemblance to this man."

The lieutenant whispered, "Hess."

"Lieutenant," Crown said, not displeased, "if you think you know the name of the person, you will forget the name. This assignment is more important than anything you've ever worked on before. And it must be kept an absolute secret. Your guess can't be mentioned to anyone."

"I understand, Mr. Crown. I should tell you that in May 1941 I was kidded a lot by friends because I looked like a certain very high-ranking German who had just flown into Scotland."

"How unfortunate. Tell me, Lieutenant, are you always this nervous when receiving letters?"

"No, sir," Stewart answered, tension draining from him, "it's just that Air Chief Marshal Hilling phoned me last night. An RAF lieutenant normally never receives phone calls from a marshal. That was bad enough, but then he told me to report here this morning because I was going to jail. That's all he said."

Crown laughed and said, "Well, to a hospital cell, not really a jail."

"I know that now, sir," Stewart said wanly, "but I put in a bad night last night."

That night, a screaming Rover ambulance pulled into the Maindiff Court Hospital's emergency entrance. Only thin streams of light escaped its hooded blackout headlights as it swerved away from the entrance, noisily switched gears to reverse, and backed under the canvas canopy. Four attendants lifted the injured man from the truck and gently placed him on a litter, then carried him quickly to the emergency door, where a

75

physician and nurse waited. Only the injured man's nose protruded from the heavy white gauze wrapped around his head. The man moaned softly. He was gently transferred to a rolling table. John Crown, dressed in white coat and pants, lifted a stethoscope from the coat pocket and plugged it into his ears and said to the ambulance attendants, "Thank you. We'll take him from here." Heather McMillan, wearing a nurse's white smock and a cap bobby-pinned to her hair, closed the emergency door behind the attendants as they left.

Through the gauze over his mouth, Lieutenant Chauncey Stewart mumbled, "This bloody war."

Flat feet kept Bertrum Atley out of the Royal Navy. So he bought specially built-up shoes and wore them for two weeks before his army physical, but his arches fell during the walk to the recruiting station, where he was examined and rejected by army doctors. His last chance to serve England was in the Royal Air Force. For three weeks before the physical, two hours a day, while he dreamed of piloting a Hurricane, Atley stood in his bare feet on whiskey bottles, trying to push his arches up.

On the morning of the physical, he took a lorry to the air-force recruiting station. He sat as much as he could during the interminable delays while his application was being processed. In the examination lines, he stood bowlegged on the edges of his feet to keep pressure off the arches. The physical lasted two minutes. His feet passed, and Atley's joy was not diminished when the doctor, who had noticed his bowlegged stance in line, ordered Atley to drop his pants so that he could, with a flashlight, look for piles. Atley passed that, too.

He was in the Royal Air Force, but as ninety percent of air-force personnel the world over will testify, there is always some test during the physical that keeps one from becoming a fighter pilot. Atley's was the color-blindness test. When the nurse held up a series of multicolored charts and asked him to identify the numbers hidden in the swirling colors, all Atley could say was "Very nice" and "Lovely."

The RAF assigned Aircraftman Second Class Atley to the Maindiff Court Hospital with a job entitled "Short-trip Pallbearer." His duty was to pick up bodies from hospital rooms, load them into coffins, and transfer the coffins to waiting trucks.

Like all hospitals, Maindiff Court hid its failures. Bodies were removed during the graveyard shift, midnight to eight in the morning. Each night, Atley arrived to find the list of deceased and a row of empty coffins. The job was not a hard one. He usually did his full shift's paperwork and loading in five hours, and he occupied the remaining time by drinking tea with the coffin truck driver, Aircraftman Howard Ross.

On this night there were nine caskets, lined in an even row on the loading ramp. His work was completed, and Ross was a few minutes late, so Atley occupied his time by carving his initials on one of the coffins. The loading-ramp door swung open, and Atley quickly pocketed his knife. A tall nurse with reddish-brown hair pushed a coffin on a roller onto the ramp.

"Here's a late one," the nurse said. "Can you get him on the truck?"

"You bet," replied Atley. "It's a little late, but I'll manage."

The nurse wore the insignia of a lieutenant, and Atley wished all lieutenants looked like her. He had a weakness for freckles.

She nodded toward the hot plate and boiling water Atley had prepared for himself and Ross. "Do you mind if I have some tea? Rolling this poor man down here has quite winded me."

Atley rushed to the hot plate. He shook out a few drops of last night's tea from Ross's cup and handed it to her. Heather McMillan looked into the cup and could not suppress a wince. She asked, "How often do you clean these cups?"

"Oh, about once a month," said the embarrassed Atley, "whether they need it or not. Here, I'll fix that."

He opened his knife and scraped the tea residue from the inside of Heather's cup. He turned it over and tapped the bottom with his palm. Heather retreated several steps.

"Let me guess," Atley said, seeing his opportunity to entertain the nurse wither rapidly, "you've lost your thirst."

"Quite, yes."

Heather turned to the approaching whir of a truck running at high rpm's in low gear. Atley said, "That'll be Ross, the hearse driver."

The camouflage-green Chevrolet two-tonner circled and backed toward the ramp. The tarpaulin covering the flatbed swayed as the truck hit a pothole and bumped into the dilapidated tires attached to the ramp. Atley squinted in surprise when a lean RAF pilot officer jumped down from the cab instead of the corpulent Ross.

John Crown held out an RAF identity card and said, "I'm Lewis. Ross was given a day's leave, and I'm taking his job while he's gone."

Atley shrugged his shoulders and lied, "Well, he usually helps me load them."

"So'll I. I'm in a hurry. Those blokes didn't let me off my other duties tonight. They just added this one. Let's get the coffins on the ramp first, and we'll load the one on the roller last." Crown lowered his voice and added, "That way, maybe we can get the good-looking nurse to hang around here long enough to get her name. She seems attached to that coffin. Must have been one of her patients."

The nurse's devotion to the casket was touching. She insisted that Atley and the truck driver move the coffin with unusual care, and she walked beside it as Atley pushed and Crown guided the box into the truck and
78

lowered it from the roller to the truck bed. As Atley secured the truck's canvas flap, Heather touched his arm and said, "Thank you. You don't know how much he means to me."

Probably not. Rudolf Hess awoke sitting comfortably in a flight seat on the Fortress. He had no recollection of the coffin.

A blue light on the cabin roof fluttered, returning Crown's thoughts to the Fortress. Waist gunner Jimmy Toland buckled himself into the gunner's seat with practiced hands. Toland now concentrated on Heather McMillan rather than Crown. Rudolf Hess roused himself from his stupor and helped Heather into the safety harness. She smiled her thanks. Josef Ludendorf's straps were so tight, he appeared to be strangling.

Iron Mike banked to port and shuddered as the landing gear locked into place. The pale light in the fuselage cabin dimmed and flickered out. A distant electric engine whirred as the flaps lowered. The engines cut back, and the bomber was ominously silent. Josef Ludendorf's hands jumped spastically as the plane touched down at Chicago's Midway Airport.

V

Iron Mike's belly hatch swung open, and John Crown dropped to the concrete. He stood in a low crouch and squinted against the sleet sweeping across the runway. A British commando came through next, quickly turned a full circle, and trotted to his post near the starboard wing. Another trooper followed and ran to his position under the nose of the bomber. Both moved with practiced efficiency despite the Thompson submachine guns under their overcoats.

At Crown's hand signal, three automobiles, parked fifty yards off the port wing, slowly approached the bomber in procession. Although it was dark, their headlights were off, and after hours of thunder from the bomber engines, the cars seemed eerily silent. Heather's admirer limped to Crown's side. He carried a submachine gun under the folds of an overcoat draped over his arm, and he pointed it at the chauffeur of the first car, a dark green Chevrolet. The trooper grinned evilly and looked for an excuse to blow out the windshield. The driver, peering through the jerking wipers, saw the weapon but did not slow. Halfway to the bomber, he signaled for a right turn. The commando reluctantly lowered his gun.

The remaining passengers were helped through the hatch by a commando who took a little too long assisting Heather. Ludendorf, drained from the ordeal of the landing, shakily two-handed himself to the ground. He mouthed a silent prayer of thanks. Hess slipped through the hatch and landed with surefooted grace. The remaining British trooper followed.

Hess began to whine as the convoy rolled away from the bomber. *"Mein Gott,"* he whimpered, *"es ist kalt."* He repeated the complaint several times, to no one, then switched to accented English. His face completely lacked animation. His thick black hair was disheveled, and heavy stubble darkened his receding chin. His eyes were dulled by the clouded, distant look of paranoia. Heather tried to draw him into a conversation, but Hess ignored her and rambled on about the cold. Crown asked himself how this shell could have been one of the most powerful men in Germany.

The convoy rolled through the early-evening sleet on Fifty-ninth Street toward Hyde Park, due east of Midway Airport. They passed block after block of small blue-collar homes with well-groomed yards. Small trees planted along the parking strips approached their first winter, and their leaves blew through the convoy.

"I hope my assistant was helpful setting up the house," Ludendorf said quietly.

"Kohler was very helpful. We did a lot of work in a short time."

"Kohler is a good man," Ludendorf continued. "He's the strong man of our team."

They used the ancient interrogation technique called strong-man/weak-man or good-guy/bad-guy. One interrogator, Ludendorf, is sympathetic and understanding. The other, Kohler, paces back and forth in front of the subject, gesturing wildly, threatening, swearing. Occasionally the good guy tells the bad guy to calm down and take a break. He offers the subject cigarettes and coffee. Soon the subject looks to the weak man for relief from the abusive onslaught. The subject continues to resist pressure from the strong man but begins to confide in the weak one, who tactfully asks the same questions. The strong-weak team is the most effective method of soft interrogation extant.

"Kohler and I go a long way back, Crown. He was a student at the University of Munich. One of my pupils. He was editor of the student newspaper in 1933, while I was chairman of the overseeing board. He received the same threats I did. Even harsher threats, because he was not a faculty member. In the early years, the Nazis found it easy to bully students, you know. I tried to help him while I was there, but things got bad for him after I fled. He was severely beaten twice. After the second beating, he contacted me in London, and I sent him a little money to escape. He was my research assistant for a while, and then I began using him at the EDC."

"Where's his family?" Crown asked, having already read Kohler's file. One of the Priest's maxims was never turn off free information, even if it seemed duplicative.

"His mother passed away years ago. And his father is still in Munich. He's got a good job there and apparently does not open his mouth against the Nazis, which Kohler resents. His father thinks Peter is a traitor. He has not heard from his father in years."

"Is Kohler a full-time interrogator now?" Crown asked, looking over his shoulder at Hess, who was still whimpering about the weather. Flecks of spittle had collected at the corners of his mouth. The commando on Hess's right was scowling in disgust. Heather jotted down Hess's complaints.

"Oh, yes, when there is someone who needs questioning. Other times, he does what most people think the EDC actually does, poring over German magazines and newspapers, gleaning facts about German society, government, and so forth. We have an impressive file, you know, and can easily justify our existence to any nosy member of Parliament."

The convoy entered Jackson Park and wound its way around the grass playfields and ponds. The park was Hyde Park's immense baby-sitter. It could accommodate a dozen baseball games and hundreds of swimmers, joggers, squirrel feeders and courters. After nightfall it also accommodated roaming bands of hoodlums.

Crown leaned closer to Ludendorf and asked, "How often is Hess like this?"

"Well, most of the time he just sits and stares. And sometimes, like now, he whines for hours about almost anything, the food, his bed, or the company, meaning me." Ludendorf smiled depreciatingly. "Other times, he is ingratiatingly polite, complimenting me on my tie, my coat, my ancestors, anything. And once in a while he will pompously lecture about the Fatherland and how it is the seedbed of Western civilization. He talks about the purity of the Aryan race and the insidious effect the Jews are having on his pure German stock. You do not know how hard it is for me to sit through that stinking pap."

"I've only heard him for a few minutes, and I'm already getting the idea," Crown answered. "I don't care what the psychiatrists say, our friend Hess is crazy."

The convoy turned north on Kimbark and continued past a few scurrying students with heads bent against the wind. College students differ from campus to campus, Crown thought. He had graduated from the University of Oregon in 1930. It was a fine academic institution, but an enterprising student could drown the academic flavor with football, beer, coeds, and sultry Oregon spring evenings. It wasn't done here. The University of Chicago undergrads Crown had seen in his days in Hyde Park were invariably intent, with brows furled in concentration even as they walked. Most looked at the sidewalk a few feet ahead of them, perhaps afraid the beauty of the Quad would disrupt their problem-solving. Their arms were always full of books on abstruse subjects reserved by other colleges for graduate students. A few had furtively glanced at Crown as they passed in the Quad, instinctively knowing he was an outsider and would never understand academic pressure and zeal. Crown had never seen so many pimples in his life.

The convoy slowed in front of a nondescript brick house on Kimbark near Fifty-sixth Street. That is, nondescript to an untrained observer. The home was heavily, though discreetly, fortified. Like Smithson's house a block away, an iron-spike fence surrounded the small yard. The spikes were made of one-half-by-two-inch iron bars set only four inches apart, thereby making it impossible to look into the yard from anywhere but directly in front of the house.

Crown emerged from the Ford and walked to the gate. After several seconds, he located the hair-width strand of wire that completely circled the house on the fence. If it were depressed or broken by an intruder climbing over the fence, an alarm would sound in the house. Crown looked up to the dormer and casually touched his nose. A dull red light flickered behind the gauze window shade. Crown's hand brushed his chin, and he heard the faint click of the gate lock being electronically thrown open.

Smithson's gardener had done an expert job disguising the second warning signal. A strip of turf crossing the front yard and circling the house had been lifted from the lawn just long enough to place a pressure-sensitive mat under it. The turf was replaced and the yard watered heavily. Only a few strands of dying grass indicated the lawn had been tampered with. Even the weight of a small dog on the strip of grass would toll bells in the house.

The draperies of the large picture window facing the porch were drawn, and a subdued light shone through the fabric. The light was a ruse. Three feet behind the window, a bulkhead made of three-inch walnut planks had been constructed from the living-room floor to the ceiling. A guard was permanently stationed between the bulkhead and the window, where he could see the yard easily through the deceptively transparent draperies. The light bulb that gave the home a lived-in appearance was in a small box to prevent light from dulling the guard's vision. A bullet might make it through the fence, the window, and the guard, but it would not penetrate the plank wall.

Crown felt under the mailbox near the front door and found two buttons. He pressed the first button three times and the second button twice. The front door clicked and Crown stepped inside.

"Nothing rhymes with orange." He said the code words, feeling ridiculous. But he had shot a man once because the code was not forthcoming, and Crown knew the bulkhead guard holding the .45 pistol had been given similar instructions.

"Nor with purple," came the reply. The agent put the weapon back on the windowsill and resumed his watch.

Crown signaled the convoy. A commando emerged and held the door for Heather and Hess. Another soldier stood near the car door and scanned the windows of houses across the street. Two escorted them quickly through the gate and to the porch.

The commandos amused Crown. They had been ordered to act like civilians doing everyday business. But they looked just like what they were—dangerous, trained men on an important assignment, keyed up, ready to explode, fingers taut on triggers. God save a plumber from walking out of a nearby house carrying a length of pipe. He wouldn't make it through the front door.

Crown closed the door behind the group and turned to face Peter Kohler.

"Welcome to our house." Kohler smiled, his English lightly accented with his German upbringing.

"Glad to be here," Crown replied, shaking Kohler's large hand. He was a wide-shouldered man in his late twenties. Kohler wore a short-sleeved flannel work shirt, and the cords of muscle were visible on his hairless arm. Crown guessed the German's neck size at eighteen inches. Kohler had receding, wispy blond hair and a nose that had been broken and badly reset. His smile was marred by a chipped front tooth. Crown knew his gentle handshake belied the power of the man. "Looks like a good job preparing the house while I was gone."

"Actually, I only did the legwork," Kohler demurred. "Everette Smithson was very helpful. He could secure a soccer field if he had to. Professor," Kohler said as he held out both hands to Ludendorf, "good to see you. You look like the trip was terrible."

"It was. It was. I haven't taken a full breath since we left Croydon Airport hours and hours ago."

They laughed together, and Kohler took the professor's briefcase. Then Kohler stopped short.

"Ah, Deputy Führer Hess, welcome to America. I understand this is your first visit here." Kohler's voice took on a hard edge as he slipped into the strong-man routine. Hess stared wide-eyed at Kohler, and the edges of his mouth turned down in fear. He locked his lips and said nothing.

"Come, come, Peter," said Ludendorf, "we can talk to Rudolf later. He needs a good meal and some sleep first."

"Let's not waste time with this—"

"Peter," Ludendorf interjected harshly, "we'll do as I say."

"Ja, Professor," responded Kohler, sounding suitably reprimanded. The little act was impressive and professional.

Crown introduced Heather McMillan, and Kohler said he was charmed as only a European can say he is charmed. Heather said she was glad to know him, and it bothered Crown. And that disturbed him further.

"We've done some work on the interior of the house, too, John. Why don't I show the three of you around? Hess can wait in the office," Kohler said as he pointed to a door to the rear of the living room. A commando gently took Hess's arm.

Kohler led them up the stairs to the second-floor

86

hallway. A heavyset man sat on a three-leg stool, and his posterior hung over the edges. He turned, nodded a greeting, and resumed surveying the yard and street. A scoped .30-06 rifle lay in a case at his feet near a telephone. A flashlight with transparent red foil taped over its lens lay on the windowsill.

"This is Jones, or so I was introduced by Smithson. I'm told Jones is a crack shot."

Kohler ushered the group into a back bedroom. It was sparsely furnished with a cot, a chest of drawers, a well-worn leather easy chair, and a sink.

"We'll keep Hess here when he's not being questioned. The bars over the window are set back a foot from the glass, and a light mesh screen covers the window. It's impossible to tell from the alley that the window is barred. We replaced the bedroom door after Jones displayed how weak it was by rapidly putting his fist through it three times. The new one is solid oak and has two throw bolts that lock from the outside."

The procession followed Kohler downstairs into what had been a kitchen. Here another agent sat in front of a bank of phones. He quickly took his feet off the table and put a novel down as Kohler entered. The man wore a revolver in a belt holster.

"The phones connect all positions in the house. And there is an outside line." Kohler lifted a U.S. Army two-way radio out of its backpack and continued, "We also have a walkie-talkie communications to our two men on the street, who hopefully you didn't see as you approached.

"I looked and didn't find them," Crown said. "I usually do."

"Very impressive, Peter," Ludendorf said. "This house is more secure than our EDC headquarters in London."

"Once again, most of it is Smithson's work. When does Hess first see Mr. Fermi, John?"

"On Monday. I have an appointment with Fermi tomorrow at his laboratory."

They entered the office, where Rudolf Hess sat in an overstuffed chair. The commando leisurely rose as they entered. His submachine gun lay on the desk, and he kept a hand on the stock. Hess was humming a tuneless drone and did not appear to notice the group until Kohler said, "Herr Hess, are you so ill-mannered that you do not rise when a lady enters the room?" nodding to the uncomfortable Heather.

Hess stopped humming and slowly came to his feet, not looking directly at anyone. The deputy führer was the picture of abject humility. His fall from Germany's high inner council to a prisoner had stripped him of all vestiges of pride. He was as crumpled as a piece of scrap paper. One side of his shirttail hung out of his pants. Both shoelaces, given to him for the transatlantic trip only, were undone and lay twisted on the carpet. The leather tongue of his left brogan was jammed to the side of the shoe, and the sock hung limply around his ankle. Hess stooped like an old man, making his tall, husky frame appear worn-out and fragile. A flash of pity passed through Crown.

"Professor, Heather, I'll drive you to your hotel rooms," Crown said. "You'll take care of Hess for the evening, Peter?"

"With pleasure," Kohler replied with a hint of malice. "Herr Hess will find his Chicago stay both interesting and . . . uh, exciting."

Crown thought the strong-man act was carried too far, particularly during Hess's first hour in Hyde Park, but then, Ludendorf and Kohler were the professionals. If anyone could get the full story of the German atom-bomb experiments from Hess, these men, with the help of Enrico Fermi, could.

Josef Ludendorf put his hand on Hess's arm and said, "Now, don't worry about a thing, Rudolf. I'll be back first thing in the morning." He turned quickly to Kohler and said in a stage whisper, "Peter, I want you to take Rudolf to his room and bring him dinner. That is all. We can talk to him tomorrow."

"Of course, Professor."

They trailed out of the office. Only Peter Kohler remained with Hess.

On the sidewalk, Heather touched Crown's arm and said quietly, "I feel sorry for Hess, alone with that Kohler."

"Kohler knows what he's doing," Crown said. "Hess is in the best of hands."

"Nevertheless," Heather persisted, miffed at Crown's insensitivity, "I don't like Kohler's eyes. And you've seen how Hess cowers when Kohler talks to him. Someone else should be with Hess."

Crown opened the Ford's rear door, and Ludendorf climbed in. Crown stopped Heather and said, "You don't know the full importance of what we are trying to get from Hess. His comfort can't interfere with our work. I hope you understand this, Heather."

Her glare conveyed anything but affection for Crown. She entered the car without saying anything further. No, she did not understand.

Rudolf Hess stared blankly at the wall as Crown's Ford pulled away. Kohler sat in the chair vacated by the commando. He looked anxiously at Hess. Kohler's authority had disappeared.

When the sound of the car faded, Hess's eyes snapped from the wall to Kohler, who jerked back in his seat as if he had been slapped in the face. Hess whispered in German, "Is this room clear?"

"There is no sound equipment here, Herr Reichsführer."

"The German bear has escaped." Hess said the code words.

"No cage could hold him," replied Kohler, who sprang from his chair into a rigid stance with his arm held upright in the fascist salute. *"Heil Hitler!"* he said fervently.

The despair and humility and fear disappeared from Hess as he rose from the chair. His eyes focused and his face lost its morose puffiness and regained the chiseled angles of decision and importance. He stood erect, with his shoulders back. Here was the Hess who had been Adolf Hitler's closest counselor for almost two decades, the Hess who could rouse a hundred thousand Germans to fever pitch with a few words, and who had overseen the German invasions of Austria, Czechoslovakia, and Poland. Hess raised his hand in the sloppy salute permitted from only the highest echelons of power and said, *"Heil Hitler!"*

Kohler remained at rigid attention as Hess said, "The Führer was right, as always, Kohler. We have duped them all. The British and Americans are youngsters at these games." Hess allowed himself a thin smile, not the smile of the idiot, half-crazed Hess in Maindiff Court Hospital, but the searing smile of a man with enormous life-and-death power.

"Herr Reichsführer, may I say how good it is to see you." Kohler choked with emotion.

"Thank you, Kohler. You have done your work well and will not go unnoticed by the Führer." Hess's eyes gleamed under the thick brows. "The next few days will tip the balance, Kohler. The next few days."

VI

Security at the University of Chicago's Metallurgical Laboratory was the tightest in the United States and perhaps the world. It took two forms: secrecy and protection.

Enrico Fermi's experiments had the highest secrecy rating given by the U.S. government, higher than the rocketry experiments in Los Angeles, the bomber factories in Seattle, and the tank plants in Detroit. Fewer than forty-five people knew the existence of the Fermi experiments, and only eleven—Fermi and eight other Chicago scientists, the president of the United States, and General Leslie R. Groves, coordinator of the bomb project—were authorized to know the purpose of the tests.

Secrecy was maintained by a strict division of labor and knowledge. Suppliers often asked the reason materials were ordered, but never received an answer. It was discovered that the graphite dust from the pile had a negative effect on the reaction, so it was decided to assemble the huge structure inside an airtight balloon. One of Fermi's young scientists visited the Goodyear Tire and Rubber Company in Akron, specialists in the manufacture of military balloons, and asked for a square balloon the size of a squash court. Because he could not disclose the purpose of the square balloon, it took him two hours to convince the Goodyear people he was in earnest. Goodyear argued there was no such thing as a square balloon, but they saw his letter of authorization and they produced the four-cornered balloon.

Contractors were equally perplexed. August Knuth, an expert cabinetmaker from Local 1922, was hired to put three-quarter-inch holes in graphite blocks. He almost went mad drilling twenty-two thousand holes at the rate of one hundred holes an hour. No one would tell him why they needed pure graphite blocks, much less blocks with holes in them. For his trouble he received the union wage and a warning that he would be swiftly imprisoned without public trial if he discussed his work with anyone. Each night that month his wife asked Knuth why he was leaving a thick graphite film on her shower walls every night after work. His story that he was sharpening pencils at the union hall was not well received.

Protection was intense. A dozen armed guards discreetly surrounded the lab, which was located on Ellis Avenue across the street from the Stagg Field west stands. The lab and the field were in the heart of the campus, so the guards easily camouflaged themselves by dressing like students. If anyone noticed the unusual number of older students carrying pool-cue cases, long objects loosely wrapped with Christmas paper, and, in the best of Chicago traditions, violin cases, they did not mention it to school authorities.

Students wandering into the lab building were politely turned away by a desk man who referred them to other labs, other professors, or anywhere else. Persistent students saw the initially courteous man quickly become angry, a tactic which always drove them away. Stray tourists were given a handful of pamphlets about amoebas. If that did not satisfy them, the desk man launched into a calculatedly boring speech about food vacuoles, contractile vacuoles, and other amoeba body parts. Only the hardiest tourists lasted more than five minutes.

One minute into the amoeba speech, Crown and

Heather showed the desk man their identification cards.

"Thank God," the man said. "I've set a record for that speech this week. One old lady with nothing else to do checked out a book on single-cell animals from the university library and now comes here once a day to argue with me." He waved them through the double doors.

A pudgy man wearing the monotony of his job on his face sat behind a card table in the vestibule near the double doors. He pressed Crown and Heather's left thumbs and index fingers on the ink-smeared glass plate, then onto print paper. He shoved the paper through a slot in the wall. Two full minutes passed before the heavy door squeaked open.

Five uniformed army soldiers sat on a bench behind the black door. The soldier who had opened the door, a gangly youth whose head was shaved almost to the skin, asked Crown and Heather for their identification cards. He strung a thin cord through the hole in each card. Anyone in the building who was not wearing his card around his neck or on his belt was immediately arrested.

"Who's expecting you, sir?" he asked as he handed the identification cards to them.

"Enrico Fermi."

They followed the soldier down the brightly lit, sterile hallway, turned right, and continued at his heels. Other guards were stationed at corners, so the hallways were under constant surveillance. All office doorways were closed and had no numbers or names on them. Every fifteen paces or so, a small alarm was attached to the wall. Crown supposed each office would have a similar alarm.

The soldier stopped in front of a door identical to all the others and knocked twice, paused, and knocked twice again. Several seconds later an electronic throw bolt clicked, and he swung the door open.

Fermi was not there, so Crown and Heather waited

in steel chairs facing his desk. The office was a disappointment to Crown, who had expected the working quarters of the famous Nobel laureate to reflect his status. The predominant fixtures were wall blackboards covered with meaningless hieroglyphics. Behind the desk, two portable blackboards on rollers hid the boarded-up windows. A waist-high bookshelf stood to the left of Fermi's desk. The desk was covered with loose papers, a telephone, the alarm box, several slide rules, and a hand-crank calculator. The only nonacademic item in the office was a pair of cross-country skis leaning against one of the blackboards. Crown looked in vain for the Nobel plaque.

"Sorry to keep you waiting, Mr. Crown," Enrico Fermi said as he entered the office through a side door and walked to his desk. He was a small man, perhaps five feet, five inches. His hairline had receded almost to the back of his head. He had a sharp nose, and his sideburns stopped at the top of his ears. He was wearing a herringbone sports jacket without a tie. The identification card was stuck on the front of his belt buckle. His pants looked as if he slept in them, and judging by the cot near the back wall, he frequently did. His Italian accent was just noticeable. "Sometimes I think the security measures are taken a bit too far. Each morning I'm given photographs of those who have appointments with me. Whenever anyone knocks, I must adjourn to the side room, click open the front office door with the switch there, and wait until they are seated, so I can look at them through a one-way mirror in the door. They don't want me to be surprised by a visitor."

Fermi leaned across the desk and shook hands with Crown and Heather and said, "I'm glad you could come, Miss McMillan. You'll have an easier time transcribing the interviews if you know a little about what's going on in this lab."

He sat down and asked, "How was your trip from England?"

"No problems. Hess is safe in a house in Hyde Park right now."

"General Groves described how you got him here. You must have been worried about the trip."

"We aren't sure of Hess's status with the powers-that-be in Germany, whether they've forgotten him or whether they want to get rid of him," Crown said. "There are enough German agents in England to have caused us problems if they wanted to."

Fermi leaned back in his chair, lifted a leg up on the corner of his desk, then glanced at Heather as if he had forgotten she was there, and quickly lowered his leg to the floor.

What impressed Crown most about the Italian was not his suitably professorial appearance, but the energy Fermi emitted. The taut lines around his eyes; the rapid tapping of his fingers on the desk, the chair arm, or whatever they came in contact with; and his darting eyes—all were symptoms of the man's tremendous energy. Crown guessed it was only with massive will-power that Fermi remained in his chair and did not pace the room.

"You are making a bomb?" Heather asked abruptly.

Fermi glanced at her and smiled. Fermi's grin involved his entire face and set his eyes at a delightful angle. He was a man who enjoyed smiling.

"That's only part of what we are doing here, Miss McMillan," he said. "Actually, what we are looking for is a cheap, compact form of energy. That energy can be released at once, as in a bomb, or released slowly, like a piece of burning wood. It is conceivable that a million-kilowatt electrical power plant with nuclear fission as its source of energy could be no larger than a power substation. Compare this with the enormity of the Grand Coulee Dam and you can see its potential. Or compare uranium with coal. We estimate that one pound of uranium can give off energy equivalent to fifteen hundred tons, not pounds, tons of coal." Fermi paused to see if Heather cared to venture a gasp of dis-

95

belief, and when she did not, he continued, "We think that one pound of uranium or plutonium can yield enough energy to supply the total power consumption of the United States for fifteen minutes."

Heather's short question had put Fermi on the defensive. He acted as if he had given this speech many times before, perhaps to himself.

"Some benefits are more immediate," continued Fermi as he switched his gaze to Crown. "Fission does not produce the smog that is Chicago's hallmark. And it's much more economical to transport two pounds of uranium than three thousand tons of coal. And on and on."

"But, nevertheless, your work centers on the production of the bomb?" Heather persisted.

Fermi looked at her with a hint of pleading in his eyes and said, "And there are a lot of nonpower uses that will be the offshoot of our work. Developments in medicine and biology will be greatly accelerated because of the large amounts of radioactive substances that will be available to researchers. It's possible that these substances can be used to treat diseases and wounds. And the availability of high-intensity radiation will have an unprecedented effect on industrial research. Who knows what can be done with chemicals that have been treated with high doses of radioactive substances? Uses of our research are endless."

Fermi paused to collect himself. He dropped his hands onto the desk and smiled broadly. "You know, Miss McMillan, you have an amazing ability to make me want to justify myself. Very few people do that. My wife, for one."

"I'll take that as a compliment, Mr. Fermi," Heather said, warming to the scientist.

"It is. She's precious." Fermi gestured to the blackboards and said, "Yes, we are working on a bomb. These things I mention, these peaceful uses, are only a secondary goal now. Our first priority is to produce a weapon that will quickly end the war, and to produce it
96

before the Germans do. I don't need contorted logic to rationalize my work on this project, Miss McMillan. I saw what was happening in Italy before I left, what the Germans were doing to Italy.

"Because of economic sanctions against Italy imposed by the League of Nations due to the Ethiopian campaign, Italy has found itself allied with the Germans. This has made most Italians gag, because the Germans are ancient enemies of Italy, and the two countries fought each other as recently as the First World War. Italians couldn't believe we were fighting on the same side as the Germans in the Spanish Civil War. We thought Hitler was a prancing idiot who was doing his best to imitate the Duce. Our newspapers led us to believe that Mussolini was the leader of this strange relationship. This delusion was shattered in 1938, when Hitler occupied Austria without even informing Mussolini in advance. The Duce could do nothing but acquiesce after the fact. Italy has slowly become Germany's slave.

"To my wife and me, the most agonizing aspect of Germany's hold on Italy was the new anti-Jew campaigns announced by Mussolini. Please remember that Italy has never been anti-Semitic. We simply didn't have traces of that German disease of anti-Semitism in our population. But suddenly the government started announcing anti-Jewish measures.

"The first anti-Semitic laws were passed in September 1938, and that's when Laura and I decided to leave Italy. Not all the laws were aimed at the Jews, however. The Duce went berserk with his laws. He issued laws prescribing proper hairdos for women and proper uniforms for civil-service workers. And Mussolini, always thinking, banned ties for men's clothing, because he said they pressed on certain nerves in the neck, which might prevent men from taking accurate aim with a rifle after they were drafted. We simply couldn't live in such a repressive, silly climate. We left Rome for the last time on December 6, 1938."

"But is a silly government enough of a reason to work on a bomb that can kill hundreds of thousands?" Heather asked.

"No, no." Fermi looked away and searched for words. "Conditions in Germany and Italy have gone far beyond being silly. I'm personally familiar with one example. Laura's piano teacher in Rome is a Jew. We received a letter from her several weeks ago saying she had been taken to a camp in Germany. The letter was newsy. But then she asked us to say hello to her brother Alexander. And she wanted to know how Laura's violin lessons were going. And she asked how I was, but called me Paul. Well, she has no brothers, Laura was taking piano lessons, and my name is not Paul. The letter was full of errors that she knew we would recognize as errors. We can only conclude she is in deep trouble and that conditions at her camp are not as rosy as the letter's censor would like us to believe. She was warning us of what is going on in Germany."

John Crown was uncomfortable. His task was to learn the layout of the experiment and see that Heather was introduced to some of the technical jargon she would encounter during the Fermi-Hess interviews, not to expose the scientist to a young Englishwoman's concepts of morality. He was sure Fermi felt ill at ease under Heather's constant gaze.

"Well," Fermi said, rising from his seat, "I seem to have run off at the mouth. Let me explain a little about our project before I take you to the squash court."

"Squash court? I've never played squash," Heather said.

"We don't play squash there, Miss McMillan. You'll see that in a few minutes," replied Fermi, glad she was not in total command of the conversation.

Fermi picked up a dusty eraser and wiped clean a portion of blackboard. He said, "Please suffer through a few seconds of physics. It'll make the squash court clearer."

Fermi drew a circle on the board and began, "You

know that all matter is composed of atoms, and that they are extremely small. A spoonful of water contains a million billion atoms.

"In 1910, Lord Rutherford first showed that the atom, which theretofore had been thought the smallest particle, was in fact made of even smaller particles—a positively charged nucleus surrounded by negatively charged particles called electrons. Although practically all the mass is in the nucleus, it is very small. And its satellite electrons are also extremely small. The orbit of an electron is not even a hundred-millionth of an inch in diameter."

"I can't even imagine those figures," said Heather.

"Well, if the nucleus can be magnified to the size of a baseball, the outermost electron would be circling it a half-mile away. So even when atoms are packed tightly together, the nuclei are very far apart.

"Later, it was discovered that the nucleus of most elements is a combination of particles—protons and neutrons. The protons and neutrons within an atomic nucleus are held together by an extremely strong force. What we are trying to do is to split them."

Fermi drew circles and straight and crooked lines as he spoke. Heather leaned forward in her chair and did not even blink as she stared at the blackboard. Crown looked alternately at his fingernails and Heather. She had thawed a little since last night's discussion of Hess, and he was glad of it.

"We've found that we can bombard a nucleus with a tiny projectile, a neutron. Heavy nuclei can be split into almost equal parts. This is nuclear fission. It isn't a hard theoretical concept."

"It doesn't seem that much energy could be released by the splitting of one atom," said Heather.

"That's true. But we're trying to set it up so that the separation of one atom causes the splitting of other atoms, and those cause the splitting of more atoms, and on and on. The potential energy of this chain reaction would be enormous."

Fermi clapped his hands together to rid himself of the chalk dust and said, "Let's take a tour of the contraption we've built, which hopefully will allow us to have a self-sustained nuclear reaction."

"You mean this hasn't been done yet?" Heather asked as she rose from her seat.

"No. The self-sustained reaction is still theory. We'll know in a few days whether my theory is correct. To the squash court."

The soldier was leaning against the hallway wall as the three emerged from the office. Fermi took a key from his sports-coat pocket and threw one of the door bolts. The soldier locked the second with a key chained to his belt.

"Sometimes I yearn for a lab where I don't have to ring six bells and unlock ten doors to go to the bathroom accompanied by a soldier," Fermi said as he led them through the hallways, past the security doors, and out onto the sidewalk. He discreetly pointed to the Stagg Field grandstand across the street.

"There's the location of our experiment, the basement of Alonzo Stagg Stadium," he said.

The backside of the grandstand was designed in the best architectural tradition of the University of Chicago. Crown wondered why a football field needed castle turrets at each corner of the grandstand. Ivy climbed up the red-brick turrets, in which were small recessed windows. The windowsills were beveled toward the ground to deny footing to a potential attacker. As with all good castles, the top eight feet of the four-story turrets were extended on cantilever beams a foot beyond the circular wall beneath, thereby making a ladder assault difficult. Archers' slits ringed the turrets and the connecting wall. Lest their work be considered too militant, the architects had infused a religious theme into the grandstand. Midway between the turrets was the main entrance, a sweeping arched doorway reminiscent of French Gothic cathedrals. The high, arched windows along the walls on both sides of the entrance continued the cathedral theme. One expected but did not see stained glass. Above these windows were more archer's slits. An architectural mess, thought Crown.

They followed Fermi under the Stagg Field entrance to a small door on the south wall of the lobby. Fermi knocked a certain way, and the iron door opened. Crown could see from the brickwork that the old door had been recently replaced with its solid-metal substitute. Crown and Heather underwent the fingerprint ritual again, and after several minutes were cleared for entry. A second door scraped open, and they walked along a long hallway past several sentries and down a steep flight of stairs.

"These are the university's old indoor courts. Handball, squash, racketball, and such. You can see the shower rooms over there," Fermi said as they walked past carpenters' tool chests and a small pile of graphite blocks carefully stacked on a canvas sheet. The hallway's dim light flickered dully off the buckles and epaulet buttons on the guards' uniforms. After a close scrutiny by two guards at the final sentry post, Heather, Crown, and Fermi walked through the door and onto a squash-court viewing platform. At one end of the platform, a curly-black-haired, spectacle-wearing technician was meticulously examining electrical components of a control panel. The parts, seemingly hundreds of them, were spread on a white cloth draped over a wooden desk. The technician did not look up as Fermi approached the viewing-platform rail.

"As you can see, this was once a squash court. The courts haven't been used for years, so most students have no idea they exist. Keeping it secret here is much easier than if we had built a new building to hide it in." Fermi grasped the rail, leaned over it slightly, and said, "That's the pile."

Hanging from the ceiling on the squash court in front of them was an immense square balloon whose thick hide concealed its contents. The balloon hung to

101

the floor of the court ten feet below them, and its side facing the observation platform was an aperture through which workmen were steadily passing. Each carefully sealed the flap behind him as he entered or left the balloon.

"The graphite gives off a fine dust that clogs the gauges and would probably interfere with the reaction. So we've sealed the dust inside the balloon, and just before the experiment, we'll pump it out and open up the balloon."

Fermi walked to the sheet-covered table and asked the youthful electrician if progress was being made. The electrician, whose curly black hair dominated his face, was myopically squinting at the structure which to Crown looked like a vastly complicated fuse box. He was digging around in it with a pair of rubber-handled tweezers and was so absorbed in his work that Fermi's question startled him.

"Oh, fine, Professor, fine. I'm just doing a routine check, probably for the tenth time. There's no problem. It may not look like it, but I can put all this together again."

"Excellent. Let's take a look at the balloon, John."

They descended an almost vertical circular stairway to court level and entered the squash court through the miniature door peculiar to indoor courts. Fermi held open the balloon flap, and Crown and Heather crouched through the canvas wall. Heather immediately felt dirty. The air was thick with graphite dust that clung to her as if she had a magnetic attraction for the particles. Her eyelids scraped as she blinked, and her tongue felt coated. She brushed her cheek with the back of her hand, and her skin was slimy.

Enrico Fermi didn't seem to notice the graphite dust. "This pile is just what the name implies—thousands of graphite blocks placed in a square pile twenty-four feet in diameter. It's very simple in appearance, as you can see, just a huge black square. But it consists of lumps of uranium spaced eight and a half inches apart,

102

separated by the graphite blocks. Right now, there are about thirty-five thousand of the blocks on the pile, and we will eventually have forty thousand or so. Each layer of solid graphite block alternates with a layer of blocks that have holes drilled through them so uranium can be placed in the holes. Now, you may be wondering why we need all these graphite blocks."

Not particularly, thought Crown.

"The reason is that a chain reaction cannot occur in pure uranium, because when the neutrons and nucleus interact, too many of the little devils escape," said Fermi, beaming at the ingenuity he was about to reveal.

"What little devils?" asked Heather.

"Neutrons. You see, the neutrons travel so fast that far too many of them escape to allow a continuing reaction. So we use the graphite to slow them down. Because the graphite does not absorb many of the neutrons, most of the neutrons it slows down bounce back into the uranium lumps. We thus can keep the reaction going, a chain reaction.

"The magic word here is 'controlled.' What must be prevented is a spontaneous reaction, where the chain reaction gets out of control. The Lord only knows what would happen if it did. So we have a control rod made of cadmium, which is inserted into the pile to prevent the reaction from beginning. The rod absorbs extra neutrons. It is our brake. When we want the reaction to start, we'll slowly pull the rod out of the pile, thereby allowing the buildup of neutrons and nuclei reacting with each other."

The cadmium control rod protruded from a pile a foot above Crown's head. For a mechanism with the importance of the rod, it had a decidedly innocuous appearance.

A workman lugging a graphite block entered through the flap. Fermi held the porthole open and gestured Crown and Heather through it. Heather swatted her skirt and blouse, to no effect. It would take

103

several showers before the dry greasy feeling of the graphite was removed from her skin. She hoped the clothes could be salvaged.

"If our experiment doesn't work, there'll be no cheap energy. None of the things I mentioned in my office will come to pass," Fermi said as they passed the checkpoints on the way out of the court area.

"What about the bomb?" Crown asked, walking slightly behind the physicist as they approached the last sentry station.

"There will be no bomb if my experiment ten days from now fails."

"My chief was vague about the potential of such a weapon. Have you calculated what this bomb could do?"

Fermi waited until they were beyond hearing range of the sentries, then said, "Yes. We figure that one bomb small enough to be carried in a conventional bomber would have the rough equivalent of twenty-thousand tons of TNT. That's enough to vaporize most of a large city. And the explosive force is not the only dangerous effect of an atom bomb. The reaction irradiates the dust particles the explosion kicks up. Anyone coming in contact with these windblown particles would die or get very sick from the radiation." Fermi's voice hollowed and seemed to drift as he spoke of the destructive capabilities of his research. It was clear he preferred to dwell on peaceful energy uses of the atom, but heightened interest compelled Crown to ask, "Has anyone considered how such a weapon will change warfare?"

"Oh, yes. A few military theorists are propounding the question to themselves. What they come up with is obvious."

"Perhaps not that obvious to some of us." Heather grinned playfully at Crown. He made a show of ignoring her.

"They believe, and rightly so, that within a decade or two after the first bomb is produced, twenty or thirty countries will have it. You see, the requirements for producing such a weapon are widely held. Many countries could produce the bomb in a decade if they had that priority. Our research, as novel as it is, will be impossible to keep secret for long. History suggests that most of what we learn and produce will be for sale on the common market within a few years."

They passed the iron door and stepped through the vestibule to the sidewalk in front of the grandstand entrance. The November clouds were breaking, and it was brighter than when they had begun the tour. Crown didn't know if he was squinting because of the sun or the graphite particles.

Fermi shaded his eyes with a hand and scanned Ellis Avenue. "I try to spot the guards once in a while," he said. "It's not that hard. They don't look as anemic as the students. There's one."

The physicist pointed to a tall man wearing a wool sweater and standing near a newspaper vendor's booth forty yards away. He carried a rolled newspaper under one arm and did not try to hide his stare. Fermi on the street made him and his partners nervous. A laundry truck stopped in front of the lab across the street, and a squat, powerful man wearing overalls climbed down from the cab, slowly walked to the rear of the truck, and tinkered with the door latch.

"The laundryman is another," Fermi said. "I only need to stand here for a few minutes before the laundry truck, a *Tribune* newspaper truck, and about a dozen men trying to be casual surround me. It's amazing. I hope they know who you are."

"They do. You were talking about how the atom bomb will change warfare," Crown said.

"Well, as I said, many nations will ultimately get the A-bomb. What's worse yet is that there will be no effective defense against it. If a country sends ten bombers against a city, surely one or two will make it past the enemy's defenses. And one is all that's needed.

"The natural result of this is that mutual suspicion
105

among nations is bound to increase. Not only will the U.S. have to worry about the heavily industrialized and populated countries, but also about any country that can afford the weapon. The bomb won't be prohibitively expensive. World politics will change, believe me, when the U.S. must concern itself with every South American despot who purchases a bomb and a delivery system."

Crown felt twelve pairs of hard eyes on the three of them. The guards were slowly closing in, wondering why the scientist was on the street, and feeling very uncomfortable that no reinforced-concrete walls surrounded their charge.

"Come on, Professor. Heather and I'll see you to your lab door. We're making these boys antsy. One last thing," Crown said. "You keep using words like 'theoretical' and 'potential.' Aren't you sure you'll have a self-sustained nuclear reaction when that pile gets high enough?"

"Well, according to my slide rule and blackboard, this will work. If I'm right, when the pile is completed ten days from now, we will enter a new age, the atomic age. And I can't foresee anything that could go wrong."

VII

Owls Head, Maine. Perhaps it is the most harshly beautiful peninsula in the United States. Jutting out two and a half miles into West Penobscot Bay, Owls Head protects the village of Rockland from the Atlantic Ocean's fierce pounding.

The November wind is relentless, tossing and confusing the shore. Tons of white water drown shore boulders and drop away, to regroup, leaving rivulets coursing down the rocks, splashing pocket to pocket, irresistibly, to the sea, only to be launched at the boulders again. Wind froths the wave crests and hurls spray at the land. Wet gusts swarm over the rocks and moan inland. Crippled and humbled by the wind, only a scattering of gnarled beach shrubs and salt grass survives the Owls Head winters.

The brunt of the winter storm hits Owls Head point, a quarter-mile outcropping on the tip of the peninsula. Here the wind rages against the stumpy lighthouse, as if in retaliation for its effrontery in breaching the point. The beacon sits on a wooded promontory fifty feet above sea level, but it is not immune from the icy seawater spray. The lighthouse normally guided ships entering Rockland harbor, but war had doused its light, and mariners relied on blue-can buoys. On this winter night, the mute buoy rose and fell implacably as giant swells raced underneath.

Owls Head's chilling winters and cool summers had beaten back the land speculators and summer home

107

owners that infested the Atlantic coastline to the south. With the exception of the tiny fishing village of Owls Head, the oceanside of the peninsula was uninhabited. Darkness and the November storm ensured the absence of beachcombers on the point. Owls Head that night was perfect.

German submarine U-513's attack periscope broke the ocean's surface two miles east of Owls Head. For several seconds the periscope alternately submerged and surfaced as the swells passed over it. Then it gained enough height to clear the wave crests, and the periscope head swiveled in a complete circle. The shaft moved very slowly through the water to avoid stirring the phosphorescent sea.

"Bridge watch. Stand by."

"Aye, Herr Kaleun."

The watch hurried into their oilskin slickers and sou'westers and helped each other into the tight rubber pants. Heavy binoculars hung around their necks. They pushed their hands into waterproof gloves. Normally the three lookouts would dread the approaching watch, a four-hour stint on the bridge, exposed to the freezing rain and spray. After a few minutes, the arms numbed from holding the binoculars to the eyes. Failing to scan the horizon every fifteen seconds was a court-martial offense. But if all went well this night, they would be on the bridge less than five minutes.

The air in the control room was stifling. U-513 had been running submerged for more than forty-five minutes. Despite the air, none of the crew complained about the submerged run. It was a welcome respite from the pitching, rocking surface journey during the three days of storm. The sub had been at sea for more than two weeks, and this was the worst weather it had encountered.

"Horizon's clear, Herr Kaleur," said the chief engineer, using the naval abbreviation for the commander's rank, Herr Kapitänleutnant. "Land directly east at ninety-five hundred meters."

"Bottom?"

"Eighty-five fathoms, sir."

"Sub depth?"

"Two fathoms."

"Prepare to surface."

A warning bell rang through the sub. Acting reflexively after scores of drills, the stokers jumped to their diesel engines, but then remembered they would not be firing them during this surfacing.

"Surface. Blow the tanks, Chief."

A low sibilation increased to a sharp hissing as compressed air rushed into the sub.

"Horizon report."

"The same, Herr Kaleun," reported the first watch officer, who had replaced the chief at the scope. "Land to east, ninety-five hundred meters. Nothing more."

"Open the bridge hatch."

Fresh, cold air was palpable as it poured through the hatch and conning tower down into the control room. The three lookouts scrambled up the conning-tower ladder and continued up onto the bridge. They immediately posted themselves on the bridge and began searching for planes, ships, anything. Five seconds later they were drenched as saltwater foam splashed over the bridge. None of them lowered their binoculars.

"Permission to enter, von Stihl."

Erich von Stihl grasped the control-room hatch panels to avoid tumbling as the boat lurched to port, dropped several feet, and rose again. He had long been over the sea sickness that had plagued him during the first few days of the journey from Germany. Despite the months of training for this mission, often on a raft on stormy seas, the first day out of Trondheim he had vomited like a rooky sailor. Some of the veteran sub crewmen had also been sick, but von Stihl suspected it was the effects of their alcoholic three-week leaves prior to sailing. He stepped inside the control room and

109

approached the commander, who was stooped looking at a gauge on the wall.

"From the pain in my ears, I guess we just surfaced, Herr Kaleun."

"That's right, Colonel. Any problems with your wet suit?"

"No, and no problems for my men, either. We're ready to disembark."

"I don't envy your journey. The sea is force five, and in a small raft, that's dangerous."

The commander did not look up from his panel of gauges. He wore nothing on his sweater or cap to distinguish him from the other fifty sailors on the sub. He had last shaved and bathed two weeks ago and looked and smelled as molted as his crew.

Whenever the ship was on the surface, the commander's face was screwed with tension, almost as if he was in pain. The U-boat was the most effective weapon in Germany's naval arsenal. The only warning to an enemy convoy it usually gave of its presence was when a tanker erupted. Then the sub disappeared, tailed the convoy, and struck again. The U-boat was a silent, assured killer.

But whenever the sub was on the surface, it was in danger from shore batteries, subchasers, and destroyers, and, most deadly, airplanes. The antiaircraft guns aft of the bridge were impotent and were used only as a last recourse. The sub's protection was its ability to dive quickly. And this depended on the spotters who stood their chilling vigil whenever the sub was on the surface. At the cry "Airplane," the lookouts would jump below deck, the hatch would be slammed shut, the ballast tanks flooded, and the sub would dive. The crew trained endlessly, until they could be submerged forty-five seconds after the first warning. Most emergency dives were caused by seagulls mistakenly identified as enemy fighters. No spotter was ever reprimanded for a false call. Rather a hundred unneeded emergency dives than one too late. Enemy planes seldom missed a sub on the surface.

Sixty seconds had passed since U-513 surfaced. The commander called above, "Report from the bridge."

"Land nine thousand meters east, nothing else, Herr Kaleun," cried one of the spotters.

"Compressor, Chief?"

"Compressor checks, sir."

"You're on your way, then, von Stihl. Good luck, whatever it is you're doing."

"Thank you, Herr Kaleun."

Von Stihl climbed out the hatch to the bridge. His two men who had been waiting in the petty officers' quarters followed him out.

Good riddance, thought the commander. Delivering the three men to this point two miles off the Maine coast had been his sole mission this time out. He had been forbidden to intercept American convoys en route, and unless he was lucky on the return trip, he would have no victory pennants to fly from the periscope when they returned to Trondheim.

Seldom were passengers allowed aboard a U-boat. When they were—typically pesty journalists—they worked as lookouts. But these three men had been deadweight. The commander's orders were that the commandos were not to endanger their health by posting lookout, by assisting the chief engineer with maintenance, or by doing anything else. They didn't have to prove themselves, and this rankled the commander and his crew.

Colonel von Stihl was icy and seldom spoke. His blond hair was close-cropped and curly. He was average height and was barrel-chested, with thick, powerful arms and legs. Cords of neck muscle stood out even when he relaxed. He had critical eyes, severe lips, and a rather large, non-German nose. He spent much of his time aboard reading economics treatises in the petty officers' quarters. During the voyage from Germany, he had engaged in several discussions with the second

111

watch officer, who had apparently read John Maynard Keynes, but the officer's knowledge and insights were soon exhausted. Many of the colonel's hours were spent staring catatonically at the sub's plumbing, lost in thought. After several days at sea, no one approached him.

Von Stihl's men had also disturbed U-513's crew. The giant Hans Graf let it be known he was in the SS Death's-Head regiment and seemed pleased that none of the sailors spoke with him from then on. The skin under Graf's right ear had been badly burned, and the scar had lost none of its purple anger. It pulled back the corner of his mouth into a small grin that gave his otherwise Teutonically handsome face a perpetual evil sneer. Graf was aware of this effect and exploited it effectively on his superiors, his lovers, and those he was about to murder in the name of the Reich.

The third stormtrooper was less sinister. In fact, Willi Lange was so inconspicuous he almost disappeared in the close confines of the U-boat. Lange was a slight man, barely reaching Graf's shoulders. He had a pug nose over a scrawny mustache. His beady black eyes never looked at the person addressing him, and his face suffered an oppressed expression, which he tried and failed to elevate to one of mere insouciance. Graf derisively called him Schwachheit, saphead. But one of Lange's peculiarities kept Graf from overpowering him and the sailors from befriending him. Lange's sole diversion aboard the sub had been to unroll the watertight oilcloth in which he kept his Schmeisser submachine gun and constantly and lovingly disassemble, clean, oil, and reassemble it. The little man even unloaded the clips and cleaned the bullets. Once, en route, when von Stihl had suggested Lange read one of his books because the cleaning was unnerving the sailors, Lange had read a chapter or so with the book resting on the mess table while his hands skillfully cleaned and recleaned the weapon. Lange's eyes never left the text, and his hands never faltered with the gun's parts. Von Stihl quickly gave up his attempts at expanding Lange's mind.

The three commandos had been cysts on the commander's ship, and now they were gone. With them would go the tension and demoralizing effect they had on his crew. The commander doubted the three would ever return to German soil. At least, he had no orders to pick them up. Just as well. It was an order he could have easily misplaced or misinterpreted.

"Pass up the raft," shouted von Stihl from the bridge.

Two seamen who had lugged the deflated raft from the bow compartment hoisted it above their heads and shoved it through the conning-tower hatch, where it was passed to Graf, who one-handed it through the hatch.

"Now the compressor hose."

Up went the long rubber hose. Bracing himself against the bridge railing to prevent slipping on the bridge's treacherous plate metal, Graf unwrapped the raft from its canvas housing and shook out the folds. He attached the nozzle to the raft's nipple.

"Air," he shouted.

The hose stiffened and the raft began to inflate. Willi Lange wrapped his arms around one end of the raft to prevent it from being carried off by the wind.

"Report from the bridge," yelled the chief, relaying the commander's request.

"All clear, Chief."

The three spotters had not even glanced at the commandos. They peered into the darkness, looking for any suspicious dot or light. Then one yelled down the hatch, "Lighthouse at thirty degrees, Chief. Light's out."

The chief relayed the spotting to the commander, who was using the magnification of the sky periscope to survey the shore and had already found Owls Head Lighthouse.

After the raft was inflated, Graf and Lange held it

113

over the bridge railing, which protected the raft from the gale. The heavy waterproof packs strapped to their backs and the wet suits made their movements awkward. Both had oilcloth bundles tied to their stomachs, the Schmeissers.

"Hand up the rope ladder," ordered von Stihl.

He deftly attached the ladder to the bridge with metal clasps and threw it overboard. The weighted end of the ladder quickly sunk alongside the sub's hull.

"Now the raft ropes."

Up came two lengths, which were quickly attached to each end of the raft. Lange and Graf released the raft and lowered it to the water. It landed upright and bobbed violently alongside U-513.

Two seamen dressed for the weather emerged from the hatch to handle the lines to the raft. Von Stihl climbed over the bridge railing and began the descent. The hull was slippery and could not be trusted for rapelling. He cautiously shoved each foot into the rope crosspieces before lowering himself another step. The wind and spray blinded him as he neared the waterline. He kicked out with one leg and hooked the raft gunwales with his foot, and then sank to his knees on the inflated tubes and steadied the rope ladder for Lange.

"Need some help, Schwachheit?" Graf yelled jeeringly over the wind.

Lange climbed over the rail without answering or looking at Graf. He arched his back forward so the package strapped to his stomach would not bang against the railing as his feet found the ladder. Von Stihl held the rope ladder slightly away from the hull, making Lange's task of placing his feet on the rope rungs easier. The swells rose and fell, lifting and lowering the raft. Lange released his grip on the ladder, but he had misjudged the swells, and he dropped six feet into the raft. One leg caught the gunwales, and he pitched wildly forward into the bottom of the raft. He heard Graf's short laugh above him.

The big German lifted a leg over the bridge railing, mockingly saluted the sailors holding the line, and grabbed the ladder. He did not use his feet, but descended the ladder hand over hand and lighted easily on the raft. Immediately, a package of provisions was lowered on a third line. Strapped to the package were two short oars. Graf unleashed them and used one to steady the raft. Von Stihl unhooked the fore and aft lines, and they were quickly withdrawn. He kicked off from the sub.

"Let's go," he commanded. They knew the routine without further orders. They had one minute to clear the submarine before it dived. If the raft was too near, it would be sucked under.

The colonel and Graf sat side by side to man the oars. As they pulled in time, the lookouts disappeared from the bridge, and von Stihl heard the dull clang of the hatch being closed. The submarine appeared and disappeared as the raft bobbed in the heavy sea.

Through the spray, the commandos saw the U-boat tilt slightly, pause, and slip beneath the surface. Not a bubble or ripple marked its departure, and not a sound reached them. They were alone in the Atlantic gale.

Von Stihl and Graf pulled against the sea. Lange alternately searched the shoreline and bailed with a half-liter tin. Sea spray steadily blew into the raft. Bailing was as exhausting as rowing. The shore was a black smudge on the horizon, visible only when the raft crested a swell. They pulled and bailed, pulled and bailed, and the smudge seemed to draw no closer.

"Christ," Graf shouted into the wind, "if I had wanted to row, I would have joined the Italian Navy." He laughed merrily, oblivious of the freezing spray.

Lange's dark eyes riveted to the shore each time the boat rose. It would be his job to track down any unfortunate soul walking on the beach who Lange would assume saw the raft. Not that their craft or its crew would be easily spotted. The raft had been colored black to blend with the night. The three stormtroopers

115

were wearing black rubber diving suits, both for camouflage and for warmth. Warmth, thought von Stihl, what a laugh.

Tests by the German Navy showed that such a raft and crew were almost invisible at night one hundred yards away. And the foul weather ensured their invisibility. Only when they were almost to shore, when the black raft contrasted with white surf, would they be in danger of being spotted. But the chances anyone was braving the inclement November weather for a walk along the beach were remote. Their landing point, three hundred yards north of Dodge Point, on the head, was not populated, so no one would be inconveniently looking out a window at ths surf.

They rowed and bailed, rowed and bailed. Trying to exclude the cold, von Stihl concentrated on the mechanical back-and-forth motion. His pumping arms began a satisfying burn as the muscles worked to and fro. The scab covering the infected sore on his tailbone, which had rubbed raw the first day of training and had not healed, was already torn off by the raft seat. The wet suit ground saltwater into the sore with each stroke.

Willi Lange bailed frantically but was losing. As they neared shore, the swells began to crest and pour white water into the raft's stern. Lange scooped water like an automaton, and his arms were on fire. It was little solace that the inflated raft would not sink even if filled with water to the top of the gunwales. No forward progress would be made. If they were to make it to land, Lange had to bail out more water than swept in. The water was gaining, and the exhausted Lange puched back the pain and redoubled his efforts.

Minute after freezing minute passed. Von Stihl fought the desperate need to let his body crank back and forth on its own volition so he could turn his mind off and shut out the cold and the gnawing ache in his arms, which seemingly evolved from the pleasant burn hours ago. At every stroke, his biceps convulsed with

116

effort, and pain shot up his arms and into his shoulders. The training is never sufficient. The thought pleased him, and he focused on it. Never sufficient. Stroke, forward. Never sufficient. Stroke, forward.

"Fifty meters to shore," Willi Lange yelled through a cold blast of spray. He pointed a new tack designed to bring the raft to shore at a ninety-degree angle to the crashing waves. Von Stihl lifted his oar out of the water while Graf took two extra strokes to turn the raft. Von Stihl's back muscles immediately cramped, and he almost shouted with pain as he dipped his oars and pulled again.

The swells gained momentum and size as they approached the beach. Now the wave crests were not frothing cold nuisances blown over by the wind, but were a force unto themselves. Tons of water spilled off the crests as the undertow from the beach topped the swells. The colonel and Graf stroked with renewed urgency as the raft was caught by the foaming surf. Bailing was useless now. Willi Lange threw away his tin bailer and grasped the gunwale straps with both hands. Despite his fear, his eye did not stop scanning the beach. He gripped fiercely as a crest of turbulent white water spilled over his shoulders and into the raft, where it rushed over the sodden rowers. The craft dived into the trough of the wave and rushed up the backside of the next watery giant. Neither von Stihl nor Graf lost a stroke as they fought to keep the raft facing the shore. Another wave and another ton of seawater boiled into the raft. The noise was deafening. Lange glanced at the pack tied tightly around his stomach and prayed that the saltwater had not breached the oilskin and soaked its contents.

"Shore's twenty meters," Lange yelled.

Now the waves were monsters lifting the raft into the air and dropping it to the troughs in stomach-wrenching descents. Lange stood precariously in the back of the raft and spotted the wave behind him that

117

they would ride to shore. The most dangerous seconds of their three-thousand-mile journey were at hand.

The giant wave, their wave, crested and began its onslaught. Unlike others before it, their wave was propelled by human anger and purpose, wanting to terrify, to humble, and finally to crush its trespassers. It thundered to them.

"Now. Stroke," shrieked Lange.

The oars bit into the water as the immense wave lifted the raft up its crest. The seething crest hovered in the black sky above them and then violently cascaded down. Whirling water smothered the raft.

Where there had been air was now bubbling, freezing, swirling water. The oar was ripped from von Stihl's grasp. He inhaled saltwater and gagged and convulsed and swallowed more water. He was vaguely aware of being thrown upside down, and then something heavy smashed into his jaw. He rolled over and over in the turbulence. Flailing his arms against the onrush had no effect. In mid-somersault, the colonel slammed into the abrasive ocean floor and felt skin on the back of his hand scrape away. Over and over he was flung. Where's the surface? Where's the shore? The questions were drowned in the overpowering, frothing tumult.

Water dropped away, and von Stihl's butt hit the pebbly beach. He blinked burning grains of sand from his eyes and saw the water rush back to the sea, preparing for the next assault. He rolled to his hands and knees and crawled up the beach just as the next wave lapped his legs, trying to pull him back to sea.

Over the roar of the waves, von Stihl heard a hacking cough. Graf was thirty yards north, bent on all fours, retching saltwater. The colonel weakly stood and looked for Lange. He saw nothing but driftwood and boulders and crashing water. He waded into the surf and felt the sand under his feet being pulled to sea by the undertow. Von Stihl looked frantically. The mission required three men. He had to find Lange. The colonel
118

waded to his knees and stupidly tried to part the water with his hands.

Another wave swamped the shore, and a submerged body plowed into von Stihl's legs and dropped him to his knees. He plunged his hands about until he grabbed Lange's pack. Von Stihl backpedaled to firmer ground and lifted Lange above the water. The diminutive, waterlogged German spasmodically coughed and inhaled great quaffs of air. Only after a dozen breaths did Lange open his eyes and try to firm his rubbery legs. Von Stihl put an arm around Lange's waist and led him to shore.

Hans Graf had climbed onto a boulder and lay on his pack propped by his elbows. He was spitting water, and his chest rose and fell like a furnace bellows. Von Stihl helped Lange onto the rock and lowered him near Graf. The colonel sat heavily and waited for his head to stop spinning.

"And if I had wanted to swim, I would've joined the French Navy," said Graf. His face assumed its evil leer. "Nice job guiding us to shore, Schwachheit. Without you, I probably would have gotten wet."

"That's enough, Graf. From this moment we speak English. No German. Understood?" asked von Stihl in accent-free Midwestern American English.

"Aye, aye, Skipper. Would ye have me talkin' with me Irish brogue," Graf said in a thick Emerald Isle accent, "or like a bloody cockney sailor 'ome after two months a' sea?" The latter sounded as if Graf had been born within earshot of Big Ben. Graf's ability at shading his perfect English into a variety of accents was duly noted in his SS file, which von Stihl had studied.

"American, Graf, just American."

"Would yew all want me ta be from the sovereign South?" he drawled in Piedmont North Carolinian, and continued in Iowan, "or from the corn belt up north?"

"Corn belt, Herr Obersturmführer."

"Aw, shucks."

Von Stihl rose to his feet, saw the raft bouncing in

119

the surf fifty feet north. "Graf, get the raft and deflate it. Lange, dig a hole somewhere in those woods."

Von Stihl slipped off his pack, broke the watertight seal, and produced a map of the Owls Head and Rockford area. Not that he really needed it. He had committed the map to memory a month before. He knew precisely where they had landed—midway between the lighthouse and Dodge Point on the tip of the head. A rough dirt road just up the hill would lead them to the tiny shoreline village of Owls Head, a little over a half-mile away. Four miles beyond was Rockland and the rail spur.

Von Stihl walked into the woods toward the sound of Lange's scraping shovel. Tiers of overhead branches filtered out the night's dim light. He moved slowly, with his hands extended to ward off tree trunks, and carefully lifted his feet to avoid vines and roots. He caught only glimpses of shadows in the black forest.

Childhood graveyard tales shivered through von Stihl as he approached the glade where Lange was hacking at the ground like a fiend. Thin gray trickles of night light broke through the forest and bounced off Lange's shimmering wet suit.

"That's deep enough. Let's change," said von Stihl as he peeled off the wet suit. He pulled a small cotton towel from the backpack and dried himself until the towel was saturated.

Hans Graf entered the glade and dropped the deflated raft into the hole. He carried his SS Blood and Honor dagger in his huge hand. He wordlessly joined the others and stripped off his wet suit.

From von Stihl's pack came an American-made wool shirt, which was old and patched on the elbows. Two buttons were missing and the collar was frayed. Next came underwear and a dirty pair of pants with a worn leather belt already in the loops. He wiped mud off his feet and donned a pair of argyle socks and scuffed brown shoes. Last came a black winter coat
120

that suffered a rip in the right forearm. Lange and Graf dressed in equally disheveled clothes.

After they dumped their wet suits and empty packs into the hole, Lange shoveled dirt into it until it was level with the surrounding ground. He gathered several dead branches from the edge of the glade and covered the fresh dirt. He deliberately wiped his muddy hands on the seat of his pants.

"Well," said von Stihl as he led them into the woods, "we look sufficiently disreputable."

"I feel grimy," Graf jokingly complained. "If my Standartenführer saw me now, I'd be sent to Stalingrad on the first train."

Without slowing, von Stihl said, "Colonel, not Standartenführer, Graf. Remember, if anyone overhears a single German word, we could be detected."

"Of course. Of course. Lange, I suggested to the colonel that we should use your regulation Wehrmacht uniforms for our American disguises. They're just as filthy and ragged as these clothes, don't you think?"

Graf laughed loudly. Lange said nothing as he brought up the rear of their single-file procession. I'm going to have to do something to get that idiot Graf off Lange, thought von Stihl.

They stepped from the woods across a small ditch onto the dirt road and followed the road south.

"What time is it, Lange?" the colonel asked.

"Five A.M., sir."

"We've got about four and a half miles to Rockland. The camp is on the railway spur just east of town. Let's pick up the pace. We want to get there before sunrise."

After a quarter of a mile the road was paved. The walk was easy and warming. Only four times in the hour did they jump into the woods on the side of the road as a car or truck noisily sped past. As they neared Rockland, they passed small homes lining the roadway. Lights shone through most windows even at this early hour, the mark of a fishing village. The wind quieted as

121

dawn approached. A slow fog rolled onto the highway from the sea, giving the streetlights ahead a blurred halo.

The trio reached Thomaston Street and turned southeast for several blocks. They crossed vacant lots and several acres of forests, skirting Rockland until they came to the Maine Central railway line. They walked east along the tracks away from town.

Several minutes later, through the first light of false dawn, von Stihl saw the distant glow of several small fires in a field near the tracks. It was the camp.

The strains of a bawdy drinking tune sung by a husky, deep voice drifted to them through the fog. " 'Oh, Mary was my brother's wife. I loved her nearly all my life . . .' "

The song stopped, and they heard the clinking of a tin coffeecup being tapped against a rock.

" 'And Mary and me had lots of fun, 'specially when my brother was gone . . .' "

The startled singer looked up and saw the three men standing over him. His fear quickly dissipated when he saw they were his kind—men, as he liked to say, similarly situated in life.

"Ah, welcome to the Road Boy's camp, gentlemen," said the hobo. "Won't you join me in the last of the morning's coffee?"

He wore four filthy sweaters, one on top of the other. Somewhere he had gotten a clean, brightly colored scarf, which he wore around his neck, with the ends hanging in front of his chest, in the best avant-garde tradition. A sooty miner's sock cap covered his white hair.

"Glad to, old man," said von Stihl as he lowered himself to his haunches near the fire and held his hands out to gather its warmth. Graf imitated von Stihl. Lange found a log in the shadows and quickly unrolled his oilskin pack.

"But, as you know, the old coffeepot gets a bit weak this late in the morning. I've got some water if you've

122

got a little coffee," the hobo said as he raised his eyebrows expectantly.

"That I do."

From his pocket von Stihl took a small, tattered paper bag and handed it to the hobo, whose eyes lit up at the offering. As he dumped a handful of coffee into the pot he said, "I'm the Road Boy. These here are some of my friends, all similarly situated, like you."

Over the Road Boy's shoulder von Stihl saw several other small fires. Each had two or three hobos around it, and each fire had a small pot held over the fire by a stick planted in the ground. A mixture of low laughter and talk drifted over the crackling fires.

"Staying long?" asked the Road Boy as he stirred the pot with a twig.

"Nah, just long enough to catch the morning train to Portland. We got some friends down that way," von Stihl said as he rubbed his hands together in front of the fire.

"Say hello to Big Petey when you get there, will you? He's an old friend of mine. Him and the Pearl. They're both old friends of mine. Tell them the Road Boy sent you and it's worth a cup of joe."

From the shadows behind him, von Stihl heard the brittle clip of a Schmeisser submachine-gun bolt being dropped into place. Goddamn kid nurses that gun like it was a baby, he thought. Probably licking the salt out of the chamber.

"Hey, Sam Son, toss me three cups, will ya?" yelled the Road Boy.

Presently the tin cups landed in the dirt near the fire. The Road Boy tapped them together to shake bits of sand out and poured coffee. He handed one to von Stihl and another to Graf. Willi Lange walked from the shadows, lowered himself to the ground, and placed the oilskin package at his feet near the fire. He nodded his thanks to the Road Boy for the coffee.

Von Stihl opened the paper bag he was carrying and brought out a loaf of bread. He tore it into fourths and

123

produced a half stick of butter. He smeared butter on each piece with his finger and passed them around. The Road Boy grinned toothlessly as he received the unexpected breakfast.

"I guess that old hag we flimflammed won't miss her bread and butter," said von Stihl.

"Certainly not as much as we appreciate it, eh, boys?" The hobo chuckled as he bit off a huge chunk of bread and palpated it with his gums.

"When's the next freight, Road Boy?" von Stihl asked.

The hobo chewed hard, muttered indistinctly, chewed several more times, and said through the wad of dough, " 'Bout five minutes from now. Maine Central short haul. It'll have 'bout twenty Johny O'Brians."

"Running empty?"

"Yep, and the doors wide open. Won't be any problem for you boys. Heads by here 'bout ten mile an hour."

The information confirmed what von Stihl had been told by the mission briefer in Germany. The train traveled to Portland, Maine, with ten stops en route. The railroad police were lax and could be bought with a cigar. Von Stihl carried a supply in his breast pocket.

"You know," said the Road Boy, "it does my travelin' heart good to see you young fellows hittin' the rails. Ever since Roosevelt's depression got over, I ain't seen many of you young ones."

"Well, when you got to travel, you got to travel," said von Stihl as he slurped the scalding coffee.

"Ain't that the truth."

As the colonel wiped his hands on his pants he heard the deep wail of the Maine Central pulling out of Rockland.

"That'll be your train," said the Road Boy. "It's been a real pleasure having you boys for breakfast."

"We'll be back," von Stihl said as he held out his hand to the hobo. "Keep the bag of coffee."

124

The train drew near and they saw black smoke spewing from the locomotive's stack into the blue dawn. It labored to pick up speed. The ground began to rumble and the train whistle pierced the camp. Lange strapped the package around his waist and Graf slung his cloth stachel over his shoulder. The engine and coal car rolled past the camp fire.

Von Stihl shot from his crouch to a dead run toward an open box car. He grabbed the door frame and kicked his feet up onto the car bed in a practiced maneuver. He pivoted and grabbed Willi Lange's arm and pulled him aboard. Graf ran easily alongside the car until they pulled back from the doorway. He leaped to a sitting position on the bed and rolled backward into the car.

The Germans leaned against the front wall and within seconds discovered what every hobo knows; it is impossible to be comfortable riding in a boxcar.

"Well, here I am, a lieutenant in Germany's finest, the SS Death's Head squadron, trained to perfection, physically fit," Graf said with his usual sneer. "And here I also am, a bum traveling across enemy territory in a freezing boxcar. Can you finally tell us where we're going, great leader?"

Von Stihl unwrapped a cigar, bit off the end, spat it out, and said, "Chicago. We've got important business in Chicago."

VIII

The Pump Room was a disappointment. Chicago's finest restaurant was everything Crown had heard and, unfortunately, more.

Ernest Lessing Byfield had decorated his restaurant with a flair quite in contrast to what one would expect from the portly businessman who invariably wore three piece, pin-stripe suits. The Pump Room's color scheme was garish blue and white and from the high ceiling hung heavy crystal chandeliers with spangled arms reaching out like grasping octopi. Murals of Sarah Siddons and Princess Amelia covered the walls.

Some waiters wore bright red, swallow-tailed morning coats given a military flavor with arm stripes and gold buttons. Tight black pants were tucked into knee-high black boots. Other waiters wore brilliant green, knee-length Indian caftans decorated with gold braids across the chests, and small matching green turbans on which perched three giant white ostrich plumes. The waiters were widely recognized as being the most professional in the Midwest.

All dishes were served from wagons: hors d'oeuvre wagons, fruit wagons, roast-beef wagons, chafing-dish wagons, and dessert wagons. Byfield liked to brag that everything but shashlik was served on flaming rapiers. The food was simply the finest in Chicago.

Located in the Ambassador East Hotel on Chicago's Near North Side, the Pump Room was a focal point for the city's nouveau society. Averell Harriman, Eddy

Duchin, Ethel Barrymore, Clifton Webb, and Mrs. Potter Palmer regularly held court in the Pump Room. Gossip columnists loitered near the doors, hoping to interview the restaurant's clientele for a story, and, failing that, to invent a story based on any recent change in the seating arrangements.

John Crown had wanted a quiet, dark restaurant where he and Heather McMillan could talk for the first time. This the Pump Room was not. When ringing laughter and boisterous conversation spilled into the lobby of the Ambassador East as the maître d'hôtel ushered Crown and Heather to the headwaiter's post, Crown knew the Pump Room would be a disappointment. The carts and waiters were constantly embroiled in loud traffic jams in the aisles. Shouts of recognition and noisy embraces filled the room. Obligatory gasps followed bursts of flame from exotic desserts. The din was overpowering.

They were led to a white leather half-circle booth against a side wall. Almost before Crown had settled himself a polite distance from Heather—an awkward maneuver, because the booth was large enough for six, and he had to slide along the seat for yards—Jimmy, the diminutive wine steward, approached their table. Crown scanned the wine list, which was written in eighteenth-century script and was almost impossible to read, and asked, "What do you recommend?"

"That depends on what you order for dinner," replied Jimmy with transparent obsequiousness, instinctively knowing Crown and Heather were outsiders. The weight of the corkscrew suspended on the large-link chain around his neck seemed to pull the little man into a deferential, subservient stoop, which regulars knew was a ruse.

"I'm going to have whatever goes with the wine you recommend," said Crown. Without waiting for the exchange to become more irritating, Crown ordered an obscure burgundy from the hills east of Paris. The supply of this French wine in America was rapidly dimin-

127

ishing, and it would be exorbitantly expensive. That is, expensive for anyone not on a carte-blanche government expense account, as Crown was.

"I haven't been in a restaurant since the blitzkrieg started," Heather said, lifting her napkin. "London hotels and restaurants aren't getting gas and electricity. And many of them have closed because the air raids empty the places every night."

"Not even an air raid would clear this place. Everette Smithson recommended the Pump Room to me and said several dozen of Chicago's high and mighty almost live here. Everyone knows everyone else. I feel like I'm crashing a party."

Heather surveyed the spangled, furred, studded, and polished Pump Room people as they gushed and gooed. She said, "You and I would last five minutes at this party. Our yawning wouldn't be considered very polite. Who's the greeter?"

"Probably Ernest Byfield, the owner. Smithson says you've made Chicago society when he can greet you by name. He also owns the Buttery in the Ambassador West Hotel. He largely dictates Chicago's taste in food and wine."

Jimmy, the wine steward, rolled a half-barrel on wheels to their table. It was filled with ice in which were buried several bottles of wine. Bunches of purple and green grapes were draped over the barrel edge and hung almost to the first metal stave. With the smoothness of decades of service, Jimmy inserted the screw, popped the cork, and poured a taste into Crown's glass. Not knowing whether his act was for Jimmy or Heather, Crown swirled the dark red wine, sniffed the bouquet, sipped it loudly, swished it around in his mouth, and, much to Jimmy's relief, did not spit it on the floor, as proper wine tasting dictated, but swallowed it. He nodded approval to the steward, who poured two glasses and placed the bottle in the tableside ice-filled replica of the half-barrel.

Heather and Crown had been together for a week,

and he knew surprisingly little about her. Their conversations had been short and without exception related to their mission. He had read her meager file, supplied by the air chief marshal. She was twenty-nine years old and had lived in London all her life. Her parents supplied her with a public-school education, and she had attended one of the London colleges Crown had never heard of. She had been working at a series of insignificant jobs and attending college parttime for six years. The file did not summarize, but Crown guessed she had been drifting, perhaps searching. When she volunteered for the British service, her life seemed to focus and accelerate. Her position with the air chief marshal indicated her proficiency for the work and her dedication. Attached to her background file was a letter from the air chief marshal attesting to her ability as an adjutant.

"How did you become Air Chief Marshal Hilling's adjutant?" Crown asked.

"I was his typist for several months. A secretary. One morning I put a memo on his desk telling how his command could be more efficient if certain positions were eliminated and others made directly responsible to his office. The air chief hardly looked up when I gave it to him, and it lay on his desk for over a week."

"He finally noticed it?" Crown was concentrating on her beautiful lips, not her words.

"Yes. There came the nasty day every executive dreads—the day dedicated to clearing off the corner of his desk, which is piled with nonurgent letters and orders. The chief usually delayed this until the pile reached a foot high. When he came to my memo, he spent half an hour studying it, and then called me in to ask questions. The reorganization began the following day."

"That must have been traumatic for Hilling's subordinates," Crown said.

"It was. Word leaked that I caused the rearrangement that sent many officers to new posts and a few to new ranks."

"And who leaked that?"

"I wouldn't know." Heather smiled wryly. "But from that moment, no other lieutenant in the RAF was treated with such deference and, by a few former antagonizers, plain fear."

"Good God, you're a devious one."

Heather laughed and continued, "And no longer did other RAF officers call me 'my little lieutenant' and return salutes while mouthing kisses. I felt marvelously secure."

Heather sampled the wine and said, "I'm glad we could be together tonight. We don't get to talk freely much."

"No, not with the deputy führer around. He's a strange case. How've you and he been getting along?"

"The same. I sat in on Professor Ludendorf and Peter Kohler's interrogation of Hess after you and I met Mr. Fermi on Saturday. Most of the time he just sits and stares, but once in a while the professor can get him to talk. He'll let Hess talk about anything, so he rambles on and on about life in Germany. He loves to tell about how he first saw Hitler and joined the Nazi party. Ludendorf and Kohler eventually shut him off, especially when he talks about the Nazis. I think it makes them sick to hear about it."

"No wonder," Crown said, absently swirling his glass by the stem. "The Nazis chased both of them from their homes and jobs. Ludendorf told me he wants to go back to Germany after the war."

"They finally got Hess to talk about the German experiments, but he gets really fuzzy about them. And he uses terms none of us know. I dutifully wrote them down, and I'm preparing them for Mr. Fermi to look at before his interview with Hess."

"Are you getting used to Kohler's interrogation?" Crown asked.

"Not really. Most of the time he glares angrily at

Hess, letting Ludendorf ask questions and steer the conversation. But once in a while Kohler yells at Hess to quit hiding information, or asks the professor to let him question Hess alone for a while. Ludendorf never lets him, but the threat is always there, and Hess knows it. Kohler really frightens him."

"Well, that's a proven technique," Crown said, reaching for the menu.

"What are you going to have?" Heather asked, purposely leaving the business talk and looking at her menu. She had never seen menus like those in the Pump Room. Not only was the script difficult to read, but the foods were grouped according to seasoning, rather than by entrée. One list was headed "Dishes Highly Seasoned with Garlic." She would not eat garlic tonight.

"Top sirloin and a baked potato."

"You won't feel like a member of the proletariat, ordering meat and potatoes here?" she teased.

"I'll have them set it on fire at our table and serve it shish kebab, if you like."

When the red-coated waiter visited their table, she ordered chicken hash.

"Chicken hash?" Crown exclaimed. "That's something my mother served whenever there was nothing else to eat. It has the parts of the chicken in it that I couldn't get down unless they were disguised."

"Don't be funny. The Pump Room's chicken hash is famous, isn't it?" she asked the waiter.

Looking like a general in his red coat with gold piping, their waiter explained, "Actually, it was famous at Jack and Charlie's Twenty-one in New York City before it came here. We do it with more flair, though."

Several minutes later the general rolled an entrée wagon to their table. He gripped a deep-dish pan with a towel, splashed alcohol into it, and brushed the hash with a punk. The flame leaped halfway to the ceiling, illuminating the booth with a yellow glow. As the fire died, the waiter swirled the hash in the pan to cook it

131

evenly and slipped it onto Heather's plate. He returned a minute later with Crown's order.

"You were raised in Oregon?" Heather asked as she sprinkled pepper on the hash.

"Yes," Crown mumbled through the steak.

"Well, tell me about it."

He swallowed and said, "My upbringing was pretty mundane. My father is a channel master on the Columbia River."

"What's a channel master?"

"The Columbia below Portland is treacherous, particularly out over the bar at the mouth of the river near Astoria. When the Columbia rolls into the Pacific, huge swells grow. They're dangerous by themselves, but they also change the sand on the ocean floor and river bottom. The lower Columbia is a graveyard for scores of ships that didn't make it. So a channel master takes a small boat from Portland out over the bar to the incoming ship. The master guides the ship in."

"I've heard how beautiful the Columbia is," Heather said.

"I used to go with my father on his trips down the Columbia. The most inspiring place I've ever seen is the last fifty miles of that river. The Columbia just doesn't lie there, like the lower Mississippi. It swirls into blue patterns as it passes, as if to show it's a force that alters the weather and slows the tide. The river is blue, but not your blue in England, or Chicago blue. It's Columbia blue, a blue so deep it sparkles."

"I'd like to visit your river."

"See it in the fog. When an opaque film obscures the banks, the Columbia is the world. The air is diaphanous, and the sky and river blend together. When boating through the fog, small islands appear and vanish as if by sleight of hand. Fog slows movement, and the river seems eerily still through the haze. But it's a lie. The Columbia is always deadly."

"It sounds surrealistic."

"I suppose so, but unlike a painting, sound
132

permeates the picture. The boat's horn booms through the fog bank every few seconds and bounces back from the hills. And the gulls and cranes squawk at the boat. The sounds are mesmerizing, and the haze disorienting. Fog enters the mind."

"Now you make it sound frightening," Heather said, nibbling at the hash.

"Once, when I was a kid, maybe eight or nine, I was standing at the bow of my father's boat as we churned through the fog to the bar. Suddenly it just overwhelmed me. I imagine it was like the instant you realize you're lost in a forest. I ran to the pilothouse. Maybe because my dad suffered the same thing once, he grabbed me, sat me down in his pilot's chair, and said, 'See these instruments. See this foghorn chain and this wheel. You and I are in control of this boat and this river. We don't fear the Columbia.' I've never forgotten that lesson."

"Where's your father now?"

"He's still piloting the river, and Mom's still cooking his dinner. They're happy."

"What about you? Are you happy?" she asked as she stopped eating and looked at him intently.

"I suppose I am. I keep busy and don't think about it much. And my steak is getting cold. You talk for a while."

"My life to date has been singularly uninteresting. Born and raised in London. Working for the air chief marshal is the highlight of my life."

"Why've you never been married?" he asked abruptly.

"How did you know that?"

"You know I've read your file. I don't work with anyone whose dossier I haven't studied."

Color touched Heather's cheeks as she remembered the embarrassing questions she had answered on her security-clearance forms. The air chief marshal must have supplied it to the Americans. Piqued, she said,

133

"Does the file say I've just never felt the need to have a husband?"

"No, but I'll add it as a postscript, if you like." Crown smiled.

She wasn't beautiful, he thought. Heather was more and less than that. Her eyes were large and green and liquid. She didn't blink. Her eyelids languorously fell and rose like wings of a summer butterfly. The physician who had reported in her file that her hair was reddish-brown didn't have an eye. Wisps of honey blond fused with light red and a tincture of brown. The shades whirled together and constantly restated themselves as light played with her hair.

Miguel Maura would have called hers an Italian mouth, the most sensuous in the world, wide, with a full lower lip. Crown guessed she had the rare ability to pout without being hilarious. The spray of freckles across her nose hinted at playfulness and sunshine and kept her from being mysteriously sensuous. She was probably a brat as a kid, Crown decided.

Heather was wearing a simple black, long-sleeved dress. It clung to her and concealed very little. The V neckline dropped just far enough to suggest the swells of her breasts. True to the ridiculous style of the day, the dress's shoulders were lightly padded and unfortunately gave her a blocky appearance. A single strand of pearls defied the mannishness of the padded shoulders.

"You look athletic," Heather said, playing with what was left of her salad. "Did you ever play football?"

"In college I played American football, not soccer, which is what I think you call football. I'm a little thin to be on the front line, and a little slow to run, so I was the punter," Crown replied, wondering why she made him feel like talking about himself.

"What's a punter?"

"He's the guy who kicks the ball when there's nothing left to do. He boots it to the other team, and they can run with it. But I was kicked off my college team."

"Why? Weren't you a good punter?"

"I was good enough, but during one game I punted to the other team, and their runner made it past all my team's tacklers, so I was the only one left between their runner and the goal. My coach didn't like how I stopped him."

"How?" Heather grinned.

"Well, I went a little crazy and punted him in a place so painful that women don't understand. He had to be carried off the field, and I was thrown off the team."

They laughed, and the waiter who had caught the story also laughed. They ordered baked Alaska, to have another ignition at their table.

"The wine is perfect."

"It was Miguel Maura's and my favorite," Crown said after sipping the burgundy again. "We spent two nights at the winery where this was made."

"Were you on a tour?"

"So to speak. Miguel and I found ourselves in front of the German advance across the hills east of Paris. It was ridiculous. By the time Miguel and I and our Free French guerrillas reached the château, we were in full retreat. The winemaker was a patriot and gave us a case of burgundy to take with us when we left."

"A nice gesture."

"It was, considering we also took his son with us as a recruit. The old man had tears in his eyes when the kid left, and he gave him the family's French tricolors, which had hung for so many years near the château. The son promised to return the flag when France was liberated."

"What happened to the son?"

"I think he's still somewhere in the Pyrenees Mountains. At least, he was when Miguel and I were called to Chicago. He was a vicious kid. He once shot a German soldier and then pissed on the . . . uh, defiled the corpse."

Heather tightly gripped the stem of her wineglass, and the color drained from her cheeks. Crown cursed

135

himself. Her eyes did not leave the glass as she said in a barely audible voice, "No one told me what you did before coming to Chicago."

"I'm a government operative. I do what my boss tells me to," Crown inadequately explained.

"What does he tell you to do?"

"Anything that needs doing. You could say I'm in the military, like you." Crown was flustered by his inability to say more.

"Is Everette Smithson your boss?"

"No, he works for my chief, just like I do. He's stationed in Chicago and runs the Chicago office."

"I don't understand what you were doing in the Pyrenees Mountains having your men do those things," she said, gazing directly at him with such intensity that Crown looked away.

He wanted to say: What the hell, the man was an SS stormtrooper, an animal. Besides, he was already dead from the ambush they had surprised his squadron with. When you're dead, you're beyond caring. But he said weakly, "I can't talk about it."

He could feel Heather withdraw. A cloud drifted over her, and her face was completely inanimate. She sipped her wine several times without saying anything or looking at Crown. It was not anger, but a reconciling and a changing of expectations. Perhaps disappointment. Not disappointment, Crown thought. Our relationship has been professional, and we haven't had the time to develop something else. Heather was controlled, as if this was an emotional dousing learned through miserable experience.

"Don't do this," Crown said forcefully.

"What?" She looked up, startled.

"You're drawing inward and leaving me. We're not going to be together alone much on this assignment. Don't retreat," Crown said, and was dumbfounded at his entreaty. Christ, he thought, let's have a little control.

Heather hesitated; then her eyes met his. "I suspected what you did for a living, John. I guess it's really no different than my job. Maybe a little more immediate."

"Can we return to normal?"

"Sure," she said brightly. "The waiter is marching toward us with dessert."

Dinner was followed by Irish coffee at an Irish bar in the Irish neighborhood of Chicago. Heather was suitably impressed when Crown mentioned there were 22,000 speakeasies in Chicago during Prohibition, mostly supplied by the Irish neighborhoods. Like tourists, they drove by the Biograph Theater, where the lady in red led John Dillinger to his fate in the alley. Wind whipped spray from Lake Michigan over the South Shore Road as they returned to Hyde Park. Crown turned the car into the driveway of the Shoreland Hotel, where Heather was staying, and parked under the awning. He walked her to the hotel door.

"When will I see you again?" she asked as she turned to him.

"Tomorrow, when you and I take Hess to his interview with Fermi."

"And when will I see you again without the Germans and Italians?"

"I'll call you tomorrow afternoon about it," he said.

"Be more definite. I don't have a phone in my room."

"Let's go out tomorrow night, then."

"Good. When you see me breathlessly jotting down every technical word the deputy führer utters tomorrow, you'll know I'll be thinking about tomorrow night and not about atoms."

There was nothing left to say that night, and Crown felt awkward as she looked up at him. She was a business acquaintance, and now a friend. Maybe more than a friend. The Priest had strictures against getting close to co-agents. "Don't stick your pen into the company inkwell," he liked to say, and he had good reason. Lovers could not be relied on to make the sacrifice plays. When the Priest suspected two agents were falling for each other, he quickly assigned them to missions half the globe apart. Heather wasn't really an operative, though, Crown thought. She's here for this one assignment, and then will return to England. Judas, I don't have time to worry about this.

As if reading his mind, Heather put her hand behind his neck and drew him near. He looked into her kelly-green eyes, and his breath caught. She kissed him lightly on his mouth and said softly, "I'm not something you have figured into your life, am I?" Crown couldn't answer, so she whispered, "Think of me and tomorrow night." She kissed him again and turned into the lobby. Crown stared after her for several seconds, then walked to his car.

Five minutes after Crown's car pulled away, Heather reentered the lobby and walked past the check-in counter to the lobby phone booth. She inserted a nickel, dialed, and waited.

"This is Heather McMillan. John Crown just left the Shoreland Hotel to go back to his apartment. . . . Yes, we have the appointment with Fermi tomorrow. Hess and the interrogators will also be there. I'll be seeing Crown again tomorrow night. . . . No, I don't know where we're going. . . . All right, I'll call you again, then. Good-bye."

Heather stared at the receiver for a long moment before slowly hanging it up. She left the phone booth and entered the elevator cage.

John Crown emerged from the doorway near the phone booth, where he had heard Heather's every word. His face was tight and flushed, and his jaws were clamped shut. The lobby's dim lighting gave his face an even more gaunt look. He fought back the sadness. The Priest was right here, too. Extend yourself, and get burned. He closed his eyes for several seconds and forced the evening from his mind. His eyes opened and were now dangerous. I'm ont step closer to Miguel's killers, he thought. And she's in it. Well, they're pros. But so am I. And I play hardball in a dirtier league.

IX

"Oh, God, my stomach hurts. These cramps. Shooting pains." Rudolf Hess clasped his stomach and convulsed forward. "Please," he gasped, "I need water. Someone get me water."

John Crown poured water from a stainless-steel pitcher into a glass and passed it to Hess. His face contorting in agony, Hess fumbled with his vials from the shaving kit he always carried, swallowed a dozen pills, and washed them down with water. He groaned and rocked back and forth in his chair as if to assist their passage to his stomach.

"When did the pains begin this morning, Rudolf?" asked Professor Ludendorf, his voice that of a kindly family doctor consoling his terminally ill patient.

"When I woke up. Even before I woke. I dreamed I had them last night. There's no hope. They're getting worse every day," Hess croaked in misery.

Hess had begun complaining of severe stomach cramps six months ago in England. He had been examined by Britain's leading diagnosticians, who had concluded they were psychosomatic. The pains usually were most severe at 7:00 in the evening, when the German war news was received on Hess's radio.

"Knock it off, Hess, for Christ's sake. You and your pains. I'm sick of them," Peter Kohler growled. He sat across from Ludendorf at the immense oak conference table at the Metallurgical Laboratory. Hess was at one end of the table, facing Enrico Fermi. Heather and her note pads were across from Crown.

The physicist was uncomfortable and concerned. Although Crown had briefed him on Hess's erratic behavior during interviews, the sight of the German twisting his face with pain, shaking uncontrollably, and whining like a spoiled child was unnerving. This was not the precise, technical interview Fermi had prepared for. Nor was it probable this burnt-out shell of a man could understand complex nuclear physics. The Italian yearned to be back at his experiment, preparing for the self-sustained reaction.

Hess scrounged in his shirt pocket and stood to feel his pants. He continued to search his clothes until Ludendorf asked, "What is it, Rudolf?"

"I need a handkerchief," he muttered plaintively.

Crown handed Hess his, feeling like a baby-sitter. Hess loudly trumpeted his nose and handed the handkerchief back. Was Crown imagining, or did he catch the faintest glimpse of humor in Hess's eyes as the German asked, "Do you think it might be possible for me to go to the bathroom?"

"God damn it, Hess."

Ludendorf put his hand on Kohler's arm to restrain him, and said gently, "Now, Rudolf, you just went to the rest room a moment ago, and we can go again in a few minutes. Mr. Fermi has some things he wants to talk to you about first."

Hess teetered back in his chair and stared at the clock behind Fermi. His jaw was slack and he repeatedly licked his lips. He began to hum monotonously.

Fermi hesitated, thinking it perhaps impolite to interrupt the drone, but at Ludendorf's signal, said, "Uh, Mr. Hess, can you hear me?"

"Of course he can hear you. This is just another play for sympathy. I've seen it a hundred times," Kohler fumed.

"Mr. Hess," Fermi began, "you were in charge of the German heavy-water experiments, is that correct?"

Hess slowly lowered his gaze and stopped humming. He blinked under his ponderous black eyebrows and then glanced at Ludendorf as if to scold him. He whispered, "I thought that was to be our secret, Professor. You told me that would be our secret. I can't have everyone knowing about heavy water, you know." A petulant third-grader.

"Mr. Fermi is one of us, Rudolf. You can tell him about the experiments," Ludendorf confided. "He's a scientist."

Hess suspiciously squinted at Fermi, who gamely endeavored to appear benign and fatherly. Crown admired the Italian's supreme effort to control his loathing of all things Nazi. Here sat a monster, once the third-ranking man in the Nazi realm and Hitler's closest adviser on war and race policies. Only Hermann Göring had outranked Hess, but despite Göring's marshal's baton and pounds of medals and swagger, Hess had had the Führer's ear day after day, decision after decision.

"You know about heavy water, Herr Fermi?" asked Hess, a triumphant smile creasing his face.

"Of course. I'm just seeing if you know about it."

Do these childish games work on Hess? Crown asked himself. He can't be that vacant.

"You know, Herr Fermi, the Führer personally appointed me to guide the Reich's production of heavy water."

"When was this?"

"I took charge in 1938, and was still overseeing the heavy-water experiments when I flew to Scotland."

Ludendorf whirled his fingers at Fermi, indicating this was the time to press with questions before Hess's mind relapsed.

"What is your heavy water used for?"

"What else? To slow the escape of neutrons and to bounce them back into the reaction. Otherwise, the
142

neutrons move too fast to react with the uranium." Hess playfully zigzagged his hands, imitating atoms, and looked to Ludendorf for approval.

Crown remembered his tour of the graphite pile in the squash court under the Stagg Field stands. Apparently Fermi was using graphite, and the Nazis were using heavy water for the same purposes.

"I know what heavy water is, Herr Reischsmarshal. Do you?"

"You're insulting me, Herr Fermi. Heavy water is just what the name implies. We pass an electric charge through normal water for many weeks. This reduces many gallons of water to a minute amount."

"How does the electric charge make the water heavy?"

"And you are a Nobel Prize winner? Come, come, Herr Fermi. Atoms of hydrogen in the water are replaced with atoms of 'heavy hydrogen,' or deuterium, which makes the water eleven percent heavier than normal," Hess lectured, enjoying his new role.

"How much heavy water was Germany producing when you took over the experiments in 1938?" Fermi tried to keep his voice conversational, but his new curiosity gave it an anxious edge.

"None."

"How much in 1939?"

"None."

"In 1940?"

"None.' '

Fermi paused, puzzled. "Well, where did you get your heavy water?"

Hess smiled narrowly and showed a glimpse of the old Hess, the Reischsfuhrer of power and prestige. "We politely asked the Norwegian Hydroelectric Company at Vemork if we could have their supply of heavy water. They produce it as a byproduct of their hydrogen electrolysis process, and they're the only place in the world where it is made."

"Did they sell it to you?"

"No, they refused for political reasons." Hess's grin spread in anticipation. Crown grimaced, knowing the cruel and true punchline Hess was baiting Fermi for.

"Well, how did you get the heavy water?"

Hess leaned forward and stabbed out the words. "We invaded Norway in 1940 and captured the plant, along with the rest of the country. Now the dumb Norwegians do exactly what we tell them to."

Hess shrieked with laughter as Fermi's face dropped. What Hess didn't mention was that Vemork and the Norwegian Hydro plant were the last bastions to fall to the Nazis in southern Norway. Kongsberg, the nearest large town, had been overrun on April 13, just three days after the invasion was launched. Norwegian troops at Vemork had been ordered to fight to the last shell. Resistance was fanatical. Vemork held out until May 3 and set the Germans three weeks behind schedule.

Fermi sipped water to compose himself. He looked at Crown, and his eyes said he would walk out of the conference room if Hess's information wasn't so vital.

"Mr. Hess, if we can continue," Fermi said, and paused for Hess to subside. The German gulped water as if to quench his laughter, gagged, and spewed water over the table, still cackling. Heather brushed drops from her note pad and arm. Hess quieted, but still wore his victory grin.

"Now, what other elements are used in the experiments?"

"Uranium."

"Where does the uranium come from?"

"From Belgium. We asked Belgium to supply us—"

Doubting Fermi would sit through another setup, Crown interrupted, "As you know, Germany invaded Belgium, and I assume they just steal whatever uranium they need. Right, Hess?"

Hess sulked at having his joke diffused. "Not stealing. We have incorporated Belgium into the Reich.

So we just transfer the urnaium from one part of the Reich to another."

"How much is . . . transferred?"

"Sixty tons of ore a month."

Fermi's head jerked up. "Sixty tons. How much uranium metal from the ore are you producing a month?"

"One full ton."

This revelation punched Fermi in the stomach. The U.S. had refined its first pure metal only a month before. If the Germans were manufacturing a ton a month, and had been for several years, we're behind. We're losing the race. He gripped the table and looked frantically around the room, hoping someone was sharing the burden of his fear. Ludendorf and Kohler absently waited for Fermi's next question, their faces devoid of understanding. Thankful for the pause, Heather McMillan furtively glanced at Crown, hoping he would look up, but he stared at the tabletop, his eyes almost closed and his mind in the Pyrenees Mountains with Miguel Maura. Only Hess knew the significance of Germany's one ton of uranium metal a month, and his eyes gleamed as he savored his effect on the physicist. In the commanding voice all Germans knew, the deputy führer expounded, "Only Germany has such an output, and only Germany has the technology to employ the metal to benefit mankind. That is, Aryan mankind." He paused to gauge Fermi's reaction and then lost himself in a fit of giggles.

"Do you know what a cyclotron is, Mr. Hess?" Fermi asked, after Hess's laugh had dissipated.

"It's a machine which gives great speed to charged particles by repeatedly accelerating them. A strong magnetic field keeps them traveling in a circle around the inside of the cyclotron. The particles are used in nuclear-bombardment experiments to find out how much energy is released from splitting an atom. Correct? Of course I'm correct."

Hess grinned broadly again, and Crown could see

why he had never seen smiling pictures of Hess. He had a bad overbite, and buck teeth.

"Where is Germany's cyclotron located?"

"Along with the Eiffel Tower, the Arc de Triomphe, and the Cathedral of Notre-Dame, the French kindly contributed their only cyclotron to the Fatherland. We have made good use of it, too."

This time he laughed derisively at Crown, who had been unable to damper the joke. Hess closed his mouth to choke off his laugh, but it sputtered through, and flecks of spittle showered the table.

Fermi leaned to Ludendorf, "Is he like this all the time?"

"No, only when the conversation is going his way. Put up with it, because he'll keep the information coming as long as he's enjoying himself. When Hess feels he's losing control of the conversation, he'll stop giving us anything useful. I know it's tough, but play along."

Fermi said quietly, "I didn't realize how hard your and Kohler's task was."

Kohler smiled gratefully at Fermi, but when his head turned again to Hess, the glower returned, and it quieted the deputy führer.

"Mr. Hess, what priority has the German government given to nuclear research?" A stupid question, one allowing Fermi to catch his breath.

"At first we had trouble getting money, because the Führer was not convinced of the feasibility of our research. Plus, our whole economy was geared for the production of tools for lightning war, which, as you know, we've been very successful at," Hess said, speaking as if he was standing behind a podium at a massive rally, gesturing widely so that those in the back row a quarter of a mile away could see him, and speaking slowly so that the public-address system would not garble his message.

"Hermann Göring promised his Luftwaffe would level London, but he had to keep setting the date back week after week. The British are resilient, too much so for their own good." Hess chuckled and coughed and reached again for the water, this time sipping carefully. "So when it became clear that total victory would not be coming in a few months, the Führer decided to fully back the nuclear experiments. By the way, gentlemen"—Hess lowered his voice conspiratorially—"the fact that Germany may not win the war this month is a high state secret and is not to be leaked to the German people." Hess rocked back in his chair and roared with laughter.

Fermi waited for him to collect himself, and asked, "Are any peaceful purposes foreseen as a result of your experiments?"

"Is shortening the war a peaceful purpose?" Hess asked, his face reflecting his enjoyment of the interview. "If so, then, yes. The German Ministry of War has conducted studies on the effect of a nuclear bomb on London. For some reason, the city is always London. I suggested New York or Moscow, but the Führer wants London. Anyway, we are convinced that as goes London, so go the Allies. In fact, we've plotted the exact block where our first bomb will fall. It's an amusing science you and I are involved in, *nicht wahr,* Herr Fermi?"

Fermi was acutely embarrassed, and he almost retreated to the rationalizations he had paraded before Heather and Crown a few days before. Peter Kohler saved him the trouble. "Listen, I've had it with you, Hess." He pushed back his chair, stood, and leaned over the table, pointing his finger at Hess's face. "You're not the goddamn deputy führer anymore," he shouted. "You're a prisoner of war, and you'll start acting like one. You answer the questions. You don't ask them. Any more of this crap, and I'm going to question you by myself in a locked room. Right, Professor?"

Rather than calming Kohler as he usually did, Ludendorf sat mute. Hess paled.

Crown's gaze shot to Hess. Something was wrong. A whiff of incredulity tugged at him, insubstantial and transient. Crown tried to fan the sensation. It was more than the strangeness of the meeting between a Reichsführer and America's leading nuclear physicist. Something here was out of place, disjointed. Or maybe the interview was too smooth and too productive. No, it wasn't smooth, not with the volatile Hess ready to explode with laughter or double over in pain. Crown shifted the ephemeral impression again, and it made no sense. It passed from him.

"Who are the scientists working on the German experiments?"

Hess looked at the ceiling and stroked his recessed chin with a purposeful display of thoughtfulness. "We ran into a little difficulty here, Herr Fermi. As you yourself know, some of the Führer's policies of racial purity have caused a few of the Reich's leading nuclear physicists to leave Germany and Italy. Your wife is Jewish, is she not?"

Fermi could not suppress his surprise. Hess chortled, put his hands behind his neck to stretch, and said, "Yes, I know about you. We were counting on your assistance with our nuclear project. But you got away. I had a personal discussion with the Duce about his emigration policies when I learned you had vanished. He promised to do better. But some do leave the Reich without permission. Some great nuclear physicists—Wigner, Teller, Szilard, Weisskopf. I would imagine some of these men are working within several meters of this conference."

Once again, Fermi's face registered what he wished it would not. All four of these scientists were in Hyde Park working with Fermi.

Hess laughed his grating laugh and said, "I thought so. Well, that's the price of a pure Germany. The price of one of the Führer's peculiarities."

The physicist choked back rage, the same rage which had dogged his last six months in Italy. He wanted to lash out at the arrogant Nazi sitting at the end of the table. This grotesque madman had helped twist the world in war and enslave entire races. And now he talked of one man's peculiarities. Hess was evil incarnate. Fermi's throat was so constricted, he could not continue.

Ludendorf said mildly, "Mr. Fermi asked you, Rudolf, what German scientists are working on your projects. He didn't get an answer."

"We have two groups—one under Dr. Diebner, and the other under Dr. Esau. They work independently of each other and largely duplicate each other's work."

"Why two groups?" Ludendorf continued with the questions as Fermi poured more water and wiped his brow with a handkerchief. The interview was draining the normally indefatigable physicist.

"In the event one group makes a mistake, the other may catch it. In addition, there's nothing wrong with a little healthy competition. Each group is acutely aware of the other. We plan it this way. There's another reason, which normally is not openly discussed. But we're among friends here." He beamed widely, scanning the room for anyone enjoying his irony, saw none, and continued, "We found that some of our scientists, even Germans, if you can imagine, were not working wholeheartedly on the experiments to produce the atom bomb. Apparently a few did not agree with the war effort. At first, we merely suspected this problem, but we had no hard proof, because obviously there was no precedent for the amount of progress that should have been made. But some of the scientists were shirking their duties, we were sure. So we set up two teams of physicists and applied pressure to the team that lagged behind. One team set the standard for the other. No one shirks now. Our pressure is enthusiastic and professional."

Fermi signaled he could continue, and in a dry, cracked voice he asked, "What company processes the uranium?"

"I.G. Farben."

"And who refines the uranium oxide?"

"Auer Company, of Berlin."

"Where are the principal German reactor experiments?"

"At Dahlem. At the Institute of Biology and Virus Research."

"Why there? Why not at the Institute of Physics?"

"People nose around. You Americans call them snoopers. No one's afraid of physics. But no one noses around a virus center. They don't know what they'll catch. Ingenious, is it not? We call the project the Virus House."

A shadow of suspicion crossed Crown again. Hess obviously loves Germany and worships Hitler. He still acts imperious and contemptuous. Yet he's divulging highly classified information, an act which makes him a traitor to the Reich. His information about German military strategy revealed during his first weeks in England proved highly accurate and very costly for Germany. His statements about the German nuclear experiments is probably just as precise. Perhaps the arrogance and cruel jokes are Hess's way of avoiding been seen as a groveling sycophant. But something doesn't fit. Or maybe Hess is just insane.

At Maindiff Court Hospital, Hess had been given batteries of tests trying to plot his freak mental processes. The psychiatrists concluded Hess had a neurotic-schizoid personality. Of course, their conclusions told Crown nothing, and only begged the issue, that being: Was Hess so far removed from reality that he would wilfully reveal top-secret information? Or was the man crazy like a fox? Crown wasn't the first to ask this question, he knew. Deserters are always suspected of being plants. But because of the invaluable and accurate facts Hess had given his interrogators during his months of confinement, the British and American officials had determined that Hess had truly crossed.

Crown couldn't argue with their conclusion, because accuracy was always the test of the genuine cross.

As Fermi's questions and Hess's laughing answers flew by him, Crown sifted through his reasoning again and again and couldn't find a fault. There were two nagging loose ends, though: Miguel Maura's death and Heather McMillan's phone call. Maura's death could be related to some other assignment Crown had worked on, but this was unlikely, because they had come to Chicago secretly and hadn't been there long enough to be found. The assassination could have been a case of mistaken identity, but this was also highly improbable. There were too many people wanting Crown and Maura dead to assign Maura's death to an accident. But these people were in Europe. So Maura's death must have been connected to their present assignment of guarding Hess. But how? Here Crown's mind went blank.

Heather's surreptitious late-night phone call was also inexplicable. Was it related to Maura's death? She was in England when it happened. Whom did she call? Certainly not anyone under Richard Sackville-West's command, because he assured Crown that all operatives working on the Hess cross in the Chicago area were identified to Crown and there would be no teams working against each other. Ludendorf or Kohler? These men's backgrounds had been scrupulously searched. They had been invaluable to the Allies in years past, so invaluable that thoughts of current deception had to be ruled out. No one produces information that costs the Axis thousands of men if he isn't loyal to the Allies.

Who she called was an unknown, but her purpose was not—at least, the short-range purpose. Someone wanted to know where Crown was at all times, and was using Heather to find out. Of course she is excited about seeing him tonight, because when she is with Crown, she and her mysterious boss know where he is. And in light of the prior assassination attempt, during

151

which the murderers were gunning for both Maura and Crown, Crown's only conclusion was that there would be another try at his life and that Heather would supply his location to the murderer.

He looked up from his folded hands and saw Heather gazing at him and transcribing one of Hess's long answers at the same time. She lowered her head slightly and looked at him with a playful, sensuous pout to tell him he had been ignoring her. He smiled warmly at her **and** regretted he would have to kill her.

"What do you mean you don't remember?" yelled Kohler, yanking Crown's thoughts back to the interview. "You've pulled that on us before, and I don't go for it, Hess. It's too convenient."

Fermi tried again. "What proportion of heavy water to uranium oxide is used to make the heavy-water paste?"

Hess's eyes were wide, and darted from person to person, seeking understanding. "I don't remember. I can't remember anything. Please believe me."

"Let's try it this way, Mr. Hess," said Fermi patiently. "Do you know what heavy-water paste is?"

"No. I mean, maybe I should, but I don't know. *Ich weiss nicht.*" Hess's face crinkled, and Crown thought he was about to sob. The German looked at Ludendorf and pleaded, "You know this happens to me. You read Dr. Rees's report. Please, Professor Ludendorf. I can't recall anything."

Ludendorf put his hands on Fermi's arm and in a confidential voice said, "Hess has these amnesia spells occasionally. He'll pull out of it in a day or two. It's useless to continue now."

"I've never heard of anything like this. A sudden attack of complete amnesia?"

"Yes. The British psychiatrists have tested him again and again and found no reason to suspect the amnesia is not genuine."

"Well," said Fermi as he gathered his notes, "I sup-

152

pose we should adjourn. John, can I see you for a moment?"

Kohler led Hess from the conference room. Hess moved like a blind man, with his hands extended in front of him, and with a wide, unsure gait. The strongman act was over, and Kohler carefully and considerately led Hess by the arm.

"I'm really stumped, John," Fermi said after the door closed. Ludendorf and Heather had also remained.

"How's that?"

"Well, Hess was an important Nazi. Most people who rise that far in any government have only one specialty, politics. It's unheard of that Hess should know so much about a complicated and new field. I can't fathom that. His knowledge is extensive, and although his amnesia spell hit him before I could reach what for me would be new ground, I'm sure he knows some vital facts, material we must have."

"So his information isn't a ruse?"

"No, heavens no. It's legitimate, and I'm sure the Germans are worried sick about what he may reveal. I can see why you have such elaborate precautions to guard him. I'll have to interview him again. Maybe a couple of times. Professor, are you sure it will take two days for his amnesia to clear?"

"Usually a day or two. I'll call you as soon as it does."

"Good. Well, this has been a productive session," Fermi said, putting his papers into a briefcase. "I'll prepare my report for Mr. Sackville-West. The Germans are much further along on their bomb project than we suspected. It's frightening."

Aware of Fermi's tight schedule, Crown asked, "How many hours of interview will it take?"

"I don't know. My own little project is due for completion in about eight days, and it'll require most of my time. But Hess's information is critical, and I'll find time to interview him. You just let me know when he can remember again."

As they left the room, the physicist stopped Crown and said, "Maybe you can review my report to Sackville-West before I send it to him? We must convince him and his superiors of the impending peril of the German atom bomb. I'm convinced that, failing any colossal blunders, the type German scientists usually don't make, they'll have the bomb a full six months before we can have one."

Kohler and four guards walked Rudolf Hess from their car to his room on the second floor of the EDC house. Kohler asked them to stand by while he assisted the zombielike Hess to bed. He would knock when he wanted out of the bedroom.

After the door closed behind them, Hess immediately emerged from his trance and transformed again into the deputy führer. "Well, Kohler, how to you think it went?"

Kohler stood at attention and replied, "Just like you planned, Herr Reichsführer."

"I thought so, too. Fermi is a bright man. But you noticed that I gave him very little hard scientific information. Most of what I revealed, he already knew."

"Yes, Herr Reichsführer."

"He was quite startled to learn of our uranium capabilities." Hess chuckled quietly. "It'll give him and the U.S. government something to worry about." Hess took off his coat and began to unbutton the shirt. "Did you notice anything about that John Crown?"

"No, sir. My job was to stare angrily and yell at you."

"That you did, Kohler. Quite impressively, too, I might add. But I observed Crown. He's suspicious. And I can tell he's dangerous. He doesn't have any hard facts, other than your fumbled attempt to kill him, but during my interrogation he was wary. I could see it in his face. He's going to pry and probe until he
154

finds something. And we can't risk that, can we, Kohler?"

"No, Herr Reichsführer."

"You know why we initially tried to eliminate him. It's even more important now that his suspicion is aroused. Kill him. Do it soon, and do it professionally, as I know you can. Don't bungle it this time, Kohler. Good night."

X

Ohio Valley farmers called the winter merely brisk. To the three German commandos rolling westward in an open boxcar, it was bitterly cold. Sliding the steel door closed would have made the journey bearable, but railroad police searched closed cars at every switchyard and passed by open cars. The lesson had cost Erich von Stihl his entire cigar supply.

"Where are we, Herr Oberst?" Willi Lange asked as he beat his arms across his chest to generate warmth.

"Call me Colonel, Lange, not Herr Oberst. We're about twenty miles west of Cleveland. We'll get to Chicago in a day and a half, assuming we keep getting these milk runs."

"A boring, drab country, Colonel." Hans Graf blew through his hands. "No Black Forest, no Bavarian Alps, no history. Just cornfields."

Drab, perhaps, thought von Stihl, but also terrifying. For hundreds of miles the train had passed cities overflowing with foundries, mills, refineries, and manufacturing plants. None of the vast countryside lay untended. Wheat- and cornfields, orchards, vast cattle herds, coal mines, and logging camps crowded the land. And the country was geared for war production. Germany was a midget by comparison. General Rommel was right about a war with the U.S. A deep sense of foreboding had settled over von Stihl.

"Hey, Schwachheit, how come you're not cleaning your beloved Schmeisser? The cold getting to you?"

Graf challenged. Crisp wind rushing through the boxcar had turned Graf's scar under his ear into a crimson sun. The ever-present malicious sneer was exacerbated by the cold.

Willi Lange sat opposite the open door with his knees tucked under his chin. His oilcloth roll lay carefully at his feet. It was impossible to ignore Graf in those close quarters.

"It's clean," Lange said, wishing the blond giant would look for something else to divert himself with.

"How do you know? You haven't put it together for at least an hour."

"It's clean, Graf. Why don't you play with your SS dick and get off my back?"

Graf's smirk lowered dangerously. "Those are big words for a little Wehrmacht corporal, Schwachheit. If it wasn't for your protector here"—nodding to von Stihl—"you'd eat them."

"Graf," said von Stihl in a tired voice barely audible over the clacking of the train, "I'm telling you again, take it easy. You'll have enough to get worked up about when we get to Chicago."

"As for you, von Stihl, I'm SS. I don't take orders from a Wehrmacht colonel."

"Graf, you received your instructions directly from SS Obergruppenführer Eicke. Those were to follow my orders. Do you understand this, or do I report to the lieutenant general you breached your loyalty oath?"

Graf was silent. He stared at von Stihl and then at Lange, conveying a threat von Stihl was sure the SS stormtrooper would someday try to execute.

Goddamn SS fanatics. Von Stihl had strenuously objected to the Generaloberst when Graf was added to the team. The general said he understood, but because of certain unmentioned pressures, the standard euphemism for SS Reichsführer Heinrich Himmler's meddling, an SS soldier had to be a member of the group.

The Schutzstaffel, or SS, was a separate entity from the Wehrmacht, the German Army. The SS was Nazi Germany's black-uniformed, sinister watchdog. It was Hitler's merciless, conscienceless strong arm that beat the German citizenry and peoples of conquered lands into compliance. German laymen and military personnel were rarely granted glimpses of the SS, which considered itself a new sect with its own rituals and customs. Their high-front black dress caps and jackboots put them above the German police and army troops. SS troops were accountable only to their superiors.

The SS was the brainchild of Heinrich Himmler, the retiring, pince-nez-wearing schoolteacher from Munich whose hobby was growing herb gardens. Himmler was a peasant mystic whose devotion to National Socialism stemmed from his fear of the corrupt web of international Jewry. He feared only one man, Adolf Hitler. So immersed in satanic evil was Himmler that few high-ranking Nazis could stand his presence. Hermann Göring once complained that when Himmler entered the room, Göring was seized with the urge to vomit.

The Schutzstaffel, or Guard Echelon, was the crystallization of Himmler's anagogic interpretation of German history and his call for a new order of German knighthood. The SS had several branches, each with a specialty. The Geheime Staatspolizei (secret state police, or Gestapo) ferreted out, interrogated, and disposed of enemies of the Reich in Germany and occupied countries. The Totenkopfverbände (Death's-Head battalion) guarded the concentration camps and later provided fighting units. The Waffen SS were elite combat troops that rivaled the Wehrmacht.

Hans Graf, the purple-scarred, overbearing commando leaning against the boxcar door frame, was a product of Himmler's vision. He had reported to the SS Junkerschule at Bad Tölz in the Bavarian Alps on November 9, 1937, the anniversary of the Munich Beer Cellar Putsch. The school at Bad Tölz accepted

158

400 officer candidates a year. Each applicant was required to show genealogical records dating back to 1750 proving he was of pure Germanic stock. Wives' records were searched back to 1800. The entrance requirements were so strict as to physical condition that up until 1936 an applicant was not accepted if he had one filled tooth. Those whose trunks were too long, noses too big, or knees too knobby were not admitted. Phrenologists searched each candidate's head for non-Aryan protuberances. Education, however, was not a prerequisite for admission. Grade-school dropouts and college graduates were admitted without distinction.

After passing the exhausting physical, Graf was issued the twenty-seven pieces of the SS uniform, which included the black trousers and tunic and black helmet. On the right lapel of the tunic were the two lightning flashes that formed the menacing double S.

Graf's transformation began at 6:00 A.M. the second day, when his blood type was tattooed under his left armpit. Then for months Graf and his classmates ran right, ran left, lay down, stood up, crawled, and jumped as they learned to follow orders. Each day had two hours of saluting practice. The right hand was in position six steps before reaching a superior and stayed rigid until three steps after passing the officer. Each day had three hours of the goosestep march. Should any of the candidates' legs not be rigid at the end of the third hour, an extra hour was added. Meals were eaten in stiff-back, chin-out position, and the silverware was moved only horizontally and vertically. These were called square meals. At any time day or night when an officer yelled "Motto" all candidates yelled back in one voice *Meine Ehre heisst Treue.* "My honor is loyalty." A late or quavering voice meant another hour goose-stepping.

Bad Tölz also stressed practical information. Graf learned six ways to break a man's neck. He spent hours on the firing range, mastering the intricacies of the Luger pistol, Schmeisser submachine gun, mortars, and bazookas. His class studied the effect of automobile exhaust on a dog that has been locked into a glass box. They saw how various barbiturates and paralyzants affected dogs. The instructor carefully noted how each ingredient would affect a human. The class learned how injections of phenol, petrol, and turpentine will rapidly kill a man. They practiced giving intravenous injections on cadavers brought from the local mortuary. A cadet who fainted was given an extra hour of solitary goose-stepping.

Evenings were occupied with political and racial education. The histories of the Nazi party and the SS were studied. The differences in the European races were explained. The marching song of the SS and the "Horst Wessel Song" were sung. Biographies of SS leaders were committed to memory: Himmler, Heydrich, Dietrich, Hausser, Steiner. Histories of the distinguished SS divisions were reviewed: Divison Lebstandarte Adolf Hitler, Division Das Reich, Divison Totenkopf, and many others. Each division had battalions whose histories were learned.

Grueling months passed. The candidates' minds and bodies were torn down and poured into the SS mold. Nazi doctrine was pounded into them. They became lean and hard. Above all, they were taught to follow orders without question.

On April 20, 1938, Hans Graf received his permanent SS pass and swore allegiance to the Führer:

I swear to thee, Adolf Hitler,
As Führer and chancellor of the German Reich,
Loyalty and bravery.
I vow to thee and to the superiors whom thou shall appoint
Obedience unto death, so help me God.

Graf's training was not as yet completed, however, for he had to earn the Reich's sport badge and learn the SS catechism, an imitation of the Catholic ritual:

Question: Why do we believe in Germany and the Führer?

Answer: Because we believe in God, we believe in Germany, which He created in His world, and in the Führer, Adolf Hitler, whom He has sent us.

Question: Why do we obey?

Answer: From inner conviction; from belief in Germany, in the Führer, and in the movement and in the SS; and from loyalty.

As did all SS candidates, Graf then spent several months in the Labor Service and several more months in the Wehrmacht. His Wehrmacht report was excellent, and on November 9, 1938, one full year after his admission to the officers' school, Graf received his dagger and was commissioned into the SS at the moving ceremony at the National Socialist shrine in Munich.

SS Untersturmführer (Second Lieutenant) Graf was assigned to the Totenkopf Battalion. Oberbayern Regiment, at the Dachau concentration camp. Here he excelled. As a youth the handsome blond had been expelled from several schools because of his remarkable talent for destruction and disorganization. His SS training captured and channeled this skill, and it manifested itself in the professional subjugation of the prisoners in his eight Dachau barracks. Graf mastered the two fundamentals of effective enslavement: change the prisoners' routine frequently, without apparent reason, to deprive them of the comfort of a set pattern; and savagely punish infractions of even the smallest rule.

Efficiency was Graf's hallmark. Punishment, whether whipping or hanging, took time and interrupted the day's busy schedule. Graf invented the lumberman's slash. Prisoners who merited whipping had the right side of their faces slashed with the SS dagger or bruised by a kapo's club, like trees being marked to be felled. Those deserving death were cut or clubbed on the left side of their faces. During lineup at the end of the day,

Graf yanked those with bloody faces from the line, and they were dealt with as indicated. Graf's innovation was duly recorded in his SS file.

Guarding the camp was monotonous, and the Untersturmführer soon longed for a break from the routine. He was also acutely aware that the SS Totenkopfverbände was looked down upon by other branches of the SS. So Graf was delighted when, in October 1939, 6,500 members of the Totenkopfverbände were organized into the SS Totenkopfdivision, which along with several other divisions became the Waffen SS, the elite fighting unit. Graf applied and was transferred to the new Death's-Head division.

During the winter of 1939–1940, the Death's-Head division prepared for Fall Gelb (Case Yellow), the offensive in the West. The division's commanding officer, SS Gruppenführer (Major General) Theodor Eicke, wanted to be at the spearhead of the offensive to demonstrate the battlefield capabilities of his much-maligned concentration-camp guards. But when Belgium was invaded, the Death's-Head division was in the second wave and saw very little fighting. In May, Eicke's luck changed. The division was pulled out of reserve and joined the Fifth and Seventh panzer divisions sweeping north across Belgium. General Rommel's Seventh Panzer Division captured Le Cateau and Cambrai on May 17 and 18. The Death's-Head division was ordered to clean up and consolidate the captured territory. Fighting small, fierce Belgian units, the division suffered sixty-nine casualties. One of them, Hans Graf, was injured when a red-hot piece of shrapnel struck him under his right ear. During the firefight, the medic applied a butterfly bandage, which pulled back the corner of Graf's mouth. The would healed slowly, permanently distorting Graf's mouth.

The Death's-Head division raced toward Dunkirk, where they hoped to capture the British Army. The SS was again immersed in battle along the La Bassée Canal at Bethune, where the British fought fanatically to allow more time for the Dunkirk evacuation. The British Fourth Brigade was responsible for holding the canal between Robecq and Bethune but was slowly overwhelmed by the 21,000 men of the Death's-Head division. British soldiers made a heroic final stand at Le Paradis and Locon. Fighting raged, but the British could not halt the Death's-Head onslaught.

The Fourth Company of the First Battalion, Second SS Totenkopf Infantry Reigment, Hans Graf's unit, under the command of SS Obersturmführer Fritz Knochlein, surrounded the 100 men of the Second Royal Norfolk at Le Paradis. After suffering many casualties, the British surrendered. Those captured were marched single file past a barn wall, where they were massacred by the fire of two SS machine guns. Hans Graf was the triggerman on one of the guns. He later bayoneted any Britisher who still showed signs of life. This was the infamous Massacre of Le Paradis.

After conquering Belgium, the Death's-Head division turned south to pursue the hastily retreating French. Engagements with French units were brief but sharp. Hans Graf's superiors noted his exceeding zeal and ruthlessness combined with his technical ability with small arms. Graf was awarded the Iron Cross First Class after the capture of Clamecy, and was promoted to Oberstrumführer (first lieutenant).

Graf's proficiency was noticed by increasingly higher levels of the SS, until Himmler, on the recommendation of Obergruppenführer Eicke, personally transferred Graf to the Berlin unit of the Liebstandart SS Adolf Hitler, which guarded the Führer. Wanting a stake in the venture in the United States, Himmler assigned Graf to the mission. Anything was better than standing at attention at the Reich's chancellory day after day, so Graf was grateful for the change. He joined Erich von Stihl in August and began the arduous two months of training.

For the hundredth time, von Stihl shifted his pack

behind him, trying to discover a bearable position. The boxcar adamantly refused to yield the slightest modicum of comfort. He stood and rubbed his buttocks, forcing blood back into the aching tissue. He raised his right knee to his chest and pulled it close to lossen the joints. Then came the left knee. Von Stihl walked around Graf and peered out the boxcar. Winter air coursing past the car pricked his face and rushed under his clothes, chasing away pockets of warmth and shocking his skin.

"To hell with riding in this freezing boxcar like cattle," Graf complained. "I say we purchase passenger tickets at the next station."

"I'll tell you again, Graf," replied von Stihl, "we stay in boxcars until Chicago. I'm not going to have any trace of us showing up on bus or train tickets. I don't want our signatures on car receipts. We can't be anywhere where we might be asked to identify ourselves. That happens at public-transportation terminals."

"What's the worry? Each of us has identification that an American cop would swear was genuine. 'Cop,' by the way, Schwachheit, is slang for 'policeman,' " Graf said as he turned to Lange.

"That's the point," von Stihl explained as he returned to his spot at the front end of the boxcar. "Our identification, as foolproof as it might be, is our last resort. There's no sense putting ourselves into a position where we have reached the last resort. So we'll stay in boxcars. If no one sees us, then no one asks questions."

"We're being too careful," Graf persisted.

"Wrong. There's no such thing as too careful on this mission. SS Major General Hausser wouldn't have issued your orders personally, had it not been important, and you wouldn't have undergone that miserable two months of training, either."

"Who needed that shit? I didn't learn anything."

True, thought von Stihl. Graf, like all Waffen SS troops, possessed an amazing arsenal of knowledge.

164

Von Stihl could teach him nothing about wiring explosives or walking silently through underbrush. The Obersturmführer's handling of a Schmeisser submachine gun was impressive. Graf was excellent in hand-to-hand combat, although, like many Waffen SS, he preferred boxing methods to swifter, surer killing techniques. Students at Bad Tölz boxed an hour a day during their training. In addition, Graf was in incredible physical shape. He could run two kilometers in an impressive five minutes and forty seconds and could scale fifty feet of rope in under twenty seconds without using his feet. Graf never perspired, just smiled malignantly. The training was vital, though, because it taught the three commandos to anticipate each other's moves. They gained a coordination and a timing which made them a team. Their competence would lessen luck's role.

The sound of crunching couplers rolled from the front of the train, through their car, and to the rear, like falling dominoes, and meant the train was slowing. Graf leaned out the door, saw the switchyard sign pass, and said, "Dammit, here we go with another stop."

Willi Lange concealed the oilskin roll behind him and slumped forward. Von Stihl took his Luger from his waistband and held it under his paper sack, pointed at the door.

Because their door was open, they had been checked only twice during the past three days, and it was unlikely the railroad police would search the boxcars in this tiny switchyard. But they were prepared.

For ten minutes their car was pushed back and forth as cars were added to the train. The roar of the locomotive's big diesel engine reverberated in their car. From the smell, von Stihl guessed a car of pigs was being shuttled into place upwind from the car.

Graf wrinkled his nose and said, "Christ. We'll smell them all the way to Chicago."

Without warning, a railroad policeman stuck his head

165

into the car. "I thought I smelled some assholes on my train. Get out," he ordered.

"Officer," Graf said, "we've got to get to—"

"Hold your bullshit and get off my train," yelled the cop as he beat his billy club against the car floor. He had an immense double chin, and von Stihl guessed the man weighed 350 pounds. "Or I'll come aboard and throw you off, and believe me, you don't want that."

Lange erupted with a phlegmatic, tortured cough. He breathed erratically and whooped sickly again, as if a hand was twisting his throat. A thin strand of spittle dropped from his lips. His eyes were open but were sightless and were raised to his eyebrows. The cough went on and on and racked Lange's entire frame. He grimaced and sank lower to the floor.

"Our friend's got tuberculosis, officer. He's gonna die in a couple of weeks," Graf said in his lunch-bucket accent. "He wants to be taken to Chicago to see his brother."

The policeman cocked an eye at Lange. The little hobo was wearing two weeks of stubble on his cadaverous face, and three days' grime on his hands. His jacket was stained and ragged, and the undershirt hanging out was filthy. One of his bootlaces was untied, as if he lacked the energy to reach his foot. Lange emitted another wrenching cough and slumped sideways, almost to the boxcar floor. He gasped for breath between coughing fits. Mucus dribbled from his nose and caught in his wispy mustache. He wheezed and coughed again, and the cough rattled to a low, exhausted moan.

"All the poor son of a bitch wants to do is visit his brother in Chicago before he dies. We got to get him there," Graf pleaded.

"Shit," said the policeman as he turned away from the door. "You bums is always sick with one thing or another." He looked back and said, "O.K., you guys can ride, but don't tell anyone along the line I said so."

After the cop disappeared down the rail, Lange sat

166

up and wiped spit and mucus from his face. He breathed hard to catch his breath.

"You know, Schwachheit, I wonder how much of that sickness is an act," Graf said with his inevitable leer.

"Nicely done, Lange," von Stihl said.

Willi Lange had been in von Stihl's Wehrmacht commando unit for a year and a half, during which time the colonel had come to appreciate Lange's single talent. On April 23, 1941, von Stihl's troops surprise-attacked the Athens airport where the bulk of RAF planes in Greece were stationed. Von Stihl and his men charged the airfield hangar. The hangar was empty, and the colonel, then a major, saw the RAF pilots racing from their huts to the Spitfires and Hurricanes on the field. The object of the Germans' mission, to capture the Greek RAF, would have been thwarted had the planes taken off.

Several of the fighters began to taxi down the runway to escape. Exasperated, von Stihl foolishly yelled at anyone in hearing distance to stop them. Before the major could retract the order and perhaps apologize for it, a little corporal whose name he had not known ran forward twenty or thirty paces, lifted his sub-machine gun, and squeezed off a short burst. The lead plane, perhaps 150 yards away, lurched and bounced to a stop on the runway, its right tire blown out. Without sighting the weapon, Lange fired several more bursts, and the next two planes in line jerked to a stop, each with a flat tire. The two planes behind them swerved violently onto the grass trench along the runway and slid to a halt. The runway was completely cluttered, and escape for the remaining fighters and bombers was impossible.

As von Stihl's men rushed from the hangar to capture the RAF pilots, von Stihl approached the corporal. "That was an impressive performance."

Willi Lange shrugged his shoulders and reached for

another clip from his belt. Each magazine had 32 bullets, and von Stihl was to learn that Lange would go to great lengths to avoid wasting a shell. Without saying more, they ran to assist the roundup of RAF pilots.

As his unit marched toward Athens the next day, von Stihl found the corporal walking a considerable distance behind the rest of the troops.

"You don't enjoy the other men's company?" Von Stihl smiled.

Without breaking pace, Lange shrugged his shoulders and said nothing.

"Do you talk, Corporal?"

"Sure, what would the major have me say?"

Von Stihl foresaw important uses for the corporal, and he was determined to get Lange to commit himself to the unit.

"The major would have you tell me the effective range of that Schmeisser you've got."

"For most soldiers, it's a hundred and fifty yards. For me it's about two hundred yards."

"How do you explain the difference?"

"If I point my gun up the road and hold it so it's exactly parallel to the road surface, do you know how long it'll take for my bullet to hit the ground after I fire?" asked Lange.

"No."

"Exactly as long as if I take a shell and drop it to the ground from my hand. The bullet's velocity has no effect on its rate of drop to the ground."

"So what you're saying is that you arc the bullets when aiming at distant targets. I could have figured that out," said von Stihl dryly.

"Maybe you could, but most don't. I have the amount of arc figured out for all distances up to two hundred yards. And I'm a good guesser of distances."

Quiet perhaps, thought von Stihl, but not unduly modest. He goaded, "Why the attachment to the submachine gun? Semiautomatic rifles are useful in more situations."

168

"Perhaps so, Major, but not German semiauto rifles. In case you haven't noticed, German-designed and -produced rifles, like the 7.92 rifle that your men up there have, are made by fools and used by fools. They're unreliable and dangerous. I once got hold of an American-made M1, and I just couldn't believe the difference in quality."

"But you're satisfied with the quality of the Schmeisser?"

"They're the finest submachine gun in history. No country can match it."

Von Stihl looked at the squat, ugly weapon hanging from straps around Lange's shoulders. With the metal stock folded in, as Lange's was, the submachine gun was only two feet long. It weighed less than nine pounds and consisted of a striated pistol grip, a small housing for the internal mechanism, a short barrel with a superfluous sight at the tip, and a magazine holder. From this holder protruded the clip, which was the size of two square pounds of butter placed end to end. The Schmeisser's official name was MP40, and it looked enough like a pistol that the German word for "submachine gun" literally meant "machine pistol."

"What caliber?" asked von Stihl.

"Are you testing me, or don't you know?" countered Lange.

The major shrugged his shoulders in a poor imitation of the corporal.

"It's a nine-millimeter Parabellum, a blowback model, which uses a thirty-two-round detachable staggered-row box magazine."

"Firing capabilities?"

"Five hundred rounds a minute, with a muzzle velocity of thirteen hundred feet per second."

"Herr Schmeisser must be proud of his invention."

"Hugo Schmeisser designed the MP181 in 1918. He had nothing to do with designing this piece. It's just a popular name."

169

"Is there anything you don't know about your weapon, Corporal?"

Lange held the gun away from his stomach and looked at it as if for the first time. With a cramped, limited smile, the smile of one who has had little practice smiling, Lange replied, "No, Major, nothing."

On von Stihl's strong recommendation, Lange received the Iron Cross First Class for his actions at the Athens airport. The major also began searching for excuses to promote Lange to sergeant, looking for the slightest traces of the desire to lead a platoon. He found none. During their occupation of Athens, when von Stihl asked him why he avoided responsibility, Lange replied absently, "I'm not a leader."

"You're better than a follower, Lange."

"I'm not a follower, either."

"Then what the hell are you?"

Lange shrugged in his inimitable way. "I don't know, Major. You'll be the first to know when I find out, though." Lange came as close to laughing as he ever did.

"Then I'll tell you," von Stihl said angrily. "You're a floater, and you'll never attach to anything. Like a goddamn French intellectual. And if you ever find any meaning in your life, it'll be fleeting, because you'll float away from it."

Lange thought for a moment, then said, "That's not really true, Major. I have a goal, and that's to be proficient at something, anything. I've tried a lot of things, and they didn't work out. So here I am in your army, and I've found it."

"The Schmeisser?"

"I can't say I'm particularly proud of the fact. It's just the way it happened. I found myself the best there is with this weapon. It's the proficiency I'm proud of. The feeling would have been the same had I been the best cobbler or the best bricklayer or the best teacher. No difference."

Several times across Greece, and later in the Western campaign, Lange had proved he was the best. The corporal developed a dependency on the Schmeisser. It was never more than an arm's length from him. He carried almost an entire second submachine gun in spare parts in his pack. And the constant cleaning. Von Stihl knew it was immaculate as it lay in the rolled oilcloth at Lange's feet.

"Little one, why'd you never try out for the SS?" Graf asked, knowing the minimum-height requirement was five feet, ten inches, and Lange was considerably shorter than that.

Lange eyed the big German and then looked past him out the boxcar door.

"Colonel, you should instruct your men on basic politeness. Here I ask a question, trying to lift the Schwachheit's spirits, him suffering from tuberculosis and all, and I don't even get an answer."

Von Stihl ignored Graf, hoping he would let the moment pass without increasing the tension.

"Answer me, Corporal," Graf demanded in his concentration-camp growl.

Graf's derisive prodding had gone far enough. Before Graf could push further, von Stihl asked, "Corporal, do you want to win that stein of beer we wagered?"

"What's that, Colonel?" Lange asked, thankful for the interruption.

"I've got a stein of beer waiting for you back in Germany if you can put your Schmeisser together in under fifteen seconds. You said you could do it once, and I called horseshit. I'm calling horseshit again."

"Colonel," Graf said forcefully, "let's finish one conversation before we get into another. I asked the corporal a question."

Von Stihl looked at Graf menacingly and said, "I'm speaking, Graf, shut up."

"Fifteen seconds?" asked Lange as he carefully unrolled his cloth.

"That's right. I'll give you the signal to start. Nod when you're ready."

Lange spread the oilcloth out and smoothed the corners. A field-stripped Schmeisser is in five parts, Lange's weapon had been broken down even further, to allow it to be rolled inconspicuously in his pack. Thirteen metal parts lay on the cloth.

Lange sat opposite Graf and the open doorway. He spread his hands out over the parts and rubbed his index fingers against his thumbs like a burglar about to crack a safe's combination.

Von Stihl waited until he was sure Graf was watching Lange.

"Go."

The corporal's hands whirred with the parts with astonishing, blinding speed. Metal snapped into metal with a woodpecker staccato. The hands were a blur. Graf's face went slack with disbelief.

Three seconds after the signal, Willi Lange bounced into a crouch and fired a half-second burst out the boxcar door. The stream of bullets tugged at Graf's sleeve, then ripped through a signpost as the boxcar rumbled past it. With an open mouth, Graf turned to see the upper half of the signpost spin away, tumble through the air, and land hard on the gravel bank.

His eyes wide and devoid of their evil glint, Graf turned to face Lange. The Schmeisser was already fully disassembled and lay in position on the cloth. White smoke drifted from the barrel. A hard smile crossed Lange's face as he stared at the giant German. SS Obersturmführer Graf knew he would never ride the corporal again.

XI

Wrenching headaches were the worst part of Paddy Flannery's new job. His foreman had told him they were caused by his inhalation of nitroglycerin fumes. Something to do with dilation of his blood vessels. The headaches would disappear in a couple of weeks. Until then, the foreman had advised, drink gallons of black coffee provided by the company. For some reason no one understood, massive doses of coffee lessened the pain.

So not only did Flannery have nitro headaches all day, he also was irritable and hyperactive from the coffee. On his long list of complaints about the job, though, headaches and caffeine were not at the top. The possibility of instant vaporization was.

Flannery was a nitro hauler at the Guy Fawkes Powder Company on Chicago's Northwest Side. Several times an hour he rolled a cart from the main plant to the nitroglycerin shed an eighth of a mile away, filled the cart with bottles of nitro, and pushed it back to the plant. If a bottle is bumped or dropped or comes in contact with a spark, it explodes with furious vengeance.

The powder company's safety measures did not assuage Flannery's fear. To reduce the chance of a spark, nitro haulers' work clothes had no metal parts. Rather than belts with brass buckles, they used strands of rope tied around their waists. The tiny metal rings on their boots had been plucked out. Boots thus prepared did

173

not last long, but the company had a closet of them free for the taking. Shirts with metal buttons were not allowed. Nor were pants with metal rivets. Nitro haulers could not wear wristwatches, rings or keychains while working. They wore white cotton tunics to prevent forgotten bits of metal from scraping against anything.

The nitroglycerin was stored in a concrete-block hut 220 yards from the plant. It was hoped this was sufficient distance to prevent damage to the plant if the hut blew. On this cool November morning, Paddy Flannery tightened the sash around his tunic, gripped the handles of the cart, and began the trek to the block house. Unlike an unstable wheelbarrow, the cart had four wheels, to prevent spills. The path to the nitro hut was made of wood planks, so no part of the cart or the hauler would contact pebbles or rusty nails that may have littered the ground. To keep the cart from veering off the track, the edges of the wood path were raised several inches.

The trip to the nitro hut was at once monotonous and terrifying. The pathway was dull, and the cart was light. The monotony left room for daydreaming. Pushing a cart was not conducive to exciting fantasies. Flannery flailed his imagination, but all it produced was a peanut vendor. He couldn't accept that, so he was forced to confront the reality of his task.

The reality was bloodcurdling. As he approached the small hut, it assumed a menacing personality, like a marine drill instructor looking for his recruit's slightest mistake. To avoid antagonizing the hut, Flannery tried to exactly duplicate the motions that had been successful on the prior trip. He found the hut accepted a three-quarter pace, not too fast and not too slow. One hundred feet from the door, he paused and gazed at the hut in homage. Before he began again, he crossed himself in the best Catholic fashion. He had been raised a Roman Catholic but had left the religion years ago. The Irishman had strong recurrences of pious zeal
174

each time he approached the nitro hut. He paused fifty feet from the hut door and crossed himself again. By this time, he was so frightened he forgot his headache. He traversed the last fifty feet on tiptoes while he intoned Hail Marys. Anyone displaying such fright on any other job would have been ridiculed by fellow workers. At the Guy Fawkes Powder Company, no one ever derided the superstitious or religious machinations performed by the nitro haulers as they approached the hut. To do so would have invited the suggestion, "Well, why don't you take the next run?"

Flannery stopped the cart in front of the hut and lifted the wood latch. The hut was not locked during the day, because having the hauler fool with a padlock and key was too risky. The door swung open, and he held his breath as he looked intently for any red vapor drifting through the door. Red vapor meant the nitro had leaked from its bottles and had become unstable. His instructions in that event were clear: get the hell away from the building as fast as possible.

There was no vapor. Flannery cautiously wheeled the cart into the hut and punched on the light switch. Rows of sinister bottles sat on heavy wood shelves. They were spaced far enough apart so the hauler would not bump into one while handling another. The only other notable feature in the hut's interior was the refrigeration coils along the walls. Nitroglycerin is much more stable when cooled. The refrigeration unit was checked twice daily, because during any transition of temperature, nitro is highly unstable. Flannery glanced at the wall thermometer, which was normal.

He was so frightened his stomach was turning over and he could feel an onslaught of diarrhea. Aware of the haulers' problem, the management had installed an outhouse to one side of the hut for those whose terror caught them in the bowels. Flannery had used it frequently.

He removed the rail from one side of his cart, then picked up a board leaning against a wall and placed it

175

across the one-foot expanse between the cart and the shelf. The board was used as a ramp. It was highly polished to prevent the bottles from catching on it as they slid along its surface.

Rarely in his life did Paddy Flannery find the mental energy to fix on one subject for any length of time, but now he concentrated with a fierce mental burn that beat back his headache. One finger went through the glass loop at the top of the bottle. The other hand went around the base of the bottle and slowly moved it across the shelf. Flannery did not breathe and his taut neck muscles pulled at his scalp. Carefully, gingerly, he pushed a bottle onto the ramp, along it, and into the cart. At no time did the bottle leave a surface. When it was in the corner of the cart bed, he repeated the motion with the second bottle. Six bottles later, he removed the ramp and reinstalled the cart's sideboard. He turned the cart around and exited the hut.

Much as a man whose automobile is nearly out of gas so he speeds to the gas station, Flannery was tempted to run with the cart. The first time he broke into a run two weeks ago, the foreman had sternly warned him that several years before, a running nitro hauler had tripped over his own feet and had toppled the cart. After the explosion, there hadn't been enough left of the hauler to scrape off the ground with a spatula. Flannery compromised by heel-and-toeing it as fast as he could down the boardwalk to the plant. As he approached the main building, his anxiety lessened and the headache swarmed back. At the gate, one of the mixers took the cart, and Flannery headed for the coffeepot.

The Guy Fawkes Powder Compnay was a dynamite-manufacturing plant, where Flannery's nitroglycerin was mixed with sodium nitrate, sulfur, and wood pulp. These ingredients stabilized the nitro so it could be hauled safely. The mixing occurred in large iron vats suspended over ponds of water, called drowning pools. If red vapor developed, the mixture was immediately dropped into the water. After mixing and drying, the powder was sealed in paraffin wrappers to be shipped to munitions manufacturers.

Flannery poured scalding coffee into his cup and sat on the bench to wait for the next nitro call. He scowled into the cup, hating everything about his new job: the headaches, the chronic fright, the coffee, the dumb secretary, and having to get up at six in the morning. Paddy Flannery was not a common laborer.

He was a gangster, and he was proud of it. It was one of the few alternatives open to a boy born in Chicago's Little Hell, a cesspool neighborhood of filth and violence officially called Kilgubbin and given its popular name from the flames of the gas-works chimneys that turned the night sky orange. Flannery's early memories were of rats, ghetto dogs, garbage cans, littered gutters, and violent asthma attacks that seized him daily. His was a cold, dirty childhood.

His life was transformed on his eleventh birthday when he was inducted into the Irish Bulls, a street gang with its hangout near the intersection of Oak and Milton streets. The Bulls dabbled in burglary, mugging, arson, and extortion, but their specialty was warfare with the "dark people," the Sicilians who had been moving into Little Hell since the turn of the century. Flannery's early teen years were spent organizing and participating in street fights between Irish and Sicilian gangs, in which often four hundred youths would engage in vicious hand-to-hand combat. Flannery became skilled with saps, chains, and homemade brass knuckles. He made his first zip gun at age thirteen and killed a Sicilian with it a week later.

By seventeen, Flannery had sufficient outlaw credentials to join the Hymie Weiss mob. Weiss was a notorious gangster embroiled in territorial warfare with Al Capone. For a year Flannery rode shotgun on Weiss's liquor trucks. One could survive as an enemy of Capone for only so long. Weiss's life ended abruptly on October 11, 1926, when he unhappily stepped in front of ten machine-gun bullets.

Paddy Flannery's young career floundered. Much as a Japanese samurai became a wanderer when his lord was killed, Flannery drifted from gang to gang. In the years that followed Hymie Weiss's death, Flannery was called on numerous times for his muscle. He was a competent strongarm man, but he lacked a vital ingredient needed to rise to the surface in a tough occupation—shrewdness. He was reliable, but he never took the initiative. He was a follower in an era when Irish gang leaders in Chicago were scarce.

To supplement his meager underworld income, he took part-time jobs, usually as a truck driver or a warehouseman. His tendency to punch-out his bosses on the slightest pretext guaranteed his work history was a transient one. In fact, Flannery had never held a job for more than two months.

Flannery sipped his coffee and leaned back on the bench praying the nitro call wouldn't come through. A rotten job. Any job was a rotten job. Particularly when he didn't know who had ordered him to take it. It was a mystery, and Flannery's mind was not adept at solving mysteries.

Three weeks ago he had reached into his apartment mailbox expecting to find the usual nothing. He didn't know that many people who knew how to write. But there was an envelope addressed to him, which had neither a stamp nor a return address. Inside was two hundred dollars in twenty-dollar bills and a brief instruction printed on note-pad paper: "STEAL A 1935 FORD TONIGHT AND LEAVE IT NEAR INTERSECTION OF WESTERN AVENUE AND THIRTIETH."

It was the easiest two hundred Flannery had ever earned. He had been tempted to keep the money without doing the work, but he thought whoever had given him the two hundred might want to start a regular business. Two hundred bucks was a lot to pay for a hot
178

car. That night it took him fifteen minutes to find a 1935 Ford. Using skills learned with the Irish Bulls, he hot-wired the car's ignition and drove the car to the intersection, where he waited two hours, hoping his new business partner would show. He gave up at midnight and took a taxi back to his apartment.

Three days later Flannery found another note in his mailbox: "PICK UP BLACK LUNCH BUCKET UNDER MAILBOX AT 2400 NORTH CLARK STREET AT 2:00 P.M. OCTOBER 29. LEAVE IT AT NORTH CORNER OF WATER-TOWER PARK AT 4:00 P.M. DO NOT OPEN BUCKET." Attached to the note were ten twenty-dollar bills.

Flannery did exactly as he was told. He was sorely tempted to open the lunch bucket, which was not locked or sealed, but anything that might irritate his benefactor, whoever that might be, was out of the question.

Flannery began to check his mailbox four times a day, and he gazed at it from his apartment window. He never saw anyone other than the mailman, who left only envelopes addressed to "Occupant."

On Monday following the lunch-bucket delivery, the third note appeared in Flannery's mailbox: "APPLY FOR JOB AT GUY FAWKES POWDER COMPANY. TAKE ANY JOB OFFERED." Five hundred dollars accompanied the note.

In 1942, when most young men were in the service, jobs for laborers were easy to find. When the powder company plant manager, Henry Harter, asked Flannery what kind of work he was willing to do, the Irishman replied, "Anything."

"Does that include being a nitro hauler?" asked Harter.

"Sure. I'm willing to do anything. I need the job."

Flannery went to work a week later. After his first trip to the nitro hut, during which the dangers of nitroglycerin were carefully explained, Flannery wished he had been more selective during the interview.

On his third working day, he found two hundred

dollars and more instructions: "BECOME ACQUAINTED WITH PLANT MANAGER'S SECRETARY. FIND OUT WHEN SHE TYPES THE EXPLOSIVES-DELIVERY SCHEDULE. LEAVE THIS INFORMATION IN MAILBOX AS SOON AS POSSIBLE."

For the first time since the mysterious notes began to appear, Flannery hesitated. Stealing a car and making a puzzling delivery were easily accommodated by his larcenous life-style. An explosives-delivery schedule, however, smacked of something truly dangerous. He wanted to protest, but to whom? His mailbox?

The hesitation lasted only a few seconds. He had made eleven hundred dollars in less than two weeks. This was the big league, which had been so elusive. This was his break. He would now be making the big bucks. Flannery decided to follow the instructions to the letter. The decision would cost him his life.

As Flannery swirled the last of the bitter coffee in his mouth, he thought of another terrible part of his job: meeting the boss's daughter. Nancy Harter was thirty-one and had worked in her father's office at the powder company for ten years. She was a true spinster—never married, always looking, never succeeding. She had grown accustomed to the role. Her life was regulated by routine. She rose at exactly the same time every morning, did exactly the same job every day, and went to bed at 10:30 every night. Weekends made her uncomfortable, because the regulation of her job was absent. Sunday evenings were the worst time of the week for Nancy. It was then she realized another week had passed and nothing had changed. It was miserable, yet it was comforting to know the following week would pass just as this one had, with no interruptions, with nothing to disrupt her schedule. She let nothing ripple her life.

Not that Nancy Harter was completely unattractive. Her hair was a rich brown and hung midway down her back. She had bright green eyes that were just begin-

ning to develop lines at the corners, which on anyone
else would have been called laugh lines. She had beautiful, even teeth, but her chin receded a bit too much.
Nancy wore clothes that were invariably three or four
years behind fashion and were what her mother called
"nice and prim."

Whatever chance Nancy's pleasant appearance gave
her was strangled by dullness. She had the spontaneity
of a wristwatch and the wit of an on-duty telephone
operator. She made even her father yawn.

She was her father's secretary and receptionist. She
took his dictation, typed his letters, drew up schedules
and purchase orders, and got his coffee. Her desk was
in the cubicle outside his office. It had a glass-and-
wood partition between it and the plant floor.

Two Thursdays ago, Nancy had been staring at the
wall clock, waiting for the minute hand to reach the
noon hour, when she was startled by a sharp rapping
on the glass pane. She turned to see one of the nitro
haulers, wearing a white coat and an awkward smile.
She assumed he was there to present a grievance,
which she would jot down and later give to her father.
When she opened the cubicle door, though, the nitro
hauler said, "Hi, I'm Paddy Flannery," and nothing
more. The Irishman had a square-jawed, handsome
face marred by a snaggle tooth. His wavy black hair
hung over his left ear to cover a V-shaped nick suffered in a knife fight years before.

She waited for him to add his complaint, and when
he did not, she said strictly, "Well?"

"I seen you working through the window here, so I
thought I'd drop by to say hello. That's all."

"Oh." She paused, not knowing how to continue.
"Well, hello."

He leaned against the door frame and tried to look
casual. "What're ya working on?"

"A letter."

"You must be pretty good at it."

She nodded.

181

"What else do ya do?" he asked.

"Whatever's in this pile." She pointed to the in-basket.

Judas Priest, Flannery thought. This is going to be harder than I planned. "Say, it's lunch hour. Why don't we go down to the lunchroom and grab a bite?"

"Oh. Well, I usually eat here. And I just bought a hard-boiled egg."

Flannery swallowed a yawn and pursued, "You need a change of scenery. Come on." He tried to smile, but the tail end of his yawn rudely twisted it out of shape.

She had eaten lunch with him that day, one of the longest hours Flannery had ever put in, and had done so three or four times in the subsequent two weeks. They had talked about the weather, her job, his job, and the weather again.

Flannery swallowed the last of the coffee and walked to the pot for a refill. Anything to lessen the headaches, even wretched coffee. He was thinking of asking the mailbox for a raise. After all, he had done precisely what it had ordered. A day after he met Nancy Harter, he had put a note in the box that said that she typed the dynamite-delivery route for the following day immediately atfer lunch each day. He grimaced as he thought of those lunch hours. She made his food taste bland. He fervently hoped that whatever the mailbox had in store for him would happen quickly. He didn't know how much more of Nancy Harter he could take. He was just about to pour the coffee when the nitro call sounded. He hung his cup on the hook and walked slowly to the cart. His stomach began to spin again.

That night after work, Paddy Flannery found the last note he would receive: "WITHOUT FAIL, TOMORROW NOON ATTACH THE ENCLOSED BLACK PAPER TO SECRETARY'S TYPEWRITER AS INDICATED IN INSTRUCTIONS. RETURN TO HER OFFICE AFTER SHE HAS TYPED

THE DELIVERY SCHEDULE AND REMOVE THE BLACK PAPER. DEPOSIT IN MAILBOX AFTER WORK."

Enclosed in the envelope was a 9½-by-3½-inch piece of what looked like very sheer carbon paper. Attached to the paper was a sheet of instructions and five hundred dollars. The Irishman retreated to his apartment to study.

The following noon, Flannery knocked on Nancy's cubicle window. With considerable mental effort last night he had determined there was no way he could attach the carbon paper to her typewriter roll without her knowing it. He had therefore devised a plan which to him sounded foolproof but which would need all the charm he could muster.

"Hi, Paddy." She smiled. His innocuous presence on an occasional lunch hour was not part of her routine. Plus, he gave her an excuse to display her teeth, which she knew to be her best part. "How's the weather outside?"

"Fine." he replied, and mentally added: For God's sake like it always is when you ask. "Say, I brought you a little gift. Not much, but you might like it."

"Oh, really, what could it be?" She blushed. In her ten years at the powder company no one had given her a gift. This was a first.

"Well, 's nothing, really." He fished in a brown paper bag and produced the black paper with a flourish.

She squinted at it for a second and said, "A piece of carbon paper? You shouldn't have. How thoughtful."

"No, no. It's much more than that." He held it closer to her so she could see it was not just carbon paper.

"It looks like carbon, Paddy."

"No, it ain't. It's typewriter-key cleaner. All you gotta do is put it around your typewriter, and it'll clean the keys as you type. Couldn't be handier."

"My keys are clean. They're always clean."

"Well, you got typing this afternoon?"

"Sure, lots of it."

"What're you gonna do right after lunch?"

"The delivery routes for the dynamite."

"That'll be enough typing to try this cleaner out. Why don't I save you the trouble and attach it."

Without waiting for a protest, he leaned over the typewriter and pressed the sticky edge of the paper onto the roll. He smoothed the edge with his fingers and then twisted the carriage knob. Just as the instructions said it would, the paper wound around the roller. Flannery pressed the adhesive on the bottom of the paper. It was almost invisible.

"Just like the salesman promised," Flannery said as he stood. "Easy to get on. You can try it out when we get back from lunch. Do just whatever you do after lunch, and you'll see your keys get cleaner as you work."

"I don't see how this stuff works," Nancy said as she bent closer to the typewriter. "I hope you didn't pay much for it."

"Hang the expense, I always say. Let's go to lunch."

Nancy commented on his jubilant mood during lunch. "It's nothing. Just the nice weather," Flannery explained. In fact, he was gloating over his success with the typewriter. Rarely had he carried off anything that required mental stealth. Here he had just duped Nancy into making his latest five hundred dollars a snap. Another person was doing his work. He had arrived in the big league.

Flannery walked her back to her cubicle after lunch and repressed the urge to stand over her while she typed. He waited inconspicuously near one of the mixing vats and watched her study a Chicago street map. Apparently she chose the truck routes at random and then typed them onto the sheet, which the escort and truck drivers would pick up the following morning. Varying the routine to the train depot was a security measure imposed by the federal government, the major purchaser of Guy Fawkes explosives. She bent over the

184

map, typed a few keys, and returned to the map. This procedure continued for a few minutes, until she twirled the roller and yanked the paper from the carriage. Flannery hurried to the cubicle and tapped on the glass.

Nancy favored him with another smile and then peered at the schedule she had just completed. Flannery came through the door, and she said, "You know, this type doesn't look any cleaner."

"Let me see." Flannery stuck out his hand.

"Oh, no." She hastily jerked the schedule to her bosom. "I can't do that. This is secret. I've got to put it right in the safe. Here, I'll type something else out on another piece of paper."

"No," he said quickly. "Don't bother. I'll take your word for it that my present ain't workin'. I'll take it back. Those bums tried to con me."

Flannery carefully peeled the black paper off the roller. He folded it and put it in his wallet. "I'll get my money back for this, you can count on that."

"Well, thanks anyway, Paddy. That was nice of you."

"No problem. I'll bring you an apple or something next time. Tomorrow lunch?"

"Wonderful."

That afternoon the nitro carting seemed less ominous than usual, because Flannery's mind was occupied with his success. His newly discovered importance, that importance that comes when one realizes a new talent, would be profitable. This money was only a beginning. He needed to let the mailbox know how competently he had managed this assignment. He could be trusted to handle something like this daily. Enough of this honest-work shit.

Midway through a trip to the nitro hut, Flannery realized that the car theft and the delivery of the lunch bucket were tests. Whoever had this kind of dough wouldn't need to have a car stolen. And they could have had a lunch bucket delivered for a lot less than two hundred dollars. These errands had been Flannery's preliminary examination. Stealing the dynamite-delivery schedule was their ultimate goal.

The Irishman thought briefly of extorting more money out of the mailbox for the schedule now that he had it in his wallet. It obviously was extremely important to someone. It would be simple. Just put a note in the box saying, "I've got the route and you can have it for another $2,000." But Paddy Flannery had spent too much time in the underworld to make the extortion mistake. Big money invariably meant ruthlessness. For the sum the mailbox had already paid Flannery, it could have had five Irishmen wrapped in chains and dumped in the Chicago River.

Flannery left work promptly at 5:00 that afternoon and took a cab to his apartment. If the cabbie wondered what a blue-shirt laborer was doing in a cab flashing a thick roll of greenbacks around, he didn't ask. The taxi stopped in front of a liquor store while Flannery bought a bottle of rye whiskey. He tipped the cabbie five dollars and waited until the cab was out of sight to approach the mailbox. He looked up and down the street, saw no one paying particular interest, took the schedule from his wallet, and dropped it into his mailbox. He gave the box an affectionate pat, and with bottle in hand climbed the stairs to his apartment. Paddy Flannery had hit the big time.

XII

St. Lazare Station loomed over the locomotive, which was belching a huge cloud of ash-gray smoke that billowed up toward the black, beamed-metal roof. Smoke and steam animated the engine and gave it an air of impatience. Hazy, cinder sky filtered through the station's ventilation ports on the ceiling. Green and blue and gray dominated the scene and suggested a coldness the train was anxious to leave.

"The Old St. Lazare Station: The Train for Normandy, 1877," Heather McMillan read aloud as she leaned over the thin strand of rope and peered at the small metal plaque on the wall next to the painting. " 'Claude Monet.' "

"I've seen another painting he did of the St. Lazare Station," said John Crown. "It was owned by the Staubs of Männendorf, Switzerland. And I think the Louvre has another. Monet painted many of his subjects a number of times."

Heather and Crown moved to the next painting. She read, *"Haystack. Winter, 1891.* 'Claude Monet.' "

"He painted seventeen or eighteen haystacks. Each was done in different light. He was obsessed with light and tried to capture the nuances of even a slight change in daylight. I've seen a number of his versions of the Cathedral at Rouen, each done at a different time of day."

"I've seen his water-lily paintings at the National Gallery in London," Heather contributed.

"He did those toward the end of his life, when his eyes were failing. They lay around his studio for years after his death. People thought their formlessness was due to his bad eyes. Their importance as a summation of his impressionistic work wasn't recognized for a long time."

"*The Morning Bath,* 'Edgar Degas, circa 1883.' "

"Degas painted racecourse and theater scenes. His favorite subjects were graceful ballerinas and ungraceful bathing women. Unlike most of the impressionists, who lived estranged from their families and penniless during their early careers, Degas's father was a well-to-do banker, who supported Degas's ambition to be an artist. So while Monet, Van Gogh, and Seurat were starving, Degas had the advantage of some income."

"Toulouse-Lautrec also had family money," Heather added.

Crown paused, looked at her with an amused squint, and said, "Say, I'm not making a fool of myself by lecturing you on the French impressionists while you know a lot more about them than I do, am I?"

"I don't mind." She grinned. "I enjoy hearing you talk. And if you make a mistake during your little lecture, I'll tactfully correct you."

"How much do you know about these artists?" Crown felt color touch his cheek.

"I studied them in Paris for a year before the war. But you're doing well. Continue." She laughed delightedly and put her hand through his arm.

Shit. He had read that in her file and had completely forgotten it. Something about her scrambled his thoughts.

"You know, you frost my butt at times," he said, shaking his head while she smiled merrily, squeezed his arm, and leaned against him as they walked into the Renoir room.

The Art Institute of Chicago was one of the many public, crowded places Crown and Heather had visited in the past several days. When not occupied with Hess, they had acted like tourists. Before the Art Institute that day they had toured the Chicago Board of Trade, where from the viewing platform they had watched insane men gesticulating wildly at one another across the tiered pits as they set the United States commodities' prices. It fascinated Crown that legally binding contracts for thousands of dollars of grain could be made with a flick of the wrist.

On previous days had been other crowded places, tourist attractions that bristled with people. Heather had suggestively complained to Crown that she was never alone with him. Crown shrugged it off, and seeing his apparent indifference, she had not mentioned it again.

Crown was far from indifferent. He was under the long gun. Someone in Chicago was looking to kill him. This was apparent, because they had tried once and failed, killing Miguel Maura, and would now be coming for him. Heather's late-night phone calls reporting his whereabouts confirmed they would try again. He was being stalked.

Revenge was not their motive. If it was, they would not have complicated their task by involving Heather. A revenge killing is the simplest. A man with a high-powered rifle waits, often for days, near the victim's home or car until he can put the mark in the cross hairs. It does not matter if the murder is public, because an experienced assassin always has an escape route, usually abetted by confusion. In addition, possible subsequent newspaper publicity of the killing does not deter the murderer, because he is long gone by the next morning's editions.

Because this was not revenge, it followed that whatever the killers' motive, Crown's death was incidental to a much more important mission. Such a mission could easily be thwarted by newspaper publicity incumbent to a public killing. The killers would try to take Crown quietly, preferably in an out-of-the-way place.

They knew that, as in all countries, an agent's death was suppressed if at all possible. If Crown went quietly, his death would not be investigated by Chicago police or the news media, because Crown's agency would quickly dispose of the body and fabricate a convincing story for his relatives.

So as long as he stayed in crowded areas, the assassin would not strike. Crown and Heather had toured the Board of Trade, the Art Institute, the Shedd Aquarium, the Field Museum of Natural History, and other teeming attractions. Heather had not asked why Crown could take time to tour Chicago with her when he was on a vital mission guarding Hess. Normally he would not have, but he was convinced that Miguel Maura's death and the imminent assassination attempt on him were connected to Hess's journey. Any other explanation was too coincidental.

Over long-distance phone to Washington two days before, Crown and Richard Sackville-West had reviewed the entire operation: Maura's death, Hess's journey to Chicago and his interrogations, and Heather's phone calls.

"That's the entire information, sir. If you can come up with anything, any possible mission or the name of whoever is behind it, you're more insightful than I am," Crown had said into the crackling telephone.

"I'd be the last to argue I was not more insightful than you, John," the Priest had chuckled. "I agree that whatever's going on has something to do with Hess. Any other explanation doesn't make sense. So we have to assume the worst—that their goal is to kill Hess. Somehow they found out he was here, and are now trying to get rid of him."

"You keep saying 'someone' when referring to the killers. Can't we conclude it's the Germans? They know how valuable Hess's information is. They must also suspect the reason Hess was brought to the U.S. was because he was talking, revealing their nuclear-experiment secrets."

"I agree," said the Priest from a thousand miles away. "So the Germans are trying to kill him. Needless to say, we absolutely cannot let this happen. He must be kept alive."

Crown asked, "Why are they after me, rather than Hess?"

"Although they know where Hess is, because Heather has obviously told them, they can't get to him. He's too well guarded. You and Peter Kohler have seen to that. So they'll try for you, hoping somehow to get to Hess through you."

"How?"

"I've no idea. But we assume they want Hess dead, and we know they want you dead. There has to be a connection. Unless they can find a way to get to Hess, they'll keep trying for you. Maybe they only want to kidnap you and force you to breach the EDC house security. Who knows? But they must feel time is running out on them. They're desperate. So they'll try anything."

"Let me see if I can read you," Crown said. "We obviously can't sit here and wait for them to strike."

"Correct."

"So we need to take the offensive."

"Right, again."

"We don't have any leads other than we think they'll try again. So we let them try again. Which means I have to make myself a target."

"You've done it successfully in Europe, and I trust you can do it in Chicago. All you need do is walk around and expose yourself. Nothing could be easier." The Priest laughed softly.

He knew as well as Crown the terrible ordeal of being a target. Anyone could be the killer—the postman, the lady shopper, the cabbie. He could be hiding behind any tree, post, building, or door. He could be watching the target from any rooftop, any car, anywhere. He could strike at any time—while the target was sleeping, eating, or urinating. Nothing, no one

191

was safe. The constant fear of the attack shortly jellied the target's nerves.

A target could not let the hunter know he was aware of the plan. Not being able to look over the shoulder every few seconds was agonizing. The target had to trust other senses to guard his rear, none of which were as acute as eyesight. Nevertheless, the target's eyes never rested. Without unduly moving his head, he let his eyes fly back and forth, searching for signs of the strike. For two weeks after his last experience as a target, Crown's eyes had twitched uncontrollably, unable to rest even after their torturous duty had ended.

Acute paranoia infected a target. It raised hackles on the neck, turned the stomach over, and made hands tremble, so that writing with a pen was almost impossible. Nights were endless, sleepless vigils. Soon a numbing ache overcame the target and dulled his senses, an ache from sleeplessness and effort. At these times the target was even more vulnerable, more prone to make a fatal mistake.

"How many days should I make them wait before setting them up?" Crown asked.

"Use your discretion. I suggest three or four days. Make them worry that you'll never expose yourself. You'll be able to predict when they'll strike, that way. If you give them only one chance to hit you, that's the one they'll take. Be careful though. You know as well as I do that this ploy requires them to have no hint you're on to them."

"What about my duties with Hess?"

"Keep at them. You're always surrounded by bodyguards and are safest when you're with him. Spend your spare time with Heather and in crowds so the assassins will think they know your every move. She'll keep feeding them information about you until they're sure that if you ever are alone and open to be killed, they'll be aware of it because she'll tell them in advance. That way, they probably won't even follow you. They'll just rely on her reports."

Crown paused several seconds, searching for words that would not be revealing. Finally he asked, "Have you come up with any reason she's in with them?"

"As best we can tell, she's never had any contact with the Nazis, so they couldn't have indoctrinated her. That leaves only one motive for her—money. They must be paying her a tidy sum."

The words had stung Crown. Not that he hadn't suspected money was her motive. He had sifted through all possible reasons why she was informing on him. Each time, he concluded she was on the German payroll, and each time, it hurt more.

At first he had been insulted. She was playing him for a fool. For the past three nights she had used the pay phone outside her hotel after she thought he had driven away. Each night, she gave succinct instructions on their plans for the next day and promised to let them know any changes in plans. She was obviously a rookie at her double life. Had she been in the business for any length of time, she would have known Crown would trust no one completely and would covertly watch her. Neither she nor her bosses respected his professional talent.

Crown's injured-pride explanation went only so far. He was too honest with himself not to admit the real and hurting reason he despaired over her duplicity. Quite simply, he was falling for Heather.

He was thirty-three years old and had never loved a woman. His affairs had been casual and brief, never long enough for emotional commitment to grow from physical desire. Women had drifted in and out of his life without affecting it. Crown entered relationships expecting at most an uneasy friendship, made uncomfortable by expectations he knew he would never fulfill. At the first sign of attachment, he withdrew, for reasons he could not understand. Perhaps he feared the responsibility of a relationship. Or he was afraid of any emotional change. He had been accused by women he was leaving of being a coward, of being juvenile, of

193

being cold. Maybe. Maybe not. He hadn't taken the time to think about it.

Heather was different. She touched him like no one before. For the first time in his life, Crown looked forward with heady anticipation to being with a woman. He was anxious when he was not with her, and wanted nothing else when they were together. Crown was falling in love.

As if Crown had been thinking aloud, Sackville-West said from Washington, D.C., "John, you'd better listen closely. I've said before that nothing can get in the way of your business in Chicago. I mean it. Nothing. That includes a pretty English girl. You've got to remember what she's doing. She's working for the Nazis. She's a traitor. And she'll pay for it. We don't have trials in our line of work, John. You know that. She's living her last days."

"I know that, sir."

"What you're seeing is what she wants you to see, what the Nazis want you to see. They're hoping you'll become attached to her. Don't get tricked. Do your job and keep your emotions out of this. Understand?"

"Yes, sir."

"Well, whether you do or not, I know you'll do your task as if you did. Remember what I said, though, when her time comes."

Crown and Heather leisurely toured the Cézanne, Gauguin, Van Gogh, Seurat, and Toulouse-Lautrec displays. She showed an amazing range of knowledge about the French impressionists. Crown tried to concentrate on what she said, but found he was keying on her lilting British voice. They hurriedly visited the rooms with paintings from the fifteenth and sixteenth centuries and paused only briefly at the Dutch and Flemish art from the seventeenth century. They overloaded on the paintings and began passing many without even a glance.

On the steps of the Art Institute they admired the

immense bronze lions guarding the entrance to the art treasures. Heather petted a lion's metal paw and sat on its concrete platform next to Crown. She leaned casually against the lion's leg and played with the back of Crown's hand until he turned it over so she could slip her hand into his. He did not look at her, so she leaned forward and peered up at him with her radiant smile. He looked away and would not play the game. She squeezed his hand and asked, "What's wrong, John?"

For a few seconds he continued to stare down Michigan Avenue. Finally he turned to her. Her auburn hair was brushed by the November wind, and her cheeks were flushed from the cold. She was wearing a tailored beige jacket over a white blouse and slim tapered pants the color of river sand, a lovely contrast to the dull, hard green and gold of the lion. A rush of emotion swelled up from his stomach and caught him in the throat. He opened his mouth to tell her how he felt, but swallowed it.

"No, nothing," he said as he forced a smile. "I have an ability to look reflective when I'm not thinking of anything."

Heather did not believe him, but changed the subject. "How do you think Hess's interviews are going?"

"I'm glad he got over his amnesia quickly. Fermi is really impatient to find out what Hess knows. Apparently he has a mass of data about the German experiments."

Crown rubbed his hands together to ward off the chilling fog rolling into the Loop from Lake Michigan. The fog bank rushed across Michigan Avenue and up Adams Street.

"What about the amnesia and the stomach cramps and all that? Is he faking?" Heather asked, scooting closer to Crown as the temperature plunged and more fog poured from the lake.

"The doctors don't think so. They say his symptoms
195

are not unusual for a neurotic-schizoid under such pressure."

"What do you think?" asked Heather in a tone implying that Crown's thoughts would be decisive.

"During both interviews, Tuesday's and this morning's, I was struck by Hess's ability to pace the flow of information. Fermi questioned him for two hours today, and he got some useful data, but nowhere near anything Fermi thinks Hess knows. Hess may have mental problems, but he controls those interviews. Kohler frightens him, but when Hess is in the interview, Kohler isn't very effective, because Hess knows we want the information and will put up with him. Kohler can go only so far in that situation."

"I think Hess is just enjoying the attention," Heather said. "He likes being the center of things, so he prolongs the interviews, because when they're over, he'll go back to his cell."

"Maybe so. He's got a big ego. No question about that. Fermi will continue to question him until Hess has revealed all he knows. Then Hess goes back to his London hospital cell. But I think he's up to something other than just being the center of things."

Heather looked quickly at him and asked, "What do you mean?"

"Well," Crown said as he turned to watch the fog, "it's just a hunch. Hess is too controlled. He dribbles out just enough information to keep us interested. When Fermi gets into the heart of the questions about the German experiments, Hess's mind goes blank or he has pains in his abdomen. Like Kohler says, it's too convenient."

"What're you going to do about it?" she asked, and Crown thought he detected an apprehensive edge in her voice.

"I don't know yet. Something will come to me, though."

It was bait. Heather would surely report his suspicions to whomever she was calling. They would be
196

prompted to act quickly, perhaps rashly. Their inability to find Crown in a nonpublic place would make them even more nervous. They would try to kill him at their first opportunity. Crown would give them that chance when he was ready. He would know when they were coming.

Over rack-of-lamb dinner at the Berghoff, conversation again turned to the deputy führer.

"He just doesn't come across as a cutthroat, like the Nazis are always depicted," Heather said while she cut tender lamb away from the bones.

"You don't know enough about him, then." Crown swallowed and asked, "Have you heard of Hess's part in the Night of the Long Knives?"

She shook her head.

"During Hitler's rise to power, he had an army of thugs and criminals called the SA, the Sturmabteilung. They started out as bouncers who beat up hecklers when Hitler spoke in beer halls or on soap boxes in town squares. The SA was headed by Ernst Roehm, a homosexual, a drunkard, and a sadist, who soon turned the SA into his private army of three million men. It grew larger than the German Army, Navy, and Air Force combined.

"Hitler used the SA to solidify his own position in Germany. Soon, though, Ernst Roehm began to flex his SA muscle. Hitler felt that he, Hitler, was losing control of the SA and that Roehm was using it to wrest the Nazi party leadership from him. It's apparent that Himmler, Hess, and others were jealous of Roehm's strength, and they fed Hitler rumors of Roehm's ambitions."

"Were the rumors true?"

"Some, maybe. Most were not. Anyway, Hitler decided to get rid of Roehm."

Crown paused to savor the lamb. Heather asked, "Well, what happened?"

"Hess and the others convinced Hitler that just getting rid of Roehm wouldn't be enough. He needed to liquidate all the SA leaders suspected of allegiance to Roehm. So Hess, Himmler, Goebbels, and Göring drew up lists of those they wished killed. If they could show that the victims had some connection with the SA, fine, but it wasn't necessary. They included on the lists those with whom they had personal grievances. Anyone unfortunate enough to have made an enemy of these men during the early years of the Nazi party was in this way condemned to die. On June 30, 1934, Ernst Roehm and hundreds of others were murdered. So Hess is just like the rest—plotting, scheming, murdering. Don't single him out for undeserved sympathy."

Crown chewed on the lamb, indicating the grisly story was over, but Heather demanded more details. "How did Roehm die?"

Crown looked at her and wondered whether he should complete the history lesson. Why not? She might as well know the mentality of her bosses.

"Even the official German story is seamy. Goebbels' press said Hitler almost single-handedly stormed the hotel in Wiessee where Roehm and several other SA officials were staying. Hitler marched to Roehm's room, stood outside the door, and yelled, 'News from Berlin, Herr Roehm'. When Roehm shouted, 'Come in,' Hitler burst into the room, where he found Roehm in bed with a young boy. Hitler screamed at Roehm about the SA chief's treacherous acts and then had him arrested and sent to Stadelheim prison. Several days later, Roehm was given a pistol with one shell in it and told to do the honorable thing. He refused. Ten minutes later someone opened his cell door and shot him several times. Rudolf Hess has bragged he was Roehm's killer."

Heather involuntarily cringed at Hess's name. She asked in a low, tight voice, "And the others?"

"No one knows how many were killed. The SS used the supposed Roehm plot to get rid of their enemies all through Germany. It was the first mass murder under

Hitler's command, and it was the night Hitler became the absolute dictator of Germany. He did it with the help of Rudolf Hess."

It was the low point of their afternoon. Telling her of Hess's infamy was not part of his grand design to flush out Miguel Maura's murderers. It was a foolish attempt to shake her loose from her employers, to put a chink in her loyalty, to make her think about what she was doing, as if he was in eighth grade telling a favorite girl nasty rumors about the boy she had a crush on. It didn't work then. It wouldn't work now. It was juvenile, but as Sackville-West had said, her time would come. She would soon leave his life, leave it violently and permanently. Crown was desperate. He wanted to be her first priority.

It was a confused, fumbling tactic, and he gave it up. Heather had committed herself to the perfidy and was probably being well paid for it. Matters of the heart rarely surfaced through sizable doses of money. Those who believed otherwise weren't familiar with a hard profession.

After dinner they walked through the lobbies of several hotels along Michigan Avenue. It was an enjoyable pastime Crown had picked up years before. He viewed lobbies of the prestigious hotels just as he viewed French impressionism—artwork that should be appreciated and preserved. It always pained him when the massive chandeliers came down to make way for more modern lighting or when the circular leather couches were replaced with sofas and easy chairs. There should be a museum of the great hotel lobbies.

They descended to the Illinois Central Randolf Street station and boarded the train for Hyde Park. As Crown knew it would be, the station and train were crowded with commuters en route to South Shore, Blue Ridge, and Rocky Island. Crown and Heather sat on the car's uncomfortable wicker seats as the heating vents along the floor pumped suffocating amounts of hot air into the packed car. His eyes watched commuters' hands.

An interminable age later, the conductor called the Fifty-ninth Street station, and they exited the car. Crown gulped the cool air as if he had been holding his breath since Randolf Street. He opened his coat wide and felt the wind chill his damp armpits. From the station ramp they saw the long row of cars winding their way through the midway. The headlights were suffused by smog and fog and were smeared together like a string of Christmas-tree bulbs seen through a frosted window. At the far end of the midway the headlights disappeared in the mist like an apparition.

They descended the ramp's steep steps to Fifty-ninth Street and walked south across the midway to Heather's hotel. Crown walked quickly to keep abreast of the five or six people walking his way. They were his shield to the hotel.

Crown paused at the hotel door, as he had on previous evenings. They put their arms loosely around each other and began the little ritual that marked the end of a day together.

"It was fun today, Heather. I'm not looking forward to you going back to London."

"I'm not either." She lightly nuzzled his neck.

Crown glanced quickly through the hotel doors to the lobby phone booth, where in a few minutes he would again confirm Heather's duplicity. That goddamn phone booth. With a suddenly tired voice he said, "Well, we've got another interview with Hess tomorrow. I'll see you then."

Once again it was a maladroit, blundering good-bye produced by the intermingling of his desire for her with his fear and disheartenment over what she was doing to him.

She clung to him longer than before, and he thought he felt her tremble slightly as she pressed into him. One of the pensioners that lived in the hotel, a gray-haired old lady with a dilapidated mink stole wrapped twice around her throat, passed them on the steps and clucked appreciatively.

Heather released his neck and looked up at him for a long moment, until Crown dumbly asked, "What?"

"John," she whispered with a voice he had never heard before, "I don't want you to go tonight."

"What?" He had heard her. He needed time to think. Was he being set up? Were gunmen waiting in her room?

"I want to be with you tonight," she said softly as she gently pulled him into the hotel lobby toward the elevator.

Crown's mind raced. He was being seduced or murdered, and he didn't know which. With his hand concealed by his overcoat, he pulled the Smith and Wesson from his waistband, pulled back the hammer, and aimed it at Heather's side. She was unaware of it as she told the elevator operator her floor. It was an old rule in Crown's profession, a rule clearly understood and honored by all countries' agents. The one who leads you into an ambush is the first to die. It makes the bait think twice before volunteering for the task. Crown's feelings for Heather caught up with his training as the elevator climbed. He lowered the gun, but only slightly. He would make the decision when forced to do so.

The elevator bounced to a halt on the fourth floor, and as the operator pulled the accordion door back, she looked at him and in a low, reassuring voice, "My room's this way, John."

Crown waited until the elevator had disappeared, and then raised his pistol behind her. She clung to him as they approached her door, and didn't notice Crown's darting eyes or his halting breath. Heather disengaged herself from him in front of room 412 and fumbled in her purse for the key. She had stopped smiling, and her hands were shaking. The key scratched against the lock for several seconds before she calmed herself sufficiently to insert it.

She swung the door open, and as she turned to him, Crown put his arm around her back, once again concealing the weapon. She wrapped both arms around his neck and said, "John, help me. I'm not very good at this."

He increased tension on the trigger and said, "Sure, honey. You go in first, and I'll be right behind you."

She looked at him sharply. "That isn't what I meant. I'm nervous. I've just made a brazen, forward fool of myself, and you're not helping." She kissed his neck and ran her hand along the flat of his stomach.

"I'm nervous, too, Heather. More than you know. You just go on into your room."

She stepped back quickly, confused by his refusal to take charge of their awkward moment. Her wide eyes reflected her bewilderment, but before she could say more, Crown smiled as best he could and with his free hand turned her shoulders and prodded her into the hotel room. He positioned the gun alongside her head and bent into a crouch as she walked ahead of him. A stupid move. She was probably nothing more than bait. The murderers would shoot through her into him. But maybe her going first would make them pause for two seconds. That's all Crown wanted, two seconds.

They entered the dark room. Crown flicked the light switch and tensed. A bed, a chair, a nightstand and lamp, and her open suitcase on the floor. Nothing more. Crown thrust the revolver under his coat and crossed quickly to the bathroom. Nothing. He jerked open the closet door. A few hanging dresses, and nothing else. He exhaled for the first time since the elevator, and felt the adrenaline pump quickly fade.

Heather stood near the bed with her mouth open slightly. Crown felt brainless.

"Are you always this jittery when entering a lady's room?" she asked, her voice devoid of the mocking tone it deserved. "I thought I was the jumpy one."

"I'm sorry, Heather. I do that all the time. I guess

I've been in the business too long." He didn't think she had seen the gun, now back in his waistband.

She looked at him with her luminous green eyes, and the full meaning of the moment revealed itself to Crown. There was no danger tonight. She hadn't been setting him up for his death, at least this time. He was alone with her in her room because she wanted him like he wanted her. Now was the time to reach for her and hold her, but he was giddy and unsure of himself.

"John," she said with a seductive half-smile, "you're as clumsy as I am."

He could not respond, so he nervously cracked his elbow several times. His throat was dry and tight, and he could feel his temples pounding. He had the sensation of being outside his body watching this romantic melodrama. He was both a player and a spectator.

She crossed the room with the walk of a woman completely in control of her sensuality. Her arms circled his waist inside his coat and lifted the shirttail. Her arm brushed the Smith and Wesson but ignored it as she rubbed the skin of his back.

Crown felt like he was leaning over the observatory railing of a tall building, deathly afraid of the height, yet pulled by the lure of a beautiful, descending, silent death. Heather was leading him to his death, yet he was powerless to resist, powerless to protest.

They kissed fiercely and he pulled her tightly against him and heard her sharp inhalation. Her hands moved to his shirt buttons, and she said, "You know, there's historical precedent for this."

"Judas," Crown breathed.

"Sure," she whispered as she pulled at the belt. "All you Yankees have come to England to entertain defenseless British women whose boyfriends are away at war. So I've come to America to reciprocate. Fair's fair."

He didn't laugh. No more kidding. No danger. Only her. There was a rush of confused hands and burning desire. No time for exploration or communication. They grapsed each other convulsively and made love violently and quickly, taking more than they gave. And after they shuddered to completion, they talked about a future together, and Crown knew there could be no future for them.

The second time was gentle and sweet, looking into the other's eyes all the while, communing with their bodies, reveling in their discoveries, loving each other. Crown's last thought before he drifted into sleep was whether she had been paid to do this, too.

XIII

Paddy Flannery was hung over before he was awake. An angry throb pulsed his temples and reached through layers of sleep to drag the Irishman to consciousness. He resisted, trying to sink back to anesthetized slumber. Through the film of half-sleep, Flannery knew this was not his current nemesis, the nitroglycerin headache. This was an old archenemy, the rye-whiskey hangover. It thundered Flannery into piercing wakefulness.

He creaked his eyes open. Even this simple movement echoed with pain. He stared at his room's ceiling and blinked several times to draw his eyes together. His nose was plugged. His mouth was plaster-dry. He dry-swallowed and worked his mouth in a futile attempt to generate saliva. His tongue was thick and uncooperative. Undulating pain worked in his eyeballs and ears and brain. There was no difference, he hazily decided, between a cheap-whiskey hangover and this expensive-whiskey hangover.

Not one of Flannery's limbs had moved since he had wrestled his shirt off, stumbled out of his shoes, and drunkenly fallen into his bed a few hours before. As he lay staring at the ceiling, he tried to recall where he had drunk his whiskey. Remembering was too painful, so he gave it up. He slowly flexed his left hand and moved it up the side of his pants to feel for his wallet. The familiar lump was there. He had not been rolled. Thank God. All his mailbox money was in his wallet.

Flannery rested his hand on his forehead, wondering whether he was sufficiently thirsty to brave the misery of moving to the sink for water. The foul yellow-brown taste in his mouth had about decided the issue when Flannery heard a sharp metal click from the other side of his room. His eyes twitched wide. It was not his radiator, which had a bass bang when filling with steam. Nor was it the draperies' pull string as it tapped against the window, bounced by the ever-present draft. This was a distinctly foreign sound. Flannery's face tightened with fright. Oblivious of the headache, he swiveled his head to the sound.

Willi Lange sat on the bedside chair with his submachine gun resting on his lap pointed at the Irishman's head. The small gunman was relaxed, and his face was devoid of expression, but his brown eyes surveyed Flannery with professional precision, searching for dangerous movement.

"Jesus," Flannery croaked with terror, "don't shoot."

He slowly rose to a sitting position on his bed, his eyes never leaving the little man's weapon. Lange did not move.

"Get up."

Flannery twisted to the terse command from the foot of his bed. Erich von Stihl stood with his hands crossed, dressed in his hobo's guise. Flannery saw the corded muscles of von Stihl's neck and his tight, curly hair and immediately knew he was not a hobo. Next to von Stihl loomed Hans Graf, a huge, dangerous-looking man a head taller than the speaker.

"Don't shoot," Flannery repeated, his voice quivering.

No one moved in the room. Seconds passed, and he was still alive. Encouraged that they weren't going to kill him outright, he added, "What do you want?"

"We want you to get up and get ready to leave. Now." Von Stihl's voice was level and in complete command.

"You guys can't come in here and boss me around, for Christ sake. I got——"

Hans Graf's arm pumped and thrust his SS dagger into the arch of Paddy Flannery's right foot. With a crunching tear, the blade sank to the hilt, and the bloody tip instantaneously popped through the top of the foot in full view of the incredulous Irishman.

In the second before his brain registered the pain, Paddy Flannery opened his mouth to scream. Graf leaned forward and stuck the stubby end of a Schmeisser almost inside the Irishman's mouth. The big hobo slowly shook his head, and Flannery knew a scream would be the end.

Graf whispered in a voice so menacing Flannery almost forgot the agony in his foot, "Next time I'll stick your throat."

Graf yanked the blade out, and Flannery spasmed with hot pain. Tears of anguish flowed down the Irishman's face as he held his violated foot. It bled over his hands onto the bed sheets. He curled his tongue to the back of his mouth to squelch a sob.

"Once again, get up and get ready to go," said von Stihl. "You have time to wrap your foot if you hurry."

Breathing laboriously through teeth clenched with pain, Flannery stripped the top sheet from the bed. Blood soaked through the sheet as he bunched it around the injury. With one hand on the sheet to keep it on the wound, he hopped painfully to the bathroom. Willi Lange followed and stood near the bathroom door as Flannery tore the sheet into fragments and used them as bandages. With the mustachioed hobo peering in at him, the Irishman knotted the strips and gingerly placed his injured foot on the bathroom tile. He winced as his foot squished and shot pain up his leg. He gripped the sink to straighten himself for a second step. His entire leg from the knee down seemed on fire as he stepped through the bathroom door. With each step, Graf's blade seemed to pierce Flannery's arch again. The gangster collapsed in the chair vacated by Lange. The first white tinges of shock flushed through Flannery's head. He breathed hard to shake it off. Failure to respond for any reason could be fatal.

"Nice work with the dynamite schedule, Flannery," said von Stihl as he sat on the mussed bed, avoiding the pool of blood. He took the black paper from his shirt pocket and tore a small end of it. He delicately peeled the paper, which Flannery saw was actually two gauze-thin pieces lightly glued together. When the sheets were separated, von Stihl discarded the carbon and with satisfaction held the white sheet in the window's early-morning light. Neatly printed on the sheet was a copy of the dynamite-delivery schedule Nancy Harter had typed the day before.

"Do you know where Addison Avenue is, Flannery? Addison Avenue at the intersection of Ridgeland?"

The Irishman nodded mutely.

"How long will it take us to get there in a car?"

Flannery flinched with sudden knowledge. He had suspected his theft of the dynamite route was for a hijacking. Now he was certain that these men, these three men dressed as hobos but who talked and acted like no rail travelers Flannery had ever come across, were the hijackers. The pleasant and distant relationship with the mailbox had ended.

"How long, Flannery?"

"Uh, ten, fifteen minutes. No more."

"Do you have a car?"

"No."

"Can you steal another one for us?"

Still clutching his injured foot, Flannery replied, "Sure, easy." Maybe that's all they want today, a car. Flannery's hopes brightened at the thought of another quick two hunderd dollars.

"Put your clothes on and let's go."

Flannery found that if he walked on his tiptoes, the gash through his foot hurt less. He struggled into a white shirt, which smelled of smoke and whiskey from the night before. He grabbed two socks from under the
208

chair and shook dust from them. He carefully pulled one over the bandage. As he cautiously tried on his shoe over the wrap, he asked, "You guys interested in a particular make of car?"

"No," von Stihl answered, "just one that'll get us to the intersection."

"You know," Flannery ventured as he reached for the coat he had dropped on the floor the night before, "I ain't honkin' my own horn or nothing, but I'm a pretty fair car booster."

"So we understand," von Stihl said with a slight smile.

A compliment from one who has ultimate control over another's life is intoxicating with its implied promise of lifesaving indispensability. Flannery swelled with hope and continued, "Well, if you guys need more cars or know any people that do, I'm your man."

"We'll see," said von Stihl easily, "but right now we've more important work to do. You're an old gangland hand, aren't you?"

"I . . . I don't know what you mean."

Of course he was, but it was not a topic of open conversation with outsiders. This was his standard answer to police questions.

Von Stihl asked again, "What I mean is, Flannery, is that you've had a little experience as a gangster, haven't you?"

Who are these guys? Flannery asked himself. They can't be cops. Not even Chicago cops lance a foot with a knife. And they can't be gangsters from any of the Chicago gangs. High-living gangsters would rather be shot than wear clothes as dilapidated as those worn by the three men. Years before, Flannery had sworn on penalty of his life never to talk with outsiders about his underworld activities. If he talked, he could die. If he did not, what would these men do? Hans Graf purposely raised his knife into view and settled the question for Flannery.

"Sure, you might say that. I do a few jobs here and there."

"During Prohibition?" von Stihl asked quietly.

"Yeah, I did some work then. Why?"

"Well, then, you must be an experienced hand hijacking liquor trucks."

How was he prejudicing himself? He was being trapped, and he couldn't see the snare.

"Uh, yeah, maybe. Why?"

"We're looking for a man with a little experience in this sort of thing."

"To help you get that dynamite shipment?"

Von Stihl nodded.

"You know"—Flannery began his protest by raising his hands palms up in supplication—"there's a big diff between knockin' off another gang's bootleg and hittin' a government dynamite truck. Jesus, I wouldn't know where to begin."

"We do. All you need to do is what we tell you. Your part of the script is already written."

Flannery shook his head fiercely. "You may have scoped me out wrong. I talk big, you know, but I'm really a small-timer. Nickel-and-dime stuff."

Von Stihl took an envelope from his back pocket and lobbed it across the room. The Irishman caught it, instantly knowing it was cash.

"Two thousand dollars for an hour of your time. Plus my guarantee the plan is foolproof. There's no way you can be caught."

Flannery lifted the envelope's flap and flipped through the twenty-dollar bills. It was more money than he had ever seen before.

"And if you play along this time," von Stihl promised, "we'll use you in the future whenever we need a car. At two or three hundred dollars a car, you're set up for life. You can quit your job at the powder company tomorrow and never lift another box or drive another truck as long as you live."

God, it sounded good. It was Flannery's dream—

210

easy money for easy crime. He had been born for this. The sharp pain from his foot prompted him to ask, "I don't suppose I have much of a choice anyway, do I?"

He looked at the giant who had punctured his foot. Graf smiled chillingly and tapped the dagger's blade against his palm. *That son of a bitch would just as soon me say no, so he can cut my throat,* thought Flannery.

Without waiting for further answer, the Irishman volunteered, "No, I didn't think so."

He glanced briefly into the filthy mirror above his chest of drawers and ran his fingers through his oily black hair a few times. His ability with automobile windows and ignitions put him in temporary charge of these three men. He milked the moment for all it was worth by slowly buttoning his overcoat and needlessly checking his wallet. He took the cash-filled envelope into the bathroom, lifted the lid off the toilet's water closet, and inserted the envelope into a clip he had jerry-rigged on the front of the water closet above the waterline. Then from the closet he produced a coat hanger and with practiced hands unwound, straightened, and bent a small snag into one end of the wire. With a stage flourish he shoved the coat hanger up his coat sleeve.

"The tool of the trade," he said proudly.

Ten minutes later, as the four men strolled down North Avenue on Chicago's Northeast Side, Flannery asked von Stihl, "You ever heisted a car before?"

"I can't say that I have."

"Well, there's a lot more to it than first meets the eye. I been doin' it for years. You can't beat experience."

"I wouldn't think so," von Stihl said, wanting to subtly prod the mick into hurrying. The dynamite truck was scheduled to leave the powder company in thirty minutes.

"You gotta find a car that can be boosted without

211

gettin' anyone's attention. More than once, one of my pals has been tinkerin' with the wiring of a car, only to have his head smashed by a cop who'd been watchin' him all the while. You got to find a car nobody's watchin'. That's harder'n it sounds, too."

Apparently it was, because they walked for ten more minutes without finding an automobile Flannery felt safe heisting. He noticed von Stihl was getting edgy, so he said, "Of course, there's another way. We steal a car no one thinks we'd have the balls to take."

"The what?" asked von Stihl.

"The balls, The guts."

The colonel nodded his understanding of the colloquialism and added, "Hurry, Flannery."

The Irishman stopped on the sidewalk near a three-story office building. He said, "You guys like Cadillacs?"

"Anything."

"You stay here. Too many people hangin' around that car would look funny. Besides, you guys look too much like bums to have anything ta do with a Caddy."

Flannery glanced casually both ways and walked purposefully toward the long black Cadillac parked against the building. The building had no windows facing the parking lot. A cinch.

A wood plaque with "Mr. Anderson" painted on it hung on the building near the Cadillac's grille. He won't miss it, Flannery reasoned. Anyone who can afford one Caddy can afford another.

He reached for the door handle. Locked. For the benefit of any onlookers, he tapped his pants and overcoat pockets searching for a key. He found none and mouthed the word "Shit!" as he exasperatedly looked around for help. Von Stihl admired Flannery's interpretation of a man in a hurry who has lost his key.

Flannery bent to the ground and seemed to find a long piece of wire. With deft movements, he shoved the looped end of the coat hanger under the rubber weather stripping at the top of the driver-side window.

When the loop caught the lock button, he jerked the wire up, and then, with the air of a longtime Cadillac owner, he opened the door of his new car.

He lay on the front seat so he could not be seen by passersby. Thirty seconds later the ignition was hot-wired. He sat up, pulled the choke button, and pressed the starter pedal. The Cadillac's smooth engine turned over. He carefully backed the car out of its owner's reserved spot. Flannery loved big Cads. Their flair was not matched by any other American car. It suited his style. He pulled alongside his three partners and leaned across the seat to unlock the doors.

As he climbed into the front seat of the car, von Stihl favored Flannery with a smile. "Well done, Irish."

Flannery painfully pressed on the accelerator. "Say," he said, trying to sound offhand, "you boys ain't Irish, are ya? I woulda seen ya around if ya were."

Von Stihl shook his head as he peered at the small houses they were passing.

"And you sure ain't Sicilian, not with your and the big guy's hair color." He inflected "big guy's" with as much friendliness he could muster. "What are you, then?"

"We're German."

"No shit?" Flannery asked as he negotiated a corner onto Ridgeland Street. "I know some damn good Germans. The Brauns. You ever heard of the Brauns? They live over on Kedzie Avenue."

"No. Never met them."

"Well, their grandparents came over on the boat forty or fifty years ago and settled in Chicago. A damn good bunch of krauts, too. No offense, o' course."

"No, of course."

"In fact, a couple o' Brauns are over fighting Hitler this very minute. Germans fighting Germans. Only in America," Flannery said as he checked a street sign. "When did you guys' families come over from the old country?"

"They didn't."

213

"Oh, yeah? You musta just come over."

"Yes."

"When?'

"A U-boat dropped us off the coast of Maine a week and a half ago."

"Oh, Jesus." Flannery gasped and would have taken his foot off the accelerator had not Hans Graf's knife pricked the back of his neck.

Ridgeland Street reflected a thousand other residential streets in Chicago that crisp Friday morning. It was a milky day, with yesterday's Thanksgiving smog still patrolling the neighborhood. The houses were simple wood and brick affairs meticulously cared for. A few had driveways and garages, the new status symbols of Chicago's working class. Most driveways were empty, the cars having transported their owners to work an hour before. Two or three prewar Buicks and Fords were parked against the curb. There was no moving traffic.

Black coal smoke poured from the chimneys and mixed with the elms before being lost to the sky. Leaves rustled in the November wind and sprinkled lawns and sidewalks. The small lawns had softened their summer green in anticipation of a hard winter. Chicago's November was a transition month, a transition from harsh autumn to harsher winter.

Small picket fences or carefully manicured hedges divided the properties. A few yards were bordered by hurricane fencing to keep in wandering dogs. A patched inner tube hung by a rope from a tree branch in a yard at the end of the block. Grass under the tube had been scraped away by little feet.

It was garbage day. In front of every house, one or two drab green thirty-gallon cans stood on the parking strip. A few lids balanced precariously on the garbage, their owners unable to stomp the pile down farther and unwilling to pay the twenty-five cents extra for pickup of a third can. Next to one of the cans was a bright red

214

wagon, which the garbage man would not mistake for garbage.

In the middle of the block an old lady wrapped in a knitted shawl opened her screen door and knelt for the milk bottle. A cat leaped out the door at her hanging shawl but hastily retreated into the house when it saw her lift the container. It always got the first milk of a new bottle. A dog across the street barked at his life-long enemy.

A mailman hurried along his route. Years of experience had taught him which hedges he could jump, which dogs he could pat, and which elderly needed a few seconds of his conversation each day. The morning was brisk, and he kept his hands in his coat pockets when he was not digging into his bag and sorting letters. The Christmas rush had started. His bag was twice as heavy as it normally was. Two times a year were hard on the mailman—Christmas and the week the goddamn Sears Roebuck catalogs came out.

Two small children skipped along the sidewalk toward their grade school. Each girl swung a Mickey Mouse lunch bucket. They kicked the crackling leaves as they danced to class.

It was a scene repeated throughout Chicago that morning. With several foreboding exceptions. Parked in a driveway midway up the block was an elegantly conspicuous Cadillac. In a Ford neighborhood, it stood out like a diamond on jeweler's black velvet. Behind the wheel was a distraught, dry-mouthed Irishman who was going over his part in the upcoming play. To fail, he had been warned, would be terminal.

Kneeling behind a hedge near the Caddy was Willi Lange. He held his Schmeisser across his stomach with the barrel pointed at the thoroughly unhappy Irishman. Lange alternated his gaze from the Cadillac to the street. He breathed evenly and showed no signs of nervousness.

Across the street, Hans Graf had hidden himself behind the trunk of an elm tree. He was as wide as the

215

trunk, so he stood sideways and occasionally peered around the tree down the street. Graf held his submachine gun in his cocked arm, with the weapon's barrel pointed to the sky. As always, he wore a sardonic grin, this time infected with a twist of concentration.

Von Stihl sat in the front seat of a Buick parked along the curb fifty feet north of the Cadillac. He had found the door unlocked. The Buick made a perfect observation post. He was slumped down so that only the top of his head was visible. Through the gap between the dashboard and the steering wheel, he surveyed the street. A strange route for a dynamite delivery, he thought, but then, who would ever think a truck laden with explosives would travel on a quiet residential avenue? Von Stihl's knees reflexively hit together. Why did he always have to urinate at times like this? He lifted the Luger from his lap to relieve pressure. With his left he gripped the car's door handle.

The scene was not unobserved. The elderly cat owner had spotted the Cadillac as she stooped for her milk. Automobiles like that belonged downtown and along the North Shore, not here. The sleek black car was sorely out of place. The old busybody petted her cat for a few moments while deciding, then did what she did almost weekly when something in her neighborhood was awry. She called the police.

Two blocks north, a 1935 Chevrolet turned onto Ridgeland Street. It was traveling slowly, as if in a parade. A few seconds behind the Chevy, a tan Dodge six-wheel truck rounded the corner and accelerated slightly to catch up to its escort car. The truck was unmarked. It carried two and a half tons of dynamite.

From his spotter's position, von Stihl saw the approaching truck and car. They were framed by overhanging elms and kicked up street leaves as they came. The colonel quickly opened and closed the car door.

Paddy Flannery tightly gripped the Cadillac's steering wheel. Acute nervousness had loosened his bow-

216

els, just like his visits to the nitro hut. He was trapped, with no way out. These were German soldiers, saboteurs. If caught, they would be hanged. Flannery was their accomplice, whose penalty would be the same. As the curly-headed one, the leader, had carefully explained during the last few blocks of their trip to this street, Flannery was in it, whether he liked it or not. There was no way out. After the hijacking, the feds would comb the powder company looking for clues. It would take them all of ten minutes to discover how Flannery had stolen the schedule, and another sixty minutes to track him down. He would hang. He could quit now, drive the Caddy away, run from these Nazis. But the little German holding the submachine gun five yards away knew his job if Flannery tried to flee.

Lange was what Flannery called a wimp—a frail, cavechested man who spent his entire life on the bottom of the pecking order. He would have lasted two days in Flannery's street gang. But Willi Lange unnerved the Irishman. The German was icily competent. On the trip to Ridgeland Street, Flannery had caught Lange in the rearview mirror assembling his Schmeisser. He did it with the precision of a watch repairman. Flannery surmised the little kraut could use the weapon with equivalent skill.

Von Stihl's slamming door snapped Flannery from his speculation. Oh, God, the truck was coming. Flannery started the Cadillac and released the emergency brake. His course was irrevocable. He turned off his mind and waited for the procession.

The escort car proceeded the truck with a solemn grace. Headlights were on. Von Stihl was reminded of a funeral. As they approached, the colonel noted there were three men in the car, two in the front seat and one in the back. Two men were in the truck's cab. They would be armed. At least one would be cradling a shotgun.

Motorcycle patrolman Frank Bates, a four-year veteran on the force, was routinely contacting precinct headquarters on a corner call box when the dispatcher told him to check out a suspicious automobile parked in a driveway on Ridgeland Street. Probably a rich relative visiting the old neighborhood, thought Bates as he climbed onto his Harley-Davidson and headed for Ridgeland, two blocks away.

The escort car crossed the intersection north of the ambush as it drew closer. Von Stihl could now make out the features of the two men in the front seat of the Chevy. The driver exhaled a cloud of cigarette smoke and said something that made the passenger laugh abruptly. The passenger looked over his shoulder out the window. Nothing was amiss. He spoke to the driver, who laughed in turn. Behind them, the driver of the truck had a cigar clamped between his teeth and appeared to be snarling. His partner in the truck was bald.

Von Stihl sank deeper in his seat as the black escort car rolled by him. It was traveling perhaps twenty miles an hour. As the deep rumble of the truck exhaust passed, he prayed the dim-witted Irishman did his part. Von Stihl's hand tensed around the Luger's grip. He braced his foot on the drive-train hump. He was coiled like a spring pushed back to its limit.

Flannery was no longer thinking. He was a machine set to turn on in three seconds. Three timeless seconds in which a faint, tinny buzz in the front of Flannery's head told him he would not survive the hour. A wave of melancholy washed over him. He had no time to savor it. The escort car reached the hedge.

Flannery punched the Cadillac's accelerator. The car leaped from the driveway into the street. The escort's driver had no time to react. The Cadillac's right fender slammed into the Chevy with a reassuring, metallic crunch. Both cars bounced back as headlight splinters peppered the concrete. Radiator water gushed from the Chevrolet. Despite his stiff-armed steering, Flannery's head struck the steering wheel. For several seconds his
218

mind faded and wandered. The dynamite truck screeched to a halt two yards behind the car.

Hans Graf sprinted from the elm tree to the collision, where he stopped in front of the Chevy, raised his submachine gun, and waited for the dazed driver to open his mouth in horror. The Chevy's windshield exploded as Graf emptied half the clip into the car. When the crystalline shards had cleared the air, Flannery saw the bloody, mangled stumps, the remnants of the driver's and passenger's heads.

At the last instant, the back-seat passenger had flattened on the floor of the car. Now he kicked the back door open, scrambled from the car, and crouched behind the open door. He carried a sawed-off shotgun, which he hastily aimed at Graf, whose attention was diverted by the truck's guard jumping from the cab. Just as the shotgun's hammers reared back, Willi Lange fired a stream of bullets through the hedge and into the shotgunner, who was blown back into the car, his side ripped away. Both barrels of the shotgun erupted as the dead man's fingers convulsed. The buckshot winged harmlessly over Graf's head and tore through brittle leaves on overhead branches. Graf saluted the hedge.

Erich von Stihl stood near his auto, waiting for the truck driver to make a predictable, stupid mistake. The colonel could not risk rushing the cab, because the driver and the guard would be armed, but the driver would soon move. Just as he thought, the truck's transmission clanged as it slammed into reverse. The truck kicked back, the driver trying to escape with his payload. When the cab reached von Stihl, the German raised his Luger and squeezed off three quick shots through the side window. The driver died instantly. His truck veered sharply, backed over a garbage can, and rammed a tree on the parking strip as the body slumped over the steering wheel. The engine coughed and died.

The truck's passenger was not accounted for. Von

Stihl dropped to all fours to look under the truck. The man's legs pumped wildly as he cleared the truck and broke down Ridgeland, running away from the massacre. The bald man ran like a halfback, zigzagging and low, to make himself a difficult target. Graf ran to the tail end of the truck and let loose a burst, but the bullets kicked up sparks from the concrete behind the runner.

Von Stihl yelled, "Lange, down the street."

Willi Lange stood from behind the hedge and lined his weapon on the bald man running madly down the middle of the street like a fool. Why didn't he take cover and give himself a chance? Lange thought. Lange's Schmeisser spit an economical half-second burst. A block away, roses of blood bloomed and quickly crawled up the runner's back. He pitched forward and was dead before his body slid to a stop.

Mesmerized by the swift violence, Paddy Flannery stood by the Cadillac and watched the carnage. When the bald runner's back sieved blood, Flannery gripped the Cadillac's fender for support. He was dizzy with his involvement and its ramifications. The Irishman's last thought before Hans Graf turned to him was: I'm going to die a traitor.

Graf's hard, taunting voice reached him. "So long, mick."

Not until the SS Obersturmführer saw Flannery had focused on his face did he let loose the rest of his clip. The submachine gun squirmed in Graf's hand. Flannery felt an odd, empty, painless bloating in his chest. The Irishman's eyes closed forever as his body sank to a sitting position on the Cadillac's running board.

Von Stihl had an almost mystical faith in Lange's ability with a Schmeisser, so without looking at the fate of the bald runner he opened the driver's side door of the truck. Sharp pieces of shattered glass fell from the door frame and scattered on the ground. The colonel grabbed the dead driver's belt and hauled him from the cab. The body bounced off the running board to the street. Von Stihl swept blood and glass from the seat, climbed in, and turned the engine over. Willi Lange hurriedly got into the truck from the passenger side and slid to the middle, to make way for Graf. The truck jumped forward, swerved around the punctured escort car, and headed south on Ridgeland Street.

Over the roar of his motorcycle engine, Patrolman Bates heard the unfamiliar staccato pounding of automatic weapons. He turned onto Ridgeland a block south of the ambush in time to see the dynamite truck pull away from the curb and wind around the riddled Chevy. It rapidly gained speed. Good God, what a mess, thought Bates as he cranked back on the accelerator and the Harley screamed toward the oncoming truck. Were those bodies? A traffic accident? What's that guy doing sitting on the Caddy's running board? Hell, he's dead. Holy damn, there's more dead bodies. And those bastards in the truck must be trying to get away.

With the truck bearing down on him, Bates jerked back on his handlebars and threw his weight to his right, putting his cycle into a sideways slide toward the approaching truck. Afraid the truck's tires would not survive a trip over the careening motorcycle, von Stihl stomped on the brakes. The patrolman rolled to his feet with his service revolver already drawn, ran to the truck window, and yelled up at von Stihl, "You're all under arrest. Get out of the truck." He thrust his pistol through the window so its blunt nose was six inches from the colonel's face.

Calmly, deliberately, von Stihl said, "Officer, if you turn around and walk away, you'll live. If not, your life ends here."

"Get out of that fucking truck before I blow your head off," Bates bellowed as he shook his gun at the German.

Von Stihl said one word, "Lange."

Willi Lange fired his Schmeisser across von Stihl's

221

lap. The stream of bullets ripped through the truck's door and tore into the patrolman's chest. The cop dropped out of sight. Von Stihl backed the truck up several yards, swerved around the motorcycle, and drove down the street.

Only two minutes had passed since the Ridgeland Street massacre had begun. Two damaged cars, a police motorcycle, and seven bodies littered the street. The old cat owner picked up her phone to dial the police again.

XIV

That Patrolman Frank Bates, whose body resembled a cheese grater, lived for four hours after the ambush was a miracle. He was rushed to Cook County Hospital, where Dr. Felix Rinder, chief of surgery and professor of medicine at Northwestern University School of Medicine, personally took charge of the policeman's care. An hour after Bates arrived at the emergency entrance, the hospital announced he had used forty pints of blood and their reserves were dangerously low. An emergency call for blood donors went out to all police precincts.

The response was heartwarming and, at least to Dr. Rinder, predictable. Uniformed cops soon filled every available space at the hospital, while nurses extracted a pint of blood from each. Even the dental clinic's chairs and the waiting-room chairs were filled by Chicago policemen with their sleeves rolled up. Queues of cops waited near each chair and bed to give blood to fellow officer Bates. Nurses drew blood from five cops at a time, rushing back and forth with needles, empty bottles, and cotton swabs. Medical students trotted over from the school to assist. A few officers would not take the nurses' word that they could donate only one pint, and had to be told the limit by the supervising physician. The streets outside the hospital were clogged with police cars and motorcycles as their drivers took fifteen minutes from their schedules to try to save Patrolman Bates's life.

By two o'clock that afternoon, 438 policemen had donated. The hospital had more blood than it could use in a week. Dr. Rinder rubbed his hands together with glee. What difference did it make that Bates had actually died the instant he was gunned down and that the bulletin about the policeman clinging to life in dire need of blood was a fabrication? For a week the hospital would not have to plead with a squeamish public to donate. At 2:30 the hospital announced that despite the efforts of the finest surgeons in the Midwest, Patrolman Frank Bates had succumbed to his injuries.

Von Stihl and his men had made their first mistake. All Chicago's criminal element, the professional underworld, the teenage street gangs, small-time burglars and muggers, torches, whiz mobs, pimps, and pushers, all knew the most important rule of survival in Chicago. It was obeyed above all other criminal mores. Gangsters served time rather than violate it. Addicts lost a week's fix rather than break it. The maxim was pounded into street urchins the day they joined the gang. It was the ultimate rule of survival, and it was simple: Never, ever, kill a Chicago cop.

Within thirty minutes of the Ridgeland Street massacre, the policemen of Chicago knew two things about the killing: motorcycle patrolman Frank Bates had been hit, and an Irish hoodlum was involved. The Chicago police force went to the streets. Cops on leave showed up to put in overtime. Others worked two shifts that day, their paid shift and a voluntary one. Arson and homicide detectives dropped their cases. Traffic cops left their posts. Retired policemen asked for special duty. Cops who had phoned in sick that day were cured and reported to their precinct stations. Their purpose: to find Bates's killer and save the courts a trial.

Chicago's outlaw underbelly paid dearly for Frank Bates's death. Their regular and generous grease meant nothing. Gang members across Chicago were rousted from their homes and clubs and taken downtown. Many suffered unfortunate bruises on the way, which on official reports were attributed to accidents on stairways. Much like a Marx Brothers movie, groups of three and four hoodlums fell down stairs simultaneously, despite their police protection en route to the stations. Gangster Mickey O'Brien broke his nose while in custody. The policeman wrote on the report, "Suspect struck arresting officer's fist with his nose."

Policy depots were raided. Underworld gambling casinos were invaded and their equipment destroyed. The Twenty-second Street precinct headquarters had so many mob hookers waiting to be booked that a street vendor made a week's profit selling them hot dogs. A Department of Health official and two policemen arrived at a mob-owned restaurant on Wabash Street and closed it for having an unsanitary kitchen. Diners were forced to leave their tables in mid-bite. A gangster-controlled garbage company's garage in Ciccro was closed with police padlocks so that the eight trucks within could be used as evidence in a possible future trial resulting from a possible future arrest. The streets dried up. Underworld patrons screamed at their aldermen but were told nothing could stop the purge.

Each collared hoodlum was asked about the massacre. Asked and reasked, with force. No one knew anything. Gang leaders, seeing their operations shrink like a slug dosed with salt, also began asking questions. Who hit the truck on Ridgeland Street? Who burned the cop? They wanted the hijackers as much as the police did. No one knew anything.

Everette Smithson paced nervously in front of the Metallurgical Laboratory. Wind blew briskly along Ellis Avenue, and a few students scurried along, their faces buried in scarves and collars. Despite the wind, Smithson's substantial bulk was sweating.

Chicago was his protectorate. For two years it had suffered fewer incidents of suspected sabotage than any other area in the country. This record was the job security Smithson needed, because he knew this job would be the last stop of his career.

Smithson had been a career army officer who retired in 1939 after twenty-five years, most of which time was served as a perimeter security officer at various bases. He had ended his army years as a major and chief of security at Fort Lewis. Because forty-five was too young to retire, he had applied to the Department of War for a job in his field. Shortly thereafter he was contacted by Richard Sackville-West, the head of a government organization Smithson had never heard of, and asked to move to Chicago to join the agency's antisabotage division.

"Division" was a misnomer. Smithson *was* the division, the only man assigned to investigate suspected sabotage in the Chicago area, which included the city, its suburbs, and, unfortunately, Gary, Indiana. It was a comfortable, secure position. Once a week he reported via coded telegram to Sackville-West in Washington. Most were single sentences announcing that no instances of suspected sabotage had occurred. Occasionally Smithson would investigate a suspicious industrial breakdown, which he usually concluded was the work of a dissatisfied employee. His job had a routineness he enjoyed and a title he was proud of.

Now this. The dynamite hijacking occurred at 9:30 that morning. He had followed the police investigation closely, and by noon they still had no hard evidence to back their belief it was a gangland hit. When the police chief told him of the one startling fact that pointed to sabotage, Smithson had phoned Sackville-West, reviewed the evidence, and asked for assistance. Smithson was not surprised when his boss suggested John Crown help. Crown was already in Chicago, and his duties guarding Hess occupied only his mornings. Sackville-West wanted a full report in two days. And he wanted that dynamite accounted for.

Smithson clasped his hands behind his back and
226

once again peered at the laboratory front door. The interviews usually didn't last this long. Hess's mind always fell apart before the noon hour. What was keeping them? He wanted to enter the building to deliver the Priest's message to Crown, but knew he could not. Nor was he allowed in Hess's presence. Smithson resumed his pacing.

A short, thick-set man wearing a charcoal trench coat and carrying a maroon blanket over his arm approached Smithson. The man had a strong jaw and a metal cast to his eyes. He paused in front of Smithson.

"Say, pal, got the time?"

"Sure," Smithson said as he glanced at his wristwatch, "it's twelve-twenty."

"You waiting for somebody?"

Smithson realized who the man was. He jerked his billfold from his pocket and held the ID up to the man. "I'm here on business," Smithson said impatiently.

"I'm sorry, sir, but your clearance isn't sufficient to enter the building."

"I'm well aware of that," Smithson replied, his heavy jowls flapping as his impatience turned to anger. "I'll wait right here."

"Yes, sir. No offense meant, but you'll be watched while you're here."

"I assumed that. When'll today's interview be over?"

The guard smiled. "What interview? Neither you nor I are aware of any interview."

"Shit," Smithson exclaimed as he looked at the lab entrance again. "You'd think that . . ."

A black Chevrolet pulled to the curb. Its passenger jumped out and opened the rear door. Two plainclothes guards emerged from the Metallurgical Lab. One immediately approached Smithson and asked if he would leave the area. When Smithson again flashed his ID, the guard became polite, but no less insistent.

"You tell Crown that Everette Smithson wants to see him. I'll be standing at the end of the building. Tell
227

him our boss has some orders for him, and they're urgent." Smithson could not keep his irritation at not being in full command of the Chicago operation out of his voice.

From a hundred feet away, Smithson saw Crown, accompanied by a tall, black-haired man Smithson assumed was Rudolf Hess, emerge from the building. Hess slipped quickly into the back seat of the Chevrolet, and a guard followed him in. The man with the blanket folded over his gun-wielding arm spoke a few words to Crown. Crown glanced toward Smithson, thanked the guard, and walked the distance to the Chicago agent. With the students and plainclothes guards, Ellis Avenue was an unlikely spot for a setup, but Crown's eyes scanned passing automobiles and building tops.

He smiled briefly as he held out his hand to the corpulent agent. "Good to see you again, Everette." Crown's eyes kept searching, never stopping. If Smithson noticed Crown's jerking eyes, he didn't mention it.

"Likewise. I understand from the boss you did a fine job getting your charge out of England." Smithson nodded his head rapidly as he spoke, and his bulbous double chin bloated and deflated like a croaking bull frog.

"Not much problem with it," Crown replied, and paused, letting Smithson know the amenities were over.

"Well," Smithson said, rubbing his hands with the relish of one about to impart important news, "you've heard about the hijacking?"

"What hijacking?"

"No, of course you haven't. You've been with your guest all morning." Smithson quickly filled Crown in on the Ridgeland Street massacre. "The Priest thinks it's sabotage, so he wants you to help me out here," he concluded apologetically. "You'll hear why we think it's sabotage when we get there and talk to an old lady."

228

"Did he say anything about the other concerns I might have?" Crown asked testily.

"Only that you can work them in with helping me investigate."

There was only one reason the Priest would order Crown to get involved with this mess. He believed it was connected with Hess and with Maura's death. Crown looked over his shoulder. Peter Kohler stood next to the Chevrolet, checking his watch, anxious to get Hess off the street. Heather and Hess were visible through the rear window.

"All right," Crown said. "Meet me at the EDC house in fifteen minutes. I'll have our guest secured by then."

Smithson used the drive to relay facts of the hijacking as summarized by early police reports. They arrived at the site at 1:45. A four-block area had been cordoned off. Crown counted a dozen police cars with flashing lights near the scene and guessed most of the others were unmarked police cars. The bodies had been removed. White paint silhouetted where they had fallen on the concrete. The motorcycle and two damaged cars had not been moved. The pools of blood were still damp. Bent over one red puddle was a white-coated police lab technician putting samples on thin glass slides. Perhaps twenty uniformed and plainclothes officers worked in the vicinity. A police photographer busily snapped pictures of the scene. An army of reporters was kept at bay by a circle of policemen. Smithson and Crown struggled to the police line, assisted greatly by the obese Chicago agent's low center of gravity. Smithson showed his ID and they passed through the line. Aching tension ebbed from Crown as if he had sunk into a hot bath. In this crowd of policemen, he was safe.

"John, this's Lieutenant Michael Sullivan, who's in charge of the police investigation."

Sullivan was on his knees between the two bullet-scarred cars, carefully inspecting the point of impact. He thrust his powerful hand up at Crown. "Glad to know ya," he said cursorily, and resumed his study. His gray-brown hair was cut extremely close, perhaps to disguise its sparsity. Sullivan's neck was drill-instructor thick, and under a threadbare raincoat his shoulders sloped like a linebacker's. Only his belly had aged, bloated with beer over the years. The pencil Sullivan used to jot down his discoveries looked ridiculously small in his hand.

"Crown's from our office. He's here to lend a hand."

Sullivan looked up. "Then you'd be wanting to talk to the old lady."

"I want him to hear it firsthand," Smithson said. "Can the three of us talk to her?"

"You won't catch me in that house again. I get enough of the mother types on weekends," Sullivan said, shaking his head and resuming his inch-by-inch survey of the collision. "But you're welcome to talk to her. The gray house." He flipped his thumb, indicating the house with the large elm tree in its front yard.

The door to the home was open before Smithson and Crown had climbed the half-dozen steps to the porch. A silver-gray cat leaped through the door, shot down the steps, and disappeared around the side of the house.

"Oh, that old cat," said an ancient voice on the other side of the screen. "Here, kitty, kitty, kitty." She made a series of clucking sounds, apparently imitating a chipmunk. "Oh, well, he always comes back. Come in, gentlemen, come in. Don't stand out there in the cold."

The woman was in her late seventies, with a face that had retained its soft prettiness. Her hair was startlingly white and was pulled back into a bun. She wore a light green print dress with a matching sash around her waist. It was Sunday wear donned to honor the occasion of visitors.

230

The heavy odor of mothballs and cat urine smacked Crown as he stepped into the living room.

"Please come in and make yourselves at home. Why don't you sit over there? Right over there." She pointed Crown to a sagging sofa under a dark landscape painting notable only because of its ornately carved wood frame. She guided Smithson to a delicate cherrywood rocking chair, but then, seeing his bulk, directed him to the other end of the sofa. Crown quickly grabbed the sofa's arm to prevent toppling as Smithson's ponderous weight buckled the cushion. Crown felt like he was sharing a hammock with Oliver Hardy.

"Tea?"

"Pardon?" Crown asked, having regained his balance.

"Would you like some tea?"

"No thanks, ma'am. We're here to ask you about . . ."

"Tea?" She turned to Smithson. Her voice had a very high, almost falsetto pitch. "Tea" sounded like a bird's chirp.

"Thank you, yes. Four lumps of sugar."

While she puttered around the kitchen, Crown surveyed her living room. He doubted it had changed in twenty years. The curtains were drawn, and the room was dim, accenting the mothball odor. A Tiffany lamp sat on an end table near the sofa. A year of *Saturday Evening Post*s cluttered the tea table in front of them. Oval-framed photographs of relatives from the last century were perched on the mantel over the fireplace. Bookshelves built into the wall near the fireplace contained a hundred or more miniature pieces of furniture collected over a half-century. An early RCA radio rested on the radiator cover near the sofa. Between the radiator and the fireplace was her chair, a gray, worn, comfortable command chair replete with footstool and knitting pouch hanging from the antimacassar-covered arm. In front of the chair was an afghan that she tucked her feet into when knitting. An August

231

Junghans eight-day clock hung on the wall across from Crown and filled the room with its soothing tick. The home was old and comfortable, the home of a woman enjoying her last years.

The old woman padded from the kitchen to Smithson, handed him a cup and saucer, and said, "Sorry, young man. I don't have any cubes. I'll pour sugar, and you tell me when."

After a sufficient time to half-fill the cup with sugar, Smithson waved his hand. She had forgotten a spoon, so he stirred the syrup with his watchband.

When she had settled into her chair and balanced her cup and saucer on the arm, Crown began, "Ma'am, I'm John Crown. My friend, Everette Smithson, and I are with the Chicago police—"

"Well, I'm always glad to see you boys, what with the neighborhood going like it is. Why, just this morning, you would not believe what was going on . . ."

"What's your name, ma'am?"

"Mrs. Falkenhausen," she answered, sipping her tea. For the first time, Crown noticed a slight accent, the light inflection of one who has spent decades minimizing that vestige of the old country.

"Did you see the hijacking, Mrs. Falkenhausen?"

"I've never seen anything like it. First I saw this big black car sitting in the Austens' driveway. I know the Austens' car, and that wasn't it, so I phoned the police . . ."

She was not the rambling, senile woman Crown had expected when first seeing her. She had witnessed the hijacking from beginning to end. Her powers of observation were remarkable. The apparent leader was thirty-six or thirty-eight years old, five feet, nine inches tall, very muscular, and had short, very curly blond hair. He had used the pistol on the truck driver. The man who had shot out the windshield was very tall, perhaps six-four or -five, and had shoulders as wide as the elm tree in her front yard he had hidden behind. She described a purple blotch under his right ear. He
232

had straight blond hair. She had not seen the smaller, dark-complexioned man until near the end, when he stood up from behind the hedge across the street. He had a small, almost invisible black mustache. All three wore shabby clothes. Both the giant and the mustached man used weapons that sounded like those she had heard on her radio shows. She nodded when Crown mentioned a submachine gun, but vigorously shook her head when he described the wooden stock of a Thompson submachine gun, the standard Chicago mob weapon.

"No, no wood."

"What do you mean?"

"There wasn't any wood on the guns. Only metal."

"Well, there has to be wood. It's the part that goes against the shoulder sometimes when you fire. It's the stock."

"No," she repeated emphatically. "No wood. I know what I saw."

Crown popped his arm several times. He said finally, "Yes, I believe you do."

"That's the clue I was talking about," Smithson said. "Sullivan told me that he has never known either an Irish or a Sicilian gang to use anything but American-made Thompsons. The gun Mrs. Falkenhausen is describing is foreign."

"That's not the only thing foreign about them," the old lady said, putting her cup and saucer down with importance.

Crown's eyes darted to her. She was a watcher and a reliable reporter. She had delivered her information like a cub newspaperman to his editor. If she regarded it as important, it was.

"What else, ma'am?"

"Well, this didn't occur to me until after Mr. Sullivan talked to me. It didn't even ring a bell when I heard it first. But later it just struck me. Funny how that works."

"What was that?"

233

"The leader, the curly-headed one, yelled, 'Lange, down the street.' "

Crown was mildly disappointed. Of course, the name of one of the men was an important clue. The Chicago police and the FBI would scour their files looking for hoodlums named Lange. But it wasn't a clue that sparked Crown's interest.

"Mrs. Falkenhausen, that's really sharp of you to pick the man's name up. Very important." Crown collected his feet under him to rise. "We really appreciate your time."

"The name's not the important part."

"Oh?"

"The leader didn't yell, 'Lange, down the street.' He yelled, *'Lange, unten auf der Strasse.'* "

"What?"

"That's right," she said, appreciating the impact of her statement. "I spent my first fifteen years in Berlin. I know the mother tongue when I hear it."

"Find anything else?" Lieutenant Sullivan asked as he wiped automobile grease from his hands with a towel. The Cadillac's front bumper was now attached to a police wrecker, which jolted forward. Glass fragments popped as the Cadillac rolled over remnants of the Chevrolet's windshield. Only a dozen or so police remained. A street sweeper was parked against the curb, with its engine idling, ready to erase the last trace of the ambush.

"Nothing important," Smithson lied smoothly. "How's your search going?"

"No results yet. All we can do is look for the dynamite truck. There must be five hundred cops doing nothing but that right now. We've formed circles. Here, let me show you."

Sullivan withdrew a street map from his pocket and laid it across the hood of the Chevrolet.

"Here's where we are. These two red circles are the lines where we have men posted. I'm pretty sure that,

234

should the dynamite truck cross any of these lines, it'll be spotted."

"How far is the outside circle from where we are?" Crown asked.

"Two miles."

"You're probably too late, then. It's been hours since the heist."

"You don't think I know that?" Sullivan snapped, reflecting the pressure he had been under since the chief of police and the mayor had personally issued his orders that morning. "But it's better than doing nothing. And nothing's all we have to go on right now. Plus, it's giving a lot of damned angry cops something constructive to do."

"What else is being done?" Crown asked, looking up and down the street, for nothing in particular.

"All the radio stations are announcing the description of the truck. There's a good chance someone will spot it. It's hard to hide something that big when the entire city is looking for it."

"What about the hood? Know anything about him?"

"Name was Patrick Kenney Flannery, known as Paddy. He's got a sheet on him two yards long, dating back to when he was fourteen. He's been charged with everything from burglary to whiskey running to extortion. Served a total of five years. When he was a kid, he was with the O'Banion gang, and as far as we can tell, after that he was associated with a series of small-timers. He was used mostly for muscle. Never aspired to anything else, at least not till now."

"Anything distinctive about him? Anything that would explain this?"

"The big thing is that he worked at the powder company."

"Everette told me about that. What about his background?" Crown asked. "His parents?"

"Irish as you can get."

"Any ties to Europe?"

Sullivan turned directly to Crown and spoke with the

235

authority of two decades on the beat. "I know what that old lady said about their weapons with no wood stocks. Sure, that sounds mysterious and international, just like your and Smithson's business. But believe me, Crown, I know this type. Flannery was a scumbag from the word go. All he did was cause trouble all his life. Not even big trouble, just nickel-and-dime stuff. Shit, if he hadn't been hauled into police stations once a week, he wouldn't have known what to do with himself.

"So I'll tell you what happened here." Sullivan's voice rose. "He and a couple other losers scratched their heads and realized that if they didn't do something big, hit somebody hard for a big prize, they'd be punks all their lives. This results—a harebrained scheme that got a lot of people killed for nothing. Those gunsels have as much use for dynamite as I do for hair on my palm."

"Then how do you explain the foreign weapons?" Smithson asked. Crown wanted to drop the subject. The lieutenant would be of little help now that his mind was set.

"I figure that's what started this whole business, those guns. Flannery or one of the others came across a couple of heavy-duty submachine guns. Maybe bought them from a fence. Who knows? The guns started it, because it gave them big ideas. They were probably thinking of the St. Valentine's day massacre and the Hymie Weiss shooting. The big time. So they brewed up this scheme for nothing more than to get into the papers."

A uniformed motorcycle policeman trotted up to Sullivan and handed him three or four slips of paper. "From headquarters and the morgue, sir."

"Assholes," muttered Sullivan as he flipped through the sheets. "Wish the fuck they'd get off my back and let me do my job. If the goddamn mayor wants to play cop, why doesn't he put on a badge and . . ." Sullivan stopped abruptly and screwed his eyebrows in concentration.

236

"What is it, Lieutenant?" Crown asked, suspecting Sullivan was confronted with evidence from the morgue that belied his theory.

"This doesn't make sense," he said after several seconds. "The Irishman was hit with the same type of bullets that killed the escort-car men. I thought Flannery had been shotgunned, but they pulled six slugs from him. No buckshot at all."

"What caliber?" Crown asked.

"It says here they're nine-double-M. What the hell's that?"

"It's the standard German caliber for service pistols and submachine guns. Any markings on the casings you found?"

"Yeah, a small K punched on the bottom of the shells," Sullivan answered, without looking up from the sheets, embarrassed by his lack of knowledge.

Crown said, "Krupp. The German munitions manufacturer."

"None of the powder-company people had submachine guns. So one of Flannery's own men killed him," the lieutenant said. "Figures. Goddamn bunch of lunatics." He paled, reached for his belt buckle, and bit his lower lip. A flaming peptic ulcer was his constant companion.

The courier-cop ran up again, out of breath and beaming. "Lieutenant, they've found the dynamite truck. At the corner of Pulaski and Fullerton."

"You still think there's something international about this, Crown?" Sullivan asked, the pain having subsided.

"I don't know." Like hell he didn't know. "I'd like to tag along awhile, though."

"Sure, sure. I figured as much. Let's go in my car. The truck isn't far from here. Inside our first goddamn ring of police." Sullivan took the street map from his back pocket, and tore it in half, and threw it on the ground.

The truck was parked in an alley behind a two-story

brick warehouse. By the time Sullivan's car arrived, the Dodge six-wheel two-tonner was already surrounded by policemen trying to keep the souvenir hunters from dismantling it.

Piles of garbage leaned against the warehouse. Curious onlookers waded through the mire to get a closer look. An enterprising *Tribune* photographer rapidly ascended a stagnant pile, precariously balanced himself atop an apple crate perched at the crest, and just as he snapped the photo, lost his footing and pitched sideways into the festering rubbish.

"Sergeant," Sullivan bellowed as he shouldered his way through the crowd, "get these people out of here."

Sullivan's reputation as an uncharitable boss must have been widespread, because the phalanx of bluecoats now moved with resolve, linking arms and pushing the throng back.

"Goddamn tourists," Sullivan said under his breath, swallowing rapidly in an ineffectual attempt to drown the stab of pain in his belly.

The curious were eventually restrained, but not before malodorous clumps of garbage had been strewn across the site. Crown lifted his feet carefully as he slowly circled the truck. He ran his hand over the ruptured sheet metal of the driver's-side door, through which a stream of Krupp products had poured.

"I think the doctors'll find that Patrolman Bates also has bits of metal in his chest from this door," Sullivan said.

"Fired from inside the cab?"

"Sure. The steel fragments are bent out. Bates never knew what hit him." Sullivan swung the truck's door open and squinted at the perforated door panel. He scraped a thin film of gray-brown particles from the remnants of the panel. "The man sitting in the middle or on the right fired, probably the middle man. He fired over the driver's lap. These powder burns are too wide to have been fired point-blank by the driver. The driver kept both his hands on the wheel so Bates

238

wouldn't suspect he was in danger. And the driver had a hell of a lot of confidence in the gunner. The bullets went above the driver's thighs but below his elbows. Look at this, too. He must have fired ten or fifteen rounds through this door, yet the hole here is no bigger than my fist. Jesus," Sullivan exclaimed. "He's one steady son of a bitch."

"Unbelievable," wheezed Everette Smithson, on his tiptoes peering at the door.

"That's a warning to us, Crown, just as plain as if it were in print," Sullivan said. "The little one, the one the old lady said sat in the middle of the cab, is extremely dangerous. Deadly."

"A professional," Crown said in a voice inaudible to the surrounding policemen.

Sullivan hopped down from the running board and looked at Crown squarely, with his basketball stomach almost touching Crown's belt buckle. "You're pretty sure about that?" It was not a challenge. The lieutenant was not preparing a rebuttal. He wanted advice.

Crown nodded. "The old lady, Mrs. Falkenhausen, told us something you don't know. She's a German immigrant. She heard one of the men, apparently the leader, the one who drove the truck away, give a command in German. He slipped, because she also heard them speak English. Good English. Plus, the submachine gun used. They're not American-made. They sound like MP40's, called Schmeissers, made in Germany and used in all the German services. And now your conclusion about the man in the middle of the seat being extremely competent with the weapon. Now, I don't know much about your Chicago gangs, but this doesn't sound like a mob hijacking. Smithson and I agree. The three hijackers were German stormtroopers."

"What the fuck are they doing in Chicago?" asked Sullivan, who believed every word Crown had said.

"If we can find that out, we can find them."

A young red-haired policeman Crown guessed had
239

been on the force all of two weeks broke through the circle of policemen and ran up to Sullivan, losing his footing several times on the slippery refuse. He didn't wait to be addressed by his superior. "Lieutenant, we've got it."

"Got what?"

"A housewife across the street saw the men change trucks. She saw the dynamite truck drive up, and then she saw three men unload boxes and put them into a van."

"When?"

"About nine-thirty or quarter to ten."

"What kind of van?"

"She doesn't know the make or the plates, but it's light blue and has 'Bakery' printed on the side of it."

"What bakery?"

"She said the name of the bakery had been painted over or erased. All it said on the side was 'Bakery.' "

"Which way did it go?"

The red-haired cop pointed over Sullivan's shoulder. "They turned around and went north."

"What else did she see?" Sullivan asked.

"She doesn't remember anything else. We've checked the other houses along the block, and no one else saw anything."

Sullivan nodded his approval and dismissed the rookie. A tired man, one who had spent his week's energy that morning, stepped up to Sullivan. He was about sixty years old. A shock of white hair hung over his ears. He wore a thin black tie and a wool sweater. As if to contradict this office wear, his hands were callused and scarred. He was a man who was assigned a desk job but escaped to the plant floor, to the days of honest labor, as often as possible.

"Officer . . ." He addressed Sullivan, but had decided Smithson and Crown were ranking police officers, so he joined their circle. "I'm Henry Harter, the manager of the Guy Fawkes Powder Company. This's my truck." Without further explanation he handed Sul-
240

livan a sheet of lined paper with figures running down one of the columns.

"What's this?"

"It's my inventory of the truck. It left the plant this morning with thirty crates of explosives. It still has twenty-eight crates. They took only two of them."

"How much dynamite in each crate?" Crown asked.

"The powder's in paraffin wrappers. Each crate has eight wrappers, and each wrapper weighs twenty pounds. So we've got three hundred and twenty pounds of explosives missing." Harter sighed as if it were his life's last breath and returned to the rear of the truck.

Sullivan worked his throat as he stared at the inventory sheet. He shook his head. "I've got to report to the mayor and the chief that we've got three German stormtroopers walking around Chicago with three hundred and twenty pounds of explosives."

"Not quite," Smithson said, his breath hitting the cold air and curling around his fleshy jowls. "You can report three men and three hundred and twenty pounds of dynamite, but at least for the time being, the fact that they're Germans is to be our secret." He looked quickly at Crown for affirmance. Crown's chin dipped almost imperceptibly.

"No way," Sullivan said, stepping closer to Smithson. "I'm charged with giving a full report. If the chief found out I'd withheld the fact the hijackers are Germans, we'd be out. Booted off the force."

"Now, look, Lieutenant," Smithson said, his voice beginning to lose itself in a whine. "We've got to—"

"Look nothing. I've got my duties out here. I can't very well lie to the men who employ me."

When Smithson looked at him for help, Crown said, "We can compromise. The three of us'll visit the chief. He'll receive a phone call from Smithson's and my boss. I guarantee you, your chief will keep our secret when he hears from Washington."

Sullivan thought about the proposal for several

seconds, then nodded. "Fair enough. As long as my ass is protected."

Crown continued, "Everette, I assume you have a list of the federal-government war installations in the Chicago area."

"Of course. That's my job."

"It only makes sense that the Germans will try to destroy one of these sites. They didn't come all the way from Germany to hijack dynamite in Chicago to use it somewhere other than Chicago."

"You're right, John." Smithson's head bounced rapidly atop the folds of his double chin. "There're fourteen in Cook County. I'll prepare a list of addresses and give it to you, Lieutenant. They're all guarded by military personnel now, but we can set up advance warning circles around them. Watch them day and night."

The Fermi experiments would be exempt from police attention. It had sufficient guards to turn back any attempt. The early-warning ring of spotters had been in effect for months.

"We won't have any trouble getting volunteers for the job," Sullivan said. "There's a thousand Chicago cops who want in on this."

"One last thing, Lieutenant," Crown said. "I want to be the first to talk to those men when they're captured. We've got to find out their motive."

Sullivan smiled faintly. "Crown, you don't know shit about cops. You don't think all these bluecoats out here are biting at the bit to find those men so they can slap handcuffs on them, do you?"

"Those hijackers can't be killed."

"Then you'd better be the first to get to them. That's the only way. You ever hear of a cop killer being tried in a court? Hell no." Sullivan paused to look at both Smithson and Crown in turn. "That includes me. Like they say in the army, I'm not taking prisoners."

XV

In one month alone, June 1942, the ranks of the United States Navy swelled by almost ten percent. The deluge of seventeen- and eighteen-year-old inductees awash with war fever was unending and threatened to swamp the navy. New training centers were built at Farragut, Sampson, and Bainbridge. The bases at Newport and San Diego were expanded. The tide of recruits still pushed against the navy's bulkheads, so in that June, the Bureau of Yards and Docks instructed the commandant of the Ninth Naval District to expand the already huge Great Lakes Naval Training Center thirty miles north of Chicago.

Great Lakes occupies a mile of Lake Michigan's Illinois shoreline between Lake Forest and Waukegan. The base extends almost a mile inland to Sheridan Road, which parallels the beach. At the outbreak of the war, the navy had acquired a 685-acre site across Sheridan Road. Within a week after the bureau's June order, bulldozers and cranes were swarming over the new acreage.

By late September, two months after the first delivery of lumber, 100 new barracks, three drill halls, a half-dozen mess halls, a sewage-treatment plant, and many other new structures had been completed. This buildup, the largest training-center expansion of the war, brought the Great Lakes Station's capacity to 68,000 recruits.

Hundreds of thousands of sailors passed through the

station during the war. When they arrived fresh from boot camp, they knew how to stand at attention and manipulate the thirteen buttons on their bell-bottom flaps. At Great Lakes they learned the arts of amphibious landing, antiaircraft defense, ship repair, submarine chasing, small-craft operations, fire fighting, and myriad other skills. When they left, they were specialists ready for assignment at sea.

Because very little at the training center was highly classified, security was porous. Perimeter defense consisted of an interlocking wire fence topped with three strands of barbed wire projecting from the top of the fence at an outward angle. The base was bordered on the south by a forest that had been cleared back from the fence for forty yards. The fence ran east and descended a rough embankment to the beach, where it traversed the sand to a breakwater jutting almost a half-mile into Lake Michigan.

Rough, waist-high grass covered the acreage just inside the south fence. A well-worn footpath followed the fence, where shore patrolmen walked the perimeter. Every fourth fence post projected ten feet above the barbed wire and served as a light pole. Hidden in reflector cones, 100-watt bulbs issued distilled light that barely reached the ground. On this November night, lengths of fence between the light poles were draped in almost total darkness.

Two shore patrolmen emerged from the night and walked into the dim nimbus of the next pole. Their black pea coats and trousers merged with the darkness, but their white caps and arm bands stood out like the breakwater beacons on the lake. Both wore cloth belts on which were attached cartridge pockets and black holsters. The holster flaps were buttoned over their Navy-issue Colt automatics. One sailor had an M1 carbine strapped over his shoulder. The other was being pulled along by an immense black-and-gold German shepherd whose training at heeling had been neglected. Like its master, the dog was anxious to
244

complete its round of the southeast quadrant. A warm rug at the foot of his master's bed waited.

The sailor held the leash from inside his pea-coat pocket. He smoked a short cigarette, and rather than expose his hands to the cold, he let the ashes fall across the coat. His companion also hid his hands from the wind. The heavy stock of the M1 banged irritatingly against his elbow. The rifleman appreciated the dog's constant tension on its leash. Shinnick always walked at his dog's pace. Three days before, the shepherd had had a case of loose bowels, and their patrol lasted an extra forty-five minutes. The CPO had a shit fit when Shinnick explained why they reported late to the guard shack. King was making up for that now as he kept the leash taut. Shinnick stumbled along behind him.

They walked briskly, silently. Their breath rolled around them and was lost in the night. They could hear the distant rumble of Lake Michigan's waves pounding the beach. The graveyard crew would take over on the next round. This was the last tour. The worst tour. Johnson wanted to kick Shinnick's dog into a run. Despite the shepherd, the sidekick, and the guns, the last round always frightened Johnson. Noises behind him crawled up his neck. Shadows lived. By squinting, he reduced his field of vision to the path directly ahead of him. Under no circumstances would he glance over his shoulder. The path, the spectral string of lightbulbs that disappeared in the distance, and the gloomy, concealing woods on the other side of the fence, all terrified Johnson. As they approached the next pallid circle of illumination, Johnson broke the silence. "This path really spooks me."

"So you keep saying." Shinnick's voice corralled Johnson's thoughts and gave them a nucleus to focus on. "And I keep telling you to transfer to gate duty."

"Nah. The CPO wouldn't buy that at all. What do I tell him? That I'm scared of the dark?"

"Tell him you're allergic to dogs. King won't mind."

"That's one great dog you got. He'd tear to pieces anybody that bothered you. But just let me get attacked, and he'd sit on his haunches laughing."

Shinnick leaned forward and patted the dog's rump. He had heard this routine before. As the southeast-perimeter tour progressed, Johnson always got antsy. He began talking almost at the same spot every round. Shinnick retorted with almost identical comments and suggestions, knowing his sidekick keyed on the voice, not the content.

"The way you act, Johnson, you'd think we're right in the middle of Germany. The only people anywhere near us are the rich folks who live on the other side of the fence on the lake."

"Then why the hell are we freezing our butts off, carrying this ice-cold rifle, and walking that monster you call a dog?"

Each time Johnson commented on King, Shinnick patted the dog's flanks. "Just in case. You never know. The krauts may decide that rather than the British coast, they're going to begin their invasion on the Lake Michigan coast." Both men laughed.

Their joke was prophetic. Fifty yards south of them, across the fence, hidden by dense forest, three German stormtroopers prepared for the assault on the Great Lakes Naval Training Center.

The barrel of Willi Lange's Schmeisser followed the guards' progress as they walked into the obscurity between light poles. Hans Graf lay in the underbrush beside him. He had made two trips from the truck. Despite having lugged the 160-pound crate of explosives from the van through 300 feet of underbrush and then repeating the journey for the ladders, Graf was not breathing hard. He turned sharply to the sound of breaking twigs. Erich von Stihl crunched toward their position. In the crystalline night, the sound of rustling bushes was alarmingly loud. Lange watched the shore patrolmen's backs as they walked away from

246

them, in and out of spots of light. The sailors heard nothing.

Von Stihl dropped to the ground near Graf. He slipped off the heavy backpack and peered across the forty yards of cleared land to the fence. He saw the shore patrolmen receding along the fenceline.

"How often?"

Lange had left the truck twenty minutes before and had kept a chilling vigil near the edge of the fence clearing. He glanced at his wristwatch.

"Roughly every fifteen minutes. At least, the guards before these guys came by fifteen minutes ago."

"Did they have a shepherd, too."

"Yes, it seems they all do."

Goddamn Abwehr intelligence. They hadn't mentioned the dogs. Against guard dogs, the stormtroopers' chances of being caught were logarithmically increased. The human threshold of awareness is very low. A shore patrolman will not see and not hear certain movements. This sensory obtuseness gives an intruder a margin of error. Not so with dogs. German commandos are taught to assume that any dog, not just a German shepherd, will detect even the slightest movement within 100 feet of him. And shepherds are not just any dog. They have a 600-pound bite that can snap an arm as if it were balsa wood.

"What do you make of the guards?"

"They might as well be in their barracks. They're not interested in patrolling tonight," Lange whispered. "They walked with their chins down and didn't look into the woods. Even the dog seemed to be in a hurry."

"What about the fence, Graf?"

The SS lieutenant held a pair of miniature binoculars to his eyes. "Just like we thought. I don't see any insulators, so it isn't electrified. But there's a thin strand of wire running through the fence about halfway up. It's a motion detector. If we jiggle it or cut it, an alarm'll go off somewhere."

"With only fifteen minutes between patrols, we'll have to hide the ladders once we're over. Let's go."

Von Stihl slung his backpack over his shoulder and grabbed one end of the ladders. He looked both ways and broke from the clearing toward the fence, dragging the ladders behind him. As the bottom of the ladders passed, Graf lifted them and followed the colonel. Lange covered them until they reached the darkness between two light poles, then left his position and ran toward them.

Their fence-breaching maneuver was called the arch. It was as old as war and almost impossible to defend against. The top strand of barbed wire was ten feet above the ground. The ladders they had purchased that day were each fourteen feet long. Graf jabbed his ladder's legs as hard as he could into the ground several feet away from the fence, then backed toward the fence until the ladder was at an angle, with its top rung directly over the topmost strand of barbed wire. After von Stihl stepped on the lowest rung of Graf's ladder to act as a counterweight, Willi Lange quickly climbed to the second-highest rung. He was totally supported by the human pylon, Graf, and counterbalanced by von Stihl. Von Stihl pivoted the second ladder so Lange could grab it and pull it up to him. Lange lowered the bottom of the second ladder to the ground on the other side of the fence. He hammered it into the ground so it would not slip and then connected the clasps they had rigged that afternoon.

"Let's try it," Lange whispered.

Graf carefully lowered his arms. The ladders settled three or four inches and stood firm. The arch was complete. Lange lifted one leg over onto the inside ladder and tested it with his weight. It held. Carrying the explosives, von Stihl and Graf followed Lange over the ladder arch.

The arch was dismantled with the same precision. Graf dragged the ladders into the tall grass fifty feet north of the fence, where they could not be seen by the patrols. Elapsed time since they had left the woods: two minutes, fifteen seconds.

Von Stihl knew the layout of the southeast quadrant of the training center as if it were his parents' backyard in Stuttgart. The most southeasterly building at the base was the security hut, located twenty yards from the embankment that dropped to the Lake Michigan beach. The hut had been built hurriedly with plywood and light beams. It was no larger than the living room of a modest house.

Thirty yards north of the security hut was a large garage containing six amphibious landing crafts used in training assaults on the beach. Fresh dirt lay loosely around the corner support posts, indicating it was one of the many new structures at the station. The surrounding grass had not fully recovered from the trampling it had endured during the garage's recent construction. The ground near the doors was compacted and rutted from the day's use of the vehicles.

The next building in line near the embankment was a weather-observation training post. An immense window for spotting weather formations over the lake had been cut into the lake-side wall. Under construction on the weather-shack roof was a three-story observation tower. The third-story floor had been installed, and two of the walls were in place. Several sawhorses and racks of lumber lay on the ground near the building.

Last in line was a four-foot-high stand made of thick beams. Mounted on the stand were three antiaircraft guns used for training destroyer-bound seamen. This was a dry training site. There were no shell carts or empty casings strewn on the ground near the guns. A wooden stand had been built behind the gun stations, so an instructor could look down at the pom-pom recruits and yell. A single-strand antenna projected above the stand, connecting the instructor to the target airplane. The double-barrel pom-pom guns were pointed to the night sky in a mute, uniform row.

The German stormtroopers ran in low crouches

249

toward the row of four structures. The terrain was uneven and pockholed, and the grass was knee-high. The year's first snow had melted and refrozen. Ice crystals snapped under their shoes. Flakes of ice caught in von Stihl's socks and melted, freezing his ankles. He yearned for his combat boots instead of his dilapidated hobo's shoes. Graf followed, effortlessly hauling the explosives. Lange lagged behind and stopped every thirty paces to check over his shoulder and listen. Lake Michigan's winter roar drowned all other sound.

Light shone through the security shack's window. It was the southeast-quadrant security chief's headquarters. He would be inside coordinating the evening's patrols. He would be their unwitting time fuse.

Von Stihl did not slow as he approached the window. The waves eliminated any need for stealth. He trotted across the dirt road that connected the four outbuildings to the main base. He tried to control his breathing as he peered through the window into the shack. No one was inside. He wiped condensation from the window and looked again. The security man was not at his post.

"He's making it easy for us," von Stihl said as Graf came alongside. "He's not here. Let's rig the matting. It doesn't matter if he's coming or going. As long as he steps on it."

Graf surveyed the shack's interior through the window, then looked above him. Attached to a corner of the shack were two sirens. Their wiring was tacked onto the hut's plywood exterior and entered the building through a small hole in the wall. There would be a switch inside the hut to throw the sirens.

A thin, peccant smile crossed Graf's face. "Nothing says we blow everything at once, is there? As long as they all go?"

Von Stihl nodded hesitatingly.

"You wire the front step like we planned, but wire only the antiaircraft guns," Graf said, helping the
250

colonel with the pack. "I'm going to make this night even more memorable for our dear security chief."

"You'll guarantee three detonations?" von Stihl asked, trusting Graf's instinct at this type of work.

"You'll wish you could see the security man's face when they blow."

They carried the explosives and backpack to the front step of the shack. Von Stihl could just barely make out Willi Lange's shadow. The Wehrmacht corporal had posted himself sixty yards down the dirt road in the direction from which possible intruders would approach. He crouched in the ditch at the side of the road, vigilant, shivering.

Graf took a small tool kit and a roll of wire from the pack. He twisted the hut's doorknob, and the door opened freely. "Wouldn't you know it?" He laughed. "Probably the only unlocked building on this whole base is the security hut."

As Graf disappeared through the door, von Stihl dug into the backpack to find the matting and another wire roll. Setting the charges should take no more than ten minutes, during which time another patrol would pass the fence. His team would exit the base in the time gap between the next two patrols. He blew on his hands, rubbed them together trying to generate warmth, and unrolled the mat.

Daniel Morgan had made his fortune early in life. Thirty years ago, he and four friends had pooled their inheritances and founded the Chicago Life Indemnity Company. Five years later the company branched out into commercial fire, theft, and liability insurance, products which soon eclipsed their life-insurance sales. Morgan's company adhered to what in those days was an unusual public-relations gimmick—dealing fairly with customers. The word spread. Ten years after the company's founding, Morgan and his friends were millionaires. Morgan rewarded himself and his family with the ultimate symbol of achievement in Chicago, a home on the lake. It took more than a million to afford a waterfront home inside Chicago's city limits, so he settled for a suburban mansion in Lake Forest. His property bordered the Great Lakes Naval Training Center.

One of the inconveniences of waterfront property in Lake Forest was that after Morgan turned off Sheridan Road, he had to traverse almost a mile of unimproved dirt road to reach home. That night, they were returning from Mrs. Potter Palmer's party at which the beginning of the Christmas season for Chicago society was officially declared. Five minutes after the storm-troopers crossed the fence, Mr. and Mrs. Morgan almost collided with the parked bakery van. Mrs. Morgan had indulged excessively and did not notice the car's violent swerve other than to smile even more sweetly and drunkenly.

"Jesus," Morgan yelped as he tromped on the brakes. The car careened to a stop several inches short of an oak tree alongside the dirt road. He quickly looked at his wife, who was still smiling, charming the jockey box.

"Now, what fucking idiot would park a truck on a one-lane dirt road?" Morgan asked angrily as he climbed out of the car. He immediately saw the truck's cab was empty. "And why park it here? We're the only house at the end of the road."

Anger turned to puzzlement. One of the truck's doors was open. It creaked as a gust of wind swung it. Nothing unusual about the cab. Horsehair tufts clung to a spring that stuck through the dilapidated seat cover. As Morgan stepped to the rear to check the truck's panel doors, a word painted on the side caught him as if a hand had grabbed his hair. "'Bakery." He stared at it for five full seconds before its import registered. Daniel Morgan ran back to his car.

John Crown and Everette Smithson leaned against their car, parked at the Glencoe police station. Thirty minutes before, the Chicago police chief had received a relayed phone call from a Glencoe schoolteacher who had been walking his dog on Sheridan Road. The teacher had spotted the bakery truck crossing the suburb's northern city limits. Lieutenant Sullivan and the two agents had sped to Glencoe, but no further sightings had been reported. The Glencoe Police Department was now in on the search. Nothing.

The Great Lakes Naval Training Station had been notified. The station's security chief ordered the three secret submarine-tracking devices surrounded by shore patrolmen. Nothing else on the base had anything but the lowest secrecy priority. The guard at the gates and on perimeter patrols was doubled. No other defense measures were ordered.

Sullivan sprinted from the Glencoe station and dived into his squad car. Crown was already in when the engine jumped to life, but Smithson had barely stuffed himself into the back seat before the car screeched away from the curb.

"One of the millionaires on the North Shore spotted the truck," Sullivan said as he jammed the transmission into second gear. "It's in his driveway, which is a long dirt road right next to the naval station."

"What's there, Everette?" Crown asked.

"Three top-secret buildings," Smithson puffed. "By now they're surrounded by shoulder-to-shoulder sailors. Nothing else of importance." Smithson shrugged his meaty shoulders. "I can't figure out why they'd head there."

"They've gone to a lot of trouble," Crown said. "And they've got a lot of powder with them. So whatever their target is, it'll be blown to shreds."

Erich von Stihl unrolled the mat and placed it on the step in front of the security hut. It was a triggering mechanism Graf had made that afternoon out of odds and ends. The mat had several layers. Topmost was a rubber mat stolen from a front porch. It had "Wel-

253

come" printed on it in raised block letters. Under the rubber was a sheet of wire screen cut from a screen door. A dozen or so thumbtacks were inserted into the screen, with the points sticking down. Next was a quarter-inch-thick piece of cardboard. Below that was another piece of screen, this time with no tacks. The bottom layer was a second piece of cardboard. Electric wire was tied to the top screen, and another strand to the bottom screen. Von Stihl connected one wire to a small battery, which he hid under the step. He began to unroll wires that would connect the welcome mat and battery to the blasting cap implanted in the dynamite. When the mat was stepped on, it would be a completed and very deadly circuit.

Inside the hut, Hans Graf twisted two screws out of the bottom of the telephone and lifted the cover off the mechanism. A phone made a perfect triggering device. Graf dug out two alligator clips from his kit and snapped them onto two screw connections on top of the phone's circuit box. He tucked a small relay box onto the phone chassis and connected the alligator clip wires to it. A phone does not have enough power to throw a switch. The relay box would cure that. He replaced a phone cover and reinserted the cover screws. He taped these relay-box wires to the phone cord, so they were almost impossible to see. He shoved the wires through a floor-level crack at the base of the wall, then placed the phone in the exact position on the desk it had been when he entered the shack.

The siren switch was on the wall next to the desk. It was a simple red-button/black-button box connected to the sirens on the roof. Graf stepped through the shack door, carefully avoiding von Stihl's welcome mat, and closed the door behind him. At the side of the shack, he found the relay-box wires and attached a battery to one of them. The phone trigger was ready.

It took Graf thirty seconds to turn the siren into the third switch by grafting a roll of wire onto the siren wire. With the telephone-wire roll in one hand and the
254

siren roll in another, he backed away from the building, allowing the strands to play out from the unwinding rolls. He followed the welcome-mat wires von Stihl had laid a few minutes before.

When he reached the amphibious-craft garage, Graf dropped one of the rolls and continued backing toward the weather-observation post. At the side of the weather post was the crate of explosives the colonel had left there. With his SS dagger he cut the wire from the roll and split the strand into its two wires. He peeled back an inch of insulation from each, then wrapped the wires around the two prongs of the blasting cap that he had inserted into the paraffin that morning. The bomb was ready. He tucked the package under a floor beam at the side of the weather building.

"Ready?" von Stihl asked. He had placed two packages under the floor of the pom-pom station.

Graf's laugh sounded like the crackling of icicles. "Let's wait to watch this."

"Five minutes after they go off, there'll be more sailors swarming over this place than there are in the North Sea Fleet. We can't risk it. Let's wire the garage and get away from here."

The last paraffin container was wired and placed inside an open window of the garage. Von Stihl whistled for Lange. The three stormtroopers began retracing their steps to the perimeter fence. The next patrol was due in three minutes, not long enough to construct the arch, so they would wait in the tall grass north of the fence.

Chief Petty Officer Bud Holz didn't envy his counterpart in charge of the sub-tracking trainers. They would be overworked and overwrought that night. Christ. A saboteur alert. The first real one in the naval training center's history. The rear admiral had doubled the perimeter patrols and stationed two armed jeeps at each of the gates. The CPO guarding the sub trackers had roused all his men to stand watch. Three shifts of angry shore patrolmen and a half-dozen yawning German shepherds patrolled the northwest quadrangle, where the secret equipment was located.

Holz's jeep growled down the dirt road toward his security headquarters. Despite the wool gloves, his hands seemed frozen to the steering wheel. His southeast quadrant was a sleeper. It was bordered on the north by a small creek and on the east by the lake. It contained numerous training facilities, but nothing that would make a likely target. The saboteurs were going after something big, concluded the rear admiral at the emergency briefing a few minutes before. He couldn't imagine what it was, and neither could Holz. Probably a false alarm from the nutso Chicago cops. But then, that truck hijacking this morning that was splashed all over the papers was real enough. The hoods had gone loco. Holz would never understand it. He pumped the jeep's accelerator, and the four-wheeler jumped forward, spewing gravel behind it.

Gunning the jeep down the short dirt road to the shack was the only action Holz got in the navy since he had been withdrawn from fleet duty. He had been on the deck of the *Arizona* almost a year before, when a Japanese bomb tore into the foredeck and blew out his right eardrum. For some reason he failed to understand, the navy considered the injury sufficient to disqualify him from Pacific duty. He loathed stateside assignments, particularly this, guarding several desolate acres of Lake Michigan shoreline.

The jeep slid to a stop in front of the security hut. Holz flipped the headlights and ignition off, then stared balefully at the shack. What an asshole job. An idiot could coordinate perimeter patrols. He spent most of his time in the shack reading or playing cards with shore patrolmen. Holz climbed out of the jeep and mockingly saluted each of his charges, the pom-pom trainer, the weather station, and the garage. He walked to the shack, wondering what variation of solitaire he would play that night. He knew every one ever invent-

256

ed. At least he had an electric heater in the shack, unlike the poor schmucks at the front gates. They would freeze their tails off tonight.

CPO Bud Holz would testify at the navy inquiry that he never saw the welcome mat. He stepped up to the shack door as he had done a hundred times before, but this time his foot pressed the thumbtacks through the layer of cardboard and into contact with the lower screen, completing the circuit. The antiaircraft trainer exploded with a horrendous roar. Holz dived onto the shack floor, a response learned the hard way last December. Bits of wood blew by the shack door, and the pressure of the explosion slammed it shut. Windows rattled fiercely. Splintered beams and twisted metal shards landed heavily on the security hut's roof. Then Holz could hear nothing else over the waves.

He rose to his feet and stupidly tapped his right ear. The *Arizona* explosion blew the eardrum out. Maybe this one fixed it. No such luck. He quickly scanned his hut. No damage. He opened the shack door and stepped outside. The remains of the pom-pom trainer were on fire. Wind rushing in from Lake Michigan fanned the flames out over the dirt road. Jesus, he thought, if it hadn't been for the two buildings in between, I would've bought it.

The rear admiral's warning came back to Holz. He shook his head to clear it. Could it be the saboteurs? What else? A pom-pom doesn't explode on its own volition. Holy shit. Real saboteurs in his southeast quadrant. He ran back into the hut and stopped in front of his desk. What's the fucking procedure? He held his hands in front of him like a wrestler about to meet his opponent, and spastically wiggled his fingers as adrenaline energy built inside him. The procedure. His eyes fell on the siren button. "Local breach requires local alert first," flashed from memory. He punched the red siren button.

A ferocious explosion tore the weather post from its foundations and hurled it over the embankment, where it rolled in a flaming ball to the beach. The blast blew out the security hut's windows and threw Holz onto his desk. Booming thunder stung his brain. His hand was numb, speckled with glass chips from the window. He could hear nothing but a dull ringing deep in his head. He forced air into his lungs. It smelled of cordite and fear. Holz rolled off the desk and stood on weak knees. Tiny crystals of glass dug into the CPO's palm as he tried to brace himself against the desk. His hand jerked back from the glass slivers and brushed the phone. Only then was Holz reminded of his duty: warn the base. With his uninjured hand he lifted the phone receiver.

Holz's head seemed to erupt with pressure as the amphibious-craft garage was torn apart by the last bomb. The north wall of the security hut ripped from its frame and flew across the room, sweeping the heater, the desk, and Holz into the far wall. The thin plywood had no noticeable braking effect. Holz smashed through it and landed in the dirt ten feet from the remains of his shack.

He lay on his back without moving, afraid to try. He thought he was conscious. The ringing in his head was gone. Now there was no sound, no waves. A sharp pain in his mouth, and the taste of blood. He had bitten clear through his tongue. His eyes opened. The sky was red from the fires. He coughed. Bits of lung whooped up into his mouth. Bile mixed with blood, and he wanted to vomit. He gagged, rolled onto his stomach, and spit onto the dirt. His chest felt as if airplane cable was wrapped tightly around it, squeezing and suffocating him. He struggled to his knees. Consciousness began to seep from him, so he spread his hands to avoid toppling. He focused on staying awake and concentrated on the ticking.

It wasn't ticking. It was the crackling of the fires. Holz could hear. Elation welled within him. There were no more buildings to blow. They'd gotten them all, but they hadn't gotten his good ear. He croaked a
258

laugh, but choked it back when blood from his tongue splashed to the ground.

It took Holz sixty seconds to rise to his feet. The back of his head pounded rhythmically. He stumbled past the wreckage of his hut, which was illuminated by the fires rapidly consuming the remains of the other buildings. Fighting numbness in all his limbs, Holz crawled into his jeep.

Hans Graf would have laughed at the sound of the explosions had it not been for the extra perimeter patrol.

"I thought you said they came around every fifteen minutes, Lange," Graf whispered. The three storm-troopers were kneeling in tall grass north of the fence. An unexpected team of shore patrolmen was walking in and out of the dim fence-post lights along the perimeter.

"It was every fifteen minutes, Colonel," Lange responded, ignoring Graf. "Now it's every seven or eight."

"It means we were discovered before the explosions," von Stihl said quietly. "They wouldn't have had time to set up the extra patrols, otherwise. Someone saw the truck." He scanned the distance between them and the fence. It looked immeasurably more formidable than when they had come in. "We'll have to break for it. Same setup formation. Lange, you go over first and cover us."

They waited in the grass. Von Stihl shivered uncontrollably. Lange nervously flicked the bolt on his Schmeisser. Now the shore patrolmen were alert, searching the grass and woods with their eyes. They had been briefed and had just heard the series of explosions. This SP's rifle was in his hands, not slung over his shoulder. The dog sensed his master's urgency and kept his nose to the frozen ground. The patrol disappeared down the line of lights.

Von Stihl was about to sprint for the fence when he

259

heard the low rumble of a jeep in first gear approaching from the east. He quickly ducked back down into the grass.

"They've called in the cavalry," Graf said.

The jeep had a thirty-caliber machine gun mounted behind the front seat. An angry SP crouched behind it, gripping the firing handle, looking for something to blow away. The jeep prowled down the fence and vanished in the darkness.

Von Stihl rose to his knees and checked the fence line. He could see no other patrols. "Let's go."

The Germans left their blind at a dead run. Graf scooped up the ladders as they passed. Navy guards would be in sight in two or three minutes.

The escape arch was erected even faster than when they had come in. While von Stihl surveyed the fence line, Lange hustled up and over the ladders. He jumped to the ground and dashed for the cover of the woods. He posted himself between two elms and looked back as von Stihl climbed over the arch. No patrols were in sight. Nor could he hear a jeep's engine. As von Stihl raced to the forest edge, Hans Graf began the ladder climb.

Lieutenant Michael Sullivan was pulled through the woods by the instincts of an Irish setter after a duck. He and the agents had heard the explosions a half-mile back. Smithson had remained at the bakery van with his pistol drawn. Sullivan and Crown lurched through the Stygian woods, stumbling over exposed roots and vines. Crown could barely see Sullivan's back as they high-stepped over the treacherous ground. The cop was puffing hard. His pistol was drawn, and he was begging for a fight. Crown hoped they weren't the first to find the stormtroopers. Sullivan and he were carrying popguns compared to the Germans' weapons. A fire fight would be short and predictable. Crown saw the flickering light of a fence post through the thick bank of trees.

Sullivan clawed through a thorny bush to the edge of

260

the fence clearing just as Graf reached the apex of the ladder arch. They saw each other at the same instant. Precariously perched atop the ladders, Graf raised his submachine gun, but was too late. Sullivan fired three times. Graf's fingers convulsed around the Schmeisser's trigger, and it spat out an aimless stream of bullets into the ground. He toppled forward into the barbed wire. His arms caught and twisted in the wire as he somersaulted down and away. The huge body almost reached the ground before it was snapped back by the tension of the barbed wire. Graf's feet swung two feet above the ground, with his arms entangled above him. His legs spasmed several times and then relaxed as Hans Graf died.

John Crown acted without thinking. He yanked Sullivan by the collar back into the woods just as Willi Lange jumped two steps into the clearing thirty yards west of them. The German fired, but the bullets careened harmlessly off trees. His targets had disappeared into the undergrowth. As the echoes of the Schmeisser blast died, von Stihl heard the jeep again. It was rushing toward them along the fence line. From the other direction, two sentries and their dog sprinted toward Graf's body.

"Through the woods, Lange," von Stihl yelled, already plummeting into the protective darkness of the timber.

Crown and Sullivan struggled back to the dirt road. Smithson was behind the car, with his pistol aimed at the woods over the hood. He jerked it toward Crown as he emerged from the trees.

"Christ, it sounds like a war in there."

"It is," Crown answered as he joined Smithson behind the car. "They'll be coming out this way. They're outgunned by the shore patrol behind them."

Sullivan produced a shotgun from the trunk of his car. He crouched behind the bakery van. From the woods came the sound of a fire fight. Several short bursts were followed by a deeper, more ferocious

261

pounding of the navy's .30-caliber. A single shot echoed in the forest. The .30-caliber answered.

Crown turned to the hoarse drone of an approaching navy jeep. It, too, had a mounted automatic weapon on its flank. It parked near the van, and the SP swung the barrel toward the trees. Crown felt as if he had captured his chess opponent's queen. The men inside the woods were trapped. They would be defeated by the only strategy they understood—hard blows with heavy weaponry.

For an instant Crown thought the dark object flying at him was a bat. He ducked, and it bounced off the car. A Luger. From inside the woods came an accentless voice: "We surrender. We're coming out."

Sullivan yelled from the van, "The little one's got a submachine gun, Crown."

That and a lot of gall if they believe I'll buy the surrender story, Crown thought. Men this ferocious don't surrender so easily.

A Schmeisser tumbled through the air and landed in the dirt at Crown's feet. Again from the woods: "There's two of us. One's injured. I'll be helping him out."

Leaves rustled directly in front of Crown. Out of the corner of his eye he saw Sullivan's shotgun raise as he zeroed in on the sound.

"Sullivan," Crown yelled, "they come out of there alive. Lower your shotgun."

"Fuck you, Crown. You know what I said about prisoners."

With a menace Crown believed him incapable of, Smithson growled, "They die, you die." The fat agent raised his pistol to cover Sullivan.

Willi Lange staggered from the woods onto the dirt road. He was holding Erich von Stihl around the waist. Blood poured from a gash on the colonel's head. His eyes were vacant, and he stumbled, almost bringing the slight Lange to his knees with the weight.

"We surrender," Lange yelled again. He raised one
262

hand above his head. He was quickly surrounded by the jeep's shore patrolmen, who violently searched him and von Stihl, oblivious of the colonel's wound. They were shoved against the car. The colonel slumped to the ground. Lange thrust both his hands above his head.

These can't be stormtroopers, Crown thought. They were bums. The little one, the one who was supposed to be so dangerous with a submachine gun, was the dregs of the earth. His clothes were worn and filthy. He was unshaven, and twigs and bits of leaves clung to his tousled hair. The blond with blood running down his face was no cleaner. His pants had been torn at the knee. One shoe was missing. The blond groaned and sputtered blood as it seeped into his mouth. Crown was disappointed. He had unrealistically been expecting men with polished jackboots and Nazi regalia pinned on their uniforms, not hobos.

"Well," Everette Smithson said as he pushed his gun into his pants, "we got them alive. Where should we put them?"

"It doesn't matter. Maybe the navy has a stockade." Crown looked at Sullivan, who was fuming behind the steering wheel of his squad car. "We can't let Sullivan or any other cops have them if we want to interrogate them, though."

Smithson looked around to make sure they were out of hearing range of the others. "Why not hold them at the EDC house? We've got another bedroom there that's as secure as the one Hess is in. Plus, we've got the best interrogator in the world there. Professor Ludendorf. If he can't find out why these guys are here, no one can."

It made sense. If the saboteurs were somehow connected with Hess's presence in Chicago, as the Priest suspected, then the sooner Ludendorf found out their motive, the safer Hess would be. Plus, the EDC house was guarded so heavily that, even if their mission was to kill Hess, there would be no way for

them to reach the deputy führer, even though he was
two bedrooms away.

"All right," Crown said.

"I'll talk to the base commander. He'll turn them
over to us."

Crown nodded. He already had a mental list of
questions he wanted Professor Ludendorf to ask the
saboteurs. Why did they go to so much trouble to get
to a training center? How did they get into the
country? Why didn't they bring their own explosives
with them, rather than risk hijacking a truck? Above
all, how are these Germans connected with Rudolf
Hess?

XVI

The phone booth was cramped, and like most men, John Crown couldn't sit comfortably. It was the telephone company's way of keeping conversations short. His knee banged against the folding door, and he muttered an expletive summarizing his feelings for the phone company.

"Pardon me?" Richard Sackville-West said from Washington, D.C.

"Nothing. I'm trying to close the door here."

"How're you holding up under the long gun?"

"Fine. I use a bathroom every thirty minutes, but other than that, just fine."

"You've been keeping busy. That should help," Sackville-West suggested.

"I guess it has. I hardly thought about it when we were trailing those stormtroopers. I was always surrounded by cops, so I wasn't an easy target. But now I'm back to the routine of taking Hess to these interrogation sessions and escorting Heather around at night."

"That doesn't sound that bad, particularly the evenings with your British girlfriend." The Priest laughed softly.

"Sure. Knowing that any minute some pro is going to launch a bullet at me is a lot of fun."

"When are you going to set it up?"

"Later today. It'll be the first time since they began looking for me that I won't be surrounded by cops or passersby. Heather knows our plans, so the assassin does, too. He'll strike this afternoon."

"You'll be ready?" A redundant question. Sackville-West could almost hear his agent's chilly smile over the phone.

"I'll be ready."

"What about the German stormtroopers you caught?"

"None of that makes any sense," Crown replied. "First, look at their caliber. I first heard about Erich von Stihl in 1939 when our intelligence pegged him as second-in-command of the German force that dressed in Polish Army uniforms and then assaulted the German radio station, giving Hitler an excuse to invade Poland."

"It was callous, but well executed," Sackville-West said.

" 'Callous,' for Christ's sake. 'Murder' is a better word."

"A little jumpy, aren't you?"

Without answering, Crown looked through the long panes of glass in the booth door to the uniformed guard leaning against the Metallurgical Lab's hallway wall. He wore sergeant's stripes and a crew cut. Crown turned away from him and said, "We also know he led the first assault on the Athens airport that wiped out the RAF in Greece."

"That we do."

"His unit didn't suffer a single casualty in the raid. That's all I know about him."

"He also spent several months training stormtroopers for Operation Sea Lion, the invasion of England, which Hitler abandoned in October 1940," Sackville-West added.

"So von Stihl is a legend that all young German stormtroopers emulate. His reputation is deserved. Apparently he's a brilliant special-task operative." Crown paused to look at the booth ceiling for a vent. There was none. It was stifling with the door closed. Rivulets of sweat were running down his back. "Did you have anything on the Wehrmacht corporal, Willi Lange?"

"No. Neither do the British."

"Well, I figure he's also very talented. Small weapons, especially the submachine gun," Crown said. "He did a couple unbelievable and very deadly stunts with his Schmeisser before we caught him."

"What about the one who was killed?"

"We don't know his name yet. From the tattoo under his arm, he's an SS member. He was huge, six-feet-five, two hundred and forty pounds. Our doctor says he was in remarkable physical shape. All his muscles were striated. No cavities in his teeth. He had a bad scar under his right ear, and, interestingly, calluses on his knucles."

"Like a bare-knuckle boxer."

"Who knows, but you can be sure he was also a specialist, probably something physical, like silent killing. So we have a team of highly talented German commandos. Another puzzling fact is that they went to a lot of trouble to get here. We know this because they left no trace of their travels. It's difficult and expensive for three people to enter this country and cross a thousand miles of it invisibly. Then, after going to all the effort to move secretly, when they got to Chicago they hijacked the dynamite truck, which splashed them all over the front pages. I can't figure out why they went to so much trouble to remain invisible, then do something so bloody it was guaranteed to make the newspapers across the country. It doesn't make sense."

"And there's the question of the explosives."

"Right. There're a lot of easier ways to steal dynamite than the way they did it. They could've broken into a warehouse or into the powder company's storage buildings. Or they could have brought it into the country with them. So why did they hijack the truck? It wasn't necessary."

"The big question," Sackville-West said, and Crown

could hear him puffing on his pipe as he lit it, "is, why did they hit the navy training center?"

"I've no idea. Neither does Smithson, and he knows all about that base. Three bombs were used, one on an antiaircraft trainer, one on a weather station, and one on an amphibious-craft garage. The third bomb also blew down the security shack. They were destroyed, all right, but why? I can't imagine buildings with less strategic importance. So we have three top commandos going to great lengths to destroy worthless targets."

"Perhaps their intelligence concerning the buildings was wrong."

"That's unlikely. Almost anyone could find out what those buildings were, much less the German Abwehr. Hell, they probably have the whole base plotted to the last inch. But even if the commandos' information was wrong, the buildings spoke for themselves. What they were should have been obvious. They were blown up anyway. Then, there's one last question, the problem of the missing dynamite."

"What?" Crown had caught Sackville-West off guard. The Priest's voice was tinny and distant as he said, "What about the dynamite?"

"They stole three hundred and twenty pounds of it. Yet, our expert says only about half that was used at the navy station. We haven't found the remaining crate of explosives."

There was silence from Washington.

"Where do you think it is?" the Priest finally asked in a voice so dry it blended with the long-distance static.

"The Chicago police are looking for it."

"Wonderful."

"Maybe the Germans simply stole too much of it and then found they needed only half what they stole."

"In light of the caliber of the men involved, does that sound too likely?" Sackville-West asked, his voice no less irritated.

"No. So they have a use for the rest of it."

"Probably. Perhaps a long-fuse bomb already planted somewhere."

"No," Crown answered. "It's easy to fuse a bomb up to twelve hours. Any longer is risky. I think there's someone we haven't caught yet. Maybe another commando."

"Which brings us to your problem," Sackville-West said. "I still say those commandos are in Chicago because Hess is there. I don't know how they know, or why they've come. But it's just too coincidental that these bizarre events are occurring at the same time Hess is there."

"And you think I'm under the long gun because Hess is here?"

"Yes."

"So Hess, the commandos, and my potential assassin are on a common mission?"

"Not the same mission, necessarily, but they've got something to do with each other. That's the only explanation that makes sense."

"I'm going to find out some answers this afternoon."

"From the assassin?" Sackville-West asked.

"As I said, he'll come. And he'll live just long enough to tell me a few things."

"John, the odds against you increase drastically if you insist on that conversation."

"Do you have any better ideas how to break this open?"

"As long as it's you, not me, no. Are you going to need backup?"

"No."

"I have a hunch if Miguel Maura was alive, you'd want a backup man. Why not use Smithson?"

"Well, despite my previous opinion of him, he handled himself well against that Chicago cop who was going to shotgun the Germans. But no, I can handle this alone."

"In other words, you don't particularly want anyone

to see your tormentor's fate." Sackville-West's laugh was brittle and cold.

The guard outside the phone booth reached for his holster and unbuttoned the cover snap. Crown's pistol was out of his belt and pointed at the guard through the glass before Crown realized snapping the flap was the guard's nervous habit. The guard's eyebrows shot up, and he backed into the wall when he saw the gun's snout aimed at his stomach. Crown shook his head, and the guard raised his hand away from the holster. He stood frozen as Crown continued the conversation.

"Getting back to the German commandos. We're pretty sure the Nazis want Hess dead because they're afraid he'll do exactly what he's doing this minute with Professor Fermi—talk his brains out. Perhaps the commandos came to get rid of Hess."

"How did they know he was in Chicago?" the Priest asked.

"No idea."

"And if that was their purpose, why did they go to the trouble of the hijacking and the explosions?"

"Maybe to get our attention," Crown said. "Perhaps they're halfway to their objective. We're keeping von Stihl and Lange at the EDC house only a few yards from Hess. Professor Ludendorf is questioning them. Von Stihl has a bad concussion from a bullet crease, and he's not very coherent."

"From what I understand, they might just as well be a continent away."

"That's right," Crown said, still pointing his pistol at the guard. "The house is guarded so heavily, nothing could happen. Plus, they're chained hand and foot to their beds. They've got a little room to move, but not enough to cause any trouble. They'll stay that way until Hess goes back to London."

"When'll that be?"

"Fermi has been talking to him for about an hour every morning. He's doing that right now down the hallway. Even with Professor Ludendorf and Peter

Kohler's help, it's a slow process. Hess's mind fades in and out. Hess's information is interesting, but not exactly earth-shaking. Fermi is convinced Hess knows more, and that's why he doesn't object to talking to Hess, even though the time of his experiment is close."

"When?"

"He told me he was going to try it this afternoon. That's why he's so impatient and excited during the interview this morning. He keeps looking in the direction of the squash court as if he could see the pile through the walls."

"If the experiment is successful, it'll be one of the greatest achievements in human history. I can't blame him for being excited," Sackville-West said.

"No, neither can I. Well, I'll get back to the interview. This is the sixth time Fermi has questioned Hess. The strain on all of us is beginning to show. I'm glad Ludendorf and Kohler handle Hess so well. I wouldn't have the persistence."

"One last thing, John." Crown knew the voice. The Priest saved the hard questions for last, and this was it. "I trust you have your plans regarding Heather McMillian worked out?"

Crown couldn't answer. After several seconds, the Priest continued, "You know our policy. You have a little discretion, but not much. This matter won't ever be released to the press, so she won't get a trial." Sackville-West again paused for Crown's response. Again there was none, so he added, "I can send another operative to Chicago to relieve you of that responsibility, if you want."

"No. No, that won't be necessary."

Heather's time was coming. His actions were to be automatic. And terminal. It was standard procedure. Following the books.

She had made massive inroads on his better sense. Crown had tried to insulate himself so his emotions wouldn't get the upper hand. As he sat sweating in the suffocating booth, he knew he had failed. The hard line

271

between work and play had blurred. He could no longer think of Heather as a tool used to trap an assassin. Yet that's what she was. A disposable tool.

She was tracing Crown. Heather was a shadow whose job was easy. She didn't have to wait in freezing Chicago sleet outside a building for hours while her mark was inside, or follow him through city traffic, or run up six flights of stairs while he rode an elevator. She was what the trade called a grace shadow, one who was in the good graces of the mark. She accompanied him openly and constantly. All she had to do was to occasionally report to her employers, which Crown had seen her do three times in the past week.

She was a traitor, and he was in love with her. Christ, what a spot. He had postponed coming to a resolution. He thought about her constantly, but had avoided the decision. The choice would soon be upon him. But there wasn't a choice. She was bought by Miguel Maura's killers. She was a paid informer, and she could have only one fate. As he sat in the tiny booth, Crown became so angry at his predicament that he unconsciously cocked the Smith and Wesson. The guard outside the phone booth went up on his tiptoes against the wall and raised his shaking hands even farther.

"Does Fermi give any indication when he'll be done with Hess?" Sackville-West's voice snapped Crown's thoughts back to the booth.

"No," Crown replied, and continued rapidly as if to compensate for the unknown amount of time he had been lost in his reverie. "The bomber crew is out at Midway, and they're ready to go on a few minutes' notice."

"Good luck this afternoon, then."

The telephone was heavy in Crown's hand as he lifted it to the hook. He felt as if he had spent thirty minutes in a sauna, and he slumped against the phone-booth wall, overwhelmed with fatigue and resignation. The effects of his long-gun vigil mingled
272

with an immense sadness, and he was enervated. He wanted to walk away from the business, go back to Oregon and become a harbormaster. Leave Hess and Fermi and, most of all, leave Heather, leave her alive. . . . Without completing the thought, he pushed himself up and shoved open the booth door. He was surprised to find the guard backed up against the wall across from the booth with his hands in the air.

"Something wrong?" Crown asked.

"Jesus," the guard blurted without lowering his hands, "you've held a cocked pistol on me for ten minutes."

Crown noticed his pistol for the first time since he had drawn it. He slipped it back into his pants and muttered an apology as he walked past the guard to the interview room.

Crown entered the conference room without interrupting Hess, who was lecturing on the National Socialist Workers' system.

"You see, it's a centralized government, with all important decisions made at the top, at the Führer's office. That's why we could proceed so rapidly with the experiments." Hess gestured grandly and leaned back in his chair. "We don't have ten levels of decision-making to hinder progress. We can—"

"If we can return to the question, Herr Hess," Enrico Fermi said, without looking up from his pad, where he was either calculating the future of the U.S. atom-bomb experiments or doodling. Crown couldn't tell which. "You said a moment ago that Professor Bothe concluded that graphite was not a suitable moderator for uranium reactors. When did he figure this out?"

"In January 1941," Hess answered, with his hands now calmly on the table, his lecture abruptly halted.

"Do you remember his calculations?"

"He used a 110-centimeter sphere of electrographite of the highest purity, but the diffusion length was not

273

seventy as expected, but only thirty-five centimeters. So he concluded that unless uranium 235 could be enriched, graphite could not be used as a pile moderator." Hess's voice was not lifeless as he revealed the secrets of the German experiments. He seemed to have switched his mind onto automatic, perhaps to avoid thinking of the consequences of his traitorous revelations.

Fermi regularly glanced at the wall clock as the questions and answers continued. He fidgeted in his chair and rhythmically tapped his pencil against an unused ashtray. He clearly wished he was elsewhere today. Crown wasn't sure Fermi was listening. The physicist's thoughts were across the street under the grandstand, where, if his years of calculations were correct, the first self-sustained nuclear reaction would take place that afternoon. Small wonder Fermi was not concentrating on the wandering deputy führer.

Heather started their little game. She looked up to catch Crown's eye. He looked away, and continued to avoid her stare for a few minutes, until with apparent complete collapse of willpower he met her eyes, and she smiled. Only Hess seemed to notice their childish game. He raised his hand and majestically swept the air in a unifying gesture, as if he had the power to marry them on the spot. He smiled benignly to give official Third Reich approval to their conjunction.

"Quit screwing around, Hess." Peter Kohler's hard voice jerked Hess upright in his chair. Kohler was Hess's constant reminder that harsher tactics were available if information was not forthcoming. But in days past, not even Kohler had been able to prevent Hess's mind from straying and receding after an hour or so of questions. Nothing, not entreaties, threats, promises, could stop him from slipping out of control. So the sessions had been concentrated efforts to drain his head of scientific data. It came in spurts. For five or six minutes, Hess would flow free with hard information that would keep Heather, Ludendorf, and Fermi

274

filling page after page. Then he would fade into pompous pronouncements about the German political system or Lebensraum, Nazi expanisonism. The sessions ended when Hess could no longer talk because of amnesia or stomach cramps. After each interrogation, Fermi had said that although he had learned more about the German experiments, he still felt Hess was not telling all he knew. So another session would be scheduled for the following day.

Professor Ludendorf and Peter Kohler proved themselves masters at soft interrogation. They managed to keep Hess on track for perhaps thirty minutes of each session. Ludendorf would lead the discussion and pamper Hess's ego, while Kohler threatened Hess if he balked. It was like prying open a brittle box. If too much pressure was exerted, the box would splinter. If insufficient pressure was used, it would never open. It was a precarious balancing act on the thin line between Hess's sane ego and his weak-minded retreats.

Long months of invaluable service to the Allies had taught Ludendorf and Kohler when to push and when to indulge in whims. They guided Hess through the conversation expertly, treating him like the fragile package he was. It was an endless give-and-take, a sparring match between the flamboyant and disturbed deputy führer and the meticulous, kindly professor and his impatient, angry assistant. It produced results. The Allies had gained vital insights into the German heavy-water and cyclotron experiments.

The sessions bored Crown to the verge of sleep. He felt like he was eight years old sitting in Sunday school listening to a nonsensical speech on being born again through faith. His butt ached, and he squirmed in his chair. Heather was his only distraction during the sessions, a burdensome one at that.

"I forget. I really do," Hess whined.

Crown stopped popping his elbow and perked up at the words. It meant the questions were about over as Hess's amnesia ended the session.

"Come on, Hess. You do this every day, and every day I don't believe you," Peter Kohler said, his voice low with menace.

"I'm telling you, I can't remember some things. My mind isn't as sharp as it once was. I can't remember." Hess's voice assumed a high, quavering pitch. "I'd tell you if I could."

"Well," said Enrico Fermi, already out of his seat and gathering his notes, "we might as well end the session. We won't get anything more today."

As usual, Fermi beckoned Crown to stay a few minutes to discuss progress. It was the only part of the sessions Crown enjoyed. Fermi was a visionary, a futurist. Their post-session discussions had on several occasions turned to Fermi's view of the future, a future aided by nuclear fission. Fermi was an optimist, a believer in man's ability to use science to better his condition. Applied science was his key to the future. Crown left these discussions feeling strangely elated.

The conference door closed, leaving Fermi and Crown alone.

"You weren't anxious to prolong the meeting today," Crown said as he poured water from a pitcher.

Fermi smiled. "With good reason. The graphite pile is completed. We'll be pulling the rod from the pile this afternoon."

"Do you ever worry that in all your figures and theories, you've made one little mistake somewhere that, although it doesn't look like much, simply means your theory is wrong and you won't have a sustained reaction? All you'll have is a big pile of pencil filling."

"That would be like you going into action with one of your pistol chambers empty. I doubt that happens often." Fermi laughed in his soft, catching way. "I think the theory is sound. This afternoon will be the proof."

"Can I supply a bottle of wine for the celebration?" Crown asked.

"We've got a case of wine already. Italian wine.

There's going to be a dozen scientists, and another dozen technicians and engineers over there. If the experiment's a success, the wine won't last long. We've been working on this for a year, and we've developed a big thirst."

"On your other front, how do you think the interview went today?" Crown asked.

"We found out something incredible today, which you may not have caught, with your attention diverted like it was."

Crown's ears warmed. "It's that obvious?" he asked.

"You don't have to be Italian to notice the electricity shooting across the table between you and Miss McMillan. If my experiment fails, it'll be because of all the charged particles streaming from this room. Even that dolt Hess notices it. I think he fancies himself the matchmaker."

"That's embarrassing as hell."

Fermi's wonderful laugh filled the room again. "Well, back to the new discovery. Remember Hess saying that a German professor has decided that pure graphite cannot be used as a moderator in a pile?"

"I remember something like that."

"Quite simply, that professor is wrong. I'm using graphite this afternoon. That's what that huge pile is in the squash court, as you know. Graphite is the perfect moderator. My tests show that. The German scientists have made a costly mistake."

"Why costly?" Crown asked, sipping the water.

"Because if they don't use graphite, they'll probably have to use heavy water, and lots of it. It's a much harder substance to come by. It means that because of a mistake in their calculations, the Germans have been thrown off the trail. That mistake might cost them a year or two."

"So you think they're behind in the bomb race?"

"Far behind. I'll send off a report to your boss tonight, after our experiment. There will be a few sighs of relief when they hear."

Crown slipped into his overcoat as Fermi said, "You're welcome to watch our experiment this afternoon. Probably at three or four o'clock. History in the making, as they say."

"Thanks, Doctor, but I've got other plans. A private organ concert that promises to be interesting."

"More so than splitting atoms?" Fermi asked as he closed his briefcase.

"The side show will be, believe me. Good luck, Doctor."

After Hess was locked in his cell, Crown met Heather in front of the EDC house. Because of the guards in the house and on the street, it was one of the few places Crown could relax. They stood enjoying the cold. She played with a button on his overcoat, and he laughed at her imitation of Hess. She blushed when Crown told her of Fermi's observation of electricity in the conference room. She asked how long Fermi would need Hess, meaning how long she would be able to stay in Chicago with him. He didn't know. He waited until a group of five or six students passed them going his way. He and Heather walked a few paces behind them toward Rockefeller Chapel. The students were his shield.

"What are we seeing at the chapel?" she asked as she reached for his hand.

"Bach's Christmas Oratorio. As I said yesterday, it's only the organ rehearsal. The choir and solo vocalists won't be there."

"Why not wait for the performance?"

"We might not be here then. It's two weeks from now. And I hate the coughing and rustling and whispering that goes on when there's an audience. This way I get my favorite part of it without the extra noise. There'll be only three people in the entire cathedral—you, me, and the organist."

"I didn't know you were such an organ buff."

278

"Sure. My parents had an old Cornish pump organ. I got pretty good at it, too."

"Do you still play?"

"No," Crown replied, picking up the pace to stay with the clot of students. "The choice was organ or football, so there wasn't any choice. Now I couldn't play a chord progression, but I still enjoy cathedral organ music."

They walked along Kimbark to Fifty-ninth Street and then west toward the chapel. Fortunately the students were headed the same way. Crown's eyes darted from tree trunk to shrub to passing car. After almost a week, the vigilance was automatic. He walked with one hand around Heather's and the other discreetly on the stock of his pistol. Perhaps he was being overly cautious. The assassin would not strike on the street, with all the witnesses. He would wait for the first time Crown would be alone in over a week. That is, alone with Heather, the assassin's accomplice. That time would be in a few minutes inside the chapel.

Rockefeller Chapel had been named after the university's largest benefactor, John D. Rockefeller, who over the course of thirty years had contributed over thirty million dollars to the school. The trustees wanted his chapel to reflect his past and hopefully future generosity. It was as tall as a seventeen-story building, and like the great cathedrals of Europe, was constructed entirely of masonry without steel support. Immense exterior buttresses flanked the arched double doorways facing Fifty-ninth Street. The gray stone reminded Crown of a fortress rather than a church.

As they approached the doors, the carillon in the tower played Wagner's Parsifal tune—the Dresden "Amen"—and then the Great Bourdon, the 40,000-pound brass bell, sounded twice for the hour. They could feel the waves of bass sound pass through them as they stood before the cathedral.

Heather pointed to the gargoyles above the panel

279

windows high on the front facade. "They're less fierce than the others around campus."

"Sure. You wouldn't want a demon on a cathedral. The one right above the doors is the archangel Michael. I don't know who the others higher up are. Maybe Rockefellers."

Heather laughed lightly and took his arm as they passed through the doors into the nave. The ceiling vaults loomed in the shadows a hundred feet over their heads. Through the ribbed arches on both sides of the nave were the side aisles. Above the arches were the long windows rising to the masonry webs near the ceiling. A row of pews extended the length of the nave. Two ornate pulpits rose from the floor near the far end. An exquisitely carved front piece separated the apse from the ambulatory at the tip of the cathedral. The north wall consisted of glass panels that allowed the nave modest illumination from the overcast sky.

Above the east pulpit, hanging like chrome stalactites, were the enormous pipes of the cathedral's Skinner organ. Lined in even rows against the wall were the smaller pipes, which at a distance looked like a row of silver needles on black cloth. The large bass pipes hung in two enormous open cylinders attached to the wall. The rehearsal had begun, and the pipes filled the cathedral with soaring billows of sound, the mystical, inspiring swells of the Oratorio, Bach's Christmas gift to Germany.

Crown guided Heather to the spiral staircase that led to the choir gallery above the entrance to the cathedral. The stone staircase was not much wider than Crown's shoulders, and was very steep. Heather gripped the handrail as they wound up the stairs. They stepped through the narrow doorway into the gallery, walked to the banister, and sat in the front pew overlooking the nave. Behind them were the gallery organ pipes rising from a cabinet in back of the last pew. The tallest pipes were near the gallery wall, and as the row neared
280

the center of the gallery, each pipe was fractionally shorter, forming a graceful inverted silver arch.

Heather asked where the organist was, and Crown pointed to the west apse behind the crossing. He said the organ was so complicated it looked like the instrument panel on an airplane.

Not, of course, to Michael Graham, the renowned organist who would accompany the orchestra and choir during the Oratorio. Graham was a master of the four-manual, thirty-six-rank organ and was known as the Organ Lion. He had been guest soloist at all the nation's major theaters and churches, including the Chapel of the Intercession in New York and the New York Paramount Theater, which housed the finest studio organ ever built. Graham was a perfectionist who demanded the utmost from the organs he played. He was known to adjust an organ for a full hour before playing the first bar. He had already done his regulating on the Rockefeller Chapel organ, and he now sat in his cockpit engulfed in the organ's resonant tones. He was unaware of his audience of two.

Heather reached for his hand, but Crown didn't respond. He seemed lost in the music, which streamed into the gallery from the pulpit pipes, to mix with the tenor pipes behind them. She playfully squeezed his hand and again received no response. His eyes were narrowed in concentration, and Heather detected something she had never seen before, a dangerous iron glint. His jaw was tight, and his cheeks were sucked in with mental effort. She absently touched his arm. It was flexed hard. She wondered if there was something to Bach's Oratorio she was missing.

The assassin entered the cathedral's south door five minutes behind them. He wore a brown trench coat and rubber-soled shoes, and he carried a Luger, which had a black silencer attached to its barrel. He stood for two minutes in the shadows of the entryway searching the pews. The nave was empty. The organ drowned all sound and made him even more cautious than usual. He stepped softly to the side aisle and then to the cloister walk. No one. There was only one place his quarry could be. The choir gallery.

With his arm cocked and pistol raised, he silently climbed the spiral staircase. At the top of the stairs, he leaned against the banister post and for the final time twisted the silencer tight. He checked the safety and raised his arms to ensure they were free. He took a deep breath and jumped through the door into the gallery. The Luger's sight swept the pews.

The gallery was empty. Empty? Impossible. He had seen them enter the cathedral. The assassin had only one second to be puzzled. From out of the corner of his eye, he saw a blur behind the gallery door. John Crown hit him in the Adam's apple so hard the slap sounded clearly over the organ. The assassin dropped to the floor at Crown's feet, and the Luger skittered along a pew.

Heather rose from the floor in front of the first pew and saw the assassin's blond hair. "My God, Peter Kohler," she gasped, and her hand reflexively covered her mouth.

As Crown dragged Kohler toward the gallery organ pipes, he said, "Meet me at the cathedral's front door in five minutes."

Heather didn't move. She stared with wide eyes at Kohler, who sputtered and coughed as he came around. Crown said more forcefully, "Leave, now."

Her gaze switched to Crown and didn't leave him as she groped down the pew toward the door. "What are you going to do?"

Crown's eyes burned as he jerked the dazed Kohler to his knees. "He killed Miguel Maura," Crown said to no one. "Killed Miguel Maura." Kohler tried to stand, but Crown yanked him off his feet toward the rear pipes.

282

"John," Heather called over the soaring organ, "listen to me. Listen to me . . ."

He turned to her and said with a ferociousness that startled her, "Leave. Get out." She scrambled down the stone stairs, frightened for her life, without knowing why.

Michael Graham had warmed to the Rockefeller Chapel organ. The stops and pedals and keys were now familiar to him, and he felt comfortable with their action. The organ was beautifully pitched and had very little lag time. The chapel's echo seemed tailored to the Oratorio. The lighting on the sheet music was just right. The hardwood seat even seemed to fit his posterior. At times like this, Graham merged with his instrument, to become the composer's ultimate statement. His hands flew over the keys with elegant precision, and his feet swept from pedal to pedal with masterful grace. Bach poured from the pipes and filled the cathedral with his spirit.

A sharply discordant note from a gallery piccolo pipe snapped Graham upright on the stool. He stopped in mid-bar and instantly determined it was the organ, not he, that had just spat on Bach. He pressed the offending key. From the gallery came a gurgling whoosh that should have been a melodious high-pitched tone. He checked the stops and pressed the key again. Same cacophonous result. He had never heard anything like it. It sounded vaguely evil.

He grabbed the organ-pipe wrench from under the stool, in case the piccolo pipe had somehow fallen off its mount, and with his brow wrinkled with concern, he walked to the south end of the nave and climbed the spiral stairs to the gallery.

Graham took three steps toward the bank of pipes before he saw the body. It was draped face-up over several of the sharp pipes. The piccolo pipe and two others protruded from the man's midsection, and their tips were covered with blood and bits of intestine. The

283

dead man's hand tightly gripped one of the pipes that had gone through his stomach. His sightless eyes were open, and blood dripped from his stomach onto the cabinet. Michael Graham leaned heavily against the back of a pew as his head went light.

Crown caught up with Heather a half-block from the chapel. He grabbed her arms. His face was grim and his voice was a feral snarl. "Now, one way or the other, you're going to tell me who you've been calling every night after I leave you."

XVII

Spreading a large plug of butter on a saltine cracker was one of Everette Smithson's true joys. He layered it on a quarter-inch high, then carefully squared the corners. He was salivating now, but he took great satisfaction in not even sampling a cracker until the plate was full. It was only 2:30 in the afternoon, a little early for his predinner Scotch, so he opened a beer and poured it into a stein.

His housekeeper, Mrs. Lacey, twittered into the kitchen and wiped cracker crumbs off the counter. Whenever Smithson was downstairs, she followed him around like a cocker spaniel cleaning up after him. She attacked his tobacco shreds, discarded newspapers, empty plates, and crumbs of all types, almost before they settled. At times he wanted to command her to sit or play dead, but she was too good and too cheap to offend.

"Mrs. Lacey, you brought your suitcase?" he asked.

"Just like you said. I'll be washing down the upstairs while you're away. If I work at it eight hours a day, I ought to have it done by the time you get back in two weeks." She was a thin little woman who owned two print dresses that she wore on alternate days.

"Now, now, Mrs. Lacey, you are overstating the case. A mere dusting is all it needs, my dear."

Smithson squeezed around the game table, where the battle of Arbela still waged, frozen since Sackville-West's visit, and climbed the stairs to his room, beer in

285

one hand, crackers in the other. He bounced up the stairs, if it was possible for one so hefty to bounce, reflecting his jubilant spirits. His small rat teeth were exposed in an unusual grin of self-satisfaction.

Deservedly so. The German stormtroopers, two of them anyway, were safely at the EDC house, being questioned this very minute by Professor Ludendorf. What's more, Smithson had played a vital role in finding them, more important than either Lieutenant Sullivan or John Crown. They wouldn't underestimate his talents again, not with that display of courage and coolness he had given them when he lowered his pistol on the cop. But then, they would never have the opportunity to test him again. Smithson was leaving next morning.

His job was done. He could take his money and leave. He was scheduled for a vacation. His two weeks somewhere. Last year he had gone to Atlantic City, for Christ's sake. This year would be different. He wasn't coming back this year. He had enough money to disappear, and that's exactly what he intended to do. Big money, too. Easy money.

Smithson kicked open the door to his bedroom, put the tray on a lamp stand, and plopped down in his abused easy chair. He flicked on the radio and reached for a newspaper, but he couldn't concentrate.

Mexico. He had never been there, but he believed the travel brochures, and they promised it would be fabulous. His train ticket was to Laredo, Texas. It had taken him ten minutes to convince the ticket agent he really wanted to go to Laredo. Smithson couldn't give a damn about Laredo, or all of Texas, for that matter. But after Laredo came Monterrey, Mexico City, Mérida. He would probably buy a little place on the Yucatán Peninsula. Maybe in Progreso. Maybe Champotón. He could afford two or three servants, a housekeeper, although he would never find one as inexpensive as Mrs. Lacey, even in Mexico, a gardener, perhaps even a chauffeur. He bit into his first cracker and rubbed the butter along the roof of his mouth. God, that was good. Do they have butter in Mexico?

It hadn't been hard. He hardly knew Sackville-West. The Priest was arrogant and cold, a killer disguised as a businessman. There were terrifying rumors about the Priest, tales of his ruthlessness and his firsthand knowledge of death. There were also stories of his power and influence. Smithson had even heard that Sackville-West had direct access to the president. Improbable. Gunmen, even smooth ones, don't rise that high.

He had also heard of John Crown through the agency's grapevine. Heard how deadly he was with a pistol, how he could have the gun out and back before the target even knew he was a target, how he was assigned to the tough ones. But Crown hadn't cracked this case and wasn't going to. Not the way he was pussy-whipped on the English girl. And the dead Spaniard. He hated those greasers anyway. And that idiot Irish hoodlum. Setting him up with those notes was plain fun. Smithson's smile returned. He reached for another cracker and opened the newspaper.

The phone rang. He swallowed hard to clear his mouth. Smithson hated the phone. It was invariably work, usually some paranoid factory boss whose ball bearings went out and who thought he had found iron filings in the works, probably placed there by Hirohito himself. Smithson pulled the phone onto his lap and lifted the receiver.

"Hello. . . . Why, yes, Miss McMillan. It's a little early for your call, isn't it? . . . What? . . . Where? . . . The cathedral?" Smithson struggled out of his seat. His face lost all its serene composure. "He's coming here? What did you say? Oh, Christ. . . . No, I don't have time now."

He dropped the phone. Sheer terror gripped him so tightly he was immobilized. Crown was coming. Blood rushed to his temples, and he couldn't inhale. His legs were made of lead. Crown was coming. But Smithson wasn't dead yet. He knew the city. He could hide where no one would find him, then catch the train tomorrow. If he could move . . . now . . .

Smithson stepped through his fear, slowly, as if walking upstream. He took several steps, very tiring steps, impeded by futility. Crown was coming from Rockefeller Chapel, Heather McMillan had said. That was only a block and a half away. Smithson could almost see Crown sprinting, pushing himself, propelled by revenge. Jesus, move!

Smithson broke the grip and began to move frantically. He opened his leather satchel and stuffed in a change of underwear and took a step toward the bathroom for his shaving gear, changed his mind, no time, and opened the bottom drawer of his dresser. He pulled out a large manila envelope. Fifty-dollar bills. Thousands of them. They barely fit into the satchel. He pushed his revolver into his waistband under a fold of stomach and draped his tentlike raincoat over his shoulders. Hurry, his brain kept screaming. Hurry.

Crown kicked open Smithson's front door without breaking stride. Mrs. Lacey was sweeping the entryway, and she jumped at the sound of the door buckling and springing open. A madman stood there, gulping air, holding an enormous handgun, looking wildly about with eyes that sparked danger. He grabbed Mrs. Lacey's broom and strode to the staircase just as Everette Smithson began jumping down the steps.

Crown shoved the broom handle through the banister rails, and it caught Smithson's ankles. His corpulent body toppled forward, spun on the rail, and he landed hard on his back on the landing. Dazed and hurt, but gripping the satchel tightly, Smithson reached for his pistol. Crown slapped it aside as he landed on Smithson and planted a knee in the fat man's stomach. The pistol slid across the entryway past the stunned Mrs. Lacey. Smithson groaned under the weight. Crown put a knife at the base of the Chicago agent's throat and whispered, "Know whose knife this is?"

288

Smithson gasped and moaned.

"I said, do you know whose knife this is?" Crown pricked Smithson's neck. The fat agent yelped. "I'll tell you. It was one of Miguel Maura's. You ordered Peter Kohler to murder him, and you've been trying to kill me for a week." He shoved the knife into Smithson's neck another fraction of an inch. "I want to know why."

The sprint from the chapel had winded Crown. His words came in bursts on the exhales. And as he spoke, he began to lose control. The anger and hatred bottled up inside him since his friend's death came to the fore and focused on the man beneath him, the man who had plotted Miguel's death, the man who had caused Miguel's knees to pop open, who caused Miguel to be run over by a fishing trawler. Crown increased the pressure on the knife and said in a voice now quivering with rage, "Why, Smithson? Why?"

"The money. This money." Smithson tried to lift the satchel into Crown's view, but his arms were trapped, and he could only wiggle the handle. "Here, Crown, take the money," he sputtered.

Blood ran freely down both sides of Smithson's neck. Crown's eyes blazed, and his thin face was merciless. He pressed the knife deeper into Smithson's throat, and the Chicago agent squealed in terror and pain.

"Why? Why? Why?" Crown yelled rabidly into Smithson's contorted face.

Heather McMillan ran into the entryway and stopped abruptly at the sight of the spectacle on the landing. John Crown was kneeling on top of Smithson and yelling hysterically into Smithson's fat face, screaming meaningless words. Crown was insane with fury. Smithson kicked his legs against the banister rail, but he could do nothing to stop his agony. Heather saw Crown dig the blade farther into the fat man's esophagus. Blood spilled inward now, and Smithson coughed and choked on it as he cried.

Heather opened her mouth to yell at Crown, but

nothing came. She stepped forward, intent on some act she had not thought of, and stepped on Smithson's pistol. She hesitated only a second, then lifted it with both hands and pointed it at the screaming bodies on the landing.

"John," she yelled as loudly as she could, aware that hysteria was in her voice. "John, stop. Please stop."

Neither man heard. Each was a prisoner of his role, screeching at the other, both incoherent, both in pain.

"Why? Why? Why?"

"John," she screeched shrilly, trying to be heard above them, "I'll shoot!"

Over the pistol sight, she saw Crown push the knife farther into Smithson's throat. Smithson's shriek was drowned in red bubbles.

"Why, Smithson? Why?"

As Heather slowly pulled the trigger, an immense calm overtook her. Now she was in control. With the gun, she could stop the torture, the pain. The pistol click-clicked as the hammer came back, then exploded. A hole the size of a quarter opened in Everette Smithson's side. His massive body jerked, then relaxed in death.

The tableau froze. The insane rage in Crown's face drained slowly as he realized Smithson was no longer responding. He had not heard the shot. A shiver passed through him as his energy receded, no longer fed by bilious vengeance. He released the knife and stood weakly over Smithson's body, fighting for breath. His hands were shaking. He blinked rapidly several times, trying to control his eyes. He stumbled over the body. His legs could barely maintain his weight.

Heather dropped the pistol and stared vacantly at Crown. He didn't move toward her, but stood away, feeling his composure return in waves. It was the first time in his life he had been completely out of control. He felt sheepish as he said, "I gave you a chance to escape a few minutes ago. Why'd you come here?"

"Escape from what?" Her voice was dull.

"You must know what we do to traitors."

"I don't know what you're talking about."

"You were reporting my whereabouts to Smithson. For a week, he and Kohler have been trying to kill me, just like they plotted Miguel Maura's death. You told him we would be at the chapel for the rehearsal. That's how Kohler knew where to find me."

"John, I didn't know anyone was trying to kill you. Mr. Smithson told me the first day I got here that part of my job was to report to him about you. He told me that it was regulation procedure and that all he did was mark it down in a book of some sort. He said all agents are watched like this at all times. It's for their own protection." Her eyes were wide, and her words were a tumble.

"You actually believed that?"

"Sure I did. Mr. Smithson was the chief of your Chicago bureau. You told me that yourself. Why shouldn't I have believed it? He said that even he was watched by someone. It's all routine."

A slow, haggard smile spread over Crown's face. "Christ, you're gullible. For the past week, I thought you were a traitor, and I was angry every time I saw you make those calls late at night."

"You saw me do that?"

"Sure. You're not very good. At secret phone calls, that is. But I must admit, your call to Smithson a few minutes ago scared him. You followed my instructions nicely. Maybe you'll make it yet."

She grinned, but it was cut short as Crown took a few steps and Smithson's body came into her view. "Why did he want you killed?" she asked.

"I'm about to find that out. His motive was money, a satchel full," Crown said, indicating Smithson's case with his thumb. "He and Kohler were working together. There was another murderer, but Miguel took care of him. Apparently they took orders from Smithson. And Kohler has worked with Professor Ludendorf for years. Ludendorf's got to be in on it."

"Where're you going?" she asked as he stepped by her.

"To the EDC house. I've got a few things to discuss with the professor."

Professor Ludendorf scribbled hurriedly across the page. He finished the sheet and paused long enough to dial Crown's number. Again there was no answer. It was imperative he talk to Crown soon, or . . . or . . . it was unthinkable. He dialed again and let it ring ten times. Nothing. He began at the top of the next page and pushed so hard the pencil tip tore through the paper. He thrust the sheet aside and reached for another from the drawer. Please call, Crown. He's probably with that British girl, Heather. Damn her. It'll be ruined if I don't contact him. Must get this report out. They won't believe it when they read it.

Ludendorf looked up at the click. John Crown stood in the doorway, aiming the Smith and Wesson between the professor's eyes. Crown closed the door behind him without lowering the gun.

"My God, John, what's going on?"

"Smithson's dead. Your pal Kohler's dead. Both by my hand. And you've got one minute to tell me what's going on."

"John, for God's sake . . ."

"Where's Hess?"

"He's up in his room. Where else would be be?"

"The stormtroopers?"

"In their room, chained to their beds. John, you've got to listen for a minute. I've been interrogating von Stihl. You know, he's got a head wound and—"

"Your minute's running, Ludendorf." Crown had not lowered the pistol.

"Listen closely, John. Enrico Fermi is in mortal danger at this very moment. I've been trying to get you for ten minutes, ever since von Stihl started babbling about the explosives they stole."

292

Crown's gun hand lowered slightly. "What about the explosives?"

"Apparently they still had half of it after the raid on the navy station."

"I know that."

"Von Stihl gave it to a technician, one of Fermi's technicians."

"When?"

"He didn't say. He wasn't very coherent."

"Did he tell you the guy's name?"

"No, he just said a technician."

"What else did he say?"

"Well, I'm putting it all in the report, and you can read it later. But he said that when a needle on their Geiger counter reaches the red mark, whatever that is, the bomb will go off."

"The self-sustained mark," Crown said to himself.

"Von Stihl said the technician wired it so none of the other scientists would know."

"Have you called the lab?" Crown said as he slipped the revolver into his waistband.

"Oh, God. I just found this out ten minutes ago, and—"

"Get the keys for Hess's cell."

As they climbed the stairs past the guard, Crown said, "It all makes sense now, Professor. Hess isn't crazy at all. He flew to Scotland and began talking about atom bombs, knowing none of his interrogators would understand a word of his scientific jargon, not even you. So Hess knew he would be brought to wherever the U.S. experiments are, so the top scientists could talk to him. Hess was used to locate the American experiment. He's got no amnesia or stomach cramps.

"Von Stihl supplied the explosives. No wonder they could buy Smithson and that technician and Kohler. German victory depends on it. They probably offered them so much money it overwhelmed them. Weak links are easy to find when tested with that much cash."

"So they're trying to kill Fermi?"

"Yes. If they do, the U.S. experiments will be in chaos. Fermi told me today that the German fission experiments have bogged down. They've made a bad mistake in their calculations. Hitler knows he's losing the atom-bomb race, so he sacrificed his deputy to gain an edge. Killing Fermi and destroying the experiment would give the Germans perhaps another year."

"Hess was just bait?"

"That's right, Professor."

They paused in front of Hess's door while the guard threw the bolts. The professor's face was open, and Crown anticipated the next question accurately.

"I was just a goat, then," the professor said.

"Regrettably, yes. All that fabulous strategic information Hess gave you during your early interrogations in London was designed to make you and the Allies think Hess was insane. His information ensured we would believe him when he began to talk about the German experiments. We swallowed it hook, line, and sinker. And who could blame us? I've never heard of anyone throwing away that many men before. But then, the Germans know they're going to lose the war if they don't get the bomb first. I suppose Hitler and Hess think the men were a small price to pay."

Crown glanced at his wristwatch as the last bolt cleared. "It's fifteen minutes to three. Fermi's experiment could be as early as three o'clock."

Rudolf Hess was sitting in the rocking chair reading an issue of *Life* when Crown entered his room and said, "It's all over, Hess."

Hess didn't look up from the magazine as he rocked back and forth.

"This magazine is much better than anything we've got in Germany," he said in his wandering voice. "Photo journalism. Isn't that what it is called?"

"Smithson and Kohler are dead. I know about the bomb planted at Fermi's experiment."

Hess blinked several times, then recast his face. The

deputy führer's eyes transformed from the vacant, staring, shallow pools of a lunatic to the penetrating eyes of one accustomed to power. His jaw firmed, and for the first time in Crown's presence, he did not assume the silly smile of a weak-minded sycophant. Crown saw the Rudolf Hess who could enthrall 100,000 Nazis at a mass rally with visions of Germany's destiny, and who could plan the invasions of Poland and Czechoslovakia. Power flowed into Hess's features, and in a two-second transformation, he became a commanding presence.

"I see," he said in his deep, resonant voice, devoid of the flecks of insanity. "So you have discovered our operation, Mr. Crown."

"Get your coat."

"My immediate superior will not be pleased."

"You'll never see him again, anyway."

"No, but nevertheless . . ." Hess's voice trailed off as the full meaning of Crown's words surrounded him. "My trip to Scotland has gone for nothing. All those soldiers we forfeited. Well, it was a gamble." He tied his shoelaces. "I want you to know, Mr. Crown, that we weighed all the risks. We knew what this mission would cost. The Führer and I did not go into this venture with our eyes closed."

"Hurry, Hess."

"It's important that you understand. We Germans are losing the war. It has gotten much worse since I left Germany. You've heard of our Russian-front debacle? That's the beginning of the end. I'm sure of it. The Führer is more far-sighted than you believe. He knew we had to have the atom bomb. The fate of the Third Reich was the stakes. Can you understand this?"

Crown nodded, to hurry him. Hess wrestled into his raincoat.

"I want you to know, I want at least one person to know, that I'm not insane and that I acted with purpose and fore-thought. History will record me as a deserter and a lunatic, but you'll know the truth."

"Do you know how the bomb is wired?"

"I have no idea."

"What's the technician's name?" Crown asked as he took Hess's arm to guide him out of the EDC house.

"If I told you that, I would truly be a traitor."

"I can simply have Fermi postpone the experiments to look for the bomb."

"Any delay is better than none for Germany."

"Get into the car."

Three minutes later they arrived at the Stagg Field grandstand. Crown was pushing it now, knowing the explosives would go when the needle hit the self-sustained mark. Fermi had said between three and four o'clock. It was 3:10. With his identification card in one hand and Hess's elbow in the other, Crown hustled Hess through the door on the south wall of the lobby. Crown rapped on the inner door with the same code Fermi had used several days before. A guard admitted them and then opened his fingerprint pad.

"I don't have time for that," Crown said without breaking step. He pushed on the next door, but it remained closed.

"I'm afraid everyone must be printed and checked," the guard said. He was wearing a brown business suit two sizes too small for him. His ink-black hair was carefully combed.

"Do you know who I am?" Crown asked, his voice stiffening.

"Sure, Mr. Crown, but this is procedure here . . . "

The guard stopped mid-sentence as the barrel of Crown's pistol bit painfully into his lip.

"Open the door. Now."

The guard forgot procedures as he clicked the signal switch and the iron door swung open. "You'll get reported for this, Crown," he yelled after them.

They descended the steep stairs to the court observation level. The piles of graphite that had lined the walls during Crown's tour had disappeared. The hall was dim and dank and smelled of mold. An army
296

guard leaning against the hallway wall nodded to Crown.

"Has anyone come out of the observation room in the last few minutes?" Crown asked.

"No, sir. Not for an hour or so. They got all the scientists in there watching the experiment. Today must be the big day. None of them is going to miss it."

"One of them will try. We'll wait here."

A small smile crossed Hess. "So you are not calling off the experiment, Mr. Crown," he said in a low voice suitable for the sparsely illuminated hall. "Perhaps my mission will be successful, after all."

"Don't count on it, Hess. I'm a great believer in the instinct for survival."

As the echo of Crown's words died in the hall, the observation door opened, and a white-coated technician walked into the hall. Crown recognized him as the curly-dark-haired white-coat he had seen working on the components at a table during his tour of the court. Crown waited until he tried to pass them, then slapped the corner of the technician's eyeglasses. A thin stream of blood spurted from the side of the white-coat's nose where the spectacles' nose rest dug into the skin. The technician grabbed for his glasses, but Crown hit his wrist with the pistol barrel. When the technician opened his mouth to cry out, Crown's pistol barrel hit his jaw. Any movement produced pain, so the technician stood still, and Crown said, "Running away from something in there? Let's go back and find out what."

He shoved the white-coat toward the door and grabbed Hess's elbow again. The guard's face reflected his puzzlement, but he wasn't about to question the flying pistol. Crown opened the observation-level door and shoved them through it.

It was a historic scene, one that would be remembered in the legend of science with the Wright brothers' first flight and Galileo's gravity experiments from the Tower of Pisa. Enrico Fermi was bent over the table, peering at the particle-counter needle. His head

297

nodded between the needle and the scientist below him on the squash-court floor, who had his hands above his head, pulling the cadmium rod inch by inch from the graphite pile.

"Try it another inch, Jack."

The rod was slipped out a little further. The needle climbed almost imperceptibly. "A little more."

Eight or ten scientists and technicians peered over Fermi's shoulder at the gauge. They stood with their hands behind their backs or at their sides, with their fists alternately clenching and relaxing. Like Fermi's, their gazes bounced between the needle and the rod. Occasionally one looked to the platform above the pile, where two technicians dressed in heat-resistant uniforms knelt with buckets of dousing solution in their hands, ready to drench the pile if the reaction became overheated. As Fermi had once mentioned to Crown, stopping a reaction that was slightly overheated was one thing. Dousing an uncontrollable fission reaction may be impossible. No one knew the consequences if it raced out of control.

Tension was palpable in the squash court. This moment was the culmination of years' work. These scientists were on the verge of unlocking America's energy destiny, and, more tangibly, altering the war's course. Other than Fermi's tense commands, no one spoke. Only the counter marked the tension, with its eerie, erratic ticking.

"Another inch, Jack."

The needle moved slightly more toward the red mark, and the ticking increased. The scientists and technicians inhaled as one. The men on the rigging never looked away from Fermi, waiting for the order to dump the solution.

None of the scientists noticed Crown and Hess and the returning technician.

"It goes off when the needle hits the red mark, Hess," Crown whispered.

"I'm aware of that."

298

"We're going to get our asses blown away."

Hess nodded. "The Führer and I went to a lot of difficulty to have that bomb placed there. You don't think I will order it diffused just because I will die with the others, do you?"

"Maybe. Maybe not."

Fermi played with a dial on the instrument panel and called for another inch to be pulled out of the pile. Once again, the dial moved closer to the red line, and the ticking increased. The sound was less erratic now and was beginning to dominate the room.

"You are a dedicated and dangerous man, Crown," Hess said, looking intently at the dial, "but I do not think you want to die today."

Crown shrugged his shoulders.

"Does a million dollars mean anything to you, Crown?"

"We're going to be blown away in a minute, Hess. We won't even know what hit us. It'll ruin our whole day."

"One million dollars. I could have it to you within twenty-four hours. Think of it."

The technician was breathing hard, and his forehead was beaded with sweat. He kept glancing at a panel of controls on his left.

"All you have to do is walk away with me from here right now. You don't have to let me free," Hess said anxiously. "Just walk away."

"Once again, Jack." Fermi's voice was on edge now. His right hand tapped the table nervously. The needle moved again. It was an inch from the red line. The ticking increased, so that it sounded like radio static. The squash court seemed steamy. "We're just a little away."

"No one would ever know the difference, Crown. They will all be dead. One million. That's everything you've always wanted."

Crown heard the tremor in Hess's voice. They were thirty seconds from being vaporized, and all it was was a tremor. Shit. Not enough. The technician might break, though. He looked ill with terror.

"Look at the needle, Crown. We can make it if we move now. Your whole life depends on the next half-minute," Hess said. There was worry in his voice now. "No more waiting for your government paycheck month after month."

Fermi was very quiet. "Half an inch more. Be careful, Jack. Get ready up there."

The scientists leaned forward to watch Jack gingerly pull on the rod. The ticking increased slightly, and the needle climbed higher. No one breathed.

Hess wiped perspiration from his forehead. "Crown, think. This is our last chance. Let's go." Almost hysteria.

Crown's face was indifferent, and his feet were firmly planted. He was going nowhere. The technician was swaying, on the verge of fainting.

"Just a fraction more, Jack. Then we'll have it."

The needle moved and almost touched the red. Hess panted like a thirsty dog. Five interminable seconds passed.

"Diffuse it, Schneider." Hess's voice cracked.

The technician jumped to the side panel. He threw a single switch and gulped air. His knees wavered. Crown and Hess exhaled in unison.

The needle crossed to the red, and the clicking bounced to a steady hum. Fermi looked up with his radiant smile and yelled, "We've made it, boys. It's self-sustaining. The nuclear age is here."

The room exploded with applause and backslapping and handshaking. The court filled with the high-pitched laughter that is tension's release. The technicians on the rigging leaned back on their haunches, lowered the buckets, and laughed. Fermi grasped hand after hand. A few of the scientists jumped up and down with joy. Someone produced a bottle of Chianti and passed it around. There were no glasses, and no one cared. One of the scientists pounded out a tattoo on the table, unable to think of a more appropriate way to express his joy. There were cries of "We did it!" and "Beautiful, Enrico, beautiful!" and "Where's more wine?"

Crown opened the door and said to Hess, "I suppose it's too late for the million dollars?"

Hess stuffed his damp handkerchief into a rear pocket. "Typical Anglo humor, Crown. Typical."

Crown pushed the technician through the door. The white-coat had trouble controlling his feet. Hess followed the technician.

The guard asked, "Enjoy the show, Mr. Crown?"

"More than you'd know." Crown could not keep the elation out of his voice.

The sound of the celebration died as the iron door swung shut, and now all they could hear was the clicking of their heels. It sounded like a prison.

XVIII

Heather winced as Crown opened the door, but Everette Smithson's body had been removed. It was a professional job. No blood on the landing or on the rug at the base of the stairs. The banister posts had been repaired, and the scuff marks on the stairs were no longer visible. Crown had not ordered the cleanup. It meant only one thing. The Priest was here.

"You came back for Miguel Maura's knife, perhaps?"

Sackville-West emerged from the living room, and Crown took his hand, relieved. The Priest's dignified banker's presence was the official signal that things were under control. When he appeared after a case, it was time to shed the pressure and tension, to reassess and rethink the mission, and perhaps to receive the next assignment. Once again, Sackville-West's traveling to Chicago was unusual, reflecting the enormous stakes of the Hess cross.

"When did you get here, sir?"

"An hour or so ago. After our conversation this morning, I decided that a journey to Chicago might be appropriate, thinking we could brainstorm the problem, but it looks like you have things under control here."

"It was close, but I think so."

"I've had to do a little cleaning up after you," the Priest said, marking his amusement by lightly stroking his salt-and-pepper mustache. "Quite a little mess in the chapel gallery, if you will remember. Our removal team had never seen anything like it."

"I was in a place of worship, so I was inspired."

"Quite. I've also had therapeutic discussions with a shaken organist and a bewildered housekeeper. They are both doing well."

"How much was in the satchel?" Crown asked.

"A quarter of a million dollars," Sackville-West answered as he pointed them to chairs in the living room. "Because Smithson headed our Chicago office, the Nazis bought him, thinking he would be in charge of Hess when he was in Chicago. They didn't expect you and Miguel Maura to step in to guard and transport Hess. If Smithson had been overseeing Hess, killing Fermi during one of the interviews would have been easy."

"So they came after Miguel and me, thinking that once we were dead, Smithson would guard Hess."

"That's right." Sackville-West could have seconded as a model, with his tailored black pinstripe suit and crisp white shirt. Only the tedious green tweed tie argued against his impeccable taste. "By the way, Miss McMillan, it's nice to see you. I trust that you and John have your little difficulties worked out."

If this was cultured American humor, Heather didn't appreciate it, but she briefly told him of Smithson's deception and her reason for reporting Crown's locations to him.

"I can't blame you for that. I would have fallen for it, too, in my younger days. So Hess was bait, John?"

"That's right. He probably had to learn the scientific data the hard way, by long cramming sessions with Germany's scientists, before he flew to Scotland. It's unlikely he was ever in charge of the German experiments, like he claimed. After his flight, he told the London interrogators enough about the German experiments so he would be shipped to the U.S. to talk to our scientists."

"Kohler was in on it. What about Professor Ludendorf?"

"I suspected him when I discovered Kohler was after me. They've been together since Kohler's student days in Germany. Ludendorf even helped Kohler escape to England. But it was Ludendorf who saved Fermi, with his incredible interrogation of von Stihl this afternoon."

"It's hard to believe von Stihl would tell anyone anything."

"As you know, he's got a head wound, one that has addled his brain, at least temporarily. He's babbling day and night, and Ludendorf managed to steer his talk to the mission. Von Stihl told the professor about the explosives planted at the experiments just thirty minutes or so before the blast would have gone off. If it hadn't been for Ludendorf, Hess would have succeeded at killing Fermi and the other scientists."

"Ludendorf must be as good as the British said."

"We also know why von Stihl and his men came to the U.S. They were the backup plan. Smithson and Hess couldn't kill Fermi at an interrogation, because I was there, so they resorted to explosives. The stormtroopers were sent into the U.S. to blow up the experiments. They were lucky to find a greedy technician."

"Why the attack on the navy base?" Sackville-West asked.

"Well, I think they hijacked the truck simply to get explosives," Crown said. "It was heavy-handed, but it worked. Then they launched that nonsensical assault on the navy station to make us think that's why they hijacked the truck. Perhaps they thought if they blew up the navy buildings, we wouldn't suspect they were going to use the explosives on the experiment."

"This has been a very costly blunder for the Third Reich. By the way, John, would you kindly stop popping your elbow? Thank you. Not only did the Nazis lose the money they paid Smithson, Kohler, and the technician, they also lost some very competent commandos, plus their deputy führer, with all the em-
304

barrassment and bad propaganda resulting from his apparent defection."

"And more. To keep us interested, Hess had to reveal secrets about the German fission experiments, the most important of which is that they've bogged down."

"But it was all for nothing. Thank God," Sackville-West breathed. "I would love to see Hitler's tantrum when he hears the Hess cross has been bungled. I understand he can throw a fit like the most talented six year-old."

There was laughter, then a pause. Heather reached for Crown's hand in an unnecessary reminder. The gesture was not lost on the Priest, who asked, "Something you want, John?"

"Now that his mission is blown, Hess won't be revealing any more German fission secrets, so we'll be flying to London with him tonight. I've already notified Wing Commander Stratton, and he assures me his crew and the plane will be ready."

"So you want some time in London, to sightsee and such, because you know someone who can show you the town." Sackville-West smiled.

"Something like that."

"In light of your very successful, if at times somewhat excessive actions on this assignment, that can be arranged. In fact, we have a little business in and around England that may keep you over there for the better part of a year, if you're interested, although I can't imagine why you would be, with all the good restaurants and such closed."

Heather appreciated the humor this time.

Sounds like a soft assignment, thought Crown.

"I'll be getting back to Washington tomorrow," Sackville-West continued as he stood. "You'll receive my communiqué within the week on your London assignment. It may require a few short trips across the channel. You know how this work goes."

So much for the soft assignment.

Sackville-West showed them to the door, and Heather asked, "What will happen to Hess?"

"He'll be kept in hospitals or safe houses until the end of the war," Sackville-West replied. "Then he'll go on trial like any other Nazi criminals we manage to catch. This little episode will never be allowed to become part of the history books, though. It makes some people high up in various government circles look rather foolish. Me, for one. And some others higher up than I. Have a good time in England, then. I'll show up in a month or so to see how things are going."

When Heather grinned, Sackville-West added hastily, "Not those kind of things."

The Priest bid them good-bye at the door, and as they reached the sidewalk Heather asked, "Do you think you can stand me for a year?"

"I'll have those brief, fun-filled jaunts into Germany and occupied France when I need a rest."

"My flat isn't very big, if it's still standing at all."

"I don't take up much room."

On the sidewalk, in Chicago's cold December, they held each other. For the first time, the joy of holding her was not overwhelmed and deadened by suspicion of treachery. His dilemma had been resolved in a way he had thought impossible that morning. She was alive and with him, with him for a long time. With his arms wrapped around her, Crown felt light and complete and contented.

Contentment. It filled him. It had been a long time since he felt this way. Years. No, only a month, since Miguel Maura was murdered. A part of him had been torn away that night on the Dearborn Street Bridge, ripped out and replaced with blue-cold revenge that had chilled him for a month. That was gone now. As they embraced, Crown could feel Heather replace that dead part of him. She healed and replenished and lifted him. A year of her in London. Maybe more. Crown laughed abruptly and squeezed her hard.

"I bet this works out between you and me," he said, looking into her kelly-green, wonderful eyes.

"I think it will, John."

An hour later, they arrived at the EDC house in the escort car, and Crown knew something was terribly wrong when the red light did not flash from the second-story window in response to his signal. Crown shoved the iron gate, and it swung open freely. Why wasn't it locked? *Oh, Jesus, no!*

"Wait here, Heather." His throat was tight.

"What's wrong, John?"

"Something bad. Really bad. Better get in the car." Crown's voice trembled, and as if to compensate, he drew his pistol.

She followed him up the porch stairs anyway. Rather than press the signal buttons under the mailbox, Crown pushed on the front door. It was unlocked, and opened under the pressure. There was no sound from inside. There should have been buzzers and code words and radio static and grumbling. Nothing.

The door bumped into a soft object and stopped. Crown pressed it again, and it gave a few inches, then stood firm. An arm plopped out from behind the door. A dead arm connected to a dead body. Moving very quietly, very tentatively, Crown stepped around the door. The window guard had been shot in the chest. That is, his chest had been laid open by a stream of bullets shot at close range. The guard's army Colt lay on the windowsill, untouched.

"Oh, God, the house has been blown," Crown whispered. He looked again at what was left of the window guard's chest. "Willi Lange."

Heather had seen too much that day to be shocked at the sight. She paused for only a moment, then asked, "What happened?"

"The German stormtroopers got out somehow. Jesus, and I thought we had Hess beat."

With his pistol in front of his face, Crown walked lightly into the kitchen. He knew what awaited them, and he was right. The radioman was slumped over his table. He appeared to be napping, with his chin resting on his folded arms. His chair sat in a pool of blood. A single knife thrust into his back had ended his life.

There was no further need for stealth. No one would be alive in the EDC house. Crown ran up the stairs to the second floor. The second-floor guard, Jones, lay on the floor, shot in the back. A pistol lay next to him, but Crown doubted he had had a chance to use it. He had fallen out of his chair sideways without turning around, completely surprised. His red flashlight had rolled ten feet down the hall.

The cell-room doors were open, of course. Their bolts were intact, which meant they had been opened with keys. Von Stihl and Lange's shackles lay on their beds. They displayed no signs of force, so they had also been opened with a key. Hess's room was empty. His kit of pills was gone, as was his change of clothes. He had casually packed, knowing someone was coming for him.

"John, where is Professor Ludendorf?"

Then it hit him, the full scope of the German plan, their full plot. He had been completely duped. He had played his hand just as Hess had dealt it. He had been led by the nose, step by step. Hess had been the puppeteer, and Crown had let himself be pulled by the strings, blinded by revenge and all the other smoke screens Hess had thrown up.

"He's gone, Heather." The words almost choked him. "Ludendorf let the stormtroopers and Hess out of their cells, and they hit the guards, and they've gone."

"Why?"

"So they could get away, for Christ's sake!" Crown felt like shooting something, and he lined the Smith and Wesson up on Hess's bed. "No, not so they could get away." The next realization made Crown's head swim. "They could have done that days ago. And they could have killed Fermi with the bomb if they wanted to, because if von Stihl and Ludendorf were working together all along, then Ludendorf wouldn't have told me about the bomb just in time for me to diffuse it unless they had another purpose. . . . "

The last words were said as he jumped down the stairs three at a time and rushed into the radio room. He pushed the dead radio operator out of the way and dialed the Metallurgical Laboratory.

"Get me Enrico Fermi's office. Hurry. . . . Yes, this is John Crown. Where is Dr. Fermi? . . . He's not? When was he due back after the experiment? . . . Yeah, I'm worried too, now."

Crown quickly replaced the receiver. "They've got Fermi."

He grabbed Heather's arm and fairly dragged her out of the house. Crown yelled instructions to the other escort cars, and he and Heather jumped into the center Ford.

It screeched from the curb, shot down Kimbark, and whined around the corner onto Fifty-seventh. "There's only one way they can get out of the country in a hurry, and I played into their hands on that, too."

"Where are we going?" Heather asked, much calmer than Crown was.

"To Midway Airport. They knew we were flying back to England tonight on the same bomber, and they must have guessed that I called the bomber crew and had them prepare to depart."

"I don't understand how Professor Ludendorf could do this."

"He was obviously in on it from the beginning. I doubt he and Kohler were paid vast sums, like we thought about Kohler, but they were probably dedicated Nazis from way back."

"How did they fool us?"

"The 'us' is very kind of you," Crown replied, winding the speeding car around a pod of startled students. "Ludendorf and Kohler were sent to England and made to look like tremendously successful interrogators. The Germans fed them supposed defectors for a year or two. The defectors told Ludendorf and Kohler military secrets in order to make them look like premier interrogators. Ludendorf and Kohler knew about it all along, of course. Hell, all of that fabulous information was planted by Hitler. Sure it was accurate, and it cost the Germans many lives, but it was planted nevertheless, to make Ludendorf and Kohler look good."

"That sounds like a lot of trouble."

"Well," Crown said as the car tore through Washington Park, oblivious of the "Slow—Children" signs, "because the professor was so productive with the other defectors, it was only natural that the British give Hess to him for interrogation. And it was only natural, then, that Ludendorf and Kohler accompany Hess to the U.S. The entire ruse was to find the U.S. experiments and kidnap Fermi."

Crown ran a red light, then another, and left several drivers shaking their fists at him. Heather dared not look at the road, so she peered at Crown and said, "I still don't understand. If Ludendorf was working with Hess, why did he tell you about the bomb at the experiment?"

"When Ludendorf found out Kohler and Smithson were dead, he knew I'd suspect him. So he simply went to his backup plan and told me of the bomb. It worked. The moment he told me about it, I no longer suspected Ludendorf at all. And after I dragged Hess to the squash court and he broke down at the last moment and ordered the bomb diffused, I didn't suspect Hess of anything more. I thought I had discovered the plan, and I relaxed accordingly. And then I reported all was well to the Priest." Crown felt like banging his head against the steering wheel. "Hell, there probably wasn't even a bomb at the squash court at all. It was just a trick to make me believe the danger was over."

310

"And you think von Stihl and that Willi Lange are in on it, too?"

"Sure. Now I know why they went to all the trouble to brutally hijack the dynamite truck. They wanted the whole Chicago police force after them, because they intended to be caught. And they left a bunch of clues no professional would ever leave, like stealing a truck with 'Bakery' painted on it and letting the neighbors see it. Von Stihl wanted to be captured, because he knew Everette Smithson would suggest they be locked up at the EDC house. That was part of their plan."

"Why?"

"You saw all the carnage back there. Von Stihl and Lange had to get inside the EDC house so they could help Hess break out. Ludendorf unlocked the doors, sure, but those guards wouldn't have let Hess out on Ludendorf's say."

Crown ran his sixth red light, and he would have enjoyed it if he had time. He had astutely, and somewhat miraculously, avoided hitting cars and trucks enjoying their rights-of-way.

"Von Stihl and Lange had another job, too. They were probably the muscle used to kidnap Fermi right after the experiment."

"Why didn't they kidnap him earlier? They would have had opportunities."

"They wanted to wait until Fermi's experiment was successful. It wouldn't have made sense to kidnap him and take him to Germany a week ago, because once there, he would've had to build his graphite pile all over again to prove his theory, before they could work on the bomb."

"Dr. Fermi would never help the Nazis, even if they could get him to Germany."

"Wrong. The Nazis can make anyone do anything. Look at the scientists making heavy water in Norway. They don't want to, of course, but they do anyway."

"Why?"

"Pressure. Incredible pressure. It works, believe me."

"So kidnapping Fermi was Hess's goal all along?" Heather asked, bracing herself against the door as the Ford swerved into the Midway Airport entrance drive.

"That's right. Finding the experiment, then kidnapping the top scientist. So far, they've succeeded because we underestimated them every step of the way."

They sped along the airport perimeter road toward hangar 17, past the DC-3's and Stratoliners and experimental air-force planes hidden under tarpaulins. Crown felt himself build as the adrenaline started to pump. He gripped the wheel tighter, and Heather could see him focus again, just as he had done in the cathedral four hours before. It seemed like a week ago.

"John, is the bomber crew at the airplane?"

His reply came several seconds later, forced through layers of concentration. "Yes, they've got it ready to go. On my orders."

"Well, I don't see how those two stormtroopers can take over a plane. There must be eight or nine crew members."

"Von Stihl and Lange will handle them just as easily as Hess handled me. The crew doesn't stand a chance, not with von Stihl's brains and Lange's skill. Not a chance."

Hangar 17's black bulk, partly disguised by the night, loomed ahead of them, and Crown turned sharply off the perimeter road to the hangar driveway. The hangar's side door was partly open, and light poured through it. The Ford skidded to a stop near a fire truck parked alongside the hangar.

"If that plane is in the air, we've lost them. It's got to be in that hangar." It sounded like a prayer.

With pistol in hand, Crown ran to the side door. He peered through it without opening it farther. *Oh, God! No bomber!* He pushed open the door, and the vast, well-lit hangar stretched out before him. The huge front doors were open, through which the plane had
312

passed, probably just a few minutes before. Crown felt small and cold and alone in the enormous structure.

He was not alone. A herd of miniature men was lined up against the back wall of the hangar, reminding Crown of a nativity scene. They weren't miniatures, they were real, but far away, the other side of the building. The men were frozen in fear. One of them, the smallest, stood apart and was pointing a submachine gun at the crowd.

Without knowing his next move, Crown walked toward the tableau. Halfway across the hangar, he recognized Wing Commander Stratton. Next to him was the surly waist gunner, but now his face contained terror identical to the others'.

Willi Lange's Schmeisser was pointed at Stratton's stomach and did not waver as Crown approached. Crown stopped twenty yards from Lange and pointed his pistol at the corporal's head, but the submachine gun did not move.

"Looks like a standoff, Lange."

Crown didn't think a Wehrmacht submachine-gun expert was capable of laughing, but there it was, crackling out into the hangar like static electricity. It ended quickly, and Crown expected a response, but got none. Lange's eyes remained riveted on the bomber crew.

"Lange, if you lay down the weapon, you might live through this."

The little German smiled under his scrubby mustache and said evenly, "Crown, I have been ordered to keep this crew here, one way or the other. The colonel did not specify how to do it. I would prefer they live, but if you fire that pistol, I promise that every one of them will die, regardless of the part of me you hit."

Crown would have risked it with anyone else but this man. Lange's trail of feats testified to his deadly ability.

313

Crown asked, "You creased von Stihl's head with a bullet, Lange?"

The corporal smiled again and said, "Just enough to make it look bad. The colonel wasn't even nervous when I did it."

No, Crown wouldn't take the chance. But he kept Willi Lange's ear in the pistol's sight. Lange didn't bother to look. Supreme confidence. Was there something standard to do in this situation? What would the Priest have done in his younger days? Hell, what would he do now? Do something, asshole.

The deep bass of *Iron Mike's* engines settled it. The sound bubbled into the hangar and shook its flimsy walls. Lange's weapon did not move from the group as Crown backed up several yards, then turned and ran to the gaping double doors. The Flying Fortress was taxiing past the row of hangars out to the end of the runway. It trudged forward ponderously, with power and purpose. At the tip of the runway, it slowed and yawed starboard to line up for takeoff. For several seconds, *Iron Mike* sat heavily on the runway, its tail almost touching the concrete and its nose high in the air, looking like an enormous metal frog about to leap into the sky. The plane's running lights were off, and no light emerged through the cockpit windows or the greenhouse. A giant, blind monster. It began to roll forward slowly, deliberately.

True inspiration comes only during times of stress. As Crown stood helplessly watching Nazi Germany's deputy führer about to pilot a stolen plane into the sky with America's top nuclear scientist his captive on board, a moment of absolute stress, the solution came to him. It was fraught with risk and danger, but then, it seemed to Crown that stopping a Flying Fortress would be inherently dangerous, regardless of how it was done. *Iron Mike's* four engines growled to a higher pitch as the plane lumbered down the runway toward Crown, picking up speed as the giant props blew back a violent stream of air over the wings.

Crown turned on his heels and sprinted to the side of hangar 17, climbed to the running board of the fire truck, and squinted into the darkness of the cab at the dashboard. The key was in the ignition. Of course it was. It was a fire truck that had to be ready on a moment's notice. Crown jumped into the cab, turned the key, and flattened his heel against the starter button. The truck's engine turned over immediately, and Crown rammed it into first gear.

The big Dodge had surprising acceleration for a fully outfitted pumper. And that's what Crown needed, because he saw *Iron Mike* rolling down the runway toward him just a hundred yards or so from hangar 17. God, it looked immense, a man-of-war about to muscle itself into the sky. Crown heavy-handed the truck through the gears, and it passed the docking trucks parked on the gravel edge and shot onto the runway.

The Fortress accelerated, gobbling up the runway. Its tail lifted off the ground as it bore down. *Iron Mike* saw the pumper at that instant. It veered to the far side of the concrete strip as it came. One tire bounced along the gravel on the side of the runway, but the plane did not slow. The four engines boomed with sound as it tried to beat the oncoming truck.

Crown aimed the pumper as if he were leading a clay pigeon at a trapshoot. The closer *Iron Mike* got, the faster it came, and the last fifty yards to the truck were covered in only seconds. A collision was unavoidable and an instant away.

Crown dived to the truck's floor just as *Iron Mike's* far starboard propeller sheared into the cab, through the seat, and into the pumping engine on the bed. A second propeller followed immediately and tore the roof off the Dodge. The sound of tearing metal rocked the cab. The propellers exploded into fragments as they churned through the truck. Bits of razor-sharp metal streaked through the cab as if a grenade had blown.

Iron Mike, suddenly without starboard power, pivoted violently 180 degress, tottered up on one wheel as the port wing scraped along the ground, and came to a dead stop, pointing up the runway the way it had come. It bounced back down to two wheels and lay emasculated and immobilized. The two starboard propellers had been sheared off.

The fire truck had been almost cut in half, and parts of it covered the runway for a radius of forty yards. It no longer even resembled the proud pumper it once was, but was a twisted and torn, grotesque heap of scrap metal. All its windows had been shattered. Pieces of rubber fire hose stuck from the tangle of metal like worms escaping from a tin can.

As if sighing in despair, *Iron Mike's* engines fluttered to a stop. Cold silence blew across the runway.

Iron Mike's belly hatch twisted open, and Erich von Stihl dropped softly to the runway. His Schmeisser scanned the ugly scene as he took several steps toward the remnants of the pumper. He planted his feet, gripped the weapon tightly, and fired an entire clip through the wrenched door of the cab. The Schmeisser's thunder echoed back from the hangars and rolled over the bomber. Nothing could be alive in the cab. He was about to insert another clip when John Crown stepped from behind one of *Iron Mike*'s wheel's in back of von Stihl.

Crown raised his revolver, paused involuntarily, perhaps to salute the legend, then ripped out von Stihl's knee. The German's weapon pitched away from him, and he spun to the ground. He lay on the concrete, blood pouring from the gaping hole in his kneecap.

The shot had not killed him. It wasn't meant to. Von Stihl fought to a sitting position and looked, not at his knee, for he knew its condition, but at the Schmeisser four yards away from him on the concrete.

He turned to Crown, coughed in pain, and very calmly, very remotely, said, "I would imagine you hang

316

enemy soldiers found in civilian clothes behind enemy lines, just like we do."

Crown nodded.

"Then this should end here."

Von Stihl rolled to a crawling position and like a dog with a wounded foot inched toward the submachine gun. It must have been unbearably painful, but his face was composed, even serene. His mangled knee left a long pool of blood behind him as he crawled the four yards. He dropped to a sitting position and very slowly reached for the Schmeisser. His hands gripped its stock, and he brought the weapon to him. Crown waited until the barrel began to slowly swing to him, then fired once into von Stihl's heart. The German lowered the weapon and lay back on the runway, dead.

Crown crawled under *Iron Mike's* belly and stuck his head up through the hatch. It was dark, darker than the night outside. He listened intently and heard nothing, then climbed up into the plane's fuselage. He struggled over wiring and piping and bomb-rack brackets, then almost tripped over the prostrate form of an alive and terrified Enrico Fermi. The scientist's eyes were wide open, and his hands were cuffed behind his back. He said nothing. Crown stupidly patted him on the shoulder, then crouched forward toward the cockpit ladder, guiding himself by holding the backs of the wicker seats.

Through the darkness, he saw an inert body slumped against the side of the plane. He grabbed its shoulder and rolled it face-up. Josef Ludendorff's throat lay open, and his shoulderblade protruded from his flight jacket. At the moment of impact, a propeller fragment had torn through the fuselage and ended his life instantly.

Crown jerked his gun up at the rustling above him. A black boot stepped on the cockpit ladder, then another. With the movement of an old man, Rudolf Hess slowly climbed down to the fuselage floor, until he was at eye level with Crown's pistol.

With a voice soft in its dignity and despair, the deputy führer said, "Crown, this time it's really over, isn't it?"

HISTORICAL NOTES

Rudolph Hess was convicted at the Nuremberg war-crimes trials of crimes against the peace and was sentenced to life imprisonment. Today he is the only remaining prisoner at the Spandau Prison.

German submarine U-513 was depth-charged by U.S. Navy aircraft on July 19, 1943, near Santos, Brazil. All hands were lost.

Fritz Knochlein, the SS captain who ordered the massacre of British soldiers at Le Paradis, was tried for war crimes. Two British soldiers, who had been forgotten under the pile of bodies, testified against him. Knochlein was executed in January 1949.

ALL TIME BESTSELLERS
FROM POPULAR LIBRARY

☐	AFTERNOON MEN—Powell	04268-0	1.95
☐	MARINA TOWER—Beardsley	04198-6	1.95
☐	SKIN DEEP—Hufford	04258-3	1.95
☐	MY HEART TURNS BACK—Patton	04241-9	2.25
☐	EARTHLY POSSESSIONS—Tyler	04214-1	1.95
☐	THE BERLIN CONNECTION—Simmel	08607-6	1.95
☐	THE BEST PEOPLE—Van Slyke	08456-1	1.95
☐	A BRIDGE TOO FAR—Ryan	08373-5	2.50
☐	THE CAESAR CODE—Simmel	08413-8	1.95
☐	DO BLACK PATENT LEATHER SHOES REALLY REFLECT UP?—Powers	08490-1	1.75
☐	THE FURY—Farris	08620-3	2.25
☐	THE HEART LISTENS—Van Slyke	08520-7	1.95
☐	TO KILL A MOCKINGBIRD—Lee	08376-X	1.75
☐	THE LAST BATTLE—Ryan	08381-6	2.25
☐	THE LAST CATHOLIC IN AMERICA—Powers	08523-2	1.50
☐	THE LONGEST DAY—Ryan	08380-8	1.95
☐	LOVE'S WILD DESIRE—Blake	08616-5	1.95
☐	THE MIXED BLESSING—Van Slyke	08491-X	1.95

Buy them at your local bookstores or use this handy coupon for ordering:

Please allow 4 to 5 weeks for delivery

B-17